LEOPARD IN EXILE

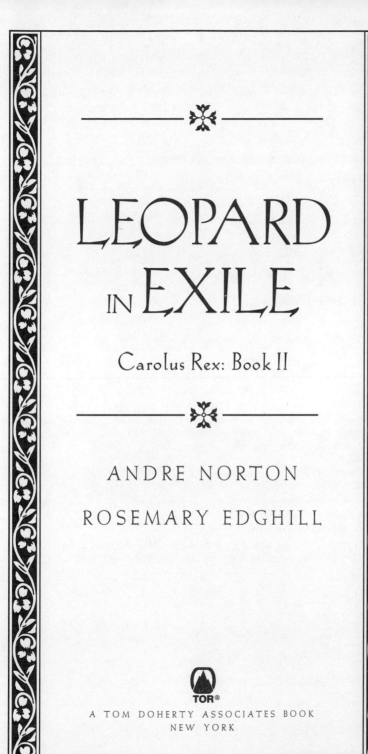

LEOPARD IN EXILE

Carolus Rex: Book II

ANDRE NORTON

ROSEMARY EDGHILL

TOR®

A TOM DOHERTY ASSOCIATES BOOK
NEW YORK

LEOPARD IN EXILE

Copyright © 2001 by Andre Norton, Ltd. & Rosemary Edghill

This book is printed on acid-free paper.

Edited by James Frenkel

A Tor Book
Published by Tom Doherty Associates, LLC
175 Fifth Avenue
New York, NY 10010

www.tor.com

Tor® is a registered trademark of Tom Doherty Associates, LLC.

Library of Congress Cataloging-in-Publication Data

Norton, Andre.
    Leopard in exile / Andre Norton, Rosemary Edgill. — 1st ed.
        p.cm—(Carolus rex ; bk. 2)
    "A Tom Doherty Associates Book."
    ISBN 0-312-86428-0 (acid-free paper)
    1. Napoleon I, Emperor of the French, 1769-1821—Fiction. 2. Sade, marquis de, 1740-1814—Fiction. 3. Nobility—Fiction. I. Edghill, Rosemary. II. Title.

PS3527.O632 L4 2001
813'.52–dc21

                                                                00-053218

First Edition: April 2001

Printed in the United States of America

0 9 8 7 6 5 4 3 2 1

*To Teresa Nielsen Hayden and Jennara Wenk
for industrial-strength eleventh-hour hand-
holding. And to Harry and Bandit, for Cavalier
Attitude and being Very Patient.*

ACKNOWLEDGMENTS

The authors would like to thank the SFF.NET Contra-historians (and various otters) for their help:

> Constance Ash (for Washington's toast and other matters)
>
> John C. Bunnell (for straightening out all my theories about where the Cree should be)
>
> India Edghill (for the third Countess of Monticello, nyahh!)
>
> Zette Gifford
>
> Sharon Lee
>
> Thomas J. Lewis (for the Ferguson rifle and general New World military advice)
>
> Anne McCaffrey (for advice and input on an earlier draft)
>
> Steve Miller
>
> Adam Pacio
>
> Beth Nachison
>
> Allen Hazen
>
> Laura J. Underwood
>
> Lawrence Watt-Evans
>
> Rose Wolf

Most of you for hand-holding and reference-pointing at short notice in my SFF.NET newsgroup, and some for other things. My apologies to all those I've omitted here, who listened to my ideas, commiserated with me about my research sources, and generally provided emotional support during the writing of this book.

And most of all my coauthor, the Lady herself, Andre Norton, without whom neither this book nor this world would exist at all.

—ree

NOTE

In writing an historical novel these days, even a contra-historical novel, the writer walks a fine line between the political correctness of modern enlightened usage and the way people actually spoke and thought at the time. In referring to tribal and slave populations of the New World, I've done my best to be clear and reasonably naturalistic while still trying to avoid terms that make me wince (complicating matters is the fact that nearly every Native American tribal name used in the East and South translates as "the People.") Only you can be the judge of how well I've succeeded at this delicate—and sometimes ticklish—task.

—ree

May this nation always be a lesson
and an example to princes.

—George Washington

An Empire That Never Was

The "If Theory" of history is that oftentimes in world history distinct and radical changes rest upon a single event or person. From that particular point two worlds then come into existence, one in which the matter goes one way and one wherein it goes the other.

The point of divergence here is the affair of the Duke of Monmouth in the days of Charles II. The majority of the English people at the time of Charles' death were bitterly opposed to the return of a Catholic ruler. Unfortunately, Charles II had not been able to produce a living heir by his Portuguese wife, Catherine of Braganza, though he had a number of illegitimate children by various mistresses, upon whom he settled dukedoms and other major honors.

There has always been a rumor that James, Duke of Monmouth, the eldest known of Charles' by-blows, is actually legitimate—that Charles, while in exile, did marry Mistress Waters, the Duke's mother. Monmouth had much of his father's charm and was strongly Protestant in his religious views. In the real world, following Charles' death, Monmouth led an uprising against his uncle, King James II

(Charles' brother and heir presumptive, a severe arrogant man determined to return England to the Catholic fold), failed, and was beheaded.

But as our worlds diverge, Charles II, during his protracted dying, realizes that James' inheritance of the throne would mean trouble for all, and finally admits to a selected body of his strongest council that the rumor was true, that he had in fact made a secret marriage with Mistress Lucy Waters, and thus the Duke of Monmouth was the legitimate heir of his body. Thus, upon Charles II's death, the Duke of Monmouth is crowned Charles III. James' followers, known to this counterhistory as Jacobites, scheme futilely to overturn the succession, and in following centuries to return England to Catholic rule. But though the new king, Charles III, has difficulties with a diehard group of strong Catholic lords, immediate events are largely similar to those in the real world. After the reign of three more Stuart kings (Charles IV, James II, and Charles V) we reach the 1800s, and a world like—and unlike—our own.

There is Revolution in France. Without the American Revolution's pattern to follow—for without the weak and unpopular Hanovers on the throne, political relations with the American colonies have never degenerated into warfare—the uprising is far more violent, more along the lines of our own century's Russian Revolution. Napoleon rises to power as a military dictator, and is soon Master of Europe. Having destroyed the anointed Royal house of France, Napoleon is master of a secular Empire that functions without the ancient land-magic based upon covenants with the Oldest People, the prehuman inhabitants of Europe. As in our world, Britain opposes the Corsican Beast, and it is Britain's funding that keeps the Triple Alliance—England, Prussia, and Russia—in the field against Napoleon.

The war's consequences reach to the New World. In this world, the Louisiana Purchase by the fledgling United States in 1805 never takes place. French Louisianne stretches from the Appalachian Chain to the Red River, a vast unruly territory still staunchly Royalist but under the uneasy control of Imperial France. West of the Red River, the land belongs to Spain, as does Florida (the Viceroyalty of New Spain) as far north as our own world's Atlanta, Georgia. As the New

England Colonies—in this world called New Albion—are still under English dominion, slavery has been outlawed in the Colonies in 1807, and the Colonial lords are more interested in selling goods to the indigenous Indian tribes than in displacing them. The economic conflict between slave-holding Louisianne and free New Albion threatens to break into war—and Napoleon, desperate for money to fund his expanding aggression, sends an Imperial governor to Louisianne to extort all he can from his New World treasury . . . the Marquis de Sade.

But all is not sanguine within the New England Colonies, either. Aware of the rich commercial opportunities of the new world, fueled in part by Napoleon's Continental Blockade, various factions, including the Jacobites, petition England to be granted fiefs and kingdoms of their own, and when that fails, plot to take them by force. The death of Foreign Secretary Charles James Fox in September of 1806 not only leaves a vacuum in British political leadership which these factions hope to exploit, but puts an end to England's secret peace negotiations with Talleyrand.[1] Though Spain retains a measure of independence, her king is dying, and she will fall to Napoleon in less than a year, granting the French Emperor a vast increase in territory that will fuel his continuing ambition and lead to Lord Wellesley— later the Duke of Wellington—taking the field against France on the battlefields of neutral Portugal in 1809.

But for the present, the long-delayed wedding of Prince Jamie of England and Princess Stephanie of Denmark, bringing Denmark firmly into the fold of the Grande Alliance, is hoped by many to herald a speedy end to Napoleon's aggression.

It is 1807. And our story begins. . . .

—Andre Norton & Rosemary Edghill

---

1. Fact.

PROLOGUE:

The Princes of the Air
(Paris, Walpurgisnacht, 1807)

The ancient house on the twisting Rue de la Morte had been an abode of the gentilesse some centuries before, but the changing tastes, first of the nobility and then the bourgeoisie, had abandoned it to the vagaries of Fate. When the Glorious '92 swept away both aristocrat and servant, the house—a thing of crumbling walls and canted floors long abandoned to mold and rot—gained a certain temporary currency, for the twisting lanes of the worst district in Paris held a real attraction for conspirators and rebels. But the star of Revolution was eclipsed in turn by the First Consul's Imperial ambitions, and the house was forgotten once more.

Or not precisely forgotten, for its brief ascendancy had brought it to the attention of a man who required just such a house, even in the days of Liberty, Equality, and fraternal love among all men.

Like many in the new government, he had prudently turned his coat years before there seemed any need of it. He had been a soldier and a diplomatist, a husband, an aristocrat, and a philosopher, and in this last role his writings had won their author some currency during the Days of Glory, as well as his release from prison.

What surprised some was that an empire should have a use for such a man. Others, though they said so with great circumspection, held that the Emperor Napoleon, having ground both Man and God beneath the iron heel of his ambition, had only the Devil left to turn to.

The Devil and his servant, Donatien Alphonse François, the Count—styled Marquis—de Sade.

Imperial France had turned its back upon both the *haut magie* that had consecrated its kings and the pacts with the Oldest People which had bound its nobility to the land. All that remained to the Emperor were those darker powers of which M'sieur le Comte had made himself master during a lifetime spent in slaking his vast appetite for pain. The Comte provided results, and so the Emperor provided patronage, and carefully did not enquire into the methods that produced those results.

Though a man who had made the Pope kneel before him must be presumed to have no fear of demons. . . .

And when the Empire did not need his services, the Comte— lately created Duc d'Charenton by his grateful master—pursued his studies and his pleasures. Age had granted him a certain wisdom— in his 67th year, the former Comte de Sade had learned the value of anonymity. He had purchased the old house upon the Rue de la Morte through the services of an agent, and if screams were occasionally heard here at night, well, such sounds were common enough in the district. And those who joined de Sade in his pleasures and survived them were circumspect for many reasons.

But this night is different.

At ten of the clock, he had ridden out from his official residence in the black-lacquered crested coach that bore him to those official functions he deigned to attend, but the coach only took him as far as the Rive Gauche before it was met by another, far inferior, vehicle. Beneath the soft April rain, de Sade transferred to the second coach. It was driven by the trusted—and only—servant to attend de Sade at his house in the Rue Morte, one Grisalle.

Another hour's jolting travel brought the shabby anonymous vehicle to its destination. Grisalle did not stop before the house, but proceeded directly to the mews behind it. Rather than be seen upon the street, the Duc preferred to enter the house through the servant's entrance, completely unobserved. In the coach itself, he had exchanged his own soberly-elegant cloak and glossy bicorne for a shabby and much-patched cape of dull fustian and a villainous low-crowned hat of battered flea-colored felt pulled low. Only his hands betrayed the disguise—white and plump like a pair of corpse-fed spiders, ornamented with a dozen costly jewels like the glistening bodies of dead insects. Despite the well-tended softness of the skin, the nails were black and ragged, as if eaten away by unspeakable vices.

Thus shrouded from view, the Duc made his way from the stables to the house, his only light a shuttered lantern that Grisalle had provided. His feet plashed through deep puddles, for the garden space was left untended and undrained. Weeds of every sort grew up over piles of decomposing waste, and the bright eyes of feral cats watched him from the darkness. Grisalle had gone before him, and the door to the kitchen was unlocked.

The house smelled strongly of damp and neglect. The kitchen was dark and empty, the fire in its great iron stove shedding the only light. No one had used this kitchen for its intended use for a very long time. On the table stood a large hamper of provisions, but that was for later. On this April night, the Duc went fasting to his work.

Grisalle ignited a spill from the coals and used it to light a branch of candles which he presented to his master. De Sade flung his hat and cloak to the floor and took the light silently, striding off into the depths of the house while his servant stayed behind.

The rooms on the floor above were as dark and cold as the kitchen and loggia, for though he was notoriously a libertine, de Sade was no sensualist. The passions he gratified had little to do with pleasure, and he passed onward to those rooms which saw extensive use.

The third floor of the old house contained a series of rooms whose doors could be flung back to open the space for dancing or card parties, and the floor had once displayed a fine inlay of exotic woods, but years of neglect had nearly obliterated its splendor. What was not destroyed by spills, burns, and the battering of heavy booted feet had been hidden beneath painted sigils of the Art Magickal.

The Duc moved into the foremost room, lighting the standing candles that stood on the tables. Here it did not matter whether it was midnight or noon: the windows were covered with draperies of heavy canvas, and painted black as well, lest the outside world intrude upon what was done here. Several censers were scattered about the room, to be lit at need, and a small fire burned in the grate, as it did nine months out of the year, for whatever his inclinations toward his own comfort, de Sade's precious books and papers could not be allowed to suffer the pervasive damp. Besides the ornate writing desk and several locked cabinets of curious and ancient books, the room's only furniture was a series of stout tables. One held an alembic and other apparatus for the distillation of drugs. Scattered across its marble surface were various boxes and bottles, each labeled in de Sade's own spidery hand.

The bitter scent that could be only faintly discerned in the kitchen was far more pronounced here—a scent as offensive to the nostrils as that of corruption, but somehow far more dry and burning. There was a choked moaning coming from the center room—wind, animal, or even human—but de Sade paid it no attention. Moving closer to the small fire, he added a shovelful of coals to its flames and began, with quick, impatient movements, to undress.

Reaching into a chest along the wall, the sorcerer withdrew an open-fronted sleeveless garment. It was made of rough undyed homespun embroidered with fine silk. Edging the opening at the front was a design of flames and Cabalistic sigils, and upon the back was a triangle of black silk upon which a goat's head had been embroidered in silver thread, its eyes sewn with rubies and seeming to glow. De Sade donned this garment and, half-clad as he was, rummaged in the trunk until his fingers closed upon the object he sought. It was a whip, its butt a human thighbone overbraided with black leather. Triangles of lead were knotted into its long leather tails, promising hideous injury to its victims.

He carried it with him to the table, and set it aside for a moment while he assembled a curious potion, grating bitter chocolate into a stained silver chalice, and adding to the shavings the crushed dried bodies of a certain beetle and several drops of oil of hashish. He then half-filled the cup with a red wine in which pieces of wormwood had been steeping, and beat the mixture into a foam with a small gold whisk. Carrying the cup and the scourge, he passed from one room into the next.

The center room was surrounded completely with black velvet draperies. The only light in the room came from the vigil candle in its red glass safe that burned at the foot of an inverted crucifix hung upon the north wall. Setting the items he carried upon the altar, the Duc took a candle, lit it from the votive, and moved quietly about the room, kindling open braziers and the candles which framed several lesser shrines about the walls of the room.

Here stood a Black Virgin, crowned with stars . . . her face twisted into a lascivious grin, her hands cupped to present her naked breasts. Beside her stood a strange figure—half goat, half human, with a burning torch between his horns and a monstrous erect phallus formed of twined serpents. Beyond them was a depiction of Luciferge Rofocalo, the Lord of This World, rising triumphant out of the flames of Hell, his black wings spread wide.

Now the room was well lit, and the crucified figure upon the inverted cross could clearly be seen. Its body was marked with deep red weals, but the head crowned with thorns was that of a braying ass.

Curls of smoke were beginning to spiral skyward from the braziers, filling the room with the scent of burning rue, myrtle, henbane, nightshade, and thorn-apple. The Duc looked upon his work with a faint smile of satisfaction. If the existence of this place were known, it would surely mean his death, for there were things that even the Great Beast who now ruled France could not be seen to condone. But soon disclosure of de Sade's small vices would not matter, for the culmination of two years of ritual and sacrifice would be reached tonight with this final sacrifice.

Turning away from the altar, de Sade felt along the wall until he had located a hidden door concealed behind the draperies. Drawing back the bolt, he opened the door to a small closet.

"And how are you this evening, Sister Marie?" he asked genially.

The woman inside the closet moaned beseechingly, falling forward into the light. Her pale hair was filthy and matted, and her naked body bore the suppurating sores of previous beatings. As was necessary to this most important of all sacrifices, she was a virgin of aristocratic blood, the by-blow of an English milord who had arranged that she be fostered at the convent at Sacre Coeur. De Sade had arranged to have her taken from there three months ago.

"In the name of God—I beg you, M'sieur—" she whimpered.

"Yes, yes. You beg and I deny, for such is the responsibility of the strong to the weak," de Sade said reprovingly. Ignoring the girl's stench, he lifted her easily to her feet and walked her toward the altar.

After so many days of darkness, even so little light was blinding to the young novice. She raised her thin arms to shield her face, too weak to otherwise resist. When the Duc pressed her against the altar, she clutched at it for support. Her eyes were bruised, her mouth puffy with blows and smeared with blood.

"Here, child," the Duc said kindly, raising the chalice to her lips. "You must drink. It will give you strength."

Grisalle had kept her without water for more than a day, so at first she sucked at the tainted liquid greedily, swallowing several mouthfuls before she realized what it was. When the bitterness of it penetrated her senses she began to struggle, but de Sade, one hand tangled in her hair and the other tilting the chalice to her mouth, forced her to drink far more of the draught than she was able to spill. When the chalice was empty he tossed it away and lifted the girl up onto the altar, the motion knocking the scourge to the floor.

The first effects of the potion seized her almost immediately: her struggles were disordered and fruitless, and he was easily able to bear her backward, until she was supine upon the black stone. Lengths of silk rope were already affixed to four bronze rings set at the corners, and de Sade bound her to them with the ease of long practice.

"Le Bon Dieu curse your name!" the girl spat. Tears filled her eyes, but they blazed defiance at her captor.

"Oh, I do hope He does," de Sade said absently. He took a cruse of red oil from the floor and began pouring it over her body.

✻   ✿   ✿

"Astaroth, Asmodeus—princes of amity—I conjure you to accept my sacrifice. Luciferge Rofocalo—master of treasure—hear my plea. I offer up to you a feast abominable to the Lord of Heaven. In this wilderness I offer you a supper of flesh instead of bread, of blood instead of wine, that my own hunger may be fulfilled. Adonai, Adonai, Adonai—"

At each recitation of the name, the scourge rose and fell softly against the bleeding flesh tied to the altar. Sister Marie was still alive, for it was important to de Sade that she remain so, at least until the end of this ceremony.

For the first hour she had met his invocations with her prayers, calling upon the Blessed Mother and all the holy saints and angels to preserve her. Then, for a while, she had only screamed, and now she lacked even the strength for that.

Each time de Sade repeated the prayers the room grew colder. The candles that had once burned brightly guttered now with a strange blue flame, and the fumes from the censers had drifted down to cloak the floor like a strange unseasonal fog, hiding the signs and inscriptions scratched and painted there.

Thirst and exhaustion dragged at his limbs like rebellious servants, but his passion for the secret delights of Hell drew the diabolist onward. Of all the prayers and sacrifices he had offered in the long months of this rite—this was the greatest: a young virgin ravished away from her vows, degraded and tormented to madness. When he had surrendered her, surely Luciferge, the Light-Bringer, would grant him what he sought.

"O reasonable Lord, just Lord, master of slanders, dispenser of the fruits of evil, cordial of the vanquished, suzerain of resentment, accountant of humiliations, treasurer of old hatred, king of the disinherited, grant me your power that I may overthrow the do-nothing King and coward God who has betrayed your followers!"

It was midnight. Between the first stroke and the last, the prayers of pious men would have no power.

"*Hic est enim calix sanguinis mei,*"[2] de Sade said softly. He took

---

2. "This is the cup of my blood."

up a small knife made of black glass and cut carefully into the vein that ran beneath the girl's breast. The dark blood welled up swiftly, and as it did he snatched up a flagon of carved jade and set it to catch the stream. When it had filled, he raised it as high as he could, and poured the blood over the figure of the ass-headed Christ.

He turned back to the girl. He must move quickly now, while she still lived. Setting aside the knife of glass, he took up one of black iron, and made a deep cut below the girl's breastbone. The girl screamed, rallied by the pain to full consciousness once more. Plunging his hand into the opening, he reached up, clutching at her still-beating heart, and ripped it from her body.

It seemed as if she lived a moment more, but if so, de Sade did not see her. He had turned, offering that which he held to the blasphemous Crucifix.

"Hoc est enim corpus meum,"[3] de Sade said, setting the heart upon the brazier of coals made ready at the foot of the crucifix. *"Aquerra Goity—Aquerra Beity—Aquerra Goity—Aquerra Beity!"*[4] The flesh hissed as the fire took it, shriveling and blackening as clouds of bitter steam belched skyward.

WHO SUMMONS ME? a Voice demanded behind him.

De Sade knew better than to turn to look upon the face of his Master. He kept his eyes fixed upon a small mirror of polished obsidian affixed to the foot of the cross. In it he could see the room, crazily distorted and reversed. He could also see what looked like a flaw of dark light, a disordering of the air, and he knew that the One he had summoned had come to him. De Sade's power would last only until the virgin's heart was burnt to ash, and he must be both quick and careful.

"I, your most faithful worshipper."

TO WHAT END?

"I beg a boon of you, infernal Lord," de Sade said. "I beseech you, in the name of the Treasure I dare not name, grant me its possession so that I may suborn the Table of Heaven, and exalt that which has been cast into the Pit!"

---

3. "This is my body."
4. "The Goat Above, The Goat Below."

There was a long silence, broken only by the sizzle of burning flesh upon the coals, as de Sade waited, almost swooning, his attention fixed unwaveringly upon the black mirror.

YOU SEEK THAT WHICH ONLY THE MOST HOLY MAY APPROACH.

"Only tell me where it lies, and I will find a way to gain it!" de Sade vowed recklessly. "I will prepare you such a feast as has never been offered to you by the hand of living man!"

IF YOU FALL OF THIS VOW, YOU ARE MINE.

The last stroke of the unheard church bell tolled, and the giddiness against which de Sade had fought overwhelmed him at last. He sank helplessly to the floor, his blood-soaked tools falling from his flaccid hands.

He did not know how long he lay in the throes of unconsciousness, but when he roused himself at last, the braziers had burned down and the candle flames once more burned yellow. Slowly, cursing his age and the stiffness of his joints, de Sade got painfully to his feet.

The floor was sticky with the girl's spilled blood. But as he regarded it, it seemed to him that the marks were too regular, too orderly, to be simply the spillage of mortal fluids.

It was a map. And glinting at its center, a small fleck of green fire.

The object he sought.

The Grail.

"And so the game begins," de Sade said softly. "All of you great men who despise me, who think that you can use me and set me aside when my use is done, I say to you that your day is done, your empire at an end! For the sorcery that has been your puppet will be your master, and on that day neither crowns nor swords will save you—this I, the Duc d'Charenton, swear to you all!"

1

Under an English Heaven
(June 1807)

The rooftops of London sparkled as if they had been polished. The spring had been wet, miring carriages in hedgerows and making travel to the opening of Parliament—and the Season—more than usually hazardous. Despite that inconvenience, every townhouse and rented lodging in every even-remotely fashionable district of Town was full to bursting by the Ides of March, their steps newly limewashed and the knockers on the doors, for this Season was to be the most glittering since bloody Revolution had struck down the aristocracy of France fifteen years before.

The Court, as was its usual custom, spent Yuletide at Holyrood Palace, but instead of spending deep winter in procession from one Great House to the next, this year the Court had returned directly to St. James Palace after Hogmanay[5], for there was much to do to prepare for a Royal wedding.

The marriage-lines, and the treaty that accompanied them, had

5. Scots New Years'.

been ready for over two years, for this was a marriage of state, one that would bind two countries as well as two persons together. Prince Jamie of England, King Henry's heir, was to wed Princess Stephanie Julianna of Denmark, securing a Protestant royal bride for England and a new support for the Grande Alliance all in one stroke. But though speed was of the essence, first social considerations, then political ones, had delayed the match again and again.

First, the Royal wedding embassy—two ships, the princess, her trousseau, and the final version of the treaty—had mysteriously vanished between Copenhagen and Roskild. Finding the princess had taken months. Soothing her brother, the Prince Regent, had taken longer, and by the time Stephanie was safe in England, all the ambassadors and dignitaries who had come for the wedding had returned home again.

Though Prince Frederick wished to withdraw his sister from the marital alliance, King Henry had the girl under his hand, and was not inclined to lightly set aside what had been organized with such pains. So Henry smiled, and delayed, and prayed that the news from Europe would be brighter—for while the Great Beast daily engorged himself upon what had once been the sovereign thrones of Europe, his northern neighbor could not be sanguine about declaring himself Napoleon's enemy.

Meanwhile, Henry must woo his own people as well, hesitant as always about accepting foreign princes into their midst. If the marriage did not have popular support, riots at home would negate any advantage England might claim upon a foreign battlefield.

Secret peace negotiations conducted by Mr. Fox had caused further delay,[6] for the making of the marriage, Talleyrand vowed, would be seen by France as an additional act of war. So King Henry had counterfeited public reasons for private caution until the negotiations had broken down completely. That had consumed the summer of the following year, and he vowed that the Princess would be married

6. Charles James Fox sent overtures to Talleyrand in February 1806, but whatever might have become of them was short-circuited by Fox's death the next month. Talleyrand was infamous for conducting independent clandestine peace negotiations with various members of the Grande Alliance.

next Midsummer Day, for the strain of attempting to preserve her countenance as an unmarried maiden was far greater than he had ever imagined it could be.

At least his heir had accepted the betrothal. Prince Jamie, once its most volatile opponent, was now the happy confederate of Princess Stephanie, though his relationship with his future bride held more of fellowship than of romance. The Danish Court was one of the most protocol-laden in all of Europe, and it seemed that the Princess had chafed under its restrictions. Despite the best efforts of Henry and his courtiers, the rumors about the Princess's behavior had multiplied daily in the weeks following her arrival, and each rumor held more than a grain of truth.

It was not, as Henry had once said to the Duke of Wessex, as if *all* these reports could possibly be true—"Though enough of them are that I have had it that vouchers for Almack's would be impossible to obtain."

"It is just as well that Prince Jamie's wife will not require them," Wessex had replied lazily. "And if the Patronesses cannot like her, then the same is not true of the *mobile*,[7] for she is cheered whenever she appears in public."

This was certainly true, and had strengthened King Henry's bargaining position with Denmark considerably, for the Princess possessed a most republican soul. She adored the people of London, and their entertainments, and the people adored her unreservedly in return. The amount of bad verse which had been written to her raking blonde good looks was a daunting thing, and had inspired lampoons and rebuttals in its turn, until it seemed that London was awash in a sea of rhyme—a far more fearsome threat, as His Grace of Wessex whimsically confided to his valet, than any French threat.

But at last all the elements were in harmony. The date of the ceremony was fixed. Emissaries from Denmark, Spain, Prussia, Russia, and even China crowded the nation's capital. Nobility from En-

---

7. "Mobile" is short for "mobile party," a witticism of this period, as only land-owners held the vote, while the "mobile party," workers and city-dwellers, were for the most part without a political voice. The phrase has been shortened further in our own time to "mob."

gland's New World Colonial possessions and nabobs from the East
India Company vied with each other to produce exotic entertainments for both the *mobile* and the *ton*.

And at last the day itself arrived.

"Sarah, where are you?" the Duke of Wessex demanded irritably,
striding down the hall to his wife's dressing room.

Herriard House, in London's fashionable East End, had been
seething with activity since long before dawn. The crush of traffic
about Westminster Abbey today required that they set out no later
than eight o'clock of the morning to be in place for the one o'clock
ceremony. In addition, Their Graces were giving one of the score of
parties to follow the wedding breakfast, and the house was already
filled with guests, borrowed servants, and chaos of the most select
order.

"Sarah!" Wessex said again, thrusting open the door to her dressing room without ceremony. "Where—"

"Here, of course. Where else would I be?" his wife asked, her
words nearly concealing the gasp of outrage from Knoyle, Her
Grace's abigail.

Wessex stopped, his gaze flickering over the room full of women.
His Duchess sat before her mirror, her back straight, her grey eyes
brilliant, and her light brown hair in copious disarray as she suffered
the ministrations of her hairdresser. Knoyle hovered indecisively, unable to decide between overseeing her lady's toilette or regarding the
seamstress who was even now putting the finishing touches on her
ladyship's glittering rose-grey gown.

"Are you not yet dressed?" Wessex demanded, though the answer was patently obvious.

"Easy enough for you, my lord—you have a uniform to wear.
I'm not so lucky," Sarah answered with acerbic fondness.

Major His Grace Rupert St. Ives Dyer, the Duke of Wessex,
dismissed his gleaming regimentals without even a glance. His Grace
was a tall, slender man with the black eyes of his Stuart forbears and
the blond fairness of his Saxon ancestors. The Dukedom could trace
its beginnings to the merry court of the Glorious Restoration, though

the first Duke of Wessex, whose mother was that firebrand lady, the
Countess of Scathach, came from a line that was already both ancient
and royal. All the Dyers possessed a cold and ruthless charm, though
the young Duke—whose sword-blade good looks had been compared
by more than one admirer to the kiss of *la Guillotine* herself—
seemed to possess it in abounding measure. His Grace had recently
married, though was yet to set up his nursery, and was said to retain
an interest in matters at the Horse Guards, though what that interest
was, there were few who could say. For many years he had held a
commission in the Eleventh Hussars, and in fact had purchased pro-
motion last year.

But his rank was little more than a screen for his more clandestine activities, and he and Sarah had spoken of his resigning it. He
was glad, now, to have retained it: the silver-laced blue jacket, scarlet
trousers, and gleaming gold-tasseled Hessians were far more comfortable than the Court dress, with Ducal coronet and ermine cloak,
otherwise prescribed for such an important occasion.

Sarah's own costume was a bulky thing of hoops and feathers, as
much unlike the current mode as could be imagined, and she was a
freakish sight in the antique garb that the rigid Court protocol insti-
tuted by Henry's Queen demanded.

"Our coach, madame, leaves in a quarter of an hour, whether
you are in it or no," Wessex said with an ironic bow.

"And the Princess will marry whether I am there or not," Sarah
pointed out reasonably. "There are seven other women to carry her
train. Oh, do go away, Wessex. Terrify the servants. I vow I shall be
with you as soon as I may, and I can be there no sooner."

The Duke of Wessex, ever a prudent tactician, retreated with a
silent flourish.

Sarah regarded the closed door with inward amusement. Her formidable mother-in-law and godmama, the Dowager Duchess, had
sworn to her often and often that all men were just alike, and would
rather face a line of cannon than a public ceremony, but until this
moment, Sarah had been certain that her own husband—whom she
had apostrophized as a hatchet-faced harlequin upon their first meet-

ing—was of another order of creation entirely. It cheered her obscurely to see him as rattled as any other man upon such an
important occasion, particularly since His Grace was in so many re-
spects unlike any other husband.

She was not certain of the precise moment upon which she had
known him for what he was, for the early days of their relationship
had been a series of shocks, riddles, and misunderstandings, complicated not a little by Sarah's occult and precipitous arrival from
another world to take the place of her dying counterpart, this world's
Marchioness of Roxbury. When she had unwittingly stepped into her
double's role, she had acquired not only an identity, but a fiancé as
well, and one had been as cryptic as the other, for the Duke of
Wessex was England's most noble . . . spy.

The craft of espionage was not a respectable one, considered,
even by those who employed its agents, to be both dishonorable and
demeaning. The fact that it was necessary as well was a terrible par-
adox that had forced Wessex to conceal his true nature and activities
even from his own family. Even now, if the truth of his endeavors
on behalf of the Crown became common knowledge, the family
would be ruined socially, and have little choice but to withdraw to
the country or even to Ireland.

But even with the stakes as high as that, Wessex had trusted his
unknown bride with his greatest secret, and that trust was the basis
of the comfortable love that had grown up between them in the two
years they had been married.

*Tendre or no, I see little future for us if I cause him to wait!
Rupert has worked so hard for this day, both as the Duke of Wessex
and as an agent of the Crown, that it is not amazing that his nerves
should be shot to flinders. I vow that mine are, and I have had little
to do but receive reports of the Princess's high jinks!*

"Is the gown ready?" she asked.

"A moment more, Your Grace," the modiste said.

Wessex galloped down the stairs two at a time, Atheling following
him with his shako, pelisse, and gauntlets. The Duke stopped at the
foot of the stair to receive his accoutrements and permit last-minute

adjustment of his uniform. Atheling settled the shako precisely upon the Duke's newly-shorn flaxen hair and made a last adjustment to the drape of the bearskin pelisse before stepping back to indicate his ministrations were at an end.

At that moment, Buckland, the butler, who was standing beside the front door with a look of ill-use upon his sallow, lantern-jawed countenance, cleared his throat and made an imperceptible movement forward.

"Your Grace has a visitor," he pronounced.

"What, *now*?" Wessex demanded, more than a little astounded. Behind Buckland, Wessex could see that the parlor door was locked. Presumably, his caller was within.

"Indeed, Your Grace." Buckland's manner assumed even more of expressionlessness, indicating how very much he disapproved of the caller. But the household staff had strict instructions to admit without question anyone who came to call upon His Grace (though also to secure those not known to them), for as a consequence of his duties to the Crown, Wessex's acquaintanceship was extraordinarily broad.

Wessex sighed, and tucked his shako more firmly beneath his arm. "Very well. I will attend to the matter at once. But let me know the moment Her Grace descends."

The butler inclined his head. Wessex stepped past him and unlocked the door to the small ground-floor parlor.

There was a small coal-fire burning upon the grate, for even in summer the ground-floor rooms were inclined to be damp. A large high-backed settee had been drawn up to face the fire, and the brandy decanter removed from the small table before the window to the floor beside the settee. Whoever Wessex's caller was, he had made himself entirely at home. Wessex shut the door with a firm click.

"I daresay, it's a trusting gentleman," a plaintive unseen voice complained in a rumbling bass.

"What the devil are you doing here?" Wessex demanded, recognizing the identity of the speaker at once.

The frame of the settee creaked as the caller got to his feet.

Though he was impeccably dressed in the sober height of morning fashion, with a blue superfine coat over biscuit-colored smallclothes, he was a not inconsiderable figure in any company, for Cerberus St. Jean was a giant of a man, well over six feet in height and nearly as wide, with massive shoulders and skin the smooth ebony color of brewed coffee.

The son of slaves brought to England a generation before, St. Jean was a native-born English freeman. He had been educated as a son of the household in which his parents had once served, and had matriculated at Cambridge. There, he had been recruited by Wessex's own master, and was one of the few of Wessex's fellow politicals with whom the Duke maintained a public relationship, for St. Jean's intelligence-gathering was of necessity confined to domestic soil, though through his startling talent for impersonation, he could take on a dozen parts and play them out flawlessly, from Limehouse slavey to *emigré* Marquis.

Wessex had been introduced to St. Jean for the first time more than a year ago, when his own duties had been focused more on the sifting of gathered intelligence and less upon the gathering of it. Since then, Baron Misbourne had decreed that Wessex must be withdrawn from the field, for on his last dangerous mission to France, Wessex's face had become too well known in high places. It had been something of a relief to move upward from the strictly-enforced ignorance of a field agent to mastery of more of the inner workings of the White Tower Group.

"I've come to give you the word about some gentlemen that you may meet this afternoon. Lord White—" (this was the albino Misbourne's work-name, in the event he must be spoken of outside the walls of the house on Bond Street) "—has received intelligence that trouble is brewing in the Colonies, and you will be in the company of many of the New Albion lords to-day."

"Trouble is always brewing in the West," Wessex answered. Wessex had only made a few brief visits to the New Albion colonies over the past ten years, and had never been briefed in-depth upon Albionese political affairs, though he knew in the most general way that the Tower was active there. "Devil take it, St. Jean, have you nothing more specific for me on this day of all days than a watching brief?"

St. Jean bent to retrieve his drink. The crystal tumbler was dwarfed by the size of his enormous hand.

"Only that you must pay attention to the Albionese lords today—who they speak to, and who speaks to them. Now that they must pay for the labor they once exacted as of right, the plantations, especially those in Virginia and the Carolinas that border on French Louisianne, complain that they will be bankrupt. Lord White is concerned that this talk may become open rebellion, which we cannot afford while the Tyrant holds Europe."

"They are squeezed very hard," Wessex commented. "With the Mississippi and the Port of Nouvelle-Orléans[8] closed to England these past four years, the cost of shipping their goods out of an Atlantic port doubles their costs. Still, I find it hard to sympathize with their distress that slavery has ended. Men are not cattle to be bought and sold."

The matter of pan-British abolition—for French and Spanish interests in the New World were still a ready market for slaves even today—had preoccupied Parliament for almost twenty years. Since 1772 there had been no slavery in England herself, and any slave brought to England was manumitted with his first step onto English soil. By 1778, this was true of all four of the United Kingdoms.

The Abolitionists, led by, among others, Olaudah Equiano of Cambridgeshire, himself once a slave, drew their membership from every level of society. Even King Henry himself had spoken in their favor, and at last the tide of special interest had turned. In March of this year, the King had been able to put his imprimatur upon the bill put forward by William Wilberforce to abolish in all its particulars the slave trade in Britain and her New World dominions—including Prince Rupert's Land and New Albion—as well.[9] No longer would British ships lawfully carry a human cargo to foreign ports, nor would

---

8. Or, as it would be known in our world after 1805, New Orleans.

9. True in both worlds, actually. Wilberforce's bill became law in March 1807. One of its less-expected results was to fuel the traffic in slaves smuggled into the Port of New Orleans from Haiti and the Caribbean by the privateers of Grande Terre. Aren't you glad I'm here to tell you these things?

any Englishman be permitted to hold slaves, no matter the country of his birth and residence.

"Still, they will resent it," St. Jean said mildly. "And to enforce the law will gain the Crown few friends. The question is, how desperate will resentful men become? We must discover who our enemies are, and what plans they entertain for our future. Spain is neutral now, but if she were to indicate that heretics such as we English are meddling in the affairs of a Catholic nation, she would declare instantly for France, and once she did, Portugal would join her, out of fear of the Beast if nothing else."

That much was true. Those countries not already under Napoleon's yoke performed a delicate balancing act of check and countercheck upon one another. Pitt's Catholic Emancipation Act six years before had been the price of peace with Ireland: nothing must be allowed to disrupt the fragile network of European alliances, neither ancient feuds nor present grudges. Spain's defection would be nearly as great a disaster as an Irish—or Colonial—revolt.

"Yet it is only a matter of time before Talleyrand gains something that will accomplish such a trick from that same informant in our midst who caused Talleyrand to lead little Mr. Fox on with the negotiations for a treaty he had no intention of making."

Though Wessex spoke of the matter so glibly, there were only three men in England who knew for a fact that there was a traitor somewhere within the walls of the White Tower. Baron Misbourne had broached the matter with Wessex over a year ago, but Wessex had already suspected the traitor's existence, and more—that the turncoat had led his double life for more than twenty years.

When Wessex's father had voyaged to France to rescue the Dauphin, then a child of eight, Andrew, Duke of Wessex, had vanished without a trace. And the only men who could have betrayed him were those who had sent him—the White Tower itself.

And so, when Misbourne asked, Wessex had agreed to hunt Misbourne's traitor and his own, using any means to do so. He had recruited St. Jean to help him because a domestic political—and one who had not even been a member of the White Tower Group when Andrew, Duke of Wessex, had vanished fifteen years before—could not possibly be their Judas.

"You have not told me all you came to say," Wessex observed. What he and St. Jean had retailed so far was no more than he already knew—not reason enough for St. Jean's visit, especially today.

"I have heard, from sources outside the Tower that under cover of this wedding, one of the Black Pope's spymasters is to come to London to meet with his agent. I have told this to no one now but you. I am to report to Lord White today—what shall I say to him?" St. Jean's face was troubled.

"Tell him nothing," Wessex said brutally. "I will take responsibility for it, if anyone must."

St. Jean opened his mouth to protest, but at that moment there was a discreet scratching at the door.

"Her Grace, Your Grace," Buckland announced.

The church-spires still cast long blue shadows as the great Ducal coach rumbled heavily along the street. It was drawn by six heavy-boned Frisians, for like many things in the Duke's vicinity, it was not at all what it seemed. The lacquered oak panels in the ducal colors of silver and green concealed armor plating thick enough to stop a round from a Baker rifle. Its axles held retractable blades that could cripple the horses of an encroaching team, and its interior harbored many secrets, among them a brace of concealed pistols. Because of these things, among others, it was not a vehicle built for speed. But on this day, speed was not a matter of concern.

Wessex sat back on the deep green squabs of the bench and regarded his bride. The roof of the coach was high enough so that her egret-feather headdress was in no danger of being crushed. Her cowled cloak of deep rose velvet, lined in satin to match the dress, was pooled about her on the seat, while her dress, stretched and pulled by the archaic hoops, was a quizzical sight.

"We shall make good time, I think, until we enter the City," Wessex observed. "Fortunately, Buckland was good enough to induce Mrs. Beaton to pack us a hamper, or else we might well perish of hunger before the wedding breakfast."

Sarah's eyes flashed in the dimness of the coach's interior as she inspected the chronometer set into the wall of the coach. "Eight-fifteen," she sighed.

Though a notorious early riser—as Wessex, given his preference, was not—the Duchess disliked both confinement and enforced idleness. The prospect of five hours spent sitting in a coach as it inched its way along the street was not one she delighted in. "I suppose we couldn't just have walked?" she said wistfully.

"Indeed we could not," her husband said repressively, though his mouth quirked. "Persons so notoriously high in the instep as the Duke and Duchess of Wessex could not be seen cavorting about the public street in the guise of an infantry regiment."

"No doubt you are correct, my lord," his dutiful spouse replied. "Rupert, who was that who called upon you this morning? I saw a horse standing in the street."

The percipient question brought Wessex's thoughts abruptly back to his distasteful duties. At the wedding breakfast this afternoon, he must be sure to speak to the representatives of the Colonies—particularly Catholic Marylandshire, chartered in 1635 and a hotbed not only of the Old Religion, but of those who still wished to see a Catholic monarch upon the throne of England. The only good thing about the accession of Napoleon was that the Catholic Jacobites who had favored Charles' brother James over his son Monmouth could no longer scheme to make common cause with France, now only nominally a Catholic nation. As for Virginia, Dutch New York, and Quaker Pennsylvania—

"Rupert, you are not attending." Sarah's voice held an edge, perceptible even over the sound of the wheels.

"I am indeed. I am merely hoping not to be called upon to answer the question," the Duke responded.

"Oh." Sarah's voice went flat with realization. "It is one of *those* acquaintances, then."

Once more Wessex did not answer. Sarah regarded him unhappily. Though she accepted his work, she hated being shut out of it.

"It is merely a matter of idle political gossip," Wessex said lightly, trying to cheer her mood. "I would be a poor husband were I to tax your patience with talk of matters as far from your interests as New Albion's factionalism."

"Far! New Albion is *America*! Rupert, I was *born* there!" Sarah said indignantly.

"But not in this America," Wessex reminded her. Not for the first time, he tried to imagine Sarah's world—English colonies unthinkably divorced from English rule to become an independent nation without a king, an ally of Tyrant France. The England she described was even more alien—a land ruled by upstart German princes, whose slothful rule and cruel taxation had driven her colonies into revolt.

As always, the attempt to envision something so unthinkably alien defeated him. The Stuarts were the true kings of England. They had ruled wisely and justly since Great Elizabeth had passed the crown to the first James, through the Great Marriage and their pacts with the Oldest People.

"It cannot be so very different," Sarah said sulkily. She had known very little of her own world's England before her journey here, and so she had seen very little difference between one England and another.

"Perhaps not," Wessex agreed. "It is certainly little different from Europe—for in your world as in mine, France and England war, and who can say which shall be the master?"

Westminster Abbey was filled with the massed nobility of England, her colonies, and her allies, as the work of more than five years of diplomatism came at last to its conclusion—the marriage that would secure a Protestant princess for England and a Danish ally for the Grande Alliance.

Inside the Abbey the air was stiflingly warm, filled with the scents of perfume and incense. The church blazed with candles, their flames adding to the heat. There was a constant rustling as the standing spectators shifted position, overheated in their ceremonial silks and jeweled velvets.

James Charles Henry David Robert Stuart, Prince of Wales and Duke of Gloucester, stood before the Archbishop of Canterbury, awaiting his bride with a good impersonation of impatience. He was dressed entirely in white satin and silver lace, against which his chestnut hair and grey eyes shone to advantage. A coronet of rose gold, newly-commissioned for the ceremony, rested upon his perspiring brow.

Supporting him upon this occasion were his four brothers in marriage, for Prince James was the youngest of five, and the only boy. His four sisters had married, variously, Leopold, a prince of Saxe-Coburg-Gotha; Duncan, a Scots laird of that country's ancient royal line; Alexander, a Russian Grand Duke; and Earl Drogheda of the Anglo-Irish nobility. Their marriages, much as Jamie's own, had been made for political reasons, for the web of kinship among the nobility was a web of expediency, as well. Three of the groomsmen were in their uniforms, and that was a sore point with Jamie also, for he had long been denied the chance to serve in Britain's army. Over the past months it had become clear that soon King Henry must permit his army-mad heir to go to war, or else go himself. The scope of the conflict expanded every year, and Wessex suspected that in generations to come, a man's measure would be taken by the list of his triumphs in this great contest.

But at this moment, all matters of battle and empire were forgotten, as Jamie's bride made her appearance at the head of the aisle.

Princess Stephanie Julianna of Denmark was tall and fair and hoydenish, but today even the most precious high stickler could find no fault in her appearance or conduct. Her wedding dress was of pale gold silk, oversewn with pearls and brilliants. Her train was edged with the same lace that made up her veil, and both stretched for yards behind her. These items were managed by eight of her Ladies in Waiting in full court dress, among them the Duchess of Wessex.

Today the princess would exchange her Danish tiara for an English crown, and those who had brought her to this place all breathed a grateful sigh of relief. Up until the very last moment it had been possible that the princess's madcap sense of humor would lead her to elope once more, leaving her household to search for her in vain. That would mean the ruin of the treaty, for her brother, Prince Frederick, was a profoundly humorless man. But in a few short moments the ceremony would be completed, and the Danish Minister waited in a private chamber within the Abbey itself to present the treaty for the Prince Regent's seal.

Stephanie reached the altar and stopped. Her ladies in waiting arranged her train and withdrew to the side.

The Archbishop pronounced the words of the ceremony, and as he did, the air of expectation among the onlookers grew. Few of them would ever participate in a magic greater than this—the joining of a Prince of the Blood Royal to his bride.

At last the vows were exchanged, the rings blessed and presented. As Prince Jamie sealed his promise with a kiss, the word was passed to the waiting citizenry, and the crowds that had been gathering in the streets since midnight erupted in wild cheering.

And the thing was done.

The Prince and Princess were presented to King Henry, both kneeling to him as his subjects. There was a moment to sign the book, and then the newlyweds promenaded from the church to be escorted back to St. James Palace through streets filled with cheering humanity.

The Palace of St. James was located between St. James Park and Green Park, just south of Westminster and the Houses of Parliament. To its east, Buckingham House had been renovated to house the household of the Prince and Princess, and would soon play host for the first time to its young master and mistress. But the seat of government still rested within the red brick walls of St. James, where the martyred Charles I had spent his last night on earth. His son had defiantly vowed that the Stuarts would reign there for ever after, and from that day to this the Stuart line had boldly held court within those same red walls.

Today the whole kingdom was Henry's guest. Pavilions had been set up on the grounds, dispensing wine and roast meat to all who cared to partake, as well as paper favors printed with the likenesses of the Prince and Princess. Dancing floors had been laid among the trees, and musicians played for all who cared to dance.

Within the Palace itself, the King hosted such important men as the Earl of Malhythe, Baron Grenville, and the Lords-Lieutenant of both New Albion and Ireland, all of whom had come to witness the treaty. Even Prince Frederick was here, to grudgingly witness his sister's wedding, and to sign the Danish Treaty into existence.

The Duke of Wessex moved about the edges of the gathering like the wraith at the feast. He had escorted Sarah here, but for the moment she was attending the Princess, and his place was here, seeking out information.

But what information? Somewhere in London a French spymaster met with his English agent: was it here? Wessex gazed at a party of Albionese lords: Jefferson, Jackson, Burr. His general briefing on the Albionese political situation had only touched on the high points of the web of New World politics, but he did recognize the three men before him—each of whom, in his way, was important in New Albion political life.

Thomas Jefferson, Earl of Monticello and Lord-Lieutenant of New Albion, looked calm and even content: he ruled Britain's presence in the New World with an Augustinian detachment, presiding over the turbulent New Albion Parliament which met in Philadelphia, the colonial capital, a location equally-inconvenient to all the delegates.

Burr and Jackson were another matter, a badger and a fox each intent upon an independent New World kingdom, each for his own purposes. Jackson had spoken openly of clearing the Indians from the land to make way for British colonists, though he had not received much support for the notion. Burr was more subtle. He spoke beguilingly of the vast mineral wealth of the New World that lay fallow for men of vision to harvest. The lure of gold was powerful, and Burr was a persuasive man. If he managed to raise enough support among the New Albion lords, and somehow raise an army. . . .

If only, Wessex thought wistfully, *it were as simple as shooting him.* But political murder created more problems than it solved. Better to watch enemies you knew than destroy them and face trouble from an unknown enemy.

He accepted a glass of wine from a server, moving on through the press of celebrants—each intent more upon his own interest than upon the wedding celebrated here today—until he had reached Lord Malhythe.

Colworth Rudwell, the Earl of Malhythe, was in some sense a colleague of Lord Misborne, though they were masters of separate fiefs in Britain's intelligence community. He was a conscious epigone, even in the 19th century preferring the powdered wig and ruffles of an earlier age. Like Wessex, the late Charles James Fox, and half the peers of England, Malhythe could trace his lineage back to Good King Charles. He was attached to the Horse Guards in some inexplicit fashion, coordinating the reports from the Army's Exploring Officers and sharing the information where needed. Malhythe and Misbourne had clashed several times in jurisdictional disputes as military and political intelligence fought for ascendancy.

"My lord Earl." Wessex bowed. "A great day for England, is it not?"

"A better day when the Heir is born. Then His Highness can extinguish himself upon the battlefield as he likes, without fear of opening the throne to a German prince."

"As you say, sir. But securing Denmark as our ally seems to me to be a great cause for rejoicing," Wessex answered with studied mildness.

"If only because England has been the midwife of peace between Denmark and Russia," Malhythe riposted. Wessex smiled to himself. The Grande Alliance fought only slightly more fiercely against Napoleon than it did within its own membership.

He was about to say more, when a motion at the doorway stopped him. He turned toward the movement, as he did hearing Malhythe bite down upon a fervent oath of displeasure.

The man standing in the doorway was dressed in black velvet and diamonds, supporting himself upon a tall ivory cane. The tail of his silvery wig cascaded down his back. Wessex knew him. All the players of the Shadow Game knew him. But what in the name of the infernal saints was Baron Warltawk doing at Prince James' wedding breakfast?

He excused himself hastily from Malhythe, moving toward Warltawk. But before he could reach him, Sarah had appeared at his side, her court dress changed for a similar gown cut *à la mode.*

"Wessex!" she said, innocently pleased at having located him in the press. "I just saw the Lord Chamberlain—" she broke off, gazing at the peculiar figure in black velvet, who was moving slowly among the press of guests. "Who is that?"

"In his youth they called him 'Warltawk Kingbreaker,' " Wessex said meditatively. "He is a Jacobite who fled abroad in '69, and has lived virtually retired since the Revolution forced him home again. And I wonder very much what he is doing here."

The bell signaling that it was time to go in to breakfast chimed, and Wessex and his lady sought their places in the order of precedence.

"Is he important, this Warltawk?" Sarah asked as they rode toward Herriard House at the end of a day of toasts and speeches. The festivities had dragged on until there was barely enough time for the wedding guests to retreat and prepare themselves for the various balls and routs of the coming evening.

"He was once," Wessex said uncomfortably, unwilling to speak of things touching so nearly upon his other life. "Sarah, I do not wish to involve you—"

"Pooh!" said his wife roundly. "You are involved—how can I not be? And if it is gossip you want, who better than I—a weak and feeble woman—to get it for you?"

Wessex sighed. His better self warred against his practical nature, and, as usual, lost. "What I want to know," he said, gazing at the roof of the coach, "is who he sees, and why. Especially if it is any of the Albionese." The Duke wondered abruptly where Sarah would stand upon the question of a New World revolution. In her world, such revolutionaries were looked upon as heroes.

"Anything else?" Sarah asked helpfully.

Wessex shook his head. He never forgot that the enemies of England could make his wife a pawn on the chessboard of Europe, and what she did not know, she could not reveal. There were secrets he must keep, even from her.

❖   ❖   ❖

Herriard House was forty covers at dinner. Tables had been brought from storage, and the doors between the dining room and the withdrawing room thrown open to accommodate the vast length of linen-draped table. Most of those attending would go from here to the Wedding Ball being given at Buckingham House this evening, and even the Duke and Duchess of Wessex would make a token appearance there before returning to preside over their own festivities.

Looking down the table, Wessex had a moment's fervent wish for the presence of his partner, Illya Koscuisko. The volatile Pole was a master of disguise, and would have no difficulty in ferreting out the things Wessex so urgently wished to know. But Koscuisko was still able to operate upon the continent, and had been away on assignment for several months.

Warltawk's presence in London complicated things. Wessex was looking for a French spymaster and an English agent. Wessex had run agents in his time, and knew that a man would have to be mad to attempt to recruit Warltawk, so it was unlikely that the Baron was a French agent. Nor could Warltawk be running agents of his own—the former Kingbreaker was too closely watched for that. But if Warltawk were neither agent nor spymaster he must be playing at a different game.

To find out what it was, Wessex needed an ally. Suddenly, he smiled.

It had just occurred to him where to look for one.

2

Legend in Green Velvet
(Paris, May 1807)

The recently-christened *Palais de l'Homme* held the treasures of a plundered Empire. The wealth of Italy, the ancient grandeur of Egypt—the jewels, paintings, statuary of a thousand years filled the Emperor's palace. As were so many constructions of the Empire, the grandly titled *Palais de l'Homme* was a makeshift thing created from the hasty joining of two older edifices: the Louvre and the Tuileries.

Those who remembered the early days of the Revolution and the glorious ideals of equality and liberty they had held in those days kept prudently silent now. The ideal-crazed revolutionaries had toppled one luxurious despot only to discover themselves replacing him with another in the space of a handful of years. And France's present Imperial master, unlike her past Royal one, would not be content until he had devoured the world and remade it in his own image. At the same time as he proposed draconian peace treaties upon his victims, Napoleon tore down the ancient buildings of Paris to rebuild the city as a second Rome, eternal monument to his glory. The im-

mense new palace that Percier had designed would not be finished
for several years: until that day, the Emperor reigned in the place
from which his predecessor had reigned . . . if not quite in the same
style.

The Emperor's court was the largest the modern world had ever
seen, and its rituals were conducted upon a stunning scale. When a
supplicant entered the vast blue and gold throne room, the occupant
of the throne at the far end was a distant and nearly-invisible figure
set against a vast gilded sunburst surmounted by the laurel-crowned
Imperial signet and surrounded by his courtiers. As one proceeded
down the long scarlet expanse of carpet that connected the throne
and the entrance, slowly the petitioner felt his own consequence
diminishing as the figure of Napoleon loomed larger and larger, until
at last the petitioner gazed up a flight of white marble steps to the
gilt and crimson throne upon which sat the Master of the World,
and felt himself dwindle into utter insignificance.

Illya Koscuisko did not feel insignificant as he gazed about the
throne room, making note of who was in attendance this day and
who was not. He had been a part of this great drama for some
months now, and had gotten used to its scale.

He only wished he could become as used to his uniform.

Napoleon rotated his ceremonial guard, but his favorite—for
propaganda reasons—was the *Garde Polonaise,* formed from the regiments of partitioned Poland—and he employed it often. Upon forming the unit, he had redesigned the uniform of the Polish hussars
from which most of its members were drawn—now the eagle-wings
were of gold, towering six feet above the soldier's heads. The wolfskin
pelisses had been replaced with whole leopard-skins lined in red silk,
and upon the fronts of their shakos the men now wore a golden
dragon's mask, an empty symbol of their stolen kingdom.

It was because of the Emperor's hollow promises that Illya had
first joined the White Tower Group, for only through the defeat of
the Corsican Tyrant could his beloved Poland live again. It was one
of the amusing paradoxes with which his life abounded that to work
against Napoleon, it was necessary for Illya to embrace the life that
would have been his if he had in fact joined the tyrant, and for some

months now Illya had been passing as a member of the *Garde Pol-onaise.*

In his *persona* as a loyal Polish *chasseur,* Illya saw everything that went on in open court and a great deal that went on behind closed doors. He kept notes of all he learned, but passing the material back to England was dangerous, and he took the risk as rarely as possible. It would soon be necessary to make the effort, however, especially if rumor did not lie.

Illya tried, unobtrusively, to ease the aching weight of his cere-monial wings. The impractical ornaments would shear loose in the first seconds of a cavalry charge, but it was unlikely that the *Garde* would ever again be called upon to fight. At least when his duty here was over he could remove the wings—and in fact, Illya had it in mind to remove rather more than that, and the prospect of agreeable company in which to do so.

"Donatien Alphonse François de Sade, Duc d'Charenton!" the herald cried.

The great golden doors of the throne room were thrown open with a booming sound, and the hunched figure of the Satanic *duc* moved slowly to the center of the scarlet carpet.

So it is true, Illya thought in faint amazement. For the last several weeks, it had been rumored about the Court that the Emperor in-tended to appoint the Duc d'Charenton the new governor of French Louisianne in the far-off Americas. It was the only reason Illya could imagine for Napoleon to summon d'Charenton to appear in open court. Even in the atheistic religious climate of Imperial France, the man was worse than a scandal.

Illya knew little about the political situation in the Americas, but from Court gossip he had learned that Napoleon's hold upon his New World possessions was sketchy at best. Louisianne was rich, but it was also more loyal to the murdered Capet line than it was to Imperial France, and so the Emperor had always preferred to con-centrate his efforts on holding the rebellious—but more easily sub-dued—sugar isles of the Caribbean. Talleyrand had long urged his master to take a conciliatory path with Louisianne, but anything less tactful than sending them d'Charenton, Illya could not easily imagine.

After several minutes, d'Charenton reached the foot of the throne and knelt. An aide handed Napoleon—his Army uniform swathed in a purple velvet and ermine robe, and a coronet of golden laurel leaves upon his brow—a set of scrolls with ornate jeweled terminals. The Emperor unrolled it and began to read in his nasal, accented Corsican French.

"I, Napoleon I, by virtue of conquest King of France, Italy, Austria, Egypt, Africa, and the New World, do hereby grant the governorship of the province of Louisianne, located in the New World, to the Duc d'Charenton, there to rule as the representative of Imperial France, to mete out France's justice and to deal with her enemies in my name."

A discreet murmur of comment rose among the ranks of the courtiers. It was, Illya reflected, quite vexatiously puzzling.

Fortunately I don't need to know why Boney would do such a mad thing. I merely need to know that the news is important enough to risk trying to get it to England.

Wessex had often had cause to be grateful that Providence had possessed him of an understanding wife, but never more so than upon this particular occasion, for after making an appearance at the Royal Ball this evening—Warltawk had not been there—he had left Sarah to open the ball at Herriard House alone.

He had stopped only long enough to change from his ball-dress to something far more inconspicuous: breeches, boots, and a many-caped dark grey riding-coat. Then, taking up black riding-gloves and a low-crowned, wide-brimmed hat that would hide his features, the Duke was off to the stables to saddle his horse.

Hirondel greeted him warmly, the great black stallion nuzzling his master and making it difficult to bridle him—though Wessex could, and had, ridden the formidable beast with neither saddle nor bridle at need. The servants who were still putting away the carriage and wiping down its team paid no attention to their master's actions—they were paid well to see little and say less.

A few moments later Wessex and Hirondel were away. Wessex led the animal through a narrow path behind the mews that led to a side street. He continued to lead his mount for another block or so, until they were well removed from Herriard House, and then mounted up and began to ride briskly eastward just as the clock on a nearby steeple began to strike ten.

His enquiries had disclosed, through the Groom of the Chamber, that Lord Warltawk had not been sent an invitation to the Wedding Breakfast, though of course he had certainly been able to produce one upon arrival. Finding out who had not attended the fete so that Warltawk could go in his stead would take hours of cross-checking, and would mean alerting Lord Misbourne, and possibly the traitor within the White Tower. If Wessex could take Warltawk and his contact himself, he might be able to settle the matter once and for all. But to do that he needed very special help.

Wessex could hear the distant boom of celebratory fireworks at St. James and Vauxhall, and every once in a while the sky above him would be lit by a cascade of artificial stars. He rode through a London alive with revelry—a good cover for any amount of peculiar activity. With so many notable personages gathered in London, the Midnight Princes would be gathered for the feast—and finding one particular demi-ruffler out of all that company was a task for which Wessex would need the devil's own luck.

In the third tavern he tried, out on Ratcliffe Highway, Wessex found that his luck still held.

The man sitting with his boots to the fire was dressed after the fashion of a Top-o'-The-Trees: high black boots with silver heels and spurs, a long, full-skirted riding coat in green velvet, and a deep-brimmed country hat into which he had stuck a long gold pheasant feather.

This garb was not that rather more theatrical costume by which five counties knew and feared him, and Wessex did not know his face, but a horse was harder to disguise than a suit of clothing, and Wessex had a keen eye for horseflesh. The proof of his quarry's identity, a silver stallion out of the Templeton stud, was standing in the best loose-box the Rat and Gauntlet could boast, placidly eating oats.

Wessex seated himself at the far side of the unoccupied table. The man in the green velvet coat looked up with quick warning, but Wessex was not cowed.

"Ah, *Merlin le Fou,*" he said amiably in gutter French. "Do allow me to stand the next round."

Morgan Tudor—known as Mad Merlin to the Bow Street Mounted Patrol and a large number of magistrates across England—regarded his unsought companion warily. There were few people who knew to call him by that name, and most of them he disliked extremely.

"You've got the wrong man," he answered briefly, draining his glass and standing to leave.

"I'm looking for the Welch[10] horse-thief who stole a horse called Moonlight two years ago, and who is a particular crony of the Earl of Malhythe," the pale stranger said without moving.

The name caused Merlin to sit back down, slowly. His hand dropped to the knife in the top of his boot. This man didn't have the look of one of Malhythe's messengers, which made it very likely that he would suffer an unfortunate accident before morning.

There was the unmistakable sound of a pistol cocking.

Merlin froze, the tips of one finger just touching the hilt of his knife.

"Please do not force me to shoot you," the stranger said sympathetically. "I wish to make you an offer that does not conflict with your present employment."

Merlin hesitated. If he resisted, the stranger would shoot him. If he ran or protested, the same thing might happen. But if he listened to the offer, he had nothing to lose. There was already a price of a thousand gold guineas upon his head and a rope waiting for him at Newgate whenever he had time to attend. He could hardly be more an outlaw than he already was.

He settled back into his seat. "Who the devil are you?" Merlin demanded ungraciously.

"As to that," the stranger said, still in French, "for tonight, you may call me Blaise."

---

10. In 1807 it's Welch, not Welsh, a usage which survived until WWI in the name of Robert Graves' old regiment, the Royal Welch Fusiliers.

✻   ✻   ✻

He'd been drinking, Merlin thought hopefully to himself an hour later. That would surely explain his present situation, although he'd much prefer never to have to explain it at all, least of all to his noble master and jailor, the Earl of Malhythe. The mysterious Blaise had given Merlin a choice: to occupy Newgate within the hour if he did not cooperate—or to gain a hundred guineas if he did. The choice had seemed simple, or as simple as his choices were these days.

Two years ago he'd been an honest villain. As a boy growing up in the mountains of Wales, his choices had been the Army or the mines, and he'd liked neither one. Morgan had a gift for horses, but no respectable Englishman would hire a Welchman to work in his stables—and to be perfectly frank, Merlin didn't much care for the amount of work involved in the life of a stable groom. So he'd become a horse-thief instead, and a vastly successful one . . . for a time.

If he'd known that choice of career would lead to another set of choices—run Lord Malhythe's errands or face the gallows without hope of transportation[11]—he might well have gone for a soldier's life. But the Earl of Malhythe had use for a highwayman, and so his career as Mad Merlin had begun.

And now someone else had found a use for a Prince of Midnight.

Merlin did not for a moment believe that Blaise was anything but a *nom de minuit* for the blond Englishman who had accosted him. Blaise had the look of the nobility about him, and Merlin with all his Welch soul knew that such men were all mad, and therefore dangerous to cross.

"And perhaps, Master Merlin, you will need a friend someday. The Earl does not care for those who cannot be of use to them," Blaise said, as if generously bestowing recondite information.

Merlin shuddered. It did not seem to him that there was much to choose between the terrible Earl and this madman Blaise. And if the man wanted to rob a coach, why the devil didn't he do it himself, instead of forcing a poor honest man from a cozy slumming-ken to help him?

---

11. Exile to one of the English penal colonies, such as the one in Australia.

Between Morgan's knees, Moonlight stamped and fretted, though the night was warm. The grey had been rubbed down thoroughly with soot to dull his coat, and the moon rolling through the heavens above did not betray his presence. A few feet away, the Englishman sat his gleaming black beast as if both had been turned to stone.

They had let three coaches cross the Heath already—fat horses drawing them and fatter lords within—and the hour was late. Blaise seemed to be waiting for something in particular, and Merlin could not imagine what. His orders for after he was given the office were quite specific, however.

"I want everything he has, and everything the coach could possibly contain. Open his luggage—strip him to the skin if you must, but disclose everything."

Merlin wondered what this could possibly be about. A bet? A loss? Outraged affections? If he was lucky, he might never find out.

There was the sound of another equipage crossing the heath. Merlin glanced over his shoulder at his companion as it drew nearer. This time Blaise nodded and gestured. Merlin was to take the coach.

Something had drawn Warltawk to London, and Wessex was betting that having now shown himself, the Baron intended to depart from Town before his numerous foes pounced—with whatever prize had lured him out.

Wessex intended to anticipate him.

The coach approached, drawn by four handsome bays. At the head of the wheeler ran a footman[12] carrying a lantern. The coach was Warltawk's.

Wessex pointed, and Merlin spurred his mount and rode out into the road.

"Stand and deliver!" he shouted. His voice was muffled only a little by the black scarf that concealed his features.

The running footman grabbed the headstall of the near leader

---

12. Yes, properly the running footman belongs to the 18th century and not the 19th. But then, so does Baron Warltawk.

as the bays shied and swerved to a halt. Merlin backed Moonlight out of the road and displayed his pistol.

The glass in the coach window folded down, and its occupant craned out, trying to see the source of the disturbance.

"Who the devil is it?" he demanded in a harsh voice cracked with age.

The coach's passenger had very much the look of a vulture at bay. His hands were covered by a foam of delicate and expensive lace through which jewels of price glinted, but the hands themselves were twisted with age, the nails thick and yellow.

Things, Merlin felt, were looking up. Blaise hadn't said anything about wanting any of his victim's possessions, and surely it would add an air of authenticity to a highway robbery if Merlin were to make off with the gold and jewels his victim wore?

"I'm a disguised highwayman," he said helpfully, as his victim continued to regard him. He had not expected to be lifting coaches this evening, and therefore Mad Merlin's gold-laced scarlet coat, plumed tricorn, and purple silk muffler were locked away in a trunk in the basement of a safehouse in Stepney, but the silver-mounted Mantons he carried should be *bona fides* enough for any man.

"And I am Baron Warltawk. Drive on," Warltawk said, rapping at the roof of his carriage with his gold-headed cane.

"I'll shoot the wheeler," Merlin said promptly. He'd rather shoot the coachman than harm any of the horses, if it came to that, but he'd learned through long experience that this was a threat that worked.

Intent upon the coach's passenger, Merlin did not see the running footman reach surreptitiously into his coat.

But his companion did.

There was a shot, the nearly simultaneous discharge of the running footman's concealed pistol, and a scream as the man fell to the ground, blood darkening the surface of his pale satin livery-coat.

Merlin kept his eyes fixed on the driver. The fact that Blaise had just stuck his neck into Jack Ketch's noose was obscurely comforting: it meant he was a stand-up gentleman who would not be betraying his confederates later.

"I've still got four charged pistols," Merlin said helpfully. "Now tell your men to come down, me lord, or I'll lay the lot o' them out upon the turf!"

There was a long moment of silence, followed by the sound from the bushes of another pistol being cocked. The coach-horses backed and fretted, disturbed by the smell of blood. The three servants still above—two on the box, one on the back—sat frozen, obviously terrified of moving.

This was not going well. Merlin had never known any soul to be more terrified of a mortal man than of a bullet, but it seemed he'd finally met one—four, in fact, for the bleeding man on the turf was crawling desperately toward his pistol, and Merlin would have to shoot him when he reached it.

Do something! he thought toward his *soi-disant* partner.

To his relief, he heard the sound of Blaise dismounting. He came forward—muffled to the eyes in a maroon scarf that gave him a headless appearance in the dim light—with one hand on a pistol and a peculiar object in the other. Merlin had no idea what it could be, until Blaise used it to shear through the harness leather in half-a-dozen swift strokes, before kicking the fallen pistol into the ditch and discharging his own into the sky.

The horses were smarter than the men—they required no further encouragement to bolt, and did so, marooning the coach where it stood.

The carriage door opened. The footman on at the back leapt down to unfold the step and help his master dismount.

"I shall see you drawn and quartered for that," Warltawk said, stepping down. "You may trust me in this."

Meanwhile, Blaise had motioned for the two on the box to descend. He forced them to lie facedown upon the damp grass and bound their hands behind them with pieces of the cut straps.

A man who knows his way about the prancing lay[13], Merlin thought with growing puzzlement. *And as that's the case, I'd give a great deal to know why he needed me to help him enact this little drama.*

---

13. Thieves' cant for the craft of the highwayman.

"And now, me lord," Merlin said to Warltawk. "If your lordship would be so good as to remove your valuables—and your clothes."

As Warltawk glared sulphurously at Merlin, Wessex moved past him and into the coach, taking down one of its lanterns as he did. He did not doubt that Merlin could handle one ancient Baron and a terrified lackey, and if he had to shoot Warltawk, all to the good. Wessex would not grieve for the old viper, whose plots had vexed England since long before even Wessex's father had been born.

The interior of the coach reeked strongly of hashish, and Wessex spotted the tall slender form of a narghile set in an ebony stand attached to the floor of the coach. He set his lantern beside it, scenting the bitterness of absinthe beneath the cloying sweetness of hashish.

He had no time to refine upon Warltawk's vices, however. Working as quickly as he could, Wessex began to dismantle the interior of the coach.

There were secret drawers beneath both seats. One contained a pistol—mercifully unloaded—and a stack of gold coins. Wessex picked one up and examined it by the lantern's light. A gold napoleon, of this year's minting. He tipped the booty into his pockets, conscious of the role he must play, but beneath the acting, his mind raced. How had Warltawk come by these coins? Had he been paid in them, or was he to pay in his turn?

The other drawer contained a small packet tied with a violet ribbon. Wessex sniffed at it, and untied the packet. A cursory inspection identified these as the letters of a lady. This, too, was bestowed upon one of the pockets of the grey coat for further inspection.

"I said bestir yourself, me lord!"

Merlin's voice. Wessex came quickly out of the coach.

The tableau upon the turf remained unchanged. Warltawk stood unmoving, glaring malevolently at the highwayman. With his coachman by his side, it would be a great risk to approach him, and one that Mad Merlin obviously preferred not to take.

"You may shoot my servants, if it amuses you. But if you shoot me, I guarantee that worse will come to you than hanging." Warltawk's voice was dispassionate.

"And if you are an invalid? Thrown upon the charity of your son?"

Wessex, coming closer, spoke softly into Warltawk's ear in a voice quite unlike his natural one. He laid the barrel of his pistol against Warltawk's leg meaningfully.

"You were a noted duelist in your day, my lord. You have seen how a wound can fester, condemning a man to see out his days hemmed in by servants and the grossest indignities. You are thought to be the last of your line, my lord, but I know otherwise. You have a living son. I am certain that he would not condemn you to the care of strangers." The identity of Lord Warltawk's secret by-blow had been a closely-guarded secret for nearly half a century, but the White Tower knew many secrets. It would be a quietly amusing sort of revenge to throw Warltawk into Malhythe's household.[14]

As the meaning of his words penetrated, Wessex felt the old man's body struck by a whiplash of rage, until for a moment he feared that a paroxysm would carry Warltawk off.

"You *will* pay for this insolence!" the old man hissed in an adder's voice.

"On another day." Wessex stepped back and gave the servant a shove. "You—move off."

The footman's nerve broke at last. He turned and ran in the direction from which the coach had come.

"Allow me to assist you," Wessex offered, reaching for Warltawk's cape.

There was nothing in the cape; Wessex tossed it to the ground. He was reaching for Warltawk's coat, when he discerned a glint amidst the foam of lace that cascaded from his lordship's throat. Wessex seized it, and flicked the long golden chain over Warltawk's head.

---

14. Lord Warltawk, his family, and his plots can be found in fuller detail in *Fleeting Fancy*, by Rosemary Edghill.

He stepped back, gazing at what he held in growing dismay.

It was a quizzing-glass, such as any member of Warltawk's generation might sport . . . but a highly unique one which, as Wessex knew for a fact, did not belong to Warltawk.

An antiquary who'd once seen it had suggested that the stone itself was possibly Roman—a disk of ruby roughly two inches in diameter, with a silvery flaw in its center whose shape had given the gem its name. The ruby called the Mirror Rose had been reset several times, though always as a quizzing glass. There were five bands along the handle engraved with letters in the Hebrew, Greek, and Latin alphabets. Once the rings were set in combination, the quizzing-glass became the engine to cypher—or uncypher—any document. Unbreakably.

The Mirror Rose was the property of Sir Geoffrey Hanaper, personal private secretary to Endymion Childwall, Marquess of Rutledge.

And Rutledge served the White Tower.

"How did you come by this?" Wessex demanded roughly.

It would be too much to say that there was a look of fear upon Warltawk's face, after the threats Wessex had made, but there was certainly a look of . . . caution.

"I am an antiquary. I recently purchased this item. And you, sir, are a most peculiar highwayman."

Wessex was fast ceasing to care whether Warltawk recognized him or not. Hanaper would not have given up the jewel while he lived, for whoever possessed it could translate England's most secret correspondence.

Wessex cocked his pistol and pressed it against Warltawk's thigh, prepared to deliver the wound he had promised. "Tell me how you stole this from Geoffrey Hanaper," he said.

"One cannot steal from a dead man," Warltawk answered coolly.

"Why should I believe you?" Wessex said.

"An impasse," Warltawk agreed. "Very well, sirrah, let me offer you this to match it: the late Mr. Hanaper's employer, one Endymion Childwall, is making a hasty trip to the Continent under cover of the nuptial celebrations. Perhaps it was occasioned by the discovery that his secretary had uncovered that which he ought not to've. Perhaps it is the desire to ally himself with the winning cause. His blood was never what it ought to be, you know."

Wessex took a silent step backward, raising his pistol and releasing the hammer. Warltawk's words made a terrible kind of sense. If Hanaper had been murdered and the death disguised— If Rutledge were the Judas-agent whose activities had so vexed the White Tower, and Hanaper had discovered that fact—

There was nothing more that could be done here, short of shooting Warltawk. And Wessex would leave that work to another. Wessex turned away, gesturing for Merlin to precede him.

"I bid you good evening, Your Grace of Wessex," Warltawk said, his voice pitched for the Duke's ears alone.

Wessex did not look back.

Wessex and Morgan rode until the lights of Town were visible. Whatever Warltawk knew—or thought he knew—was a problem for another dawn. For now Wessex put it behind him. At the edge of Town, Wessex drew rein and turned to his companion. Both men had rearranged their dress as they rode, giving themselves a more respectable appearance. If luck was with them, it would be hours before Warltawk could report his encounter with a pair of highwaymen. And it would be best for all concerned if the *Prince de Minuit* could prove he'd been entirely elsewhere, for Warltawk's reach was long.

"If I were you, my lad, I'd get Malhythe to send you somewhere safe—such as Paris," Wessex said with a faint smile.

"I was thinking more of Coronado," Merlin said fervently. "I'd rather live under the Dons than be torn to gobbets by that wizened old hellgrammite."

"Coronado might be far enough," Wessex allowed. He passed Merlin a heavy wallet that bulged with stolen gold. An experienced gentleman of the high toby such as Merlin would find ways to spend the gold napoleons without attracting undue attention. "This should see you there and more. If I were you, I'd leave now."

Merlin smiled a crooked smile and touched two fingers to his hat-brim. "And so I shall. And I thank you for an evening I'd not care to repeat, Master Blaise."

He wheeled his horse and trotted away. Wessex wasted no time in spurring Hirondel on his own path.

At this hour, it was not possible to use the regular entrance to the White Tower Group, which was a haberdashery on Bond Street. Instead, Wessex spent precious minutes locating a certain coaching inn that lay along High Holborn. He did not stop in the Globe and Triangle's innyard, but rode Hirondel directly into the stable.

A surly ostler looked up, reaching for the lead-weighted club with which he kept order in his domain.

"The Scarecrow has business with England," Wessex said, and the ruffian subsided. He jerked a thumb over his shoulder.

Wessex dismounted—to have dismounted before giving the code-phrase would have been to ensure his immediate execution—and led Hirondel through the stable. The Globe and Triangle was a busy inn, and for the most part its traffic was entirely ordinary.

A second groom watched carefully as Wessex led Hirondel into the last stall on the end, taking with him the lighted lantern that hung on the peg there. It was a loose-box, scrubbed clean and with thick straw strewn upon the floor. Wessex went quickly to the manger in the back and pushed it toward the left. There was a loud click as the mechanism engaged, and then the entire back wall of the stall swung inward as if it were a door, to disclose a long downward-sloping narrow passageway, just high enough for a mounted man, if he were a careful one.

Wessex led Hirondel through the opening, then shoved the wall back until he heard the click that meant the mechanism had engaged once more. The stallion nosed at him inquisitively, and Wessex took a moment to reassure the beast before he swung into the saddle again.

The passage was damp and close and smelled pervasively of horse. Hirondel's hooves made only the faintest of sounds, for the passage was floored in thick rubber tiles. It led from the stables at the Globe and Triangle to the cellars of the Bond Street house, a passage of no little distance. Wessex had used it only once before, but tonight he had no choice: there could be no possible reason for the Duke of Wessex to call upon his tailor at this hour of the morning—and he could not approach Baron Misbourne at a public function even if he knew where the White Tower's master might be.

A quarter of an hour brought him to the end of the passage. The passageway seemingly ended in a solid wall, but Wessex knew its secret. He dismounted, tied Hirondel to a ring set into the wall, and cast about until he found the pulley-ropes that worked the dumbwaiter. As Wessex strained at the counterweighted ropes, an open-sided box that only moments before had appeared to be a part of the tunnel walls began to rise skyward, bearing Wessex with it.

It was just as well that my lord of Wessex had dressed the part of a low fellow when he had gone seeking the highwayman, for no Pink of the *Ton*[15] would have been able to work the mechanism without imperiling the work of the impeccable Weston. But Wessex's coat was slovenly loose, and a few minutes of exertion saw the open elevator rise into the lowest of the cellars of the Bond Street establishment.

Charteris was there to greet him as always, the impeccably-liveried White Tower butler giving no indication that there was anything amiss regarding the hour or fashion of Wessex's arrival.

"Good evening, Your Grace," Charteris said imperturbably, reaching for Wessex's cloak and hat.

His Grace surrendered the items reluctantly. The Mirror Rose was in the inner pocket of his coat. "I need to see Lord Misbourne. It is a matter of the utmost urgency."

"Of course, Your Grace. If you will come with me to the Yellow Parlor, I shall enquire if His Lordship is at home. I shall send a servant to see to your horse."

A few moments later, Wessex stood in one of the four small rooms on the ground floor of the premises. Except for the colors for which they were named—Red, Yellow, Violet, Blue—and which were carried out in their decoration and appointments, the four rooms were

---

15. In the corrupt Anglo-French of the period, it signifies the Upper Ten Thousand, the titled and noble society that was composed of England's aristocracy.

virtually identical. Even at this hour there were fresh candles burning on the mantel, and from behind the velvet curtains, the faint sounds of late revelry could still be heard on the streets without.

He supposed that Charteris was waking Misborne as he waited. He doubted Misbourne would be any happier to receive this news than Wessex had been to gain it . . . assuming it were in fact true.

He drew the Mirror Rose from his pocket and studied it. In the light of the clustered candles, the flaw that so resembled a silver rose in the heart of the ruby could be clearly seen. With this and its counterparts, Britain had an inviolable code to use in communicating with its politicals on station in Lisbon and elsewhere. Without it, they did not. It was bad enough that the secret should be known at all. Worse, that it should be compromised.

The door to the Yellow Parlor opened.

"My lord will see you now," Charteris said impassively.

Wessex dropped the quizzing-glass into a pocket and followed Charteris up the curving staircase to the first floor of the town house concealed behind the haberdasher's facade. No doors gave onto the corridor save the one at its end. That door was covered in padded red leather, and as always, Charteris pushed it open and allowed Wessex to pass through without announcement.

Also as always, the room was frightfully dim, for Jonathan Milo Arioch de la Forthe, third Baron Misbourne, had been born an albino: strong light hurt his eyes, and sunlight blinded him. But these disabilities were insignificant in the face of Misborne's formidable intellect, a mind which had placed him as the spider in the center of the web that held the Grande Alliance together: the white knight who had taken the field against the Black Pope and the prospect of a globe-spanning French empire.

Wessex forced himself to stand still, waiting for his eyes to adjust. The room was lit by several cobbler's lanterns; the candle flames reflected through flasks of spirits, filling the room with a warm, diffuse, brandy-scented glow. As his vision cleared, he saw Lord Misbourne seated at his desk. If the Baron had been roused from sleep by Wessex's visit, he gave no sign of it, rising to his feet when Wessex took a step forward.

"Your Grace. What business brings you here at such a late hour?" Misbourne asked mildly.

"This." Wessex stepped forward and laid the Mirror Rose on the desk.

Misbourne did not touch it. "How did this item come to be in your possession, Your Grace?"

"I held up Baron Warltawk's coach," Wessex said without further explanation. "I found it when I searched him. He gave me to understand that Geoffrey Hanaper was dead, and that Lord Rutledge cannot now be found."

"And did Christian have any suggestion of where we should look for Lord Rutledge?" Misbourne asked, using Warltawk's given name. "The other is true, by the way. Mr. Hanaper died three days ago. We have been able to keep it secret thus far—with so many visitors in London, I felt it wisest. It is an unfortunate matter."

"Lord Warltawk suggested that the Marquess had taken a repairing lease upon the Continent," Wessex said.

Misbourne sighed, and rubbed his eyes. Endymion Childwall had been the closest thing to a friend that Misbourne had permitted himself, Wessex knew. It was the Marquess's own father who had recruited Misbourne for the Shadow Game, years ago.

"Then we have lost him," Misbourne said with a sigh. "He was in Town this morning, but undoubtedly he was only awaiting Warltawk in order to flee. By the time I can contact Paris Station he will already have gone to ground upon the Continent; we will never take him then. I can only be grateful we have not lost this." He picked up the Mirror Rose. "Though I do not know how much use it will be to us once Endymion tells Talleyrand its secrets."

Misbourne gazed at the quizzing-glass for a moment, then put it in the drawer of his desk. "But I know that you will find some good in all this. We have found our mole, at least. It is Rutledge.[16]"

"Have we?" said Wessex. "Somehow it seems all too pat: Hanaper's suicide, Warltawk's arrival, Rutledge's departure. We are meant

---

16. Endymion Childwall, Marquess of Rutledge, is properly referred to in conversation as "Lord Rutledge" or "Rutledge," of course. Aren't English titles wonderful?

to think that, certainly—yet if the Marquess were a traitor in French pay, he would hardly have omitted to take so valuable a bargaining chip as the Mirror Rose with him. And Warltawk is no French agent: he's a Jacobite, if anything, and lives to amuse himself. I cannot see him conniving with *le Pape Noir* to any purpose. This is a ruse. Let me follow Lord Rutledge to France—"

"No." Misbourne spoke decisively. "You are too well known to be of any use to me in France. Paris Station will have to do what it can to apprehend Rutledge . . . and we to mend the damage he has done."

"You're right of course," Wessex said smoothly. He turned a bland countenance to Misbourne, but behind that facade his thoughts were spinning. Rutledge made a plausible mole, but all of Wessex's instincts told him that the Marquess had not betrayed them . . . or if he had, it was not in that way. There was still a traitor, somewhere within these walls. And he must find and exonerate Rutledge to prove it.

"If that is all, my lord, then I pray you will hold me excused. I am thought to be giving an entertainment this evening, and it would look well if I were actually to attend."

Misbourne smiled dutifully, but the thought that Rutledge had been the pawn of France for two decades hit him hard. He waved dismissal, but when Wessex had turned and reached the door, he spoke again. "When you are through playing, come and see me, Your Grace. I have a mission in mind for you."

"What sort of mission?" Wessex could not keep himself from asking.

"An execution."

3

The Game of Kings
(Paris, June 1807)

✤ The *Palais de l'Homme* held public rooms, private rooms, and those that were simply secret. In one of those rooms that did not exist, two men sat talking.

Charles-Maurice de Talleyrand-Périgord—the butcher with the face of an angel and the manners of Satan himself—had been born into the French nobility half a century before and had been nearly as oppressed by it as any impoverished peasant. The Revolution had freed him from the duties of a priest and allowed him the chance for revenge upon the parents who had disinherited him because of his lameness.

Since the days when Napoleon was First Consul, Talleyrand had consolidated his own power, a power he meant to be more enduring than that of either Church or State. Napoleon had made himself Master of Europe, but if Napoleon were to fall tomorrow, Talleyrand would survive. Without his master's knowledge he had treated secretly with both England and Russia. His reach was as long as his ambition was vast, and he feared nothing.

Not even the man who sat before him.

"So. As I promised, the Emperor has made you Governor of Louisianne. All he cares about is the New World gold that will keep the Grand Army in the field and buy the loyalty of his agents in Spain. You are to provide it any way you can—including taking the Spanish treasure ships, if you can do so without implicating France. You may do whatever you like with the colonists—they are a surly and ungrateful people, as much Spanish as French. And now, d'Charenton . . . what of your promise to me?"

The man who sat opposite him was some fifteen years his senior. He had been born into a noble Provençal family, and served both in the Army and then the government before his . . . proclivities . . . became known. The King had reprieved him, but it was the Revolution which had freed the Marquis de Sade from confinement in the Bastille. When the People had cast out the Holy Church, those forces which the Church had kept at bay had been freed to flourish. In the atmosphere of libertine humanism that flourished in the days before the First Consul had begun his climb to power, no act was unthinkable and no practice forbidden. By the time Napoleon had found it politic to make his peace with Rome, d'Charenton had rendered himself indispensable to the apostate madman determined to become the master of Europe.

"I assure you, Monsieur Talleyrand, the Holy Grail is in the New World, and I will find it. Who has the Grail is the master of the world. No army will be able to stand against him. With the Grail in his hands, the other Hallows will quickly fall to the Emperor—and with them, victory eternal!"

"And having such power in your hands, you will instantly turn and give it to the Emperor?" Talleyrand's voice was mocking.

"I have no interest in the things of this world," d'Charenton said sullenly. He was as much vain as proud, and loathed being the object of ridicule.

It was fortunate that the man was mad, Talleyrand thought, for if d'Charenton had not been, Talleyrand could not even have pretended to believe him. Of course d'Charenton wanted the Grail for some purpose of his own. Anyone who did not was too foolish to have any hope of gaining it.

It was Talleyrand's business to encourage d'Charenton to seek the prize, and his business also to assure himself of its ultimate possession. Talleyrand was that rarest of creatures, a true atheist. He believed the Grail to be a fantasy, but a fantasy for which men would kill and die—and a fantasy that would ultimately ensure the supremacy of France.

And thus, Talleyrand had placed an agent in d'Charenton's suite, an agent who would share the Imperial Governor's highest counsels. An agent who would report to Talleyrand and d'Charenton even as he planned to betray both of them; trustworthy because he believed he deceived them all, and acted only for himself.

A man whom Talleyrand would betray in turn when he no longer had need of him.

"Then there is no reason for us to quarrel," Talleyrand said smoothly. "The Emperor desires to rule this world, and you desire to rule the next. And I exist only to fulfill the desires of each of you. Now," Talleyrand said, suddenly practical. "I shall send you and such ships and soldiery as France can spare to Louisianne at once. You will move at once to secure the colony, suppress rebellion, and end collaboration with the English. The *Occidenteaux* will find you a hard master, I hope?"

D'Charenton smiled and rubbed his hands together. His rings glittered. "And there will be no interference?" he repeated eagerly.

Talleyrand shrugged. "Louisianne is far away, and news travels slowly across the ocean . . . when it travels at all. Why should the Emperor care what happens to a rebellious colony—providing his revenue continues uninterrupted? Give him the Spanish treasure ships, increase the taxes, and you may do with the people as you choose."

He thinks I am a fool. D'Charenton regarded his longtime adversary-turned-ally. Talleyrand meant to turn the Grail to his own use, and thought he could steal it from d'Charenton to do so. But d'Charenton meant to put it beyond his or any man's reach the moment he gained it, in a way Talleyrand could not foresee.

As Talleyrand said, the New World was far away . . . a land without a King to make the ancient land-pledge, and hold the power of the soil and the Ancient Races at his command. But if there were one who knew the ancient ritual, who knew what payment would be asked, and who could lay his hand upon that payment at need, such a man would be a power to challenge not only the Emperor, but the very Powers That Were.

"Then there is nothing more to say, Monsieur Talleyrand. I shall leave at once for Nouvelle-Orléans," the Duc d'Charenton said.

The street was quiet when Wessex and Hirondel passed through the dooryard of the Globe and Triangle once more, and for a moment Wessex thought longingly of Sarah and home. He did not think she would easily forgive him for abandoning her so completely tonight, but he could see no other choice. Right now Rutledge was only a few hours ahead of him, and it was three days to Paris. If he could catch his quarry before he went to ground, Wessex might yet repair some of the damage done this night.

If he did not delay now.

If the luck was with him.

With a sigh, Wessex turned Hirondel in the direction of the Dover road.

Herriard House glittered with light, and the line of carriages waiting to disgorge their guests stretched for almost a mile. Tonight all the Polite World celebrated the Prince's wedding, and if the revelry was not unmixed with relief, then that was a truth that went unspoken, especially among the Prince's Circle.

Sarah had viewed Wessex's departure some hours before with a certain wry amusement. She had as little taste for these social set-pieces as he did, but fewer duties that would permit her to avoid them. Fortunately each of her guests this evening had been willing to believe His Grace to be elsewhere in the grand crush, so Sarah had not been forced to admit to his absence. And so as the night passed she smiled and danced, and played the proud hostess, and counted the hours until the house would be her own again.

It was comforting to know that her husband's sense of duty was equally strong, and that he would not be so derelict unless the need was dire. Unfortunately, when he did return, she would have no good news to greet him with. Despite her best efforts, she had learned nothing of what Wessex wanted to know, for no one at all had the least thing to say about Baron Warltawk.

The sun was peeping over the housetops as the last carriage trundled away from her door.

"Has His Grace returned?" Sarah asked Buckland hopefully.

"I regret, Your Grace, that he has not." Even Herriard House's formidable butler showed signs of exhaustion after the events of the last twenty-four hours.

Despite herself, Sarah's shoulders slumped. What predicament had Wessex become entangled in now? And what could she do about it?

"Doubtless he is roistering with low company, and will join us in his good time," Sarah said, forcing a smile. "Tell the servants to clean up later, and tell Knoyle I will not be needing her tonight. I am sure that all of you are as tired as I!"

Sarah turned away and ascended the stairs to her bedroom. Safe behind her own door, she plucked the feathers and jewels from her coif and ran her hands through it until her light brown hair lay free over her shoulders. She shook her head, savoring the freedom, and began to undress.

Damn the man! Where the devil was her husband?

He'd been one jump behind Rutledge every step of the way, but Wessex did not waver in his belief that the Marquess was not the traitor he sought.

When Hirondel had begun to tire Wessex had stopped to bespeak a fresh mount from among those the White Tower kept stabled along the main road. He ordered Hirondel led on to Dover by slow stages—for if Wessex returned at all, it would be to that city. He scribbled a hasty—and entirely cryptic—note to Sarah that he stared at for a long moment before consigning it to the common-room fire. Words were a dangerous thing, when commended to a scrap of paper that might fall into other hands than those of its intended recipient.

Then Wessex was on the road again, riding after a man who seemed simply to have ceased to exist.

By late morning of the following day Wessex had reached Dover and satisfied himself that Rutledge was not here. No English ship openly sailed to a French port in these troubled times, but Spain was still neutral, and many times Wessex had sailed to Spain as a preliminary to visiting France. Rutledge, it seemed, had not—nor had any man answering his description left Dover in the past three days.

Wessex gazed about the bustling port with mounting exasperation. *He might be dead. In London, on the road . . . there are a thousand ways for a man to let himself out of life. All I have is Warltawk's word that Rutledge fled to the Continent!* But all his instincts told Wessex that Rutledge was alive, and still somehow ahead of him, though nothing told him why the man had fled.

If I were Lord Rutledge, what would induce me to throw everything over and take a moonlight flit to the City of Light?

Money, position, and devotion to Revolution Wessex considered and discarded. Rutledge had as much of the first two as any man might reasonably want, and as for the third, he was no fool. The Goddess Revolution devoured all her lovers, and France was no friend to the English aristocracy, even to one who turned his coat to join her. The French reception of Lord Byron's notorious missives to the *Gazette* had proved that much. No, Rutledge was not so foolish as to believe a welcome waited for him in France.

Yet still he went.

That left blackmail. Someone, somewhere, had leverage he had used to force Rutledge to this course. Which was, Wessex reflected, a strong indication that Rutledge was not their mole—at least, not the one who had doomed Andrew, Duke of Wessex, so many years before. There were few levers that would hold good for twenty years.

Rutledge was not the traitor. He *knew* it.

But he needed proof.

He needed Rutledge.

❄   ❄   ❄

The Duke of Wessex sat at a table in The Moon and Lantern, the largest (and only) inn in the village of Talitho. It was a small fishing village like a hundred others in the fen country, but it had the added distinction of being the primary embarkation point for agents which the White Tower wished to insert directly into France—and if Wessex knew that, Rutledge certainly did. If Rutledge were going to France clandestinely and directly, he would leave from here.

"Good evening, Capting." A grizzled old party—one of the local fisherfolk—joined him uninvited. Wessex raised a languid hand to the tapster and indicated his guest. Mine host hurried over with a pewter tankard—from the scent, it was the local beer heavily spiked with gin, a popular beverage—and set it before the fisherman.

"They says you're wishful to take a sea voyage," the man continued.

And so he was. But on this particular occasion Wessex found himself without the passwords and tokens that would see him safe to the Continent under the aegis of the White Tower. Improvisation was indicated.

"Indeed. I have urgent business east of here." Reaching into his pocket, Wessex placed a small stack of gold guineas upon the table.

The smuggler's eyes widened at the gleam of gold, and Wessex knew well what the man was thinking. Where there was some gold there would be more, and a body weighted and slipped into the waters of the Channel would not quickly return to give up its secrets to the local magistrate.

"It might be I knows someone who can accommodate you, Capting."

"I would, of course, be appropriately grateful," Wessex said, sliding the gold toward the man with the tip of one slim finger. "And more grateful, could you provide me with certain information."

It was raining in Paris.

Illya Koscuisko gazed moodily out the window of the barracks. There was a rumor circulating that the *Garde* would be sent to Louisianne with the new Governor. Illya doubted Napoleon would send his pampered show-regiment so far away, but *something* was certainly up. The *Garde* had been confined to barracks except for duty and parade for the last three days, and Illya couldn't find out the reason.

He had urgent intelligence for England, and he couldn't get it out. He was impersonating a soldier, and the fact that he was merely a spy wouldn't save him if he were caught off-post in civilian clothes. If he weren't flogged to death, he'd be hanged.

Still, the matter was becoming urgent, as several previous attempts he had made to pass the information had been peculiarly thwarted. And so in the last few hours Illya had arranged to lose spectacularly at dice, with the result that he had taken Stefan's place on watch at the stables.

Any regiment that did not place a guard on its horseflesh would find it missing in short order, and the matched greys of the *Garde Polonaise* were famous, so a strict watch was in order. A little laudanum in a brandy flask took care of his fellow guard: when Janocek began to slump and mumble, Illya dragged him inside and covered him tenderly with a saddle blanket. Sleeping on duty was a flogging offense—even if he woke before Illya returned, Janocek wouldn't advertise his own negligence. If Illya were lucky, he could get to Paris Station to send his report and make it back here before he was missed.

Quickly he unbuttoned his uniform jacket and turned it inside out. He left as much of his uniform behind as he could, and covered the rest with a plain dark cloak. The hour was late and the weather raw. Both factors worked in his favor. He walked quickly but did not run, a trick to avoid attention that he had learned long ago, when he still hoped to win freedom for his homeland by himself.

But one man has little power in the world, unless he is a madman. Freedom is a thing forged of alliances, not swords. England cares nothing for Continental possessions, and much for a balance of power. If she wins, it is she who will draw the boundaries of the nations, and my people will be free once more.

But if the Great Beast wins, there will be room for only one nation in Europe, and that is France. . . .

A few minutes later Illya relaxed: it seemed certain now that at least he would not be caught on the way to his destination, and if he should die afterward it would not matter as much. He walked faster, and within half an hour he had reached the location he sought, a rowdy bistro in Montmarte called the Moulin Rouge.

In English the name meant "Red Windmill," and at one time, before the city had surrounded it, perhaps this structure had been one. Certainly it was shaped like a windmill. Its skeletal blades were silhouetted against the sky, creaking faintly in the storm. Despite the inclement weather, business was brisk, with many people coming and going. With a confidence he did not feel, Illya joined them.

The inside of the bistro was hot and dim, lit as it was by oil lamps high on the walls. Illya made his way toward the stage, where a handful of ballet-rats, scantily costumed to represent the seasons, capered on stage exchanging bawdy jokes with the crowd.

Illya pushed himself forward until he was pressed against the stage. Freeing his arm after some struggle, he tossed a coin to the *jeune fille* dressed as Spring. She was a plump, brown-eyed brunette with a saucy expression. Female agents were rare, but they did exist, and Paris Station was one of them. Illya wondered what her story was, not that he'd ever know it.

She caught the coin expertly, glancing in his direction. Her face gave away nothing as he made the recognition sign.

They'd made contact. Now all he had to do was wait.

Their rendezvous was established smoothly: no one thought anything of one of the Moulin Rouge's *filles de joie* picking up a drunken patron and taking him away with her for a leisurely fleecing. Illya climbed the steps to her shabby lodging feeling a certain distant relief. Whatever happened to him now, he had delivered his information.

"Your name?" she asked him.

"Eagle," he answered, giving the only name she needed to know.

"You can call me Avril," she answered. "Avril" was the code-name for Paris Station: any operative manning it would be called that.

She set her candlestick on the table, then closed the door behind him and locked it. Illya lit the lamp with a spill as Avril closed the shutters and drew the curtains. The building had once been a grand *hôtel* for the elite of the City of Light: now it was old and shabby. Avril did not draw attention to herself by living beyond the means of a cabaret dancer.

Illya began pulling thin sheets of coding paper out of his tunic. In case of detection, water would reduce the material to a pulpy unreadable mass. Paris Station would transfer the code groups to a more durable medium before sending them.

"This needs to reach London immediately," he said. "It has a Gold Priority." Gold was for the most urgent traffic a field agent could send: routine messages were sent as Copper or Bronze.

Avril looked at the pages and sighed faintly. "I won't be sleeping tonight—and neither will you. London Station has put out a Most Urgent All Agents, and I suppose that includes you."

"My heavens," Illya said mildly. A "Most Urgent" required all agents—even those who had spent months building cover identities—to drop what they were doing and respond. "Has Princess Stephanie defected?"

Avril shot him a deadly look, scooping up the papers he'd brought and slipping them into a drawer. "No. Some *Duc d'Anglais* has run mad and he's over here. Apparently he's quite deadly and can pass for a Frenchman as well. Anyone who sees him is to take him down before *le Pape Noir* does and ship him back to Angle-terre—dead or alive. Here's his description."

She brought out a sheet of paper and placed it before Illya, along with a tankard full of rough red wine. He took a drink before he looked at the paper, and as a result he choked and sputtered, spraying the paper and the table with red wine as Avril whisked his coding papers frantically out of the way.

The man the White Tower wanted—dead or alive—was the Duke of Wessex.

It was good to be back in Paris once more, Wessex reflected, even if he were here on a wholly-unauthorized mission with an unsuitable companion. He'd caught up with Rutledge in Talitho, not that doing so had gained him anything.

Wessex had been right: it was a case of blackmail, and Warltawk had been its agent. He had passed a message to Rutledge that Marie Celeste was in danger, but could be saved if Rutledge came to Paris and offered himself as a hostage.

Wessex had not been able to discourage Rutledge from his single-minded determination to rescue his child, and so had found himself with two choices: murder Rutledge on the spot, or accompany him to France and hope to get all three of them out safely.

"We have to reach the convent!" Lord Rutledge insisted.

"Patience, my friend," Wessex murmured, putting a minatory hand upon his companion's arm. To the casual observer, the two men were nothing more than casual *flaneurs* beside the Seine. "There are social calls we must make before we call upon the good Sisters of the Sacred Heart. Each thing in its own time."

Including, perhaps, their arrest. Rutledge was no trained field agent, and Wessex had not been briefed for insertion in over a year. Alone on the Continent, without identity papers or most of his special equipment, funds running low, the two of them could expect to give Talleyrand's Red Jacks a run for their sport, but that was all. Imperial France was documents-mad, changing the papers and passes one needed to travel or to reside in Paris with malignant whimsy. If they were challenged, they were doomed.

The only saving grace of the matter was that Rutledge spoke French with a Parisian accent, a relic of his days manning Paris Station. That alone had kept them unmolested upon the road to Paris. But to reach Paris was not to reach the Convent of the Sacred Heart twenty miles outside it. And Rutledge's daughter Marie was there.

Years before, Rutledge had fled to England with Paris Station's vital documents, but the swift ferocity of the Revolution had taken everyone by surprise. In order to get out, Rutledge had been forced to leave his opera-dancer mistress and their young daughter behind. The mother had been executed as an *aristo,* but Rutledge's influence had brought the child Marie Celeste to the Convent of the Sacred Heart, where she had grown safely to maidenhood ignorant of her still-dangerous English connection.

" 'Good time?' " Rutledge said fiercely. "There *is* no time! Once the Jacks take her not even Grenville and all the army will be able to get her out of Talleyrand's clutches!"

"In God's name, keep your voice down!" Wessex hissed. "How are we to proceed without knowing what lies ahead of us? She may be dead, or taken already—it is four days since that message reached you. Think, man!"

Rutledge rounded on him. "When I agreed to let you accompany me, you told me you had a plan to save my Marie. If you do not, then *I* must bargain for her life with my own."

And I must kill you before you fall into Talleyrand's clutches. He will gut you like a deer and have all you know in an instant.

Wessex repressed a sigh. "We must have travel documents and information to proceed. I think I know where we may get them."

It was purely a bluff, of course, but he and Rutledge were both well-dressed, and French fashion was not so far from that of England as to render them completely outlandish.

Wessex headed for the *Palais de l'Homme*.

The imposing and dignified old building—nursery to kings—resembled a harlot bedecked to ply her trade, its upper stories swagged in colored bunting while the Emperor's banners—the crested "N," the stylized honeybees—belled in the hot breeze created by the clusters of burning torches. Guardsmen in fantastic uniforms more suited to a Vauxhall rout stood at stiff attention, the blades of their sabres glittering in the firelight.

"How are we going to get in there?" Rutledge asked hopelessly.

"By behaving as if we belong," Wessex said calmly. "So many freakish things happen in Paris these days that no one can say what is *convenable* and what is not."

"But what about—"

"As for M'sieur Talleyrand, he is unlikely to be in his chambers at this hour. The man is a notorious rake," Wessex said disapprovingly. "Now come! With courage and luck, we will be on our way to the convent by midnight."

The bluff got them through the gates and into the *Palais* itself.

The most Wessex hoped for was to be given a few minutes alone in a room while the guard sent for someone in authority, but as he and Rutledge followed a uniformed soldier through the twisting back-passages of the Palais, Wessex found that his luck was still with him in a most unexpected fashion.

"Here, fellow! Where are you taking those men?"

It was a hussar—one of the *Garde Polonaise,* by his uniform—in full fig and a fiery temper. Ferocious auburn moustaches and flowing sideburns concealed most of his features, and the brim of his shako was tipped roguishly forward. His leopard-skin was slung off one shoulder to make way for the enormous gilded wings that threatened every movable object in his vicinity.

"I—Sir, I—It is a matter of National Security," the guardsman said. "Citizen Vidoq and his assistant—Citizen LeCarre—are demanding to see Minister Talleyrand. And they have no papers."

"What?" the hussar demanded haughtily. "The insolence of it! Return to your post—I will handle this matter myself."

"But—" the corporal began.

"*Go.* You fool, this touches upon the honor of France!"

The guardsman cast one last terrified look in Wessex's direction, saluted smartly, and left at a near-run.

"It helps that they think we are all mad," Koscuisko announced conversationally. "In the devil's name, man, what are you doing here? Do you know I've orders to see you dead or in London?"

"Interesting," Wessex said noncommittally. He'd known Misbourne wanted to keep him home, but he hadn't expected to be hunted so ardently by his own people. He cast an eye up and down the deserted hallway. No doubt Koscuisko was trying to decide where to take them. Well, that was something Wessex wondered himself.

Koscuisko made a face of dismay. "It's more than interesting—it's a disaster! Whatever am I to do with you, m'lord? And who the devil is this fellow?" he demanded.

"Allow me to present a colleague of ours from London," Wessex said.

Koscuisko drew himself up very tall and clicked his heels. "Captain Jerzy Kouryagin of the *Garde Polonaise,* at your service," he said formally, making a short sharp bow. He shot another puzzled glance at Wessex as he straightened.

"Blackmailed into coming to Paris to rescue his daughter," Wessex explained laconically. "The Black Pope is getting lazy in his dotage. He asks his victims to come to him."

"And you came along to rescue him. And now I'm to rescue you both. Ah, well, I was getting bored with Army life," Koscuisko said philosophically.

Freed from the need to blend into Court life inconspicuously, Koscuisko was prepared to provide abundantly—and been just as appalled as Wessex at the thought of the White Tower's Number Two on the loose in France.

"Warltawk arranged it, but I don't know how much he knew. I suspect our mole knew I was getting close and put up Rutledge to lead me off the scent," Wessex said.

"Or to make it look as if you were the garden pest yourself. It's unlike our master to have colleagues who can be so easily leveraged."

Koscuisko had disclosed the details of the "All Agents" bulletin that had come through Paris Station: Wessex knew that there would be a reckoning to settle, but not for the first time he blessed the fact that Koscuisko was something of a loose cannon. The volatile Pole was entirely capable of ignoring orders from London if he did not feel like following them. Apparently he did not feel like following these, but Wessex knew he was still in danger from any of the other agents the White Tower might have in France. Luck had been with him—extraordinary luck, in fact—but now their only safety lay in speed.

"He undoubtedly thought it was a sustainable risk. The girl was safe in holy orders, after all. We'll need four sets of papers, one set for a girl named Marie Celeste. *Sister* Marie Celeste, of the Convent of the Sacred Heart."

Koscuisko stared at him. "Wessex, it's bad enough I'm letting you live. Do you actually mean to say we are on our way to kidnap a *nun*?"

His partner smiled. "You'll manage. Think of England."

※   ※   ※

"Misbourne would give his eyeteeth to see this," Wessex said a quarter of an hour later.

"Ah, well. I dare say he'll see it in Heaven, for we certainly won't get out of here alive to present it to him."

The three of them stood in the Holy of Holies—the private chambers of the Black Pope himself. As Wessex had predicted, it was untenanted at this hour, and it had been easy enough to get in— the Imperial Guard were convinced that no one without the authority would dare. And considering the death that would await a transgressor, Wessex supposed that most people would not.

But if they were to reach the Convent of the Sacred Heart they needed travel papers that would be unquestioned—and the only place they could reach that held the proper stamps and seals was Talleyrand's own office.

The desk and the safe had been locked, of course. But neither mechanism had withstood Koscuisko's clever fingers. The Polish hussar had removed the more ornate portions of his uniform and stuffed them in a closet. They should serve to baffle the Jacks when the break-in was found.

Now Koscuisko labored carefully with pen and inks as Wessex and Rutledge ransacked the files. The most sensitive stuff would not be here, of course, but even what they could find was a feast for British Intelligence.

"Hullo." Wessex was mildly surprised. "It says here d'Charenton's been confirmed governor of Louisianne. Why is that, do you suppose?"

"Court gossip says it is to punish the *Occidenteaux*," Koscuisko said abstractedly. "It is more likely he will drive them into open rebellion, and we shall have new allies."

"D'Charenton hasn't held a government post in years. He's more valuable to Bonaparte as a sorcerer," Wessex said, frowning. He passed the papers to Rutledge.

"There have been rumors about the reason for his posting, but to find them confirmed. . . ." Rutledge said slowly. "Dear God, I had never imagined things to have progressed so far!"

The tone of his voice caused even Koscuisko to look up from his work.

"Perhaps you had better not say anything more, my lord." He did not know who Rutledge was, but that he was here at all in Wessex's company argued that he held a high place in the shadow world of political agents.

"No. I know very well that your duty is to keep me from falling into the hands of the French by any means. But this information must reach London at any cost, and so I must disclose to you more than it is good for you to know. For many years there has been a kind of . . . truce in effect upon the battlefields of the Continent. Bonaparte's generalship has been terrifying, but it has been wholly mortal. He has never brought the *Art Magie* onto the battlefield. And so we have refrained from doing so as well, for if by our arts we were to intrude our quarrel into the Unseen World, the consequences would be destruction on an unimaginable scale. But we believe that he now intends to do so."

"How?" Wessex asked. He had only a gentleman's acquaintance with the *Art de Haut Magie* and a nobleman's knowledge of the Oldest People, nothing more. But even Wessex knew that magic was a fickle thing, as likely to fail as to work its weavers' will, and that to call upon the Great Powers was not to command them.

"There are certain . . . Hallows. Objects that are not of mortal creation, or which have been infused with Divine power. Their guardianship is a sacred trust; many such are guarded still, in places far from this. But of them all, the most ancient, the most sacred, is the Holy Grail.

"Hugh de Payens was led to it in 1188. For many years he and his brethren kept it safe, but Philip le Bel, hearing word of the treasure, desired it for his own, because of the legend that to bring the Grail onto any battlefield ensures victory for him who wields it. To keep it safe, Jacques de Molay sent the Grail, with other treasures the Order had in keeping, to safe harbor in Scotland. But the fleet never reached our shores. It vanished, and the Grail with it.

"When the New World was discovered, it was speculated that those lands might have become the destination of the Templar fleet instead, and those who succeeded the Templars have searched New

Albion as they were able, seeking the Grail. If Bonaparte is sending
his demonolator to the New World, it must mean he, too, realizes
the Grail must be there, and is seeking it out."

"And if he seeks it, he means to use it," Wessex finished slowly.
"And that means that if he is balked of this achievement, he will only
move on to another." And if that were so, this war that had taxed
England for so many long years was about to become terrible beyond
imagining.

"Ah. There we are." Koscuisko got to his feet, blowing upon the
last of four sets of documents to dry it. "Shipshape and Bristol fashion, as *le mode Anglais* would have it." He held out the papers to
Wessex, and only then took in the expression on the Duke's face.

"Is something wrong?"

An hour later three men in dark cloaks rode eastward out of Paris.
There was considerable traffic on the Lyons road, but the passes they
carried had been signed by Talleyrand himself—or at least, would
pass for that under the eyes of anyone but the Black Pope himself.
And if that were not enough, they had brought a goodly number of
his personal papers with them as well. It was best, Koscuisko had
said wisely, to make things a hanging offense immediately, to save
their enemies the trouble of inventing charges. Accustomed to his
partner's fey wit, Wessex had not risen to the lure.

They reached the convent just after first light.

It was an odd thing, Wessex reflected, to see an establishment
of religion here in Imperial France. The Revolution had been based
upon sweeping all such institutions away—Church, Crown, even the
very calendar—and at the beginning of his rise to power the First
Consul had sworn to uphold the ideals of the Spirit of '89. But the
Corsican Beast was a pragmatist after all, and the Church would
make an uncanny enemy. And so Napoleon had ignored the com-
munities of religious that had survived, and had tacitly resumed com-
munication with Rome. France had been a Catholic nation ever since
the Legions withdrew from the West; her excesses and her perver-
sions were all cut from that same seamless cloth. She would go atheist, but never Protestant.

The convent building showed the scars of anticlerical feeling—
the statue of the Virgin which had stood outside its gates was chipped
and battered, and the high stone walls were scarred by fire and de-
faced with paint—but the thick wooden gates were solid and un-
broached.

"Now how do we get past those?" Koscuisko murmured quizzi-
cally. He had shaved off the sideburns and moustaches that would
instantly betray him as a military man, and his glossy chestnut hair
was clubbed severely back. He looked like a wayward scholar.

"I imagine," Wessex said, "that we knock."

Leaving Koscuisko to hold the horses, Wessex and Rutledge approached the gate. A chain with a wooden grip fed out through a
hole in the wall, and when Wessex pulled on it, he could hear a faint
tinkle far away.

After several minutes, the Judas-window in the door opened.
Black eyes in a seamed yet ageless face bored into his.

"My name is Rupert Dyer," Wessex said mildly. "May I come
in?"

"She is not here." The Mother Superior—a serene woman in dove
grey robes—spoke simply.

The doorkeeper had been a lay sister, who had quickly brought
the Mother Superior to deal with this strange and possibly dangerous
intruder. Wessex had known better than to try a bluff on the Mother
Superior, whose loyalties lay with Rome rather than France in any
case. He had simply told her the truth, omitting personal names
wherever possible.

"How—When did they take her?" Rutledge looked like a man
in his death-agonies.

" 'They,' m'sieur?" The elderly nun looked puzzled.

Wessex held up a hand to keep Rutledge from saying more. "You
say that Sister Marie Celeste is gone. Where did she go—and when?"

The Mother Superior regarded him sorrowfully. "She vanished
from her own bed in the dead of night on Candlemas Eve. I fear
that some terrible fate has overtaken her."

The disappointment was as sharp as a blow. Five months, and

the girl missing every day of it! The trail was worse than cold. Had Warltawk known that when he baited Rutledge with the news of the girl's peril less than a week ago?

"No. I will not believe it." Rutledge staggered slowly to his feet. "She cannot simply have vanished."

"Was her bed slept in?" Koscuisko asked unexpectedly.

The Mother Superior frowned, thinking. "Yes. I believe it was. But the most peculiar matter—that which causes us to have such worry—is that her habit and shoes remained when she had gone."

Wessex and Koscuisko looked at each other, and each had come to the same conclusion. The girl was dead, though they might never know how, and there was nothing to be done now but get home as fast as possible. It had been foolish for Wessex to come so far, risking Rutledge's capture and his own. To remain would be worse than suicide. It would be black treason.

"I thank you for your help, Madame," Wessex said. "Come, my friends. We have far to go."

4

The Queen of Heaven
(Wiltshire and Baltimore, 1807)

The house that was nestled into the rolling Wiltshire downs had been called Mooncoign for time out of mind, for long years before it became King Charles III's gift to the first Marchioness of Roxbury over a century ago. It was Sarah's favorite place in all the world, even though she had only seen it for the first time two years before.

Who were you—and who am I? Of your line, or I could not have been drawn here to take your place . . . but who were you? Am I like you? Rupert will not say.

Sarah stood alone in the Long Gallery, gazing upon the painted portraits of her ancestors—or at least, of someone's ancestors. The portrait of the last Marchioness—of *Sarah*—hung at the end of the line, a splendid study by Romney. Sarah had ordered it removed from the Hall and hung in this out-of-the-way place as soon as she had recovered her true memories. The painted stranger in the gilded frame was not her, but the likeness of a woman who had sacrificed her name and her life so that Sarah could take her place in this half-like world.

Why? That was a riddle to which she had no answer.

Sarah sighed heavily, wrapping her cashmire[17] shawl more warmly about her shoulders. It might be the end of June, but it was still chill in the Long Gallery when the sun moved around to the west.

She'd come here to tease herself with old riddles in the hope of taking her mind off the other matter, for a week had passed, and there was no word at all of—or from—her husband.

When Wessex had not appeared by the morning after the ball, Sarah had decided it was best to continue on with the plans the two of them had made together. She would remove to the country, even though it was the height of the Season, and do her best to make it seem that Wessex was with her. He would know to seek her at Mooncoign as soon as he could.

If he could. Did he lie dead even now, an unrecognized corpse in some back alleyway of London? Had what Wessex called "The Shadow Game" come to him?

Oh don't be a goose, Sarah Cunningham! He took Hirondel with him, and I wager the beast has the sense to come home if there is trouble—even if Rupert does not! I shall write again to London to see if he has arrived there yet.

Rather than going home to Mooncoign, Sarah ought more properly to have removed to Dyer Court, for that, not Mooncoign, was the Duke's principal seat. But the two estates marched together—one of the reasons Wessex and Roxbury's parents had betrothed them so many years ago—and Sarah privately thought Dyer Court to be chilly and over-formal. She preferred Mooncoign, with its long rambling wings refaced in Italian limestone a century ago, and its fantastical rooftop Sphynxes.

And this *was the house in which that other Sarah grew up. If I am to know her at all, I must find her here.*

Sarah gazed on the unliving face of the woman who might be

---

17. Cashmire, or Kashmire shawls are what we know today as cashmere shawls, though in the 19th century they were named for their (supposed) place of origin rather than for the fabric. Clear?

her twin—who *was,* in some sense, her twin, though their kinship lay across dimensions, rather than space or time. After a long moment, her shoulders drooped. The painting kept its secrets, as it always did, and after several hours spent here in solitude Sarah was no closer either to an explanation of her husband's absence, or to the serenity to accept it.

With a last look back at the portrait, Sarah walked resolutely to the stairs.

The gardens of Mooncoign, in the time of the last Marchioness, had been redesigned by no less an artist than "Capability" Brown. They did not now reflect the stiff formalism of previous ages, but what passed on these civilized shores for a Romantic and tumbled naturalism.

Sarah crossed the terrace and passed down the long slope of lawn. There was an apron of white gravel at the foot of the swale, and beyond that a low boxwood maze. Reaching the other side, she circled left to strike the Ride, a long straight stretch bordered by double plantings of tall yews that led down to the shore of the ornamental water, making a pleasant gallop that had ended in soggy disaster for more than one horseman. From hints Knoyle had let drop, Sarah suspected that her other self had found her death in Moonmere, for the abigail still spoke of how sick Sarah had been two Aprils gone following a mock sea-battle staged on the lake.

Beyond the ornamental water the tame garden ended. Plantings had been arranged to suggest a dense woodland, but they gave way quickly to such true wilderness as England could fairly boast. Sarah had often gone into the spinney to think, but today she had not stopped to change her day-dress for a walking dress, and neither her shoes nor her skirts would survive the expedition. With a sigh, she stopped at the edge of Moonmere and looked down.

Barely a ruffle of wind marred its surface, and so Sarah saw her reflection mirrored against the sky: a plain brown-haired, grey-eyed girl in a simple white calico day dress.

Who is Sarah? she wondered. *Who am I?*

Suddenly the light failed. Sarah looked around, and saw that the surface of the lake was steaming. Veils of mist were rising from its surface, forming a thick cloud that was moving quickly to envelop her. She took a swift step backward before realizing that whatever danger the mist represented, it was moving too fast for her to escape. Resolutely, Sarah steeled herself to face what came.

The fogbank broke over her like a chill caress, blotting out sight and scent. Sarah looked down, and even the grass beneath her feet was gone, enveloped in the all-concealing greyness. In that moment Sarah recognized it for what it was.

Magic.

"*Sarah. . . .*"

The voice seemed to come from everywhere and nowhere.

"*Help us—help them—help yourself. . . .*"

The mist drew back a little, and now Sarah could see her surroundings once more, but they were terribly changed. The close-cut grass beneath her feet was a sparkling silver, and the colorless trees across the lake sparkled as though they had been dusted thickly with sugar. The water at her feet was mirror-still and mirror-silver: no sunlight danced upon its surface, nor did it reflect the blue of the sky.

Neither sun nor moon.

"Where are you? Show yourself!" Sarah cried.

"I am here."

He was as she had first seen him: a man as small as a child, dressed in a sort of short deerskin toga, his skin stained dark in a dappled pattern that was meant to match the pattern of moonlight through trees. His hair was long, and carefully braided with leaves, and around his throat he wore a torque of pure gold, with terminals of clear amber carved in the shape of acorns. He reached out a hand to her.

"Walk with me, Sarah."

Unhesitatingly, Sarah put a hand into his. She had met him—or his like—before. This was one of the Oldest People, the race who had held this land before her own people's ancestors. That Sarah's kind now walked its green hills was by the sufferance of these elder kin, to whom she owed a daughter's respect. He had come to her once before when she was new in this world . . . but what was his purpose now?

The mist dissolved before them, but it did not show Sarah the familiar lands around her home. Instead, they walked in silence through a forest of oaks whose trunks were larger than three men together, where the mist swathed the great branches like bridal veils.

"This is the land as it once was, before Men came out of the East with their flint and bronze and steel," the fairylord said. "Once it was ours, then you came to take it from us."

"Why are you showing me this?" Sarah asked. She pulled against his grip, but it was as if the land itself gripped her. Now he was taller, wearing green velvet instead of spotted doeskin, his face hidden by a golden mask with branching jeweled antlers.

"It is the nature of Man to take, just as it is the nature of Time to send each race through the Grey Gates in the end. But oh!—not yet, Sarah!—do not send us away yet!"

"I will not banish you ever," Sarah said, puzzled. "Mooncoign is yours for as long as you wish it, and I think—I have heard—that the King has said your lands and ancient rights here in England are to be respected by all men."

"The generous words of an English king, but no King rules in France," the fairylord said sadly. "The Great Marriage has not been made there, and the land suffers. We *are* the land, Sarah, and so we daily dwindle and die!"

"But what am I to do?" Sarah asked, confused.

"Come." As she followed him once more, the great oaks slowly vanished from the landscape. Now the land was gently rolling, forested in pine and birch . . . and hauntingly familiar.

"I know these woods!" Sarah burst out, coming to a stop.

She had hunted this forest—or its twin—through all the years of her childhood. American state or English colony, the land itself was unchanged: these were her home woods as she had seen them on many a misty Baltimore morning, with the yellow leaves beneath her feet and the faint tang of woodsmoke on the air. Tears gathered in her eyes: this was home—*home!*

"Why do you bring me here?" she demanded, her voice suddenly harsh. The longing for what she had so casually given up was a dull pain in her heart, destroying her carefully-cultivated serenity. Never to walk these woods again, never to breathe this air . . . !

Now her companion's hair was a white, lime-stiffened crest over his skull and down his back. Rings of blue paint around his eyes gave his gaze the staring intensity of an owl's and he wore a goatskin kilt and a collar of bones and feathers strung upon a leather thong.

"In the West there is a land where Men do not yet take so much from their elder kin, where the worlds of man and beast and spirit live all in harmony. Do not let this war which destroys us here seek out our kindred as well. We beg this of you." He dropped her hand and stepped back.

"Me?" Sarah demanded incredulously. "How can I—?"

"You have lived in the world that will come, but in this world, those things are not yet as they are there. Stop them, Sarah—or all is lost!"

He had been moving away from her as he spoke, and now his body was half obscured in the mist. The white of his hair and kilt merged into the whiteness of the fog, making him a ghostly figure.

"Wait! Don't go!" Sarah took several stumbling steps after him before realizing it was hopeless. Where the Fair Folk wished to dissemble, no mortal could pierce the veil.

When the mist fell away, Sarah found that she had somehow been transported into the woodlot on the far side of the lake. It seemed as if the last few moments might not have happened, but she knew better than to dismiss this vision as nothing more than a vivid day-dream. The fairylord had come to warn her—or to ask for her help.

"You have lived in the world that will come. . . ."

He must mean her own world, where the colonies had achieved independence from the Crown, and forged a new American nation. Did that mean that such a revolution would come in this world as well? And how could she it if that were indeed so? *He wants me to stop Napoleon,* she realized incredulously. *He wants me to stop the war that the King himself cannot end. How in heaven's name am I to do as he asks?*

"Oh!" Sarah made a small sound of frustration. "And I might as well have gone for a walk in the woods at that," she said ruefully, "for my dress is ruined and I have lost one of my slippers into the bargain." Kicking off the other dainty shoe—meant for floors of wood and marble, not a trek through the outdoors—she began trudging back to the house.

It was after tea-time when she reached Mooncoign again, and she was no closer to understanding what had happened beside the lake than she had been before. The feelings of homesickness that the fairylord had kindled made her both melancholy and angry, though who the subject of her anger must be, not even Sarah knew.

"*There* you are, Your Grace!"

At the sound of the familiar voice, Sarah halted. Knoyle bustled up to her, the abigail's brown eyes going wide as she took in Sarah's disheveled state.

"And without your shoes, Your Grace?" she cried piteously. "And you in such delicate health!" She flung the shawl she carried about Sarah's shoulders in the same way a fowler would fling his net, and with much the same intention. Knoyle defended Sarah as fiercely as an only chick—and was convinced despite all evidence that Sarah's constitution was a fragile one.

To keep the peace, Sarah allowed herself to be cosseted with hot tea and a hot bath, letting the strange experience on the bank of Moonmere fade away from the surface of her mind. The warm water soothed the scratches left by the brambles that had reduced her gown to a sorry rag, but Sarah drew the line at being bundled off to bed.

"I am quite recovered," Sarah said firmly, pulling on a warm day-dress in blue and white flannel. "And I have not yet finished my letter to the Dowager Duchess. I promised faithfully to send Her Grace a full account of the Royal wedding. Nearly a week has passed and I have not done so. I must begin before the light is gone—for I hate writing by candlelight!"

In fact, Sarah hated doing anything by candlelight—the larger the house, the gloomier it was once the sun had set. In the spring she had attended a lecture at the Royal Society that had suggested that one day streets and homes would be illuminated by burning gas, but Sarah had found the harsh blue-white glare and loud hissing of the lamp that was demonstrated at the lecture to be worse than candlelight. A terrible prospect, if all homes were lit so!

It required more firmness than she would have liked, but at last she made her escape from Knoyle and scurried downstairs to her private parlor.

When she had taken possession of her double's house, Sarah had removed the heavy ornate furniture that the other Sarah had favored from the room, and had the thick velvet curtains taken down. Now light blazed into a spacious high-ceilinged room with eggshell-yellow walls and floor to ceiling windows looking out upon the vistas to the west and south. It held no more furniture than a Chinoiserie writing desk with its delicate gilded chair, and a long recaumier[18] covered in brown velvet poised invitingly before the fireplace.

Sarah gained her refuge and closed the door firmly behind her, turning the lock for good measure. The room was filled with the blaze of afternoon sun, and Sarah took a deep breath, forcing herself to relax. Sometimes the thousand restrictions the nobility was hemmed in with chafed her so! She was no petted aristocrat, but an American who had been born free of crowns and thrones. . . .

But if this is a cage, it is a pretty one. And I am loved, Sarah reminded herself. She would survive the estrangement from her birthplace—after all, those who had settled her homeland had left homes behind to do so, and had made new homes in a strange and alien land. She could do no less.

Sarah seated herself at her desk, frowning slightly at the packet of folded and colored papers dropped there beside her unfinished letter to Grandanne—letters from the Duchess of Wessex's vast correspondence, for Sarah enjoyed writing letters nearly as much as she liked to receive them.

The servants would have brought the post, of course. She sorted through the missives, hoping for some word of her husband, but only two were franked as the nobility of England had the right to do, and neither was in his hand. She put them aside, intending to deal with them later, and turned to the others. Three bore no stamp. Two were invitations from local families to some festivity or other. One was not.

Its covering was of rough stained paper, of the sort one might

---

18. A couch to you.

find at a coaching inn, and it had been bound in thin twine before it was sealed with thick yellow candlewax. But despite its rude contrivance, the handwriting was patrician and even.

Sarah picked up her pen-knife and cut the cords. The pages inside were of the same poor-quality paper and ink, but the lines were written boldly and not crossed, as if the writer did not dare chance that her message be unclear. The pages crackled as Sarah carefully unfolded them. The letter was dated two months ago, and—

From Baltimore! Someone writes to me from home!

" 'Dearest Sarah—' " the letter began.

I wish I were home. The shamefaced realization that neither love nor duty were enough to suppress the unworthy pangs of homesickness made Lady Meriel smile wistfully before returning to her letter. If only that were her only problem! The tiny attic room was the meanest in a lodging that was very far from the best to be found, but its landlady asked no questions of a young schoolmaster and his wife, and Louis had felt that the two of them would be safer here than in a more respectable establishment.

For almost two years she and her husband had traveled carefully to this destination—from France, to England, to Ireland, to Portugal to throw pursuers off their trail, to Huy Braseal in the New World, and thence, by slow stages, their money by this time almost gone, north to Baltimore, where they had gone to ground.

The near-tropical heat[19] of Baltimore in April made Meriel's thin woollen dress cling damply to her body and her hair break loose from its smooth coif to riot in tendrils about her forehead and neck. The oppressive humidity made the paper soft and moist, difficult to write upon. Despite the greyness of the day, Meriel had opened both the windows her little lodging possessed, and the damp air brought her the smell of the sea, hoping it would remind her of home, but even the sea was not the same as it was at home in Cornwall. Here the smell was softer, greener, tinged with woodsmoke and river.

Meriel gazed ruefully around herself. She had been raised as

---

19. Which is to say, temperatures between 60 and 70 and muggy.

befit one sprung from a line of kings, and if she had been a pawn most of her life, she had been a pampered one. Before she had eloped with Louis, she had never suspected the existence of such a rude chamber as she now inhabited, much less that she would be living in it. The ceiling of the tiny room slanted sharply downward— even Meriel, no giantess, could not stand upright at the window, but must sit crouched over a shabby table, its surface rough with knots and adze-marks. The only light came from the two narrow windows, wide rather than tall, whose panes were of oiled parchment and not honest glass. Though her exile had taught her caution, Meriel wished she dared to be reckless, for prudence left her reduced to circumstances in which she would not have kept her own servants at home.

And I may become a servant myself—or worse—for who knows if this letter will reach Sarah? She is my only hope, but it is not much of a hope when all is said and done.

The air in the room was heavy and close, and the open windows seemed only to admit heat, not dispel it. Meriel would rather have waited to discharge this task until night had brought with it some vestige of coolness, but she did not wish to spend any of her remaining budget of coin upon candles, and the charge to convey this letter all the way to England would take more than half the money that remained—all she had in the world. Soon she would be forced to earn her keep by the work of her hands—she, the daughter of a belted Earl, raised to be no more than an ornament to a titled husband!

But I am more than that—Louis had taught me that. And Sarah will not desert me. She swore she would always stand my friend— she and the Duke both, and I am so afraid of what the villains who have my Louis now may do to him. . . .

No! I will not despair! The Holy Mother will aid me if I am friendless on Earth. I know She will.

Meriel's family, like the royalty of France, followed the Old Religion, and Maryland's population was predominantly Catholic. Since the grimly Protestant years of Charles III, those of the Old Religion who had chafed under the restrictions England placed upon their faith since Cromwell's day had found a new homeland here in which to practice their religion without constraint. If her trouble were not so terribly political, Meriel would have gone to the parish priest for help days before. But she dared not. Anyone here might be her friend—or enemy—for the best of reasons.

" 'Dearest Sarah—' " Meriel wrote, and stopped. It was hard to know what help to ask for, when she did not know herself the full extent of the blow that had fallen upon her, only that it made her heart ache.

She and Louis had arrived in Baltimore by ship a week before. Funds were waiting here for them through the good offices of His Grace the Duke of Wessex, enough to settle them respectably anywhere in New Albion, for land in the New World was to be had nearly for the asking, and few here, so far away from the courts of Europe, were likely to guess their terrible secret.

But some will guess, for His Grace was never the only one who knew my Louis' secret! If only Louis had listened to me—we should have gone to Coronado[20]—it is so far away that no one there would care who either of us was. I begged him—

Tears gathered in her eyes and Meriel quickly turned away from the table lest she blot the paper. After a moment she composed herself and turned back to her task. She must choose her words carefully, for Louis had told her that he had long suspected they were watched and followed, and her letters might be intercepted.

And he was right to fear, for he was stalked by the wolves that harry our every step. Oh, my poor husband, captive in the hands of those who will seek to use him for the unlucky accident of his birth!

Tears welled up afresh in Meriel's eyes. Three days ago Louis had gone to Nussman's, the Baltimore banking house where their money lay waiting for them. It was the most dangerous part of their entire journey, since to claim the money Louis must reveal himself under a name known perhaps to too many. They had delayed it for as long as they could, but at last Louis had gone.

---

20. In this world, this is the Spanish-held land stretching from the Rio Grande to the Pacific Ocean and south into Mexico. It is bordered in the north by Oregon Country, which stretches from our world's northern California up the coast to Alaska and eastward as far as Idaho. In 1807, Oregon Country is disputed land claimed by England, Russia, France, and Spain.

And he had not returned.

Sarah—Sarah, help me! He is a pawn in the dreams of mad-men—do those who hold him mean to make him their puppet-king, or is it Bonaparte, yearning to destroy the last of the true bloodline once and for all?

Fifteen years before, Louis-Charles of France had been a child of seven, in Revolutionary custody with his mother and sister, but he had been Louis XVII from the moment the blade fell upon his father's neck, and as such, a valuable pawn to both Royalists and Revolutionaries. But somehow the pawn had vanished from the chessboard, to grow secretly to manhood in the house of the Abbé de Condé. Chance had tangled his life with Meriel's, and happenstance had grown into love. Raised as a commoner, Louis had formed no wish to assume a role for which he was not trained, to rule over a people who did not love him. So when fate had offered him the chance to escape that burden and marry the woman he loved, he had seized it eagerly.

We were fools to think they would leave us in peace! Meriel thought bitterly. Louis was too valuable as a symbol—to the Royalists, to the Emperor, even to the English. Whosoever held the last rightful king of France held a sword at the throat of Napoleon's Empire.

With new determination, she dipped her quill in the inkwell and set pen to paper once more.

'Dearest Sarah, I write to beg your help for my husband and myself. He has vanished—I know not where—and I am alone and friendless in a foreign land, in fear of my own life. . . .'

Meriel awoke at first light. She had worked far into the night upon her letter to Sarah, reduced to finishing it by the light of the inferior tallow candles with which the landlord had grudgingly provided her. Once she had tied the thick packet shut and waxed all the knots with the stub of a precious saved beeswax taper, she had been unable to sleep, and had knelt on the uneven floor for hours with her rosary, begging the Blessed Virgin to keep Louis safe and bring him back to her—or failing that, to bring Meriel to him to share whatever fate

God had ordained for him. At last, exhaustion had driven her to her bed, where she had fallen asleep in her underclothes, the jet beads of the rosary twined around her fingers.

When sleep deserted her at dawn's first light, Meriel rose and dressed carefully, brushing out her long black hair and rebraiding it into a tight coronet that would disappear beneath her scuttle-brim bonnet. The bonnet was an old-fashioned style, of printed calico over plaited straw, but the deep brim and the veil pinned to it concealed her face from casual inspection. It was important to appear respectable, when the appearance of respectability was the only thing you had left.

When she was ready, Meriel examined herself as best she could in her hand-mirror. She wore a plain traveling dress of indigo-dyed cotton *de Nîmes,* and over that a grosgrain pelisse in a darker blue, trimmed in scarlet satin lace. Her tan gloves, a carefully-hoarded luxury, had cost more than the rest of her clothing put together, and fit her hands with sumptuous sleekness.

She picked up her ridicule[21] and hesitated. The small bag would be easy for a thief to steal, and she could afford to lose neither the letter nor the money. At last, thinking hard, she wrapped the gold coins that represented all her wealth in one of Louis' handkerchiefs—to muffle them—before tucking money and letter into the bag. Lifting her skirt, she tied the ridicule's strings carefully to the waistband of her petticoats, so that the pouch hung down among her skirts.

She could delay no longer. Meriel opened the door and walked from the room.

She was no longer the sheltered girl who had fled her uncle's plots as she would flee the pains of Hell. With the confidence of much practice she made her way to the Harbormaster's office, and

---

21. "Ridicule" or reticule—sometimes called a *budget,* from which comes the country expression "a budget of news"—is the ancestor of the modern handbag. It was formed by cutting a circle out of a piece of cloth and sewing a drawstring around the edge. When the string was drawn shut, a small pouch was formed. The pocket inside a muff was often used for the same purpose, but it's too warm in Baltimore in April for a muff.

there secured the direction of the fastest England-bound ship.

A few minutes later, Meriel stood at the foot of the gangplank of the *Jahrtausendfeier Falke* and asked to see Captain Pendray. Pendray was a Cornish name, and when he appeared on deck, Meriel took the chance of addressing him in that language.[22]

"*Durdatha why! Fatla genough why?*"[23]

"*Ea, ma Yehes genam,*"[24] Captain Pendray said. "So you are a countrywoman!" His green-hazel eyes were startlingly pale in his deep-tanned face, and he regarded her with friendly watchfulness. "You're a long way from home, *Madama wheg*.[25] Are you in trouble?"

The truth was that she was, but Meriel did not want to say so openly. "May I come aboard?" she asked instead.

Pendray conducted her to his cabin and poured her a glass of wine from a decanter on the sideboard. The cabin, tucked under the stern, was as well-fitted as if it had been carved to be a giant's jewel box, and through the open door of the cabin, Meriel could hear the sounds and shouts of the men on deck.

"You're a trusting missy, 'tis truth," the captain said. "To come below deck with a rough seafarer such as I."

Meriel regarded him steadily. "I am desperate," she said simply. "The Harbormaster said that your ship sails regularly to England, and that she is fast."

"None faster," Pendray said proudly. "When the tide goes out today, I go with her, and we'll see Bristol in five weeks—but I'll not involve the *Falke* in any shady doings."

"All I ask is that you carry a letter for me to the Duchess of Wessex, in England. I have written her direction upon it—her house lies in Wiltshire. She is a friend of mine."

Pendray regarded her skeptically. Meriel knew what he was thinking. Though she was respectably dressed, she did not look like the sort of person whom Duchesses befriended.

---

22. It's a dialect of Gaelic, and the last native speaker died in the late 19th century. It wasn't Dolly Pentreath, though.

23. "Good morning! How are you doing?"

24. "I am well."

25. "Dear Madam (lady)."

"It is urgent that my message reaches her. I will pay you to carry it, and as much more as will hire a messenger to bring it to the Duchess."

"And what will keep me from taking your money and tossing your letter over the side as soon as I've hauled anchor?" Pendray said playfully.

"Your honor," Meriel answered. *"Onen hag Oll."* "One and all." It was Cornwall's motto, and no more than the simple truth.,

Captain Pendray's face went slowly red. He turned away quickly to cover his contrition. "Aye, missy. You'll forgive an old sailor for speaking up so freshly to a Cornishwoman. There's them among us that still remembers what it was to fight for Trelawny."

"I know," Meriel said. Decades and even centuries could not blunt the memory of that great rising, when forty thousand Cornishmen had marched against the King to save one of their own. That honor was in their blood, as much as was the wild music of the ocean upon the rocks.

"Give me your letter and I will see it safe," he said roughly.

"You will have to turn your back," Meriel said with relief. When he had done as she had asked she got to her feet and fumbled beneath her skirts until she had freed the ridicule. She opened it and placed the letter upon the table.

"I will give you ten guineas if—"

"Nay!" The captain's voice was harsh. "I will do it for the love of hearing the Old Tongue spoken again. Give me two guineas to pay the messenger at land's end, and I vow your Duchess will have your letter not six weeks from today."

Though in fact she was no better off than she had been, Meriel left the *Jahrtausendfeier Falke* in better spirits than she had been since Louis disappeared. She was a victim of powerful forces far beyond her control, but she would not be a pawn.

Sarah blinked, coming back to herself as she gazed at the letter. The room was dim, the last rays of the setting sun shining through the line of trees to the west.

Meriel's words had been written weeks and miles away—what had happened to her in all the long days it had taken her letter to reach Mooncoign? She might be dead already—or Louis might be— or both of them. . . .

No. Think, Sarah! Wessex would know the thing most likely to have happened in Baltimore, but he is not here, the disobliging man. And Meriel's case cannot wait until he is: were I in Bristol at this very moment, it would be six weeks to America. Three months since Meriel wrote by the time I reached her . . . !

Sarah got to her feet and began to pace restlessly, trying to imagine what had happened. Louis was too careful to have fallen prey to the footpads or press gangs which were an inevitable feature of port cities, so she dismissed that possibility at once. So he had to have been taken by someone who knew who he was, for plain Mr. Capet would be of no use to anyone's plots.

But who?

Sarah made a hissing sound of exasperation between her teeth. She could guess until she was sick with it and be no closer to the truth! She turned back to the writing-table, and hesitated as a realization struck her.

You can reach Meriel yourself as fast as a letter could. And in this Baltimore, the wishes of the Duchess of Wessex will carry far more weight than those of plain Sarah Cunningham in your own.

Yes. She would leave a letter for Wessex, but she would start for Baltimore this very night.

Less than two days later, Sarah stood upon the deck of the *Triskelion*, watching the Bristol wharf dwindle behind her. The *Triskelion* carried the Royal Mail, and passage aboard her was dearly bought, but with a following wind she might reach Boston in as little as four weeks. Sarah's trunks contained a large quantity of coin, and such items of clothing as would allow her to make a grand show, in case someone might need to be overawed by the apparition of an English Duchess under full sail. She would travel alone, for the matter was too dangerous to involve an innocent servant in it, and hope a Duchess's eccentricities would excuse all. But Sarah did not count upon that card trumping all, and so she carried with her also her most prized possession: a Baker rifle, taken from one of Wessex's enemies on a truly memorable occasion.

Sarah had learned to shoot almost as soon as she had learned to walk, but, as with most of her fellow Americans, the weapon she had inherited from her dear papa had been a musket, the same Brown Bess that most of the British Army still carried in the field today. The Baker was as unlike Brown Bess as a racehorse was unlike a plowhorse: accurate at more than three times the standard-issue Army musket's range, and capable of being loaded and fired at the startling rate of three times a minute by an expert shot. Sarah had made herself just such an expert, and she dared to swear that the Baker would speak as loudly on her behalf as it did on General Wellesley's.

Now all she could do was wait, and try to figure out what she could possibly do to find Meriel's husband.

Out of hard-learned caution Meriel followed a different path to return to her lodgings, and her steps took her past the staunch brick and limestone facade of an unfamiliar church. The doors stood open, and Meriel could smell the familiar scent of incense and see the flickering light of vigil candles flickering within.

She frowned. This was not Our Lady of the Angels, in which she had spent so many anguished hours beseeching the Blessed Mother to save her husband, yet it was undeniably a church of the Old Religion.[26] Willing to be curious, Meriel crossed the street and entered.

It was cool and fragrant within. The tall stained-glass windows cast mosaics of brilliantly-colored light over the pews and the pale stone floor. At the end of the center aisle she could see the High Altar, its furnishings gleaming, flanked by banks of candles. The church seemed to be empty, but perhaps the priest was hearing confession, or occupied in the vestry. Meriel advanced to the altar and curtseyed, crossing herself, and then turned right to enter the Lady Chapel.

---

26. As Catholicism has been known in England since Tudor times.

The blue-robed statue of the Virgin welcomed her with its out-stretched hands and gentle smile. Golden stars were painted around the hem of the blue mantle, and one bare foot rested in the curve of a crescent moon half-hidden in the draperies of her robe. Banks of vigil candles burned on either side of the statue.

Meriel knelt and crossed herself, then rose to her feet to light one of the candles. She dropped a sovereign into the box beside the pile of unlit candles, and after a moment's thought, added six more. Captain Pendray's unexpected generosity had left her with more money than she had anticipated, and it seemed greedy to keep it. There were others far worse off than she, even in this darkest hour of her life.

Only keep Louis safe, Blessed Mother! He is your dutiful son who kept God in his heart even when all of France descended into the madness of atheism. Help him now. Help me.

She knelt again before the statue, her senses lulled by the flick-ering lights and comforting surroundings. She shook her rosary out of her sleeve and began to say her prayers, the beads slipping easily through her gloved fingers. Slowly the panicky fear for Louis' safety, the terrible uncertainty about her own fate, stilled beneath the eter-nal reassurance of the ancient words.

She had reached that moment every supplicant knows, when the contemplation of the Mysteries opens the gate to the Eternal, when she became aware of the light shining through her closed eyelids.

It was not a sudden jarring apparition. The light appeared so slowly that it was several minutes before Meriel realized it was there. When she opened her eyes, it was with mild curiosity, not sudden fear.

BE NOT AFRAID.

A glorious Being of light stood where the statue had stood just a moment before. Though the light was intense, somehow Meriel could see the figure clearly. It was barefoot, draped in pure white robes, and it carried a gleaming sword that shone brighter than the sun. The shadow of great wings mantled the Being's back.

BE NOT AFRAID, it said again, and somehow she was not. Goodness radiated from this Being along with the light, and Meriel knew that she had been called to witness a glorious miracle. This was one of God's own holy angels. Tears of joy welled up in her eyes.

"Have you—Why have you come?" she corrected herself, stumbling over the words. Angels were messengers, and she both desired and dreaded this one's tidings.

The angel smiled, and Meriel felt a wave of good humor and kindness touch her like a loving parent's caress. FEAR NOT FOR YOUR HUSBAND. THOSE WHO HOLD HIM WILL BECOME HIS GUARDIANS, THOUGH AS YET THEY KNOW IT NOT. I COME TO ASK SOMETHING OTHER OF YOU.

"Anything!" Meriel answered instantly.

It will be a hard road, the angel warned her. WITH DIFFICULTIES YOU CAN NOT YET IMAGINE. I WILL ASK YOU AGAIN. THINK CAREFULLY BEFORE YOU ANSWER.

"I will do anything you ask," Meriel answered. Her heart beat faster with the angel's warning. Why did it caution her? It was a holy messenger of God—how could she refuse to do what it asked of her?

A moment of terrible doubt struck her. What if it hesitated because it knew she would fail? Suppose this creature asked more of her than she could do? The angels were greater than Man, but only Holy God was omnipotent.

"If you ask for my help I will give it, as much and as well as I can," she answered, her voice quivering with fear.

The angel smiled at her. BE AT PEACE, LITTLE SISTER. I ASK FOR YOUR SACRIFICE, BUT NOT YOUR FAILURE. SEE WHAT I HOLD IN MY HAND.

Meriel looked, and though it had not been there before, she now saw that the angel held a great Cup, like that into which the good father poured the water and the wine at Mass. But this was not a cup of gold or silver. Instead, this cup seemed to be carved whole out of one enormous emerald. From the rim to the base golden letters were carved in a long spiral, flaring star-bright against the rich green of the Cup.

"It is the Grail. . . ." Meriel whispered.

THOSE IN WHOSE CARE IT WAS PLACED LONG AGO CAN GUARD IT NO LONGER. NOW YOU MUST SEEK IT WHERE IT WAITS, LEST IT FALL INTO THE HANDS OF EVIL. SEEK IT WESTWARD, OVER WATER, AND YOU WILL NOT FAIL TO FIND IT. FARE YOU WELL, DAUGHTER OF EVE.

As it spoke the brightness and the form both seemed to fade, though Meriel could not say, if she had thought about it, at what moment it had begun to fade and at what moment it vanished. She only knew that at some moment she found herself alone in the Lady Chapel, staring up at the painted statue of the Blessed Mother with wide, unbelieving eyes.

Wait! Meriel longed to cry. This was a charge far greater than any she had ever expected would be laid on her. She barely knew where to begin.

But she *did* know where to begin. That much she had been told. She must go west, into the broad, unmapped, wild Virginias, which stretched all the way up into the Great Lakes.[27]

And what of Louis? She thought the angel had sworn to her that Louis would be well, but what if that were only her own hopes smoothing the way for her? How could she abandon her search for him when she did not know? How could she be sure . . . ?

There is no certainty this side of Heaven, Meriel reminded herself stalwartly. She rose to her feet, her mind made up. There was much to do.

When she left the church, Meriel realized that she must go upon her quest as simple pilgrims went. She returned to her lodging and changed to her oldest clothes, taking with her no more than she could knot into a shawl, and began to walk westward. And in her excitement she forgot, until it was too late to recall it, the letter she had sent aboard the *Jahrtausendfeier Falke.*

As she walked, she worried over Louis' safety and her own sanity, but to have refused the angel's summons would have been to refuse all that she believed in, and so she went forward, praying for a sign to soothe her heart. When the sun was high overhead she paused to drink from a stream, and to eat the bread and cheese she had brought with her. When these provisions were gone, she would have no more, except what God should provide.

---

27. In New Albion, the County of Virginia covers all or most of what in our world would be the following states: Virginia, West Virginia, Ohio, Indiana, Illinois, Wisconsin, and Minnesota.

In our world, the original English settlers were quite the optimists: the lands granted to Virginia originally ran all the way to the Pacific, despite competing French and Spanish claims.

As she hesitated on the bank of the stream, Meriel heard a rhythmic crackling through the underbrush. She froze, visions of wolves, bears, or even lions filling her mind. But all that appeared was a large white mule, upon its back a man wearing the broad-brimmed black hat of a Jesuit priest.

"Good afternoon," the priest said calmly. "Can I be of assistance to you?"

Meriel shocked herself by bursting into tears. Angelic visitations and heavenly missions were foreign to her experience, and with the best will in the world, her nerves were sadly shattered.

The priest dismounted, and waited while she cried herself to a stop. "Tell me how I can help you," he urged gently.

"I don't know!" Meriel cried. She dropped to her knees and clutched at his hand, kissing the ring that was the symbol of his holy office.

"Are you a Believer, my child?" the priest asked kindly. "Would it help you to confess yourself to me?"

"Yes—no—I don't know, Father," Meriel said wearily. "I scarce believe it myself, and I do not know what I am to do. I know that I am to go west, but that is all."

"And how do you know this?" the priest asked.

"An angel told me, in a church in Baltimore," Meriel said miserably.

There was a moment of silence.

"I am Father MacDonough," the priest said. "Are you quite certain it was an angel?"

"I have never seen an angel before—but it looked like one. How can I disobey?" Meriel answered helplessly.

"You must pray for guidance," Father MacDonough said. "And you must consider those whom your actions may hurt. Your parents, perhaps?"

"No." Meriel shook her head. "There is no one left in Baltimore to worry about me." She spread her hands in a gesture of submission. "I must go west. Beyond that, I do not know."

Father MacDonough frowned, considering. "Well, perhaps we can travel together for a time. I am heading into Indian lands to offer the Word of God to the native peoples. I mean to travel as far as the border of Louisianne, if God so wills. Perhaps you would care to accompany me?"

"If God so wills," Meriel said with relief.

That night they made a simple camp beneath the trees, and said their prayers together. Father MacDonough had shot a brace of pigeons, and roasted them as the twilight deepened into night. His mule was laden with trade goods, for he brought more than God's word to the tribes, and he gave Meriel a blanket in which to wrap herself against the evening chill. As the fire burned low, the two of them lay down to sleep. Weary from her fears and the long day of walking, Meriel fell asleep at once.

The song of the nightingale and the overpowering scent of roses awakened her. She sat up, opening her eyes.

Over the embers of the fire, the emerald Cup hovered, its surface aflame with the golden letters of fire. Through the trees of the forest she could see the mountains, and could feel the Cup drawing her south and west as if it were a magnet, silently demanding that she retrieve it.

Then she awoke in truth.

Courting birds sang in the tree branches. It was still dark, but she could see the shapes of the trees against the sky, indicating that the sun would soon be up. On the far side of the fire, Father MacDonough slept on.

Meriel sat up, shivering as the blanket slipped and the cold air pierced her to the skin. She rubbed the sleep from her eyes. The Cup was nowhere to be seen, but she knew where it was. West— somewhere west—and she would be led to it. She no longer doubted. With a lighter heart, Meriel got to her feet and began building up the fire.

For the first few weeks their path took them past isolated farmsteads, villages, and trading posts. Everyone they met was friendly, feeding them and often giving them a bed for the night in exchange for fresh news from Baltimore. Meriel's muscles toughened under the constant exercise, and though her problems remained as pressing and unresolved as before, she learned not to worry about them. Each night she saw the Cup, leading her onward into the next day's travel.

Then one morning she awoke, and realized this was the last day she would be able to travel with the kindly Father MacDonough, for his path tended north, into Ohio country, while hers led her southward. The miles she had already traversed gave her the confidence to greet this new challenge; one of the things Father MacDonough had taught her as they walked was which plants were edible and which were not. It was late spring, now, and though the land did not yet carry its midsummer bounty, there were birds' eggs, roots, and herbs enough to feed her.

"I will leave you today, I think," Meriel said over breakfast.

Father MacDonough looked troubled. During the time they had traveled together he had never pressed her for confidences she had been unable to volunteer, but Meriel had always known her explanations of her mission did not satisfy him.

"My child, this is land over which no European has ever traveled. The tribes we have met so far are peaceful trappers and traders, but not all Indians are so pacific. A woman alone would be subject to such terrible danger as you cannot imagine."

"But that is the way I must go, Father. Surely God would not lead me into peril if that were not a part of His design?" Meriel answered.

"Perhaps your faith is stronger than my own," Father MacDonough said tartly, "But you are walking into greater danger than you can imagine."

"God leads me there," Meriel said patiently, though she believed what he told her and her heart beat faster in fear. "I cannot turn my back upon Him."

"And if it is not God Who sends this message to you, but the Devil, leading you on through your own pride?" the priest said at last.

"Then I will ask God to forgive me that," Meriel answered. "And I know that you fear for me so much that you have followed me south these last four days, good father, away from your own chosen road. But today we must part."

Father MacDonough sighed, looking utterly weary. "God defend me from the faith of the young," he muttered, raising his hand to bless her. "And God defend you, child, if folly and not faith drives you."

That night Meriel slept alone after a cold supper, curled up at the base of a tree. Her faith did not keep her from spending an uneasy night, and she sorely missed the Jesuit's company. When morning came, she rose and continued walking through a forest that seemed still to exist in the morning of Creation. For three days she did not see another human being, then she fell in with a Jewish peddlar who led two heavily laden mules and carried the most enormous pack Meriel had ever seen. He told her that he meant to trade for furs along the banks of the Ohio River, and then take a packet-boat into Nouvelle-Orléans to sell his cargo.

He seemed to accept her appearance without question, though Meriel knew that after so many weeks in the wilderness her appearance certainly would not pass muster anywhere in polite society. She lost track of the days the two of them followed the narrow deer-track along the floors of the narrow valleys. The mountains around them seemed to unfold in endless ridges, until Meriel wondered if they continued, chain upon chain, all the way to the Pacific.

But at last, when the mountains were only a blue smoke-smudge upon the horizon behind them, she parted company with him as well. Meriel had only the vaguest idea of how long or how far she had walked, and in her heart, the faith that had sustained her so long was beginning to waver. How could the Grail be here in this immense wilderness? And if it were, how could she possibly find it? And even if she were led to it, what could she possibly *do* about it?

Somewhere, Louis' fate had already been decided, and she might never know what it was. Those who played the Shadow Game were certainly capable of making one man vanish without trace or record.

Do not think of that! she told herself fiercely. *You made a promise. You must fulfill it as best you can. You are not worthless—is Louis' love a worthless thing, that he should give it to a worthless person? Trust, and believe, and you will prevail.*

But her brave self-adjurations were hard to obey. Meriel's husbanded rations ran out at last, and none of the plants she encountered were familiar ones. Water was becoming harder to come by as well, for the few creeks she passed were at the bottom of deep ravines, behind protecting screens of thorns, almost impossible to reach. As the days passed, it began to seem to her that the wilderness might be the only victor.

5

The Duchess and the Dirtwater Fox (England and New Albion, July 1807)

At Dover, Wessex and Koscuisko went their separate ways, Koscuisko to bring Lord Rutledge to London, and Wessex to his country estate.

He ought to have gone directly to London and taken his caning for this mad start. That he'd gotten away with it, and brought Rutledge and much valuable intelligence home with him was sheer luck, and Wessex knew that this detour to see Sarah was only a temporary reprieve from Lord Misbourne's anger. At the worst, he might be dismissed from the Tower's service. He was not certain whether the possibility dismayed or relieved him.

Wessex had always known that the perilous double life he led could not endure forever, but he had always thought it would end in death, not retirement. Politicals died in service. A retired spy, stripped of the protection his former masters could afford, could not expect a long life . . . but might a Duke endure where one of the commons would be cut down?

The notion might be worth considering.

"Cheer up, lad. We're home," he told Hirondel.

The proud brick towers of Dyer Court flared ruby-bright against the westering sun. The house was as new as Mooncoign was old—built in the time of Charles II for the first Duke of Wessex to be a model of comfort and efficiency, for the Dyers had long been a forward-thinking family.

Sarah would be waiting for him there. His errand in France—and the need to cover his traces so thoroughly on his return, as well as evade their own operatives acting under the "All Agents" order—had eaten weeks. It was now the middle of July, and his lands drowsed in the long approach to an English summer. Wessex wondered whether his reception would be as warm as the weather, or as cold as his doubts.

As it happened, it was neither.

"Does Her Grace dine at home tonight?" Mills, his chief groom, was waiting as Wessex rode into the stables to turn Hirondel over to him.

"Her Grace do'ent lie here, my lord. She'm come down to lie at Mooncoign a month gone." The craggy old ostler looked embarrassed to correct his master.

"Yes, of course," Wessex said quickly. So his wife was beneath her own ancestral roof and not his? It would not do to draw a hasty conclusion as to her reasons, nor to let the servants see he was out of countenance. Nor would it do to present himself before her in the dirt of the road. "I shall need a chaise and team in an hour."

His wife's property was the erection of a more exuberant age than Dyer Court, and had been improved out of all recognition by succeeding generations of Roxburys. From its cladding in white limestone to the ornamental Sphynxes that guarded its roof, Mooncoign bespoke the excesses that sprang from absolute license. The arrogance of the Conynghams was legendary throughout the county and the Ton.

But the present Marchioness, his Duchess, was forged of a different steel entirely, and Wessex knew better than to expect arbitrariness or spite from her. Her actions were always considered and thoughtful—whether they were to his taste or not. He was more grateful for her stubbornness than he would ever willingly let her know, for in some sense Wessex felt it protected her from him. No one who ever knew her would need to waste a moment's worry about running roughshod over the Duchess of Wessex. She was as unyielding as the bedrock itself.

A little over an hour and a quarter after his arrival at Dyer Court, His Grace of Wessex, a vision in grey from foot to crown, arrived at Mooncoign. It was nearly dark when he drew the chaise-and-pair up before the portico, but no torches were lit, nor had he seen the banner displayed that would proclaim Sarah as resident beneath her own roof. Yet the servants at Dyer Court had been certain that Sarah had come down from Town following the Royal wedding, just as the two of them had planned in what now seemed another lifetime.

A groom came running to take the horses' reins, and Wessex dismounted from the carriage. He walked quickly to the door, which was already swinging open.

Buckland was standing ready to greet him. Wessex's spirits lifted. If Buckland were here, then Her Grace certainly was. But his hopes were to be almost immediately dashed.

"Good evening, Your Grace."

"Good evening, Buckland. Is Her Grace at home?"

"No, Your Grace. But Her Grace left a letter for you, should you come to receive it."

Buckland showed him to the Duchess's parlor, where Wessex waited while Buckland fetched the key that would open the strongbox hidden beneath the hearthstone and presented him with Sarah's letter and its enclosures. The letter was admirably terse—Sarah had never been one for long drawn-out roundaboutation. His wife had packed herself up without so much as a by-your-leave and left for the Americas, to entangle herself once more in the dangerous affairs of the French King in exile.

Wessex could not fault her caution at any rate. She had not left the information lying about for anyone to find. Now a cheery fire crackled upon the hearth and Wessex, fortified by a strong whiskey-

and-soda, studied the letter that had sent Sarah upon her quest.

As he read it, Wessex groaned inwardly. No wonder his beloved lady had taken off without even a maid to bear her company! Lady Meriel's letter sounded half-demented—and with good reason, Wessex had grudgingly to admit. For Louis to vanish was bad enough. For him to vanish while on an errand touching so nearly upon his true identity was a dark omen indeed.

His conscience, what there was of it, did not trouble him for his part in the Young King's disappearance from the chessboard of Europe. Louis had been missing for twenty years: it would not unduly change matters did he continue absent, and Wessex had come to like the lad and understand his wish to live free of crowns and intrigue. But to vanish well, one needed funds. Earlier in his career, Wessex had spent some time in the New World on the White Tower's business, and one memorable adventure had left him with a Spanish ransom in gold to be disposed of. He had deposited it at a convenient bank, using his identity of the moment, and thought little more about it. Having little use for the money himself, and having resolved to set the Young King beyond reach of either the Corsican usurper or Wessex's own English masters, Wessex had given Louis the passwords that would allow him to claim the gold that Don Diego de la Coronado had deposited at Nussman's Bank years before.

Only he and Louis knew the money was there. But Don Diego was known—at least within the Tower—as one of Wessex's cover-identities. The All Agents warrant for his capture, dead or alive, was still in effect. Did the unknown enemy mean to strike at Louis . . . or at Wessex?

Either way, Sarah had gone sailing into danger a fortnight past. Wessex flung both letters into the fire and watched the flames consume them, then rang for Buckland and began giving orders. The White Tower, the mole, d'Charenton, Talleyrand's new ambitions, all vanished from his mind in an instant. Whatever dangers Sarah faced, he would share them with her.

It lacked a few days of the Lammastide when Wessex's preparations were complete, aided by the fact that the one place the White Tower was not searching for him was in his own country. Even if Koscuisko or Rutledge betrayed his whereabouts, it would take Misbourne time to put someone into the field to snare him, and before that event could possibly take place, his yacht, *the Day-dream,* was crewed and provisioned.

Wessex had prepared a wide selection of weapons and documents that should suffice for any occasion, and he had enlisted the aid of his very superior manservant, Atheling, to accompany him upon his quest, since on this occasion Wessex was afforded the luxury of traveling in his own persona. All the Duke of Wessex lacked was peace of mind, for if he had possessed no warrant to risk himself in France, he had even less to intrude upon the affairs of New Albion. There was trouble brewing there, Misbourne had told him, and even so far from Europe there were those who knew him for what he truly was and would take the intrusion of the Duke of Wessex into their affairs as a violent insult.

But he had less choice than if a gun were pointed at his head. If he arrived too late to save his Duchess, Wessex swore he would not arrive too late to share her fate.

Though the tide was against them, Wessex had no intention of waiting one moment more than he must to sail. The moment he was aboard, he gave Captain Tarrant the office, and the ship began to move.

Day-dream had been his father's yacht; a sixty-foot racing sloop that had made many a clandestine Channel-crossing at the height of the Terror. Captain Tarrant felt it could make the crossing to Baltimore without difficulty, and Wessex had liked the freedom and privacy that using *Day-dream* would give him. No political agent was ever sanguine without a secure rat-line down which he could retreat at need, and *Day-dream* would give Wessex such an avenue of escape.

The dyked meadows of the fen-country, still thick with morning mist, slid away and vanished into the soft grey of sea and cloud. The sail-canvas snapped and wuthered as it filled, and the ship began to move upon the wind with the inexorable grace of a racehorse. Slowly the marsh-smells of *Day-dream*'s quiet anchorage gave way to the sharp scent of the open Channel. He felt as much as heard the ship sing beneath his feet as lines and masts took the strain of the sails. A strong vibration passed through the deck beneath his feet, the bow-wave sent a fine tingling salt-spray over the exposed skin of Wessex's face, and he heard the hissing of water along the hull.

Yet some faint precognition warned Wessex that all was not as it should be. He had just turned to seek Captain Tarrant when the sailor's shout reached him.

"Hoy! Captain! Stowaway in the hold!"

Without thought, Wessex dropped his hand to the pocket of his greatcoat, where a pistol reposed in a scabbard of chamois leather built into the pocket. Two seamen were coming up from below, a disheveled and struggling figure held between them.

A familiar figure.

"Hullo, Koscuisko," Wessex said resignedly.

Koscuisko glanced toward him and smiled irrepressibly. The young hussar was dressed in rough fisherman's garb, his bare feet and cotton smock indistinguishable from those of a thousand other such men.

Wessex motioned to the sailors. "Never mind. He's in the way of being a friend of mine."

"You must have burned your candle at both ends to get Rutledge to London and find me in so short a time," Wessex observed idly.

The two men had gone below to Wessex's cabin, where they could obtain some privacy. Koscuisko sprawled at his ease in a chair, a glass of French brandy in his hand. Wessex stood. He had removed his greatcoat, but it—and its concealed pistols—hung near to hand. Koscuisko was his friend, but Wessex had never made the mistake of assuming their loyalties were identical.

"You don't know the half of it," Koscuisko answered gaily. "Misbourne had some maggot in his bonnet about you doing a moonlight flit, though he was glad enough to have my Lord of Rutledge returned to him. Our friend d'Charenton has been more than active of late—Paris Station says a number of young ladies have made their

last trip to a certain address in that city, and they suspect that
Mam'selle Marie was one of them. I'd thought he might be working
to get the governorship, but now I wonder if he mightn't have two
strings to his bow."

"D'Charenton almost always has," Wessex answered absently, his
mind elsewhere. "This nonsense about the Grail, for example."

"Are you so sure it is nonsense? At any rate, I barely had time
to make my report before I had to turn around and head back to
the fens to find you. I swam out to the ship last night—and deuced
cold work it was, I assure you!—and thought I'd best lie low until
we were well away. Shouldn't want to disturb good Captain Tarrant
at his work and all. And it's ho! for the colonies." Koscuisko leaned
back in his chair with the look of a man well-pleased, but though his
tone was light and his words idle, the expatriate hussar's dark brown
eyes watched his friend consideringly.

"I hope you've brought more luggage with you than that, or it's
going to be a long voyage," Wessex said, willfully ignoring the undertone of their conversation. "Illya, I know why I'm here and I have
no intention of confiding in you. But why are *you* here?"

"We're going to Louisianne to assassinate d'Charenton and start
a rebellion, you and I," Koscuisko said cheerfully.

"Are you quite mad?" Wessex asked, after a long moment. "How
could . . . oh. I see."

This was undoubtedly the task that Misbourne had wished to
brief Wessex for: a political assassination, in a colony where the situation was volatile at best.

It was a known fact of the Shadow Game that one executed a
sorcerer at one's peril. The executioner tended to die within the
year, and worse: if the sorcerer were of an especially vindictive or
malignant disposition, his curse did not restrict itself to his killer,
but spread to blight the land all around . . . unless the executioner
were of Royal blood. Wessex had acted as executioner against a sorcerer twice, once in Paris, and once—a particularly memorable affair—in Scotland. On those occasions he had gone forth with the
blessings of King and Church, with silver bullets in his pistol and
runes marked upon his sabre, and his foe had died safely, cleanly,
and eternally.

So far as he knew, Wessex was the White Tower's only clandestine operative able to perform such sanctions. While it was true that Koscuisko was closely related to Poland's Royal family, the blood-magic and the land-magic ran differently there. If Koscuisko were to kill d'Charenton, there was every chance he would die, and place Louisianne under a curse as well.

Such a thing would lead to violent unrest, perhaps even Revolution. Which might be Misbourne's ultimate goal. . . .

Koscuisko refused to explain by what means he'd conveyed his equipment to the ship, but he'd brought a great deal of it, as well as a copy of the briefing book on the Louisianne Colony. As the *Daydream* plied her way west, the two men studied it carefully. That his own country should become the handmaid of foreign Revolution disturbed him greatly, but if Wessex were heading into a seething cauldron of unrest he wanted to know it,

"Of course, revolution in Louisianne would be to England's benefit," Koscuisko said provocatively.

The weather was good, and the two confidential agents spent many hours on deck stripped down to singlet and trews, only partly from choice. Life in New Albion was of necessity a thing much conducted in the open air, and neither man wished his drawing-room pallor to expose him as a foreigner.

"Force France to withdraw resources from Europe, open the Western Frontier, bring Spain into direct opposition with France," Wessex ticked off the points impatiently upon his fingers. "In short, war in the New World, and there has been none there for nearly a century."

The land had been peaceful since France and England had sorted out their spheres of influence. England's colonies were primarily matters of trade and of creating markets in the native populations, with which they had excellent relations. Spain and France, however, saw the inhabitants of the New World less as trading partners and more as the slave labor to found a vast mining and agricultural empire.

With time enough, the New World natives would be on a technological par with their European brethren, and no easy prey for adventurous nations. But it would be a generation, perhaps more, before the Iroquois, the Cherokee, and the Mohawks had the industrial base for equal competition with the East. Until that great work was completed, they were vulnerable . . . and the Crown must protect them.

Perhaps even against itself.

"We are all at war," Koscuisko said with unwonted gravity. "Is it kinder to place our cousins under an artificial protection, or to treat them as men?"

He did not press Wessex further to take up the mission. Perhaps Koscuisko feared what the Duke would say. For himself, Wessex had no doubts.

During the long weeks at sea aboard *Triskelion,* Sarah relearned the skills that had been so much a part of her other life, the skills of patience and stealth. She voyaged to America as a hunter, and it was a hunter's skills she would need.

This trans-Atlantic passage was very different than her first. She traveled as a woman of privilege and property instead of as a terrified orphan. She traveled not into an uncertain future, but back to her childhood home, and if, deep inside, a warning voice told her there was something she overlooked, Sarah ruthlessly shunted it aside.

She had come to regret her hasty action in leaving Knoyle behind. This world expected great ladies to travel in state—with servants—and regarded anything else with deep suspicion. Sarah doubted that her story of a maid taking sick at the last moment truly convinced anyone, but her confidence and obvious wealth silenced wagging tongues, and no one was foolhardy enough to present her with the cut direct.

Her fellow travelers were mostly Anglo-Albioners who had traveled to England on business and were now returning home to their plantations and estates. A few women journeyed to rejoin their husbands—Sarah discovered that the tropical climate of the New World was considered unhealthy for children, and many of the upper classes sent their children home to England for the first years of their lives.

It was on the tip of Sarah's tongue to denounce such foolish nonsense, for certainly no American had ever entertained such a pernicious notion, when self-preservation stopped her. Sarah Cunningham might know what it was like to have been born and raised in a free New World nation, but the Duchess of Wessex should have no notion.

But the masquerade—for such was her life—was often very hard.

Her one consolation was the company of one of her fellow passengers, a man whom Sarah instinctively liked, even though she was sure he flew beneath colors falser than her own. He was a tall piratical-looking gentleman, black haired and grey eyed, with the look of being more comfortable on horseback than shipboard.

Morgan, *soi-disant* Marquess of Carabou, traveled with only one servant, a thin nervous boy whom Sarah privately felt he must have acquired from the nearest pothouse. The Marquess had a silver tongue and winning ways—he was undoubtedly a rogue and a scoundrel, but Sarah had little else to distract herself with in the next month, and vowed she would know the truth about him before they docked in Boston.

"The man's no more a Marquess than I am, Peter Bronck," a woman's voice scolded angrily. Sarah ducked back out of sight and eavesdropped shamelessly.

Dorcas and her husband were fur traders; each year Peter Bronck traveled from his offices in Nieuw Amsterdam to Fort Chingcachook along the Great Lakes to meet with his suppliers and to buy furs. Dorcas had been the most suspicious of Sarah's claim to be the Duchess of Wessex, for she and her husband were members of the rising middle class—what the *Ton* called Cits—and Dorcas, at least, held herself far higher in the instep than any queen. It was a particularly American attitude, Sarah realized with an inward shock, and that it was strange to her was a sobering benchmark of how strange the whole world had become. When had she become used to the groveling deference from her fellow men that she had always used to mock?

"Now Dorrie," Mr. Bronck answered. "Surely a man may call himself as he pleases?"

His wife's response to that was an indignant snort. "He may call himself the King of Spain, so long as he does not ask me for money! But that has nothing to say to the point—the man is no aristocrat, and I'll be burned if I treat him as one!"

Sarah smiled to herself. Each scrap of information was another clue she could use to weave her snare for him. But the Marquess was a slippery fellow. His table manners were direct, but no worse than Sarah had seen elsewhere in polite society; no clue to his background there. He wore a sabre at his hip, but so did many men. The most interesting thing she knew about him was that he had four silver-mounted horse-pistols and the harness to match. Perhaps he was a highwayman fleeing the notice of the Bow Street Mounted Patrol.

All Sarah was truly able to discover was that he had spent his early years in Wales—and that only because she had chanced to be nearby upon the occasion when he spilled a full lamp's-worth of oil down the front of his new velvet coat. *Then* there had been language of a pungency Sarah had not heard for some time, but even upon that memorable occasion my lord of Carabou had not beaten his servant, whose fault the accident had been. Sarah decided she liked him, whoever he really was. Marriage to Wessex seemed to have given her a taste for the company of rogues and scoundrels.

"The captain tells me we shall be docking in Boston Harbor in a day or so," Sarah said to Morgan one evening. It had become her habit to take the air with the mysterious Marquess each evening after dinner. Her cabin, while lavish by shipboard standards, was cramped and confining, and she spent as many hours away from it as she could.

"I suppose it's as good a place as any to find a ship heading south," the Marquess said.

"I'm heading south as well," Sarah offered. The tactical difficulties of making her way to Baltimore to search for Meriel, which had seemed so negligible at Mooncoign, now seemed to loom insurmountably.

"Are you suggesting that we travel together?" Morgan asked.

"Perhaps I am," Sarah admitted. "I need to get to Baltimore immediately. I'd thought to charter a ship, but. . . ." *But I'm not certain that this America is at all like the one I remember,* she admitted, if only to herself.

"The Royal Mail would be faster if you can flash the ready," Lord Carabou said frankly. "Or if Your Grace has New World properties, perhaps your man of business would be kind enough to put one of your ships at your disposal."

Sarah bit her lip in consternation. Perhaps Wessex did own land or commercial enterprises in what in this world was still the British colonies, but she'd never thought to ask, and now it was too late.

"I'm sure you think me the veriest greenhead—or worse?" she suggested.

"A rank impostor like myself?" Morgan grinned impishly, to take the sting from the words. "No, I don't doubt you're every inch a duchess. Nowt but the nobility can get quite so tangled in its own schemes. Why, I recollect the last time I was in a position to help out a member of the gentry—t'was the Duke of Wessex himself, as it happens, little though he'd care for the likes of me to know his proper handle—"

"I don't actually doubt you," Sarah interrupted with a sigh, "as my husband gets himself into the most peculiar scrapes. And I don't care who you truly are, or where you're bound. But I need to get to Baltimore as fast as may be!"

Morgan studied her face in silence for several moments before a slow smile of acceptance broke over his lean, weather-tanned features.

"Aye, well, I can help you as far as that, my lady Wessex."

And so it was that barely a week later, Sarah prepared to descend the gangplank of a second vessel onto the bustling Baltimore docks. With her were a manservant and a maid hastily hired in Boston by her enterprising companion—a necessity, or so Morgan had told her, to handle her baggage and uphold her consequence.

"Well, Lord Carabou. I suppose we shall not meet again."

"Not if either of us is lucky," Morgan answered with a grin. "I'm bound for Corchado—I'll buy me a large *rancho* and a pretty wife, breed blood cattle, and end my days at peace in my own vineyard."

"It sounds an excellent plan," Sarah answered solemnly. She held out her hand, and after a moment, Morgan took it. "Fare you well."

"Farewell, Duchess. And good hunting."

He turned away, and Sarah followed her trunks down the gangplank and onto the Baltimore docks. They seemed much larger than she remembered them, with large numbers of British and Danish ships docked for loading. To her surprise, she saw large numbers of The People working side-by-side with the colonial dockworkers.

This is not the same world I left, she reminded herself. She had accepted all the bowing and curtseying her rank commanded when she was in England, but she found it oddly jarring to receive the same deference from those she unconsciously thought of as her countrymen and peers. It brought home to her as nothing else could have that the America she had unconsciously expected to find was not here at all.

With Morgan's worldly-wise assistance, Sarah had messaged ahead by heliograph, and so a coach from the Royal Baltimore was waiting for her at the foot of the dock. Her trunks were quickly loaded, and the coach moved off toward the hostelry from which she would begin her search for Meriel.

So far she had weathered all her surprises with at least the appearance of equanimity, but now, as she moved through a landscape she had once known so well, the differences struck as hard as blows. Instead of rows of whitewashed brick or clapboard houses surrounded by orchards and gardens, the town she saw could have been London in miniature. Sober English tradesmen and their ladies walked the streets in equitable company with Native men and women in their own accustomed dress—another extraordinary sight to Sarah's eyes.

I feel as if I've fallen through a mirror, Sarah thought in bewilderment. She realized that she had unconsciously counted on her familiarity with Baltimore to aid her in coming to Meriel's rescue—but this was a world utterly alien to her. Here no Revolution had divided America and England to make them two separate nations, nor set the colonists in opposition to the land's first peoples . . . but what was such an America like?

It does not matter, Sarah told herself fiercely. *All that matters is rescuing Meriel . . . and Louis.*

"Where is she?" Sarah demanded, hearing her voice go shrill with stifled anger.

"I'm sure I don't know, your fine ladyship," the woman said. Her manner was more than insolent, despite the fact that Sarah had provided a *douceur* of good English gold in recompense for her time.

"But she *was* here," Sarah said desperately. She had come directly to the address Meriel had given in her letter, and only now began to realize how out-of-place even her sober traveling dress and plumed bonnet were in this shabby neighborhood. She had never feared to walk wherever she would in Baltimore when she had lived here, but both the town—and she—had changed.

"Not these four weeks gone," the woman repeated. "Happen it you'll be wanting to pay the rent herself left owing? You can have away her traps for that."

Sarah grimaced. She doubted extremely that there was any rent owing to this slatternly landlady, but she wanted Meriel's luggage. It might contain some clue to where her friend had gone.

"How much did she owe?" Sarah asked resignedly.

Three days passed, and Sarah spent them exhausting every official avenue she dared to employ in her search for Meriel. She had investigated workhouse, madhouse, prison, and hospital, and found no sign of either Meriel or Louis. If not for having taken possession of their luggage—for Louis' had been lumped in with Meriel's—she would have begun to doubt they'd come to Baltimore at all. But even Meriel's diary failed to give her any clue. It ended abruptly five weeks before, just before the date on the letter that Meriel had dispatched to her.

Today she had managed to get an audience with the Governor-General, and to her despair, he had also been unable to help her.

Sarah trudged up the street to her lodgings, her steps heavy with weariness. She had chosen to walk rather than to be cooped up on the jarring stuffy coach, but now regretted her impulsiveness.

I cannot believe they are gone! I cannot stand by and do nothing! Sarah told herself stormily. For one painful instant, she longed for Wessex. Surely he would have some notion of what she could do next!

'Someone knows something. Depend on it. All that remains is to ask until you find them.'

She could almost hear Wessex's lazy drawl in the words, and slowly she realized there *was* someone left for her to ask. Sarah's steps quickened with new purpose. She was not defeated.

The brief time she had spent in Baltimore had taught her the need for circumspection. She was no longer Miss Sarah Cunningham, a nobody whom anyone might easily overlook, but the Duchess of Wessex, a Personage whose comings and goings were matters of note. She dismissed her maidservant and waited until the hour was late and the hotel was quiet—it was the same coaching house that she had left Baltimore from a lifetime ago, but the Royal Baltimore was a far grander establishment than its American counterpart. Discretion was called for.

While she waited, Sarah took down her hair and combed it out into two long braids. She garbed herself in a pair of tight-fitting moleskin trousers and a shirt of rough homespun she had provided herself with back at Mooncoign. Over the shirt she wore a vest of chamois leather into which had sewn much of her gold during the long sea voyage. The vest fit as heavily as a medieval coat of mail, but the wealth it concealed could be transported silently, and the coins would turn a bullet if need be. Last of all, Sarah retrieved her beloved Baker rifle from its concealment in the false bottom of her trunk, and slung the bag of cartridges[28] over her shoulder.

---

28. Not what we would think of as a rifle cartridge, but a paper packet containing powder and shot. The packet itself functioned as the wadding. To load, the packet would be torn open, the powder poured down the barrel, and then the

She caught sight of her reflection in a mirror and grimaced. A fine Duchess she looked—more a raw Colonial hob-goblin, did this world possess such creatures. All she needed was to paint her face with hunting magic and braid some gull-feathers into her hair to complete the picture. But this Sarah could go where Duchess-Sarah could not, and ask help of the only folk there were left for her to ask.

When she was certain she would not be interrupted or seen discovered, Sarah opened the window and slipped out onto the roof. Her bare feet found easy purchase on a drainspout, and in a moment she had slipped down the side of the building and trotted across the yard.

In another universe, Sarah had been the daughter of Miss Charlotte Masham and Master Alisdair Cunningham, and had grown up in a small house on the edge of Baltimore. Her father had lost all but his life at Culloden, and his health had been broken in the battles for American Independence, so from an early age, it had been Sarah whose woodland skills had kept the family larder filled. She had been more at home among her Indian playfellows than among her fellow settlers, and when cholera had carried off her parents, had found herself toiling as an unpaid servant in her cousin Masham's household. Dame Alecto Kennet's intervention with a tale of a mysterious legacy had started Sarah on the long journey that had led her, in the end, back to her own beginning. Now Sarah would see if anything at all of the world she remembered still existed in this one.

She moved noiselessly through the deserted nighttime streets of the town—in this world, Baltimore had a curfew—and quickly reached its edge. The moon above gave her enough light to see by until she reached the edge of the trees. She had planned to conceal herself there and wait for dawn to search for the village, for she wasn't quite sure if the this-world analogue of her Cree playfellows

---

wadding, followed by the bullet—a ball of lead about the size of a child's marble. The load would be rammed into place with the ramrod, and then fired off, the powder ignited by means of a spark struck from the flint.

would even be here. The tribes native to the Maryland area were the Conoy, the Nanticoke, and the Shawnee, all of which were members of the Algonquin Confederacy. The Algonquin and the Iroquois held an uneasy truce all up and down the East Coast, though the power of the Five Nations had been decisively broken before Sarah was born. For as long as she had been alive, land-hungry Europeans had pushed the Iroquois and the Algonquin westward, leaving only isolated pockets of native settlement behind, such as the Cree village above Baltimore.

The *Eeyou Istchee*—the Cree—were not native to the Atlantic Seaboard. The main body of that nation lived far to the northwest, in what Sarah knew as Canada, but a generation ago a forward-thinking leader had sent a band of his people south to form a trade outpost on the outskirts of Baltimore, and it was they who had befriended first Alisdair Cunningham, and then his daughter.

Sarah realized that in this world, the First Peoples and the Europeans lived in far greater harmony than in her own. Here there had been no burning and dispossession of the Mohawk nations, for the English valued the native peoples as a market for the goods from European mills instead of seeing them as unwanted tenants of land they could better use themselves.

But even if the two peoples lived in harmony, Sarah did not presume they trusted one another. Cree scouts had made good spies in the American Revolution, and Sarah only hoped she could call upon their skills herself.

So lost was she in her own thoughts that she paid no heed to where her footsteps led her, for if Baltimore had changed, the land was just as she remembered it. It was only when she realized that the light had grown brighter that she stopped and looked up.

Sarah caught her breath in wonder. The whole forest gleamed with a silvery light, and the trees looked as if they were made of jewels. Each leaf gleamed like a dull emerald, and the tree bark had turned to rough silver. Every detail she saw was impossibly sharp, down to the brown curl of last year's leaves upon the forest floor and the coiled gold of the mosses.

Sarah clutched her rifle tighter. *What has happened here?* she wondered, her heart beating faster. She knew she ought to be afraid, but all she felt was a sense of wonder and excitement. The world had become more itself, not less. This was the world she had always unconsciously expected to see when she was a child, and seeing it now gave her a shock of recognition, not of strangeness, as if something she had given up hoping for had finally happened.

All the peoples of this world take magic for granted, as if it is an everyday occurrence. And so I suppose it must be. I stand on the edge of the Spirit World, the world as it was in the moment of its first making.

If that were truly the case, then a tool had been placed into her hands. The People held that all the world was sacred, and did not wall off their gods in churches as the white settlers did. Sarah leaned her rifle against a nearby tree, clasped her hands together, and prayed.

Spirit of the land, spirit of the Oldest People, hear your child. Help me to find what I seek, so that I can keep my promise to aid my friend, for you know that the world was first made from words and that a promise is sacred.

When she opened her eyes, she saw the bear.

It stood on its hind legs at the edge of the clearing, the transcendent moonlight silvering its ash-brown fur. Grandfather Bear stood nearly twice as tall as a man, his long black claws gleaming like glass.

Grandfather Bear was the patron of the Hunting Societies. Without his leave, no game could be taken from the forest, the sky, or the stream, and so the people danced to him each winter. He was the greatest of the Elder Brothers who watched over the People and taught them how to live. Until Corn Mother had come up from the south, Grandfather Bear's medicine had been the only resource the People had to feed themselves. He did not help the liar, the oathbreaker, or any hunter who did not generously share all he had with his fellows.

She reached into her pouch and took out a quid of tobacco. It was used as both offering and currency among the People, and she had thought she might need it to trade for information. But now she realized she had been too long away from her childhood companions, and forgotten their ways. Kindred did not buy the help of kindred.

She held out the tobacco on both palms toward Grandfather Bear, and now she could see the necklace of beads and shells that he wore. The colorful designs of hunting medicine striped his mask and muzzle and formed a bright dapple upon his shoulders. Sarah shivered with inward awe, and carefully placed the tobacco on the ground before her, backing away.

Come, daughter.

The voice in her head was rough and low, such speech as stones or wind might make. Bear dropped to all fours and turned away, vanishing into the forest. Where he had stood, there was now a path through the wood, the white shells and polished stones of its surface gleaming in the moonlight.

Feeling insensibly lighter of heart, Sarah picked up her rifle and followed it.

6

In the Land of the Fallen
(Louisianne, August 1807)

The city had last burned in 1794, when Baron de Carondelet was governor, and been rebuilt out of the private purse of Don Andres Almonaster. The Spanish city that had risen from the ashes of the French trading post boasted a public school, a charity hospital, a Capuchin convent, and the great cathedral dedicated now to Saint Louis that towered above every other structure in the city. The courthouse was still known as Cabildo House, even though the Spanish dominion of the city had ended seven years before, for though the colony had been ceded to France seven years ago, Napoleon had sent no governor, preoccupied as he had been with problems at home.

And so Spain had continued to govern her former colony, though with increasing laxity. Seeing that, the great pirate fleets moved north from Cartagena to make Grand Terre their new base from which to prey on the rich shipping in the Gulf, and in a matter of months, Nouvelle-Orléans became a hotbed of criminals. These stalwarts received the news that France was at last to send a Colonial Governor as the office to steal everything that wasn't nailed down. They were opposed by a Civil Guard drawn from the ranks of the city's French, Creole,[29] and Free Black inhabitants, and the street fighting was bloody and inconclusive.

The Duc d'Charenton arrived at the city in July with three well-gunned ships and several hundred infantry under the command of General Victor. To divert the pirates' attention from the arriving ships, Victor instructed Admiral Jerome Bonaparte to land his troops at the Bay of Mobile. As Victor marched overland, investing the city from the north, the Emperor's young brother, Admiral of d'Charenton's little fleet, acquitted himself admirably, driving the pirates' ships from their stations at the mouth of the Mississippi and freeing the Port for the new Governor's arrival.

Once in the city, d'Charenton settled into spacious apartments in the Cabildo, scorning the house at the corner of Toulouse and Levee that the Spanish governors had previously occupied in favor of proximity to the courthouse and prison. The traditional pillories on Chartres Street were replaced with the stake and the gibbet, and the new governor began his reign by emptying the prison, and executing the prisoners his army had taken. Those who were burned alive, so it was rumored, were the lucky ones.

At first the city welcomed him. The Duc was of noble French blood, and surely harsh measures were the only cure for the lawlessness and anarchy that had beset the city for several long years. And the Duc d'Charenton did so many good things. His soldiers patrolled the streets day and night, so that any woman, Creole or French, might walk the streets unmolested. Tradesmen opened their shops without fear, and the port regained its former vitality. Goods that had moldered in dockside warehouses were loaded and shipped to Europe, clearing the docks for new arrivals.

Most of all, to the delight of the *Occidenteaux*, the new Governor placed an enormous tariff on Yankee goods. For years the western settlements of New Albion had shipped their goods down the Ohio

---

29. The term "Creole" has had many different definitions over the course of New Orleans' history. For convenience, if not strict historical accuracy, I am using it to refer to residents of Spanish descent.

and the Mississippi for loading upon the great Trans-Atlantic ships, and the flatboats, crewed by *mauvais Kaintocks,* rendered certain districts of the city unsafe for man, woman, or beast when the crews were in possession of them. Now the Kaintocks discovered they would be charged half their cargo's value for the privilege of discharging it in Nouvelle-Orléans—and the French customs officials were careful to set that value high. Half of every English cargo—furs and hides, tallow, tobacco, indigo, flax, copper—went instead to France, while French and Spanish cargoes used the port for free.

And so the days passed as, like a fat white spider in the center of a golden web, d'Charenton consolidated his power.

Almost twenty years before,[30] Father Antonio de Sedella had been appointed Commissary of the Inquisition, and voyaged to Nouvelle-Orléans to establish a tribunal of the Holy Inquisition there. His mission had met with no success, as Governor Miro, too familiar with the excesses of the Holy Office in his own country, had deported him the moment de Sedella made his mission known. But before he had departed, Father Antonio had prepared all the machinery of the Inquisition, including a network of secret passageways that ran from the Capuchin friary to the Cabildo, to the Cathedral de Saint-Louis itself.[31] All his preparations had lain dormant, awaiting the arrival of the man who had discovered their existence from the records of the Inquisition itself.

The underground room was large, surprisingly cool despite the heat of the season. Lanterns filled with perfumed oil burned, filling the room with the sickly scent of burning roses, and the walls had been draped with gorgeous fabrics, giving the chamber the look of the tent of some oriental potentate. A large carved and gilded chair had been brought down from the room above, the arms of Spain still picked out in gold and silk against its red velvet back, and a child's

---

30. December 6, 1788.

31. The tale of the Capuchin Inquisitor and his hellish labyrinth can be found in *The French Quarter,* by Herbert Asbury. As Anna Russell was wont to say, "I'm not making this stuff up, you know."

painted china doll sprawled carelessly upon its seat. Beside it stood a delicate gilded table, with a decanter and cups of gold and crystal upon them.

The worst is dat he keep de little p'tit wid him, even here, d'Charenton's secretary thought. Charles Corday was not certain which of the two terrified him more: the ancient, degenerate nobleman, or his golden, elfin protégé.

One of the ways d'Charenton had amused himself since his arrival was by surrounding himself with the young daughters of the city's prominent families. Little Delphine McCarty was the cherished daughter of a powerful Nouvelle-Orléans family.[32] She was perhaps seven, certainly no more, and in her the mingling of Scots and Creole had produced a child who showed promise of being an astonishing beauty. Most of the children had been terrified and repelled by the secret chambers beneath the city, but little Delphine had been fascinated, and slowly d'Charenton had initiated her into his more terrible pleasures.

"I had heard that the weather in Nouvelle-Orléans was unpleasant during the summer months, but I confess I do not find it so. In fact, I would say that the weather is quite delightful. Do you not find it so, Madame?" d'Charenton asked. Delphine giggled, a high thin sound like the death-screams of mice.

The woman the Duc addressed uttered a low groan and turned her face away. Her name was Sanité Dédé, and until last week she had sold sweetmeats in front of the Cabildo and around the Place d'Armes. How d'Charenton had discovered that she was also the *Regina de Voudoun* for this parish was something Corday did not know. But d'Charenton's spies were everywhere, and as soon as the Governor possessed that information, he had Sanité arrested.

---

32. Delphine Lalaurie, née McCarty, was a real person, and at the center of one of the greatest scandals in New Orleans history. In 1834 she was discovered to have been responsible for the systematic torture-murder of dozens, perhaps hundreds, of her slaves. She barely escaped the (white) mob which clamored for her blood, and vanished from the pages of history, perhaps to Europe. The house on Royal Street, which stands to this day, is rumored to be haunted by the ghosts of the children she murdered there.

At first he had offered her money to give up her secrets. She had laughed in his face, secure in her power.

That had been a mistake.

Broad bands of livid purple now stained Sanité's golden skin where the muscles had been torn beneath the flesh. Delphine reached for the wheel at the head of the table, and d'Charenton swatted her hand away, beaming avuncularly.

At first, the Duc had difficulty in utilizing Father Antonio's legacy, for the engines had rusted in the humid air of Louisianne. But he had brought with him men who understood their repair, and there had been an unending stream of criminals and rebels to practice upon, until now every hinge and crank and pulley moved with the satin suppleness of precision machinery. Now the wheel was delicately balanced, and would move at a touch. Even a venerable old man like himself could operate them, once the subject was secured to the framework, and he had many strong soldiers to perform that task.

"Madame Dédé?" he repeated. "Perhaps you do not find the weather comfortable?" Almost caressingly he reached out to the great four-spoked wheel and tugged upon it gently. Counterweights moved, and the iron gears at the heart of the Procrustean Bed racketed forward a notch.

The woman shackled to the mechanism threw back her head and screamed. Mademoiselle McCarty clapped her hands, beaming.

"So, Madame. You do have a taste for conversation after all, perhaps?" d'Charenton said genially. "You will remember the nature of our last discussion?"

The Voudou Queen moaned despairingly. The light of the lamps glittered off her eyes and her sweating skin, and the white-crusted tracks of tears gleamed upon her cheeks.

"M'sieur Corday? You can refresh her memory, perhaps?" d'Charenton asked, turning to his secretary. D'Charenton knew his secretary despised his pastimes, and for that reason insisted upon Corday's attendance at his little inquisitions.

Charles Corday—who had, in another life and time, been known to a select few as "Gambit" for his reckless bravery—hesitated. He did not wish to be here at all, either in this chamber or in the city itself, but for many reasons he dared not disobey his latest master or interfere with the Duc d'Charenton's unspeakable notions of sport.

"You wished to know de secret of de *Voudous,* Your Grace," Corday said dutifully. He drew a silk scarf from his sleeve and wiped his forehead. It was cold and damp here in this subterranean chamber beneath the Cabildo, but Corday's fine French linen was already soaked with sweat.

D'Charenton regarded him with a sparkling, feverish gaze, and Corday shuddered inwardly. People liked to consider the Duc d'Charenton a madman, but Corday knew that he was not. A madman was not in control of his appetites, and d'Charenton controlled his as a coachman might govern spirited horses. Corday enjoyed Talleyrand's own patronage, and while that was true, d'Charenton's private secretary was entirely safe from d'Charenton's whims . . . at least, so long as his true sympathies remained unsuspected. For "Gambit" Corday was neither French nor Creole. He was Acadian, and for many years his people—descendants of those settlers dispossessed from French Acadia when it fell into English hands—had dreamed of a homeland of their own, a land in which they would be more than despised and landless refugees.

Louisianne could be that homeland, if its bonds with the Emperor across the sea could be broken, and so for years Corday had served two masters—the Black Pope, with his self-serving Imperialist ambitions, and his fellow Free Acadian conspirators—hoping for the day that his countrymen would rise in revolt to throw off Imperial chains.

But the lessons of the French Revolution were too bloodily recent for that. The *Occidenteaux* were reluctant to try to cast off the yoke of tyranny, fearing wave after wave of frenzied executions in reprisal. It had been a stroke of fortune when Talleyrand had sent him to Nouvelle-Orléans with d'Charenton.

D'Charenton's habits were notorious among Talleyrand's circle, and Corday had known that d'Charenton's rule would be all that was needed to drive Louisianne into open revolt at last, so though he could have struck d'Charenton down and taken his place a dozen times on the voyage here, Corday had withheld his hand. But now he feared that in doing so he had made a pact with the Devil himself.

D'Charenton was searching for something, and whatever it was made him willing to flout the power of *les Voudous*. D'Charenton's powers must be great indeed, that he had not already been struck dead by the power of the Conjure Doctors and Voudou Queens against whose gods he offended.

"Very good, Corday! Delphine, isn't he the very best of servants? You see, Madame Dédé, M'sieur Corday is eager to continue our chat, as am I. I beg you, satisfy my curiosity. You are *la reine Voudou*. Your house has been searched. The apparatus has been found. The Church rebukes. But I do not—" Here the Duc leaned toward the woman, so that their cheeks nearly touched. Corday swallowed hard and turned away, but try as he might, he could not shut out d'Charenton's wheedling voice, Delphine's laughter, nor the moans of their victim.

What did he seek, here in Nouvelle-Orléans? What prize could be worth the undying enmity of the *Voudous Magnian*?

Could anything? Could freedom?

The woman screamed once more, and this time Corday heard the finality of death in her voice. He felt sick with relief. He had gone to a conjure doctor as soon as Sanité Dédé was taken, and bought herbs to make her heart race and fail. He had steeped them in the water he gave her, but he hadn't dared to give her enough to kill her immediately, or d'Charenton's suspicion would have fallen upon him, and after the last month, Corday was willing to do nearly anything not to fall into the governor's clutches. What was done in these dungeons had even driven him back into the arms of Holy Mother Church herself, and Corday would have been willing to swear that no power on earth could do that.

"You faint like a woman, Corday." D'Charenton's voice was amused. "What a pity. I was told that the Africans were of hardier stock, but this creature lasted barely a week. She told me nothing."

"Do another one, *cher oncle*," Delphine begged. "Take my servant, my Letty! She is strong, and—"

"Perhaps there was nothing to tell," Corday offered desperately, to still that terrible lisping voice.

"No. There was something. I know it. Are you a student of magic, m'sieur?"

With an effort, Corday kept his hands from the blessed saint's medal he wore against his skin. Like many of his generation, Corday hated magic as a sly and unpredictable science. It was a way of cheating, just as aristocracy and money were ways of cheating.

"No, Your Grace. I 'ave nevair 'ad time for such studies, me."

"That barbarous accent of yours, Corday! Before we are through, we will teach you to speak French like a Parisian, won't we, Delphine? But first we will broaden your education."

d'Charenton stepped away from the dead woman, and took a decanter from a table beside a black cabinet. He poured a glass full of red wine and offered it to his secretary. Corday shook his head, not trusting himself to speak. D'Charenton drank deeply before continuing.

"In the *Art Magie*, it is commonly held that one evokes the infernal powers and invokes the angelic powers to gain mastery over the material world. But that is to overlook the fact that this world—what Hermes Trismegistus called the Mesocosmos—hosts powers of its own. In the barbarous days of Royalty, did not the King upon his Coronation make pact with the powers of the land, so that the destiny of King and Land were one?"

King Louis had been executed when Corday was only a boy, but the fact that France Herself had not risen to her master and bridegroom's aid had been one of the factors that propelled the Corsican into power. Reluctantly, Corday nodded. D'Charenton grunted in satisfaction and poured himself another glass of wine.

"Well, then. This is a new land. By what ceremony shall we bind ourselves to it, so that its powers are ours to command?"

Delphine, bored with the turn the conversation had taken, had climbed up into the red plush chair and was cradling her doll, scolding it in a voice that was an eerie echo of d'Charenton's own.

Corday stared at him for a moment before realizing some answer was required. "But . . . I thought . . . only the King—someone of Royal blood. . . ."

D'Charenton laughed unpleasantly. "But this is a new age, my excellent Corday, and we must put superstition behind us and bring the science of magic into the 19th century! A king is no different than any other man, and so it follows that any man may approach

the spirits of the land to become their vassal and master. These ignorant savages have learned to treat with unknown spirits, and I will
gain their secrets and use them to approach the spirits of this land
and bend them to my will. If not now, then soon. I have more than
one way to gain the information I seek. Always remember that I am
an inventive man, M'sieur Corday."

"I nevair forget dat, Your Grace." *And to what use will you put
what you learn, my lord Duc?* Corday wondered. This was terrible
news, for if d'Charenton proposed to rule Nouvelle-Orléans by
magic, even the power of guns and swords might not be enough to
win her freedom.

For a long time, Louis did not know where or even who he was. He
awoke in darkness, to the sick swaying of a ship, and did not know
for how many hours or days he drifted in and out of consciousness
before his mind cleared enough for him to remember why it was so
wrong for him to be here.

He remembered walking down the street in Baltimore—the imposing portico of Nussman's Bank. He was not sure, but he thought
he remembered the portly smiling figure of the Director of the bank,
the scent of coffee. . . .

Then nothing.

Drugged. The thought floated to the top of his mind. He had
been drugged, and kidnapped.

The thought was enough to galvanize him into full wakefulness.
Louis groaned and rolled over, painfully forcing open his eyes.

He wore the good linen shirt and velvet trousers he had donned
to attend the banker, but his plumed tricorne, his silk stockings with
decorative clocks, his silver-buckled brogues, and his silk coat and
vest were all gone. Whether he was the victim of robbers or kidnap-
pers, the result was so far the same, and Louis blessed the lifetime
habit of caution that had kept him from venturing out with any identifying papers about his person. His captors would not have gained
so much as the direction of his lodging from a perusal of Louis'
personal possessions.

The ship shifted again, and Louis heard the gunshot-snap of canvas above. Each movement brought a fresh surge of nausea, though he was normally a good sailor.

At least there was light to see by. A candle in a water-filled safety lantern hung from its hook on an overhead beam, and by its wan aqueous light Louis was able to make out his surroundings.

He lay on a straw-filled canvas pallet, in a stall such as was commonly used to transport horses by sea. The scent of ancient horse was still strong, mingling with the odors of tar and brine. A tin plate and cup lay upon the straw beside his head, and Louis recovered a confused memory of someone sitting with him to feed him. They had undoubtedly kept him drugged so that he would be tractable . . . but for how long? Where was he now?

And who this time has determined that Louis Capet will be of use to them? he wondered grimly. For a moment fear for Meriel consumed him—what had they done to his wife?

Perhaps nothing—but that is nearly as bad as what they might do. He forced the thoughts from his mind with an effort. There was nothing he could do to save Meriel—and the fact that she was not confined here with him argued that the conspirators had overlooked her.

His mouth burned with thirst, and he knew his first act must be to find water. But when he tried to get to his feet, Louis discovered that his captors had not been as negligent as they had first appeared. His ankles were in iron shackles, a short length of chain between them. Despite this, Louis forced himself to his feet, holding to the wall of the loose-box for balance. Just as he gained his feet, the ship heeled over sharply, flinging him to the straw again. Through the deck above, he could hear the shouts of sailors.

It is night, or else the sun would be visible through the hatches. No ship sails so at night unless it flees a storm, and I hear no sound of wind and ocean.

Unless it flees a storm . . . or is fleeing something else.

Pirates were a common problem along the coast of the Americas, and in their travels Louis and Meriel had been menaced a number of times. If his captors had been fleeing pirates—and such pursuits could cover hours or days, each ship hoping for a favoring wind—it would explain why he had not received his customary ration of drugs this evening.

It also meant that whoever had kidnapped him had not taken him across the ocean to England or France—unless of course those who pursued this vessel belonged to one navy or the other.

His thirst overrode all other immediate considerations. Dragging himself to his feet once more, Louis shuffled from his improvised jail, his fettered ankles making his movements snail-slow. The men on deck were shouting now, but Louis could not make out their words over the creaking of the ship.

He stumbled through the dark of the hold, guided as much by touch as by the feeble illumination of the lantern. It was worth a flogging to the sailor that had left it here unattended, but Louis was grateful for the guidance it gave him. He reached the ladder nearly by accident, and followed his nose to a barrel of brackish water chained beneath it. There was a wooden dipper pegged to the barrel, and Louis filled it and drank deeply, holding to the ladder to maintain his balance. The water was laced strongly with vinegar to keep it from going bad for as long as possible, but Louis didn't mind. He drank until his stomach was stretched tight and his head had cleared. Now to free his ankles, for bound as he was, he would go straight to the bottom if the ship sank.

Perhaps that had been his captors' plan for him, Louis thought soberingly. Whoever they were, they would not want him to survive as a witness if their plans went awry. The thought galvanized him to search for some tool with which to free himself.

A sailor he had traveled with had once explained to Louis that only constant maintenance kept sailing ships from springing apart and sending their crews instantly to Davy Jones' Locker. From this he understood that the ship's carpenter was the most important member of a ship's company, and his tools were always kept ready to hand. Shackles that had been put on a man would surely be simple to remove with the proper tools.

A few moments search—to the accompaniment of increasingly-frantic sounds above—located a mallet and a chisel, and with a few deft blows Louis had cut through the bolts that secured his bonds.

Had they been of felon's iron and not sailor's lead, he could not have managed the feat, but the soft metal sheared through easily.

At that moment a great crash shook the vessel, the shock making the hull moan with stress. The lantern tore free of its mooring and smashed into darkness, but now there was a spill of firelight down the ladder leading to the deck.

It is pirates, Louis thought, his guess confirmed. *And now they have boarded the ship.*

What should he do? The men aboard this ship were no friends to him, but those who had taken it from them might be even less so, for Louis was entirely without false modesty, and knew that he was the most important man in the world.

Not for what he might do, but for the fact of who he was. The last King of France—unanointed, uncrowned, and in exile, but King still. And there were those who would try to use that fact to their own advantage.

A lesser man would have despaired long ago, but a life spent in hiding, the only survivor of his murdered family, had made Louis a fighter. He hefted the hammer and grimly made his way up the ladder.

On deck, a scene of slaughter and chaos the like of which he had never seen save in his nightmares greeted him. The vessel upon which he had been held captive was bound to another with a network of grappling hooks, and its decks were awash with blood. Though it was night, both ships were so brilliantly illuminated that every detail of each could be easily seen. Here and there the clash of steel still rang out, but most of the fighting was over. The air reeked of blood and the burnt gunpowder whose smoke still hung over the ship in an acrid bluish haze.

All about the deck, men stood gazing at the carnage with torches in their hands, and the enemy ship—a rakish, black-hulled sloop—was lit with lanterns until it resembled a saint's-day float. The legend Pride of Barataria was written upon its bow in large golden letters, and it flew two flags—one of red and gold that resembled that of Spain, and the other one Louis had never seen before: on a red field, a silver skull surmounting crossed sabers.

Nothing worse could happen to him now, Louis thought with a strange pang of relief.

"Here! You! Another one!" a voice called in French.

Before Louis could react, he was seized from behind, the hammer jerked from his hand. He struggled weakly, but nausea and sickness overcame him, and the pirate had no difficulty in subduing him. He was hustled across the blood-stained deck, to where the man who was obviously the pirate king sat in a chair brought from the captain's cabin below.

"Caught him sneaking up from the hold, Captain," his captor said, shoving Louis forward. He fell to his knees and looked up.

The captain was a tall man, a few inches over six feet, and had the look of Gascony about him. He was clean-shaven, with long curling black hair and a large gold ring in his right ear. He was barefoot, in the fashion of an ordinary seaman, but his garments were of fine white calico, and he wore a coat of fawn-colored doeskin that was spattered with the blood of his enemies. He held a heavy naval cutlass in his left hand, resting its point on the deck.

"He does not have the look of a seafaring man," the Captain observed. "Are you sick, my little cabbage? I won't tolerate fever on my ship."

Louis shook his head, resisting the urge to wipe the drug-sweat from his face. Around him, the dead were being thrown overboard. He tried to keep from looking.

"Ah? Well, we will see." The captain reached down and seized Louis' hand, inspecting it critically for a moment. "I was right. You are no sailor," he decided. "I will have more of you anon—for now, take yourself out of my way. I have business with the good Captain, and I will deal with you later. Take good care of him, Robie—you tend to bruise your playthings."

The sailor who had brought Louis before the pirate captain gave a short bark of laughter and hauled Louis to his feet. The one the pirate king had called Robie was a youth several years Louis' junior. He had pale blue eyes, and his hair hung in a thick cream-colored braid to his hips. A diamond the size of a cherry-pit winked in one ear.

"Like what you see?" Robie asked mockingly.

"I meant no offense," Louis said.

"Doesn't matter," Robie said, smiling. "If Jean wants to be offended, it won't matter what you want, you'll be feeding the fishes before sunrise. Come along."

Robie led Louis to the foredeck and seated him upon a crate. The young pirate wore a blue silk sash with a pistol and a dagger thrust through it, but it was his own weakness, not the other's weapons, that rendered Louis so completely his prisoner.

"Please, can you answer for me a question?" he asked humbly.

"Maybe," Robie said grudgingly.

"What is the name of this ship?"

"*This* ship? Oh, you'll have a tale to tell Jean when he gets to you, I have no doubt. This is the *Merchant's Luck* out of Baltimore. And we—" he bowed low, doffing an imaginary hat with a flourish "—are the *Pride of Barataria,* licensed privateers of Spain."

"But you are not Spanish—nor is the captain," Louis pointed out. At the throat of his shirt, Robie's skin showed paler than Louis' own. He had the look of a Dane about him.

"What does it matter where we were born, if Spain will give us letters of marque and England will oblige by being our enemy? And if we take a treasure ship or two out of Corchado, who's to know? Now be quiet. I want to watch."

From his vantage point, Louis could easily watch the disposition of the *Luck*'s crew. With an effort, he kept his face impassive. The fighting was over, now, and the pirates ransacked the ship, carrying chests and kegs and bales up from below and over to the other ship. The pirate crew sluiced down the deck with bucket after bucket of seawater as the dead were flung overside, and in the water below, Louis could hear the thrashing of sharks.

Those sailors who had surrendered were herded to one side under guard. The living were brought before the enthroned pirate captain in small groups, and either went over the side to the sharks or joined their fellows huddled on the foredeck. The screams as the sharks took their prey made Louis wince, but he knew that the men thrown overboard wouldn't have lasted long in any event, for most sailors couldn't swim.

But I can, Louis thought. *If we sail near enough to the coast, I will leap overboard and take my chances.* From Robie's words, he knew that they must still be off the coast of the Americas. He still had a chance.

Most of the ship's officers had died—pirates strutted around the deck wearing their hats and coats—but the captain had so far survived. Now he was brought before the pirate king, struggling and swearing, and forced to his knees.

"Now we'll see some fun," Robie said. "No cargo to speak of and nothing in the strongbox. The men aren't pleased, and Jean will put on a show for them."

"So, M'sieur le Capitaine—"

Louis could hear him clearly; Jean had raised his voice so that every man on the deck could hear him.

"Jean Lafitte! You barbarous bottom-feeder—"

Captain Lafitte struck him to silence. *"Non,* my good Captain. Jean Lafitte is a patriot who fights for France. Ask any man. But you, my good *Albionnaise*—what can be said of an Englishman who flies a Spanish flag in French waters? Surely he is a masterless dog, to be put down like the vermin he is."

"I—I—" Louis' captor stammered himself into silence, at last realizing the magnitude of his peril.

"Why should I keep you alive? Eh?"

"D'Charenton pays me!" the captain burst out. "If I am harmed, the Governor of Louisianne will take revenge upon you all!"

Lafitte yawned elaborately. "As if the *Royal Orléans* had not attempted that already. My dear Captain Franklyn—you will have to offer a better ransom than that for your life. Tell us of your cargo."

Louis tensed, and felt Robie's hand come down hard upon his shoulder. But still Franklyn hesitated.

"I'll tell!" one of the sailors yet to be judged shouted out. "It's the King—'e's got the True King o' France, an' he's taking him to the Governor. That's him up there!" the sailor cried, pointing to Louis.

Vainly Franklyn attempted to silence his crewman, but was himself struck down for his pains.

"Little cabbage?" Lafitte called to Louis. "Come down here, my own, and unbosom yourself to me."

"And don't try anything even remotely amusing," Robie breathed in his ear.

Once again Louis came before the man he now knew to be Jean Lafitte, Terror of the Gulf. The journey he and Meriel had made north from Huy Braseal a few weeks before had been complicated by fear of the pirate's raids, for despite Robie's pious talk of letters of marque, it was well-known that Lafitte was a law entirely to himself, and took whatever prey he chose.

"And are you the King, my little Frenchman?" Lafitte asked.

"There is no king in France," Louis said coldly. "Robespierre and *les canailles* saw to that many years ago."

"Yet there are those who would welcome King Louis XVII back to the throne," Lafitte mused. "Those who say the Dauphin never died, but was spirited into hiding by those who loved him. He would be a man of much your age, would he not, my brave? And you have as much the look of the Old King as one can take from coins and statues. No doubt it has been a great trial to you in the days of your life. And for my part, I should like to know what prisoner is of such importance to the Governor of Louisianne that he would devote a ship entire to his secret transport."

"I can't tell you," Louis said evenly. "I have never met the Governor of Louisianne. And no man can help his features."

Lafitte threw back his head and roared with laughter. "So the monkey would bait the lion, eh? You are as brave as a king, I will grant you that much. Throw him to the sharks."

For one horrified moment Louis thought that last remark was directed to him as well, but it was the sailors holding Captain Franklyn who moved forward, carrying the captain of the *Merchant's Luck* to the rail.

"No—No, I beg you! I will tell you all!" he cried as they lifted him.

Lafitte raised his hand, and the pirates set Franklyn back down.

"Talk, then," he advised genially.

"I—I—D'Charenton is a warlock! He has forbidden me to speak—he will kill me if I do!" Franklyn babbled. Even Louis had to feel sorry for him. Franklyn had obviously never thought to meet the terrible dilemma that faced him now.

"Fear neither God nor devil, and always cut the cards." Lafitte raised his hand again, and Franklyn's nerve broke completely.

"No! I beg you, sir—I can make you rich!"

Lafitte shook his head, smiling.

"For years I have traded with France—" The words burst from Franklyn as if he could no longer contain them. "Early this year I was told to be at a certain establishment upon a certain day to take this man—" he jerked his head toward Louis "—into custody. I was to bring him as quickly as I could into Nouvelle-Orléans, letting no man see him, and bring him to the Cabildo by night. D'Charenton would pay a thousand gold napoleons for him—it is because he is the Dauphin Louis Capet—"

As he uttered the name, a terrible thing happened. His face swelled and darkened as if a garotte had been placed about his throat. The blackness spread across his skin as ink would spread through a glass of water, and in seconds he fell to the deck, dead.

There was utter silence from the sailors.

"I correct you, Captain Franklyn," Lafitte said gently. "Old Louis is dead, so there is no Dauphin, only a King. We must always observe the niceties of correct address, my dear Captain. It is what separates us from the beasts. Put him overboard." He gestured, and with only a moment's hesitation the pirates took hold of the bloated and already rotting corpse and heaved it over the rail in one smooth movement.

"Do you wish to join him?" Lafitte asked Louis with a lazy smile.

"You know I don't," Louis said, forcing the image of the captain's unnatural death from his mind. D'Charenton . . . where had he heard that name before? "But I tell you again, France has no king. And any man who wished to proclaim himself the heir to the Bourbons had better have more to back him than a trick of likeness. The Corsican is hardly likely to resign his honors for a simple request."

"True," Lafitte conceded. "We thought we might be free of his attention here in Louisianne, but as you see he has sent us a governor to scourge us into fealty to his Empire. It is in my mind that this d'Charenton should discover the manner of man he has displeased, but how this is to be arranged will require some thought. It will not disturb you to remain my guest while I discover just what it is that the governor wants with you?"

"How can I refuse such a charming invitation?" Louis asked ironically, bowing elaborately. Traitorous relief surged through his veins at his narrow escape, but beneath it was a puzzlement as great as Lafitte's own. He could not imagine what use he could be to the Imperial Governor of a province still loyal to the Bourbon kings.

And he wasn't entirely sure he wished to find out.

Scratched and sunburned and close to starving, Meriel finally reached the banks of an enormous river, the widest she had ever seen.

The thick mist of morning—by which she had found it—still hung over the water and spread across the plain beyond, making the world a thing of grey shadows, and the river itself seemed to steam. It stretched before her as smooth and glassy as a lake, but white ripples out near the center of the river warned her that she dared not try to ford it. She knelt in the mud of the riverbank near a stand of reeds and scooped water into her mouth. Her thirst, at least, she could assuage, if not her hunger.

The mud before her was patterned with deer-slot and bird tracks, but though game was here in abundance, Meriel had no way of taking any of it. She had no skills in woodcraft. She had been very lucky to get as far west as she had.

But now, perhaps, my luck has run out, she told herself fatalistically. She did not despair—for the nuns had told her as a child that despair was the most grievous of sins—but she was confused, and held that to be no fault. From the first, she had not been certain why she had been brought into this wilderness, and now that she had reached the end of her trail—or so it seemed—she was no more enlightened. She had followed the Grail, and the Grail was not here.

There was a rustling in the reeds. Meriel turned in that direction, wondering if she would be lucky enough to find a bird's nest with eggs there.

A man stepped out of the mist. He was tall and bronze-skinned, nearly naked after the fashion of the savages. His hair was stiffened with clay into a high ridge that was stuck with clusters of duck feathers. He took a quick step toward her, reaching out.

Meriel sprang to her feet and tried to run. But her skirts tangled her legs, and she was hungry and footsore. She didn't get far. The savage seized her, bearing her to the ground.

Meriel struggled in his grasp, terrified. He was shouting at her in a language she did not know, and at last she closed her eyes and waited to die.

But whatever the savage intended for her, it was not to be that. He hauled her, not ungently, to her feet, and pushed her ahead of him along the shore.

"What do you want with me?" Meriel asked despairingly. "Who are you?" She received no reply, but when they had gone a few yards, Meriel realized he was leading her to his boat. She had seen native canoes before on her travels—long, narrow boats made of birch-bark or deer-hide. When they reached it, her captor motioned to her to step into it.

Meriel glanced around herself, hoping there was something else she could do besides comply. Once in the boat and on the river, she would be entirely at his mercy, for if she tried to swim to safety, her heavy skirts would bear her to the bottom of the river. But as much as drowning, she feared what other fate the savage might be bringing her to. But there was nothing else she could do but obey, and so Meriel got into the boat, arranging her muddy skirts as modestly as she could around her ankles. She held very still as the savage pushed the narrow boat into the water, and then climbed into it.

What a fool I was! Faith is easy on a sunny day, and trust is a simple thing when one has nothing to lose. Was Father MacDonough right all along? Is it pride that has brought me to this?

She shook her head, trembling with weariness and fear. The canoe rocked furiously, and Meriel gripped the sides tightly, her heart hammering. With swift smooth strokes, the savage thrust the little craft out into the center of the current, which seized it and pulled it more swiftly down the river than any man could have done. They moved forward in silence, wrapped in the mist, one with the river.

After a time the sun began to burn through the mist of early morning, and Meriel could see the land that rolled past them on either side. Not so much as a plume of woodsmoke broke the flawless blue of the sky, and the animals that came to the river's edge to drink stopped and regarded the travelers without fear. Plainly, this was a land that had not known the touch of Man.

It would have been a very pleasant journey if only Meriel could have put aside her fear, but dread of what was to come blinded her to the beauty that surrounded her. Surely the angel had known this was what would happen when it sent her out into the wilderness. What purpose could such a death serve?

I am no one! Not a religious—certainly not a saint! Why am I here?

At last the turbulent absurdity of her question made her see it was foolish to ask such a thing. 'Why am I here?'—was this not a question everyone asked, even those who were *not* sailing down an uncharted river as the helpless captive of a New World savage? The answer was always the same: it is not for you to know.

Her rosary had survived her latest misadventure, and after a while Meriel looped it around her wrist and began to tell her beads, finding a measure of comfort in the familiar prayers.

The sun had traversed a significant portion of the sky—and the river widened even farther—when they reached their destination. For a long time Meriel had been able to smell smoke, and now, when they rounded the bend, she could see the source. On an island in the middle of the river, there stood a city.

Father MacDonough had told her that the natives of the New World did not build in stone, but before her she saw a stone city as great as any in Old Europe. Four round towers like chessboard rooks, bounded a set of handsome palisades crafted from dressed timber. The gates stood open, and Meriel could see more stone buildings within, square and strong with thatched roofs. A short stone quay had been built to jut out into the river, and the canoesman paddled strongly toward it. He did not tie up his canoe at the quay—something it was not designed for in any event—but used the jetty to break the force of the current so that he could beach his frail craft.

He drew it up on a sandy bank and then gestured for Meriel to follow him into the strange city.

The long hours spent in the tiny canoe had stiffened her muscles, and her slowness made him impatient, for he reached out and seized her wrist, dragging her ashore by force. He spoke to her in his strange language, searching her face for any sign of comprehension. Free to observe him at last, Meriel realized there was something about him that was different from any other native she had ever seen.

He had blue eyes.[33]

Realizing that she could not understand him, the native shrugged in disappointment and gestured for her to precede him into the city. Meriel stumbled forward. For the first time in many hours, curiosity overwhelmed fear. In her travels she had heard tales of lost colonies—could this perhaps be one? An outpost of Christian men here in this pagan wilderness? The sight of so well-built a settlement reassured her. The city was filled with people. Children played in the street, their shouts and laughter sounding like that of children anywhere. Men and women dressed entirely in the native style went about their tasks, paying little attention to Meriel. Many of them had blue eyes, and their hair was not black, but shades ranging from light brown all the way to blond. They were a tall and handsome people, and if they had only been wearing European dress, they could have passed her on the Baltimore streets and Meriel would never have given any of them a second glance.

At the center of the village was a large stepped pyramid, its grey stone surface carved with rows of symbols in an alien alphabet, and inlaid, in places, with carved and colored stones. A wide row of steps led up to a dark archway surmounted with a carving of some winged creature.

At the foot of the steps stood two men holding spears. On their heads they wore queer conical helmets whose rims were carefully

---

33. The Mandan tribe, of the Mississippi/Ohio valley area, was reported to be a tribe of blue-eyed, blond Indians who built in stone. Only sketchy reports of the tribe exist, for the Mandan succumbed entirely to smallpox in 1843, disappearing from the American scene, and their island city has since been lost. Lingering Vikings? Far-ranging Templars? No one will ever know. . . .

trimmed with animal teeth. On the bare chest of each, a large circled cross was painted in red earth. Her captor spoke to them at length, and as she listened to their conversation, Meriel was possessed of the taunting thought that she could almost understand it. She was fluent in English and French, and could get along in Spanish, and it was none of these, but though she did not know the tongue they spoke, she could not escape the feeling that it was familiar, nevertheless.

Their conversation ended, the man who had brought her here turned and walked away. He paused for one last look at Meriel, as if he were willing her to understand through will alone what he had been unable to communicate through language. But Meriel paid no attention. While they had been talking she had been looking at the pyramid. The design above the door was not a bird, as she had first thought.

It was a cup. A cup of green stone, surrounded by flames.

Without a thought for her safety, she ran up the stairs. The guards had not been expecting that, and she was past them before they could react.

The stairs were carved for show, or for ceremony, but certainly not for use. They were too high for her to climb easily, and Meriel slowed as she came near the top. But when she glanced back, the guards had halted several steps below her, as if unwilling to proceed.

Puffing and out of breath, Meriel reached the top. There was no one in sight—only the carved representation of the Cup she had followed so far, set above the lintel like a taunting signpost.

More timidly now, she ventured inside, despising her rash actions but unable to disavow them.

The interior space of the pyramid rivaled that of the great cathedrals of Europe. It was dimly lit by smoking rushlights set in niches carved into the stone. These interior walls were covered with painted pictures too dim for Meriel to make out; she walked through the center of the vast shadowy space as if drawn by an invisible call, and then she saw it.

It stood on a squat altar of black stone, illuminated by a beam of sunlight that shone down through an opening in the roof far above. It was not the Cup she had seen in her vision, and yet it was. The shallow bowl was shaped from a single slab of cloudy emerald-colored stone, and an aura of great age radiated from it. The bowl stood upon a pediment that represented the masterwork of some unknown medieval goldsmith—the stem of the cup was crafted in pure gold, in the shape of a jeweled falcon with outspread wings that cradled the bowl, and whose ruby eyes seemed to glow warningly at Meriel in the dimness of the room. The carving on the body of the bird had been worn away by the touch of many hands over the years, until all that was left was a soft golden curve where once sharp-cut feathers had lain.

Here it was—the treasure the angel had sent her to find. Meriel came forward, entranced, hardly daring to imagine touching so holy a thing. As she gazed at it, the golden falcon seemed to burn brighter, until it glowed so dazzlingly that Meriel could no longer see the Cup.

"Kessae!"

The shout made Meriel recoil. A man, his hair the soft cream-white of age, came running toward her out of the darkness. Upon his head he wore a tall conical headdress of red-dyed feathers, and his features were a strange mingling of European and Indian. Meriel saw with surprise that he wore an iron cross on a thong about his neck.

"Are you a Christian?" she asked with surprise. Fumblingly, she held up her rosary.

The man's eyes widened with surprise. *"Dona de rella geon alinerr?"* he asked her suspiciously.

Meriel shook her head hopelessly, unable to understand him. She held out her rosary, hoping the holy symbol could speak where she could not.

"I have come such a long way," she said softly.

Suddenly there was a sound of angry shouting, and the slap of many footsteps. A second man, dressed as the first but many years younger, appeared at the head of a troop of painted soldiers. One of them seized Meriel, jolting the rosary from her hands, and the Young Chief covered the Cup with a painted drape, shouting angrily at the older man.

Following the Young Chief's orders, the guards bore her deeper into the temple, forcing her at last into a small room—one of a row of identical cells—whose door was a formidable lattice of copper bars. Though Meriel screamed and struggled, it was useless. They flung her inside, her momentum carrying her to the far end of the prison. Meriel scrambled instantly to her feet and ran to the door. People spoke of copper as a soft and malleable, but the bars beneath her hands might as well have been iron, so immobile were they.

"Please!" she cried, stretching out her hand.

The Young Chief turned to regard her, yet if he understood her impassioned pleas for freedom, he gave no sign of it. After a moment, he turned away and left her.

Is this to be my fate? To have come so far only to become a captive of a strange lost tribe, my fate forever unknown?

BE NOT AFRAID.

In the middle of the night, the Voice awakened her once more. Meriel gazed up at the angel, and her eyes filled with tears. She had come all this way to protect the Grail, only to find herself the prisoner of savages, and the Grail guarded beyond her own modest means to do so.

It has all been for nothing, she thought rebelliously.

NOT SO, SISTER, the angel rebuked her gently. The glowing Being spread its wings wide, and in their dazzling light, Meriel saw visions.

She saw Europeans come to the city in the river. The city was much smaller—mounds of earth and grass stood where carved stone buildings once had been, but the people were the same. The whites came in peace, to trade blankets and guns for furs, as happened in so many other places.

Then Meriel saw the River People lying ill in their stone houses, the sores of smallpox bright upon their skin. She saw the streets of the city choked with the dead, the few survivors fleeing in fear of the plague, vanishing into the wilderness, until nothing remained but a city of ghosts. Even the dead vanished, their bones scattered by scavengers until no man could say who had died here, or when.

NOTHING LASTS FOREVER, SISTER, the angel told her. THE PRIESTHOOD

WILL DIE AND THE PEOPLE WILL SCATTER. WHO WILL GUARD THE GRAIL ON THAT DAY? YOU MUST TAKE IT NOW, TO A PLACE I WILL SHOW YOU.

"How?" Meriel demanded in exasperation.

But there was no answer. The glorious Being was gone, and she was alone in her cell—more alone than ever before, her task unfinished.

7

Savage Enchantment
(Baltimore, August 1807)

Sarah followed Grandfather Bear down the white shell trail. The forest she moved through was one she had hunted many times as a child—or a version of it, at any rate. This was the path that led—in her world—to the Cree village that had been the second home of her childhood. But why had Grandfather Bear come to lead her to a place she knew so well?

She remembered the Elderkin's words. Perhaps Grandfather Bear also sought her help in that tangled matter—in which case her destination might be a very different place.

But soon the trail she followed became broad and well-worn, as it was near the village. She could smell water and woodsmoke and the scent of cooking. When she looked around, she could not see Grandfather Bear, although she would have been hard-pressed to say when he had disappeared.

The quality of the light was different as well: the fragile, pale light of early morning.

Have I walked all through the night? Sarah wondered. Suddenly unsure of her welcome, she moved forward slowly.

She could just glimpse the roof-lines of the longhouses when the village dogs began to bark. The village was home to about a hundred people. Beyond it were the orchards and fields belonging to the People, the well-tended fishing pools and traplines. The colonials often thought that if land was not well-marked by scars of habitation it was not in use, but such was not the case among the People. The forest was their ever-filling Grail, and they saw no reason to remake it in their own image.

Knowing that her presence was no secret, Sarah walked quickly into the clearing. The People had a saying that only hunters skulked, and Sarah had come to ask a favor.

Unexpected tears of homecoming prickled at her eyes when she saw the village. Everything was just as she remembered it—the three longhouses roofed in bark and skins, the stretchers of green hides drying out of the sun, the smokehouse woven of green pine branches reeking fragrantly of herbs and aromatic woods. Until this moment, Sarah had not realized how homesick she was—not for America, or Colonial Baltimore, but for *this*.

The dogs rushed forward, and Sarah held out her hands in a gesture of friendship. The leader sniffed and bounded away, barking frantically. People began to appear, drawn by the commotion. There were many familiar faces among them, men and women Sarah had known her entire life, but among them were two she did not know: a tall sandy-haired man in European dress accompanied by a striking woman wearing a long robe of beaded and painted white doeskin.

"*Wachiya*," the robed woman said in Cree, though with an accent strange to Sarah. "Are you she whom we have journeyed far to meet?" she asked.

"I am Sarah Cunningham," Sarah answered, puzzled, in English.

"Then come, for I and my husband have much to speak of with you."

Though these two guests were not Cree, Sarah realized that she knew them well by reputation, for in their way, they represented the hope of the People as well as of their own tribe. Alexander Mac-

Gillivray was the son of Lachlan MacGillivray, who had married a daughter of the Wind Clan of the Creek nation. Now his son Alexander, whose Creek name was The Beloved Man, ruled the whole Creek nation as the consort of the Sahoya, The Daughter-of-the-Wind. The Americans of Sarah's own world had been glad to treat with MacGillivray, whom they had named "King," and so had been willing to treat the peoples he guided as their equals, meeting with them in council and setting their hand to treaties of mutual benefit.

Whatever had brought the Sahoya and her husband eastward, it was a matter of importance great enough to command an alliance between two tribes that had maintained little contact with one another in the past. And obviously they had expected Sarah's arrival, for to journey here from their tribal lands in (as it was known here) Western Transylvania was the work of many weeks. Their journey would have begun as many weeks ago as Sarah's own, long before she had realized she would seek out her kindred.

Soon Sarah was seated around the council fire in the Chief's House, with Alexander McGillivray to her right and the Sahoya on her left, and the elders of her own tribe grouped before her. The requirements of hospitality must first be met before business could be discussed, so Sarah sat impassively through a token meal of corn porridge and venison, washed down with a smoky birch-bark beer. Though her face remained impassive as good manners demanded, within her, Sarah's heart was singing. She was home—*home!*

But this was not the home in which she had spent her girlhood. If the village and its people were familiar to her, then the reverse was not true, as she discovered a short while later.

"I greet you, brother," Sarah said formally to the young warrior who offered her the pipe of tobacco that signaled the fact that business could now be discussed. Meets-The-Dawn was her foster brother—they had grown up together.

But the man before her met her gaze with no hint of recognition. Shaken, Sarah took the pipe without saying anything further. The harsh tobacco burned the inside of her mouth, and she was careful to inhale shallowly. Her own brother did not know her. If she had needed any more proof that she was far from the land in which she had been born, Sarah needed it no longer. She knew these folk, but they did not know her.

"You have traveled a great distance to come to us, Sarah Cunningham," The Daughter-of-the-Wind said, when at last all the formalities had been observed.

Sarah turned to meet the sachem's eyes. The Sahoya was the medicine-sachem of the Creek, and fleetingly Sarah wondered what powers such a one could command in this world.

"I did not think it was so far as it is," Sarah answered, striving to keep her disappointment out of her voice. She was still a daughter of the People, and among them it was the height of rudeness to wear one's emotions upon one's brow, forcing everyone they met to share them.

The Sahoya's gaze rested upon her with cool approval.

"Is this a tale that can be shared? Since before the Courting Moon grew large in the sky the spirits have spoken to me of you, telling me that you journeyed to our younger brothers, the Cree. The spirits have said that I must aid you, for the sake of all who live in this land—not only the People and the Anglais, but our elder brothers of the land as well."

It seemed that The Daughter-of-the-Wind was also privy to that same prophecy that the Elderkin had shared with her back in England, Sarah thought in despair. It was a great pity no one seemed to know just *how* it was she was to accomplish whatever it was she was to do!

"I will tell you the whole tale, as I have never told it to any man or woman before. There is much in it that remains a mystery to me, and I humbly beseech your guidance." Sarah bowed her head.

"Go on," the Sahoya said, and the Cree leader nodded in agreement.

"In this world I am known as Sarah, Duchess of Wessex, though in truth I was born in Baltimore in a world very different than this—a world where America rebelled against King George to become a free and independent nation."

"King George?" MacGillivray said in his strong Scots burr. "Who the devil is King George?"

Sarah cudgeled her brains for the scraps of English history her mother had dinned into her in the schoolroom. It had not seemed important to her, here in America, to memorize the history of a country she would never see. "He is a German king, who rules England because there are no more English kings to govern her. It was his folly and tyranny that drove my countrymen to rise up against him."

MacGillivray shook his head in wonder. "Englishmen turning on their king like a pack of Frenchmen? It's a hard thing to believe—not that the Sassenach don't deserve it," he added with a faint smile.

Sarah spread her hands in a broad shrug of dismissal. "It is a tale long past, of no moment save to illustrate that there is world upon world, each lying close beside the next like the pages of a book." She placed her palms together to illustrate, then spread her hands again. "And so I came from that world to this, and here many strange adventures befell me."

Sarah told the tale of being recruited by Dame Alecto Kennet and the Dowager Duchess of Wessex to take the place of her dying counterpart in this world, and how despite their best efforts she had seen through the masquerade to take her own place as herself in this new world. She spoke of her husband, the Duke of Wessex, and of how the scheming of an ambitious nobleman had entangled her with Lady Meriel Highclere and Louis of France.

"The Dauphin—alive!" MacGillivray exclaimed. "How can that be?"

"A distant relative hid him in the country for many years," Sarah said. "Both the English and the French would have used him for their own purposes if they could, but all that Louis wanted was to live his own life, free of the fear of death."

"Aye, I reckon the puir wee bairn'd have little taste for a throne after the life he'd led," MacGillivray said sympathetically.

"And the English Duke—your husband—had this man in his power, and freed him?" the Sahoya asked. Her tone indicated disbelief. It was unlike the People to so lightly surrender so great an advantage.

"The Wessexes," Sarah observed drily, "have long been accustomed to doing precisely as they please. And neither of us felt it was right to hold Louis against his will. The French would kill him—the English would make him a prisoner."

But for the first time she questioned that decision. It was what Louis wanted—to marry Meriel and live his own life, free of kings and crowns—but was it right to help him do so? Was a year of freedom worth whatever terrible fate had befallen him afterward? And what of Meriel? Had the villains who seized Louis returned to kidnap her as well? Where was she?

Sarah shook her head, dismissing such thoughts. "It is done now. Louis married Meriel Highclere, the daughter of a noble English Catholic family, and went with her into hiding. But it seems that they were followed to the New World, for Louis vanished three months ago in Baltimore. Meriel wrote to me for help, but by the time I arrived, she had disappeared as well. I searched for her, but no one seems to know where either of them has gone—or who has taken them." Sarah tried not to let the hopelessness she felt show on her face. "I know it is a simple matter for people to just . . . disappear, but I must do all I can to find them."

"And where is yuir Duke in all this, Yuir Grace?" MacGillivray asked. "It seems to me that a man of his consequence—with the ear of King Henry tae boot—could do much to make things run smooth."

"I left a letter for him, for he was away on business when Meriel's message came," Sarah said tactfully. "I only hope he will follow me here as quickly as he can."

"Why did you come to us?" the Sahoya asked. "And how do you come to speak the tongue of our younger brothers as one born to it?"

"Because I *was* born to it," Sarah said, rather tartly. "I grew up in this village, though not this world. My father's house was just over that ridge, and Alisdair Cunningham was always a great friend to the People." A friend they had needed, for the city had been expanding at a great rate, and there had been talk in the Town Council for as long as Sarah could remember of forcing the native tribes to move westward so that more land could be put under cultivation.

She had seen no sign of such expansion here, and in fact she had discovered Baltimore was smaller—if grander—than the town she remembered from only a few years before. The British, it seemed, did not share the appetite of their American cousins for farming everything in sight.

But they will. A cold thrill of foreknowledge coursed through her. This world's development might run behind her own, but sooner or later the British would wish to turn New Albion into one vast network of agricultural plantations. And then here, as there, the People would be pushed out of lands they had not chosen to cede to the Europeans.

Could she stop that? Could *anyone* stop that? She thought this might be what the Elderkin had asked of her, but how could any one person do such a thing?

"Sarah? You look as if ghosts walk upon your burial-ground." The Sahoya looked grave.

"I am afraid of what may come . . . and afraid for my friends. Can you help me find them?"

"I have sworn that I will not tangle the future of my people with that of the white man. We fought the wars of the French against the English, and many *Eeyou Istchee* died. And in the end the English prevailed, and thought of us as their enemy. I will not let that happen again. Not even if the First People bid me to help you."

It was a hard decision to make, but it was the decision of one who must speak truth and fairness for all. Sarah nodded, realizing the justice of it.

"I would not ask you to endanger your people, for I consider them mine as well," Sarah said. "I cannot call upon ties of kinship in this world," Sarah admitted reluctantly, "but I would still beg you to do what you can to help my friends, for I have nowhere else to turn for help, and this quarrel is not of their making."

The Sahoya studied Sarah for a long moment, her dark eyes impassive. At last she nodded. "You must rest now, and sleep. I will think on this matter."

And with that, Sarah had to be content.

Everything must be paid for. Nothing came without a price. That philosophy underlay all that the People did, whether in this world or the Spirit World, and so Sarah was not surprised to find that her journey through the forest with Grandfather Bear, though it seemed so short a distance, had left her aching and exhausted. She was happy to curl up in borrowed blankets in a corner of the Young Woman's House and let the life of the camp wash around her like a familiar ocean.

It was dusk when she awoke. Now was the time for the People to gather together, to smoke and tell stories and sing songs. Work ended with the setting of the sun, and now was the time for family.

She sat up, still a little fuzzy-headed, and saw that a young girl knelt before her, head modestly bowed.

"Winter Fawn!" Sarah exclaimed without thinking.

The girl stared at her, eyes wide with wonder. Sarah could guess her thoughts. Here was a mysterious stranger, a European brought by spirits, who spoke Language like one of their own and knew the names of everyone in the village. How could she not be a mysterious and powerful being?

"Thank you for coming to waken me. That was most kind," Sarah said gently.

"The Daughter-of-the-Wind has sent you fresh clothing. She bids you join her in the Council House when you are refreshed."

Sarah thanked the girl again as kindly as she could, but it was painfully obvious that Winter Fawn only wanted to get away. Once the girl was gone, Sarah looked at the garments she had left.

They were a queenly gift indeed—red flannel leggings trimmed with silver buttons and sturdy, well-made moccasins decorated with blue glass beads. A skirt of soft doeskin trimmed in red wool and a short poncho of dark green cloth completed her outfit. Once Sarah was dressed, she felt as if she had shed another layer of illusion, coming closer to her true self. But that only raised once more the awkward question of who Sarah Cunningham truly was. American? English? Cree? The America she was born in did not exist, her Cree family did not know her, and she had never felt less English.

Sarah sighed, and began to rebraid her hair with the aid of the comb the Sahoya had sent. When she was done, she got to her feet and went to look for her sponsor.

The adults were gathered around the fire, still occupied with the evening meal. The elder children tended babies, and the younger chased fireflies and puppies. It was a mild night. Dogs attempted to remain unnoticed as they worked their way closer to the fire and to the food set in beechwood bowls set beside it. The good scent of tobacco mingled with the smell of woodsmoke and roasting meat. Through the trees, Sarah could see the evening sky glowing in shades of peach and jade, with the first stars of evening sparkling against the light like diamonds on jewelers's velvet.

If only everything could stay just as it is now, Sarah thought wistfully, but even as her mind formed the words, she knew that such a thing was not what her heart craved. There was no place in this world for the Duke of Wessex, and Sarah would not even consider abandoning him. She loved her exasperating, secretive husband—their marriage was what paid for all the rest in this topsy-turvy world. If only she could have true home and husband both!

The Sahoya saw her and raised a hand, and Sarah went to kneel beside her upon the fine bearskin robe that was the place of honor. The Daughter-of-the-Wind served her with her own hands—roast venison and hominy, and the small tart apples that grew along the riverside. Sarah ate gratefully, for she was still hungry after her journey through the Spirit Lands.

"Some have thought to ask what help you would ask of the People," The Daughter-of-the-Wind said formally, when Sarah had finished. "For it is in their minds that you have told us much about yourself, and little about what brings you to our fires."

It was ever the way of the People to approach a difficult matter slowly and carefully, but now Sarah's spirit chafed under the restriction. Still, she chose her words carefully.

"I came here hoping that the People might have word of my friend Meriel, for I know that the eyes of the People see that which others do not, and the ears of the People hear that which others do not."

"And what would you do, if you had this knowledge?" the Sahoya persisted.

"That would depend on where she was," Sarah said drily, and there was quiet laughter from the folk gathered around the fire.

"Well!" the Sahoya said abruptly. "In so much we can aid you—as for the rest, we shall see."

As Sarah had half-expected, The Daughter-of-the-Wind meant to use magic to find Meriel. Sarah had brought Meriel's diary with her, knowing that many forms of magic relied on a tangible link to the person sought.

Three days later, when the moon was full, Sarah stood with the young sachem in a forest clearing far away from the village. The two of them were there alone, for The Daughter-of-the-Wind feared to expose her people to the powers she would call.

Both she and Sarah had fasted since yesterday's dawn, and had spent most of the day ritually cleansing themselves with powerful draughts of herbs that had left Sarah feverish and disoriented. Well might one see anything in the grip of such drugs! But she knew that the magic that she would see tonight was no illusion, but instead as true and real as anything in the world.

The thought frightened her. It was as if the world she knew had suddenly doubled in size, and now encompassed so many things that she had never imagined. The familiar had become strange, and the ease with which Sarah had once moved through the world was gone. This new world was a stainless mystery of sunlight and shadow, and in its presence, Sarah felt as if she were a child again.

Together with the Sahoya, Sarah made offerings and sang prayers to the nine points of the compass, calling upon the guardian of each direction—stag and bear, hare and hawk, turtle and owl, fox and wolf. . . . As each representative of the First People came to take his place around the circle, Sarah could feel the power grow, could see each spirit with its stylized mask-face and painted fur, as if each was the animal whose spirit it embodied, but also more. The preparations took a long time, and Sarah's voice was hoarse from chanting the prayers by the time the circle was complete.

Then the Sahoya handed her a gourd filled with a thick dark liquid, brewed from holly leaves, tobacco, and many other herbs. Sarah filled her mouth with it three times, and each time spat the liquid into the fire in a fine spray. The steam that rose through the flames was bluish and acrid, and her mouth and lips were numb when she finished.

Next, she followed the Sahoya around the flames as the woman sprinkled the rest of the gourd's contents upon the ground around them. It seemed to Sarah that the earth smoked where the liquid hit, and the bitter smell filled her nostrils, making her dizzy. When the gourd was empty, the Sahoya flung it into the fire, for such implements were never used twice. It smoldered for a moment, then burst into a bright greenish-white flame.

The numbness was spreading across her face and neck, now, and Sarah could feel her heart thudding heavily in her chest. The deer-hoof bells on the Sahoya's leggings made a rhythmic clattering as she danced her slow pattern, and despite Sarah's best efforts, her own steps slowed and stopped, until she was staring motionlessly into the leaping flames.

When the Sahoya saw that she had stopped, she looked up into Sarah's eyes. The fire struck red sparks from the back of her pupils, and she smiled triumphantly.

In that moment Sarah felt a pang of terror. Betrayed! She struggled to remain conscious, to stay on her feet, but felt herself falling to the ground.

Sarah dreamed. In her dream she was a hawk, flying above the forest, soaring through the sky, borne aloft on the wind. Her keen sight saw for miles, saw everything down to the smallest mouse scurrying through the fields.

But as she flew through the heavens, the land beneath her began to change. First the trees vanished, and farms covered the rolling hills. Then the farms vanished in their turn, until the hills were covered with buildings—first small wooden houses, then large brick houses, then gleaming towers of glass bound together by roads that gleamed like stone and traversed by carriages that moved of themselves, carriages that resembled gigantic gleaming insects.

The rivers died, and the air became thick and dirty, and Sarah realized that the animals were all gone, save for a few foxes and raccoons that scavenged the corners of this new man-made world for food. Bound in steel and stone, its times and seasons ignored, the earth itself sickened and groaned beneath the weight of so many people. And still they came, more and more of them each year.

Where are the People? Where is my family? Vainly, hawk-Sarah sought for them, her flight carrying her west and north. All she saw was bloodshed and tears. The Algonquin, the Iroquois, the Cree, all driven from their lands. Driven across the plains, across the mountains and the deserts, hunted into extinction by those too frightened and selfish to share, until only a few remnants of Earth's Children remained, huddled on reservations little different from prisons, cowering in fear and despair while sickness and poverty harried them like starving wolves.

The living land dwindled, until only a few small islands of life remained in the vast sea of poisoned stone, until even the European usurpers began to suffer as their victims had, dying as the land died.

This was the future, of which men spoke with such hope—the future in which war and disease would be abolished, when all men would live in peace and brotherhood, and all the secrets of Nature would be unfolded.

Sarah's soul recoiled in horror, revolted beyond measure by the visions she had seen. How could they come to this? Not even Napoleon's legions, not even the hated House of Hanover, could be so barbarous. . . .

This is how Time ran in your own world, a voice spoke within her mind. *Before Men realized what they had wrought, it was too late for many . . . so many . . .*

"Who are you?" Sarah demanded. The response was confused, a flutter of images, as though a million voices spoke at once. *This is how Time will run in your own world,* the chorus of voices repeated, and Sarah was overwhelmed by sorrow and loss, as though it was her own future that had been destroyed. The contrast between the blackened wasteland of her vision and the pristine Arcadia she had walked through only that morning was too heartbreaking to bear.

She struggled to close her eyes, to shut it out, but the magic coiled through her remorselessly, showing Sarah everything—and more. It was as if she somehow understood the inward meaning of everything she saw, and so she saw war follow war, and war turn to plague, until at last the sprawling cancerous cities began to fall in upon themselves, like a fire that had burned too hot and fast.

It is too late for that world, from which magic was driven out so long ago. Without the knowledge that the Hidden Wisdom brings,

*the people of that world have rushed into folly from which the re-
covery will be long and painful. They have forfeited all that they
might have been.*

"*But it is not too late for this world!*" Sarah hoped desperately.
Surely she had seen what she had seen to provide a warning to the
people of this world to turn back before it was too late.

But what could one lone woman do?

*You have power, if you will accept it. From strength comes bal-
ance that gives freedom to all things.* . . .

As the last words of the Voice echoed through hawk-Sarah's
mind, she felt a tide of weakness filling her, dimming the terrible
world of her vision and at last blotting it out entirely.

The strong sun of afternoon shining full upon her face roused Sarah
at last. Her body still ached with exhaustion, and each movement
required a supreme effort. When Sarah opened her eyes, for a long
time all she could do was gaze passively about herself.

She still lay in the clearing, between two blankets upon a soft
bed of pine boughs. All trace of the great magic done here the night
before was gone. The only fire was a small cookfire smoldering gently
upon a bed of sand, a leather cooking pot suspended above it. The
Sahoya knelt before it, cleaning fish as though she were any woman.

At the sight of her, a strong surge of emotion welled up in Sarah,
but it was so intermixed with puzzlement that even Sarah could not
put a name to it. The Seeking Medicine had not gone as she willed
and expected. The vision she had experienced had faded from her
mind, leaving behind only its imprint of sorrow and loss—but she
did know that whatever else she had done last night, she had gained
no word of Meriel's whereabouts.

Seeing her awake, the Sahoya rose gracefully to her feet and
came to kneel beside Sarah. She brought with her a gourd filled with
water, into which she dipped a rag and bathed Sarah's forehead.

"The weakness will pass," she said. "Your spirit has journeyed far,
and is weary."

"What . . . what did you do to me?" Sarah's voice emerged in a
hoarse whisper.

"Forgive me, Sarah, but if I had told you what I purposed, your will would have worked against my magic. I sent you to the Crossroads of the Worlds, to the land from whence your spirit came. It would be a far harder thing for me to travel there than for you to return there, and so I sent you to learn what I would know. It makes evil hearing, Sarah of Baltimore."

"I know," Sarah whispered, closing her eyes against the tears that memory brought.

"But you will speak for us to the English King who has made himself overlord of these lands." It was not a request.

"I will do what I can," Sarah promised. "But what of Meriel? I owe her my help as well."

The Sahoya lowered her eyes in shame. "I promise you, I sought for your friend until the moon passed below the Western Hills, but all that I found was the image of a cup as green as spring leaves and as gold as autumn leaves, that flamed as bright as sumac in winter. Your friend is cloaked by greater magic than my own, whether for good or for ill I cannot say. All I know is that the one whom her heart seeks is still in this land, and not beyond the sea as you feared."

"Louis," Sarah said. "Meriel must have gotten word of his location and followed the trail while it was still fresh." She fell silent. Where in the New World could Louis be, if he were not in Baltimore?

"Louisianne," she said. Though it seemed a thousand years away, gossip about the volatile French province had dominated London in the months before the Royal wedding, and so Sarah knew that the rebellious colony was on the verge of secession from Napoleon's Empire—and who better to lead such a rebellion than the man everyone would acknowledge as the true king of France?

Louis.

It was a hunch—a wild guess based on hope much more than fact—but the more she thought about it, the more Sarah was convinced this must be her answer. If Louis had been kidnapped and not taken back to Europe, Louisianne was his only logical destination.

"I think I know where to look, now—for both of them," Sarah said.

She tried to sit up, but was still too weak. The Sahoya supported her, and brought the gourd of water once more to her lips. As Sarah drank, she felt strength return.

"If you go into French territory, you will need help. You cannot pass for one of the People, and the French are at war with the English," the Sahoya said.

Sarah had not considered that, so used had she been to thinking of America as one great country, but what the Sahoya said was true. Even if she could get to Nouvelle-Orléans, the Duchess of Wessex would certainly not be welcome there. Yet she must go, and the only way she could go was overland, on foot, as one of the People. The Duchess of Wessex could not sail to a nation with which her own nation was at war, even if she could find a ship in Baltimore Harbor that would accept Nouvelle-Orléans as a destination. But with the Sahoya as a guide, the journey would be a quick and peaceful one.

"Will you aid me?" Sarah asked.

"Yes. For I think we will all need to learn to help one another in the times to come."

When Sarah was once more strong enough to travel, the Sahoya led her back to the Cree village. If she shared the details of her dream-quest with anyone, Sarah did not know of it.

It took the two women three days to make their preparations. Where a European would prepare for a similar journey with hundreds of pounds of supplies and a string of pack mules, Sarah and The Daughter-of-the-Wind would go in little more than the clothes they stood up in. In addition to blankets, flint and steel, and tinder, they would carry salt and a few days of trail rations. With the Baker rifle that Sarah carried, they could easily live off the land, and shoot enough fresh meat to trade to the villages they might pass through for the supplies they might lack.

There was a great feast made to see them off, and Sarah received many presents—a tinderbox, a good steel knife, a buckskin sheath for her rifle, beaded and fringed and greased to keep moisture from damaging the Baker's delicate mechanism. In return, she shared out all that she had brought, including the gold sovereigns, which the

People prized as much for their intricate beauty as for the value of the gold. She wrote a long letter to Wessex, telling him all that she had discovered and where she was going, and gave it to one of the Cree, an older man named White Badger, to take to her hotel, there to await her husband's arrival.

In the dim light of morning, Sarah rose from her bed in the Young Woman's House and gathered her possessions for the journey. Around her, the unmarried daughters of the Cree slept, and in that moment, it was easy for Sarah to believe that the last few years had not happened—that her parents were still alive and well, that she had never journeyed across the sea to an England far stranger than her imaginings.

She stepped through the curtain that covered the longhouse door and looked around. The Daughter-of-the-Wind was waiting for her, but another figure stood beside her. As she approached, Sarah saw that it was Meets-The-Dawn, her foster brother.

"I ask to accompany you," he said.

Sarah schooled her face to stillness. "This is not your journey," she said gently.

"You speak our tongue. You follow our path. I will have it said, when you go before the White King again, that the Cree gave help where it was needed."

"Let it be as you say," the Sahoya said impatiently. "Come, Sarah. The way is long."

"I suppose you won't change your mind?" Koscuisko said coaxingly.

The two men stood on the deck, savoring the sultry September air and the bustle on the dock. *Day-dream* had slipped into Baltimore Harbor at first light. Though a far smaller city than either Boston or New York, Baltimore was a thriving port. Wessex hoped with all his heart that he would enter the city to find Sarah waiting for him, but he had another matter to deal with first. No matter how much Koscuisko might pretend otherwise, they were not in New Albion on the same mission.

He was not even entirely certain that Koscuisko's mission was what he said it was—after so long in the Shadow Game, Wessex distrusted everyone without prejudice. He regarded his sometime partner unyieldingly.

"Our paths diverge," Wessex said. "I wish you would not go to Louisianne, Illya," he continued, surprising even himself.

"But the women are beautiful and I hear the food is sublime. And I would be remiss, do you not think, did I not to renew my acquaintance with the excellent Duc d'Charenton, especially since he provided us with such a splendid hunt for Princess Stephanie and her yacht?" Koscuisko said.

It was d'Charenton's sorcery that had led the *Queen Christina* into French waters in an attempt to seize the Danish Princess before her wedding. D'Charenton could call upon formidable, unnatural powers if he so chose, and Wessex's grim humor deepened.

"Are you refusing the assignment? You never have before, you know," Koscuisko added in a different voice.

"I never took this assignment in the first place—and if we begin this game of hired murder, Illya, where does it end? Shall the King and his ministers be forced to live behind prison walls, lest an assassin's bullet end their lives? Shall we fill our armies from the gallows and let every rookery[34] be a breeding ground for future diplomatists? It is not a happy future you paint for us, my friend." The life of a political agent, who must sometimes kill to perform his duties, was one thing. To become a casual assassin was quite another.

"Better any future than none," Koscuisko answered, equally grimly. "If Napoleon continues his adventures unchecked, he will gobble up your country as he did mine, until only France is left, presided over by the Great Beast and his Black Pope."

Wessex sighed. The reason they so rarely had conversations of this sort was that the arguments each raised were unanswerable. "Tell Misbourne—should you see him before I do—that I did not find this latest adventure to my taste, and so have decided to amuse myself elsewhere."

Koscuisko shook his head regretfully. The scapegrace sailor who had stowed away on the *Day-dream* was gone, and Koscuisko was

---

34. Slum.

his elegant, dandified self once more. "I hope, in that case, that the next time I see you, it will be in circumstances at least as happy as these."

"And I'll hope that I see you again at all," Wessex said bleakly.

"Oh, you will," Koscuisko said, laughing. "For I was born to be hanged, and from all reports, d'Charenton's tastes do not run in that direction at all. I shall be perfectly safe. For now, I see that my trunks have made it securely to shore, and there is a gentleman I must meet in the city. His name is Fulton, and the White Tower has been sending him money for some time. I suppose I will go and see what use he has made of it."

Wessex raised his hand in farewell. Koscuisko was always mad for gadgets, from Babbage's Difference Engine[35] to the latest mechanical theories of the Royal Society. They worked as often as not, which was a surprise, but Koscuisko's future plans had no bearing on Wessex's.

The Duke had kept his own counsel during the voyage over. If Koscuisko knew that Wessex was bound for New Albion, he knew little more than that. Sarah's gambit had left her husband little choice of how to play this adventure. When Wessex ventured forth from the yacht, he would do so in his own persona, playing the unfamiliar part of himself. Only as the Duke of Wessex could he reasonably expect to hear news of his Duchess, and that would make him very easy to find.

When he had seen Koscuisko and his waggonload of trunks vanish into the teeming downport, Wessex had returned to his cabin to allow Atheling to complete his Ducal toilette to the manservant's exacting standards. At a few minutes shy of noon, he strolled down the gangway, the image of an indolent, haughty English Duke. Captain Tarrant had already called at the Harbormaster's office, but there had been no letters for either the *Day-Dream* or the Duke of Wessex.

Wessex thought he might go and do some banking.

---

35. A real invention of Charles Babbage's, which the British government funded until its inventor died, his dream of a mathematical engine still, alas, unrealized.

✳   ✳   ✳

There was a wreath upon the door of the venerable Nussman's Bank when Wessex arrived, and it was not long before the Bank's august visitor was put in possession of the intelligence that the Bank's Director had met with an unfortunate end only a few months before.

"He was always an *intemperate* gormandizer, was Mr. Nussman," said Mr. Freedman in tones of gloomy relish. The Bank's interim Director was as gaunt and cadaverous as Mr. Nussman had been plump, and had received the Duke with an almost mortuary relish. Now the two men sat in the late Mr. Nussman's office, a chamber whose windows were so densely shrouded with layers of Venetian blinds, lace curtains, and velvet draperies that it was a very brave and determined ray of sunlight that could gain admittance.

"I may collect, then, that the death was unexpected?" Wessex asked. On the surface, all he showed was polite interest, but within, his hunter's senses had sharpened. Had Nussman been killed to keep him from talking of his meeting with Louis?

A few moments idle chat established that Mr. Nussman had met his fell end after Louis would have called at the bank. His death was ascribed by Mr. Freedman to an excess of rich food, but he was easily led to describe Mr. Nussman's last hours, and those symptoms sounded far more to Wessex like poison.

"I am, as you know, contemplating the deposit of a substantial sum with the Bank, and am glad for you to reassure me that the establishment is still in prudent hands . . . but perhaps Her Grace has already attended upon the matter?" Wessex asked delicately.

No, the Duchess of Wessex had not called. No, neither had Wessex's good friend, Don Diego de la Coronado. Wessex left Nussman's very much as he had arrived, suspicious and unsatisfied.

It would be some hours yet before Atheling had terrorized the servants at the Royal Baltimore to his liking, and Wessex wanted to stretch his legs after the long sea voyage. He had spared Louis from entanglement in Britain's schemes, but such forbearance had not secured liberty for the young King in exile. Now Louis was in someone's hands, no matter whose. He had vanished in April. Five months later there should be news, and the next thing Wessex must do in the hunt for his Duchess was gain it.

At the Turk's Head he took a cup of coffee—the bitter stimulating brew was far more popular here, where the tariffs were lower, than it had ever grown in England—and asked after news. He heard a great tediousness of crops and weather, and of the ruinous burden of complying with the new Bill of Abolition, which had first been read out here in May, and of the Crown's intention to found a Freedmen's Bureau to help defray the costs.

Many of the newly-freed slaves meant to go to Africa, either to return to their homelands or to colonize a place of which they had only vaguely heard, but as many more had firm ties to New Albion, and meant to make homes of their former prisons. Fortunately the Lord Protector's Monticello had for many years been run with free black labor, for the Lord Protector did not keep slaves, so the complaints of plantation-owners that the thing could not be accomplished were devalued at the start.

"And the Froggish darkies are as r'iled up as damme," one speaker said, "for all they think of is to get across the Freedom River into Virginny or Transylvania—they may starve here, but they are bound to starve as free men. I hear the French Governor hangs a thousand a week."

"If he did, who would be left to get in the crops? Come to that, who will bring them in here in the Carolinas? Enjoy your pipe, my friend, for I am afraid you will find tobacco very dear in the future," another answered.

There was general laughter at that remark, and the conversation turned upon the ruinous tariffs recently imposed at the Port of Nouvelle-Orléans. There was not much sympathy extended to the farmers and trappers whose goods had been lost, for if Nouvelle-Orléans were closed to English shipping, the Atlantic ports—such as Baltimore—would flourish accordingly. Feeling he would hear nothing of note here, Wessex moved on.

At the Royal Monmouth, the talk turned more to the war with France, for the recruiting sergeant had lately passed through, striving to bring colonial regiments such as the Royal Americans up to strength. Here Wessex heard laments of the impressment gangs that preyed on the unwary near the docks to fill Royal Navy quotas, and complaints of the necessity of sending their young men to England when their own borders needed protection from French and Spanish invasion, and even protection from disaffected Indian tribes in the pay of the enemy. The war news was all stale or garbled, and Wessex moved on once again.

At the Delaware Arms the clientele cared little for the larger issues of life. Wessex drank a pint of excellent beer and heard about a mysterious fire on the docks, a rash of minor thefts on the outskirts of town—since iron and silver had been left untouched, the locals were inclined to blame piskeys—and a general chorus of blame to the natives for not earthing their Powers in the same fashion the English did.

"I'd sooner have a yellow dog in the house than a Native girl, letting in who knows what across the hallowed threshold sweet as never you please," a stout woman said indignantly.

"Ay, it's not what comes across the threshold as worries me, but what a man may meet on the road," another gossip complained.

There was a brief discussion of a highwayman who had held up the Royal Mail the month before and seemed impervious to both pistol and musket. Opinion differed as to whether this was because the highwayman had been wearing steel armor beneath his coat, or because he was a ghost to begin with.

Frustrated in all directions, Wessex gave up and turned his steps toward his inn. Nothing at all seemed to be going on in Baltimore. Certainly there was no sign of either Louis or Sarah in the gossip, which meant that Louis, at least, had not turned up. Certainly Misbourne had never taxed Wessex with having left a valuable pawn unsecured, which argued that Misbourne—and thus all of Europe—did not know of Louis' existence.

It would be a great joke on us all if he has simply fallen prey to footpads or highwaymen, and now lies dead in Potter's Field with no one the wiser as to his true identity.

But in that case Meriel would still be awaiting his return, and Sarah would simply have retrieved Meriel and returned home. Wessex thought highly enough of his wife to suppose that she would have left word for him that she had done so.

But there had been no such word. In which case, where the devil was she?

He was within sight of the inn, when the unmistakable sound of a trigger being cocked caused him to freeze in his tracks.

"Ah, there's prudence. Show a measure more, Your Grace, and you'll live to dandle the grandkiddies on your knee—"

His loquacious assailant had made the fatal mistake of talking long enough to let Wessex gauge where he was. The Duke struck out behind him and then spun, flinging himself upon his surprised attacker.

From the alleyway came a roar and a flash of flame—the gunman whose weapon-cock had alerted Wessex had fired, his ball going wide in the confusion. But by then Wessex had closed with his attacker.

A stiffened strip of buckram and leather sewn into the sleeve of his coat deflected his assailant's first slash, and when Wessex landed atop him, the knife went skittering across the hard-packed earth of the street.

The man fought with too much skill to be a common thug. He had known precisely who he was after, and had been bold enough to try to take his prey in broad daylight. This was a professional.

Wessex chopped at the other man's face, feeling his ducal signet twist and cut him beneath his glove as he did so. At the back of his mind, a clock was ticking off the seconds until the second man could reload and fire.

"Back off, unless you wish to kill your comrade!" Wessex barked sharply. He staggered to his feet and lurched toward the alley-mouth, away from both his assailants.

Pocket-watch pistol and garotte were useless, and the delicate mechanism of his throwing-knife had been damaged in the scuffle. His rapier would be useless against a gun or even a heavy stick at such close quarters. He had a second knife in his boot, but to gain it would take seconds he didn't have. He saw an enormous figure come forward out of the shadows, holding a long gun by its barrel, as the first man leapt onto his back.

The fight took a long time, as such fights went—almost two minutes—but the outcome was never really in doubt. Wessex was entirely willing to kill both of them if he had to, and after the first few clashs he realized they wanted to control, not hurt him. Wessex wrestled the gun away from the man before him and used it as a club, downing the gunman as the man on his back sought to strangle him. For all his lean height, the Duke of Wessex was ferociously strong. He slammed the second assailant into the brick wall, and then spun and swept his feet out from under him.

"Who sent you?" Wessex demanded, kneeling over his victim, his hand about the other's throat. The man was dressed in country fashion, obviously a native Albioner or trying hard to look like one.

"They want you to come home," the man gasped. He had received much the worse from the encounter—his lip was split and bleeding, and a red welt that would soon blacken was forming around his eye.

Wessex ripped ruthlessly through his victim's coat and vest, his fingers vising tight about the other's throat to discourage resistance. He found what he expected to—money, documents identifying their bearer as one Thomas Wren, and a badge with a silver tower erected upon a field of blood: the device of the White Tower.

"Misbourne sent you?"

"No!" Wren's eyes grew wide with fear. "T'was Lord Q who set us on—oh, lord, you haven't killed Barney, have you, sir? He's my brother, and Ma'll be cross if she finds I've gone and got him kilt."

Wessex rocked back on his heels, torn between laughter and disgust. Lord Q, the son of Sir John Adams, was the head of Boston Station, and so the de facto head of the White Tower's activity here in New Albion. Wren and his brother Barney were low-level field agents, the lamplighters upon whose work so much of the high-level politicals' successes were based. The boy couldn't be more than two-and-twenty, if that, and suddenly Wessex felt a thousand years old.

"Now listen to me, young Thomas. Take your brother, and yourself, and go and tell Quincy to mind his own business. Assure him that the next man he sends after me might well not be as lucky as the two of you have been. Explain that when I am entirely annoyed I tend to kill people. Tell him you have no idea what I am doing in

Baltimore, but that you are very certain I do not wish to be interfered with. Assure him I have no intention of renouncing my estates, and so may be expected to return to London in my own good time. Do you quite understand?"

"I—I—I—Yes, my lord. Yes, I understand!" The boy's face was so white that faint freckles stood out on it like sun-shadows, and his bravado had vanished like the snows of yesteryear.

Wessex suppressed all impulse to sympathy. The boy was alive, and a good fright now could save his life later. Besides, Wessex suspected his coat was entirely ruined, and the thought of what Atheling would say made him irritable. He got to his feet and tossed the identification badge carelessly onto Thomas Wren's chest.

"Now go away," Wessex said, turning his back upon the boys and stepping toward the street. He took a moment to bless his luck that New Albion followed English fashion, not French. Had this street brawl occurred in France, he would already have been seized by both secret and uniformed police and hustled off to some dungeon. But the English relied still on magistrates and night watchmen, and neither was likely to interrupt a private fracas.

A young street urchin, who had watched it all with interest from his perch beside the door, came running up to Wessex as soon has he had gained the street.

"Is you the Duke?" he demanded inelegantly.

"Yes," Wessex said shortly, straightening his coat and attempting in vain to brush the mud from his sleeve. Hopeless.

"H'it's your manservant, me lord. He said I was to find you, and tell you your ship was burning."

By the time Wessex reached the harbor, the *Day-dream* had burnt to the waterline, and hung, a sorry derelict, half sunk in the water, still smoking faintly. The scent of burned pitch and tarred rope hung sourly over the harbor.

"I'm sorry, Your Grace," Captain Tarrant said. He had been standing on the dock, watching his ship burn. The casual onlookers had left when the best of the show was over, but Tarrant had waited for Wessex in order to make his report.

"She went up like wildfire. Between one second and the next the whole ship was aflame. She burned like kindling. I've never seen anything like it."

I have. "Were any of the crew hurt?" Tarrant's arm was in a sling, but he looked unharmed. In better trim than young Thomas Wren, at the moment.

"A few singed. Nothing to speak of. Most of the crew was ashore, Your Grace having been so kind as to give them leave."

Wessex reached for his purse, and passed it to Tarrant unopened. "See that they stay out of trouble, and out of the Royal Navy. As for the ship . . ." he gazed toward the remains of his father's yacht.

"I do not think she can be salvaged," Tarrant said reluctantly.

"Well, see they remove the wreckage as soon as she stops burning. I won't be called before the Harbormaster and scolded for making a mess." Wessex smiled faintly. He doubted any Harbormaster would presume to scold the Duke of Wessex.

"Yes, Your Grace. Do you have any further orders?" his captain asked.

"Buy me a new boat," Wessex said simply.

The fire aboard the *Day-dream* had sprung from no natural cause, Wessex was certain. Such opportune fires could be timed, with a mechanism of glass bubbles and vitriol, to ignite several hours after the device was left. A slow match leading to many small charges of gunpowder could make a ship burn that way . . . or phosphorous-cloth rags, soaked and left to dry. There were a thousand ways to set such a pyre, and a gentleman-spy knew most of them.

The only question remaining was, which side had burned his boat? The reason itself was plain enough: whoever it was wanted him held in Baltimore, tied up with the legalities of the arson investigation at the very least, imprisoned for committing it at most.

So the only question that remained was who—the White Tower, the Red Jacks, or some as-yet-unsuspected contender?

Even if it were the Tower's doing, Misbourne might not know about it. Wessex had not forgotten that he had been originally tasked to investigate the mole who had plagued the Tower for two generations. Misbourne thought it settled now that the Marquess of Rutledge was no longer being blackmailed for his daughter's safety, but Wessex suspected the mole still flourished, and might now be turning his attention to his hunter.

It was dusk by the time Wessex returned to the Royal Baltimore, and this time his arrival was unimpeded. Aching and weary and filthy, he thought most of a bath.

Atheling had obviously been watching from the window above the street for Wessex's arrival, for the most superior manservant was on the doorstep to usher Wessex into their temporary accommodations. One glance at Atheling's studied expressionlessness, and Wessex knew that Sarah was not here, nor anywhere Atheling could have discovered in the last few hours.

"Have we had a spot of difficulty, Your Grace?" Atheling inquired, as soon as they had ascended to Wessex's rooms.

"More in the nature of colt-fever,[36] Atheling," Wessex answered, stripping off his coat and kicking it across the room. He paused a moment to work the mechanism of the throwing knife; the delicate metal of the sheath, which allowed it to drop into the wielder's hand for throwing, had bent. He slipped it off and tossed it to the couch. It was a fine trump-card when it worked, like so many things in life. "I shall require a bath, and you may tell me your other news at once. The boat is a loss, by the way."

He sat down and began dragging at his boots. After a moment, Atheling took over the task.

"So one was given to understand," the valet murmured over his shoulder. "Your Grace is bidden to dine with the Governor tomorrow evening. A selection of horses is waiting for you down at the stable, and if none of them is satisfactory, a Mr. Bulford has a champion hunter, Further, which he might be willing to sacrifice, Mr. Bulford having recently sustained certain losses at the gaming table. Mr. Ashley will bring Her Grace's trunks to the room as soon as he locates the strongroom key, and—"

"What did you say?" Wessex demanded, sitting up and pulling his foot from Atheling's hand. "She is here?"

---

36. Youthful high spirits.

"No, Your Grace. But she *was* here, and, ah, decamped without paying her shot, as Mr. Ashley was so bold as to make known to me. She was not here above three nights, and he cannot say where she might have gone."

"Devil take and blast the man!" Wessex swore. His valet regarded him impassively until he sat back once more and suffered his second boot to be attended to.

"There was a young person—from Boston, one surmises—who accompanied Her Grace to this establishment. I am endeavoring to discover this person's direction so that Your Grace can interview her."

"Tell Mr. Ashley that if my wife's possessions are not returned to me immediately I shall come and shoot the lock off his damned strongroom myself," Wessex growled.

"As Your Grace wishes. May I offer my regrets that one of Your Grace's trunks was still aboard ship at the time of the conflagration?"

Even without seeing Atheling's face, Wessex could imagine the faint air of self-congratulation with which the manservant delivered himself of this ornate locution. He allowed his valet the change of subject.

"Did we lose anything of particular importance?"

"It would be some of the heavier hunting gear, Your Grace."

"Damn," Wessex said softly. Atheling had always affected to believe that the special weaponry that could not be disguised when it came to his attention was simply hunting equipment. No wonder the ship had burned so merrily, if that had been aboard—Wessex knew what he had packed. They were only lucky the harbor was still there.

"I am very sorry, Your Grace," Atheling said, removing the second boot and straightening up. He regarded their condition sorrowfully and shook his head minutely. Wessex wondered if at this rate he would have any item fit to be seen in by suppertime.

"There was nothing you could do—unless you were the one who set fire to my ship in the first place?" Wessex suggested.

"I will see to your bath, Your Grace," Atheling pronounced. "You will find your dressing gown laid out in the next room, along with a can of hot water."

Dismissed, the Duke went to inspect the rest of his accommodations. They were rustic, filled with the cumbersome furniture of local craftsmanship, but the whitewashed rooms were clean. Through small round panes of bubbled glass—also of local manufacture—Wessex could see the faint flecks of the lit streetlamps below. With a sigh, he completed the task of undressing himself, and washed the worst of the dirt away before putting on his dressing gown. Fortunately, the encounter with young Thomas Wren had left his face unmarked—bruises would be an awkward business to explain to the Governor tomorrow evening.

If Sarah had been here, why had she gone? And where? Why would she take ship for England again without her luggage—if that was what she had done?

Sarah, my love, where are you? How could you have vanished and left me no way to find you?

When Wessex emerged from his bath, two of the hostelry's servants were carrying in the mooted trunks under Atheling's watchful supervision. A personage Wessex took to be Mr. Ashley hovered in the hallway, presumably in the hope that the Duke would restrain himself from shooting anything.

Wessex's heart twisted at the sight of the trunks—the green leather stamped in gold with the Roxbury crest proved beyond doubt that Sarah had in fact been here.

"Was there nothing else? A letter?" Wessex demanded, more sharply than he had intended.

"Your Grace—" Mr. Ashley took the opportunity to insinuate himself. "A terrible misfortune! Indeed, had we known this lady truly was the Duchess of Wessex—"

"Did you not?" Wessex cut in sharply. "Forgive me. I had been under the impression she had declared herself."

"I—Well, of course. However—"

"You did not believe her." Wessex cut him off ruthlessly. "I will speak to you in the morning, Mr. Ashley. Good evening."

The innkeeper retreated in disarray.

"A difficult puzzle, Your Grace," Atheling observed mildly, once they were alone.

"The—infernal—presumption—of that creature." White-lipped

and shaking with sudden fury, Wessex turned away to compose him-self. How dare any man presume to judge the Duchess of Wessex, no matter how she chose to present herself? Wessex was an aristocrat to the very marrow of his bones, and believed that the nobility, like Caesar's wife, was not only above reproach, but above suspicion. The thought that Sarah might have been forced to endure the contempt of her inferiors was maddening.

But Sarah would not have minded, Wessex realized. Indeed, she might not even have noticed. He shook his head at the thought of his wife's Republican upbringing. Men needed kings to rule them, just as bodies needed minds to govern them.

After a moment he sighed, and spoke without turning. "Bring me my lockpicks, Atheling. Let us see what she has left us."

Mr. Ashley had brought not only Sarah's luggage, but two other trunks unfamiliar to Wessex. He ignored those for the time being. If Sarah had left him a message, it would be among her things.

A few minutes work with the probes opened the heavy locks, for they were meant to discourage casual thieving, and not a determined assault. Wessex opened the lid, and was greeted by a strong scent of lavender and roses, the scent Sarah wore.

He tore through the trunk's contents ruthlessly, but found noth-ing that would help him. Some sturdy traveling clothes, one fine satin gown, a few second-best jewels in a small traveling case, the pistol he had given her on their anniversary, with a goodly supply of powder and shot . . . but no letters, documents, no message of any sort. The items that had—so he guessed—been lying about her rooms had been tumbled will-y-nill-y into the trunk when it had been taken away—he found her French soap, a flask of toilette water, some hairpins, and her brushes. As much more, Wessex guessed, had fallen prey to servants' pilfering, but the Royal Baltimore did not retain its reputation by allowing its guests to be stolen from, and so most of Sarah's possessions were intact.

He opened the catch to raise the false bottom of the trunk, but found it empty save for a thick layer of blossoms of unspun wool.

He lifted one and sniffed at it.

"Gunpowder," he said aloud. He suspected her Baker rifle—such an unsuitable prize for a Duchess, little though Wessex was in a position to judge—had been carried to New Albion in that compartment.

The second trunk held much the same as the first had. Here there was a small case of medicines and bandages, and the false bottom of the trunk contained a quantity of gold coin and an expertly-forged Royal warrant to release a prisoner into the bearer's hand.

"Burn this," Wessex said, passing the document to Atheling.

He sat back on his heels, puzzled. Sarah had certainly come prepared for a wide variety of trouble. She had been prepared to retrieve prisoners from royal justice, to physic an injured man, to bribe a great many men, or to fight. If the Baker was missing from its place, it must be with her. But where was she?

He got to his feet, and approached the other trunks.

The first held men's clothing—few pieces, and those of average quality. Wessex felt a tingle of suspicion. These items were too featureless, too . . . ordinary . . . to be the possessions of an innocent man. He searched it again more carefully, and found where the lining had been cut away and reglued. He ripped it loose, and found a thin leather secretary[37] that contained a journal and a few letters, both in French. He glanced quickly through the journal. Its writer had been as circumspect in his journal as he had in his person, but it provided clues enough.

"Burn this as well," Wessex said, handing the journal to Atheling. It would not do to leave proof of Louis' continued existence where it could be easily found. He had known from Meriel's letter to Sarah that she and Louis had reached Baltimore—now he knew that Sarah had tracked them down somewhere in the city and brought their luggage away with her.

Wessex read over the letters very carefully, but there was no clue in any of them that their authors had known Louis' true identity. The letters were addressed to a variety of names, and Wessex memorized them before handing the letters to Atheling to burn as well. Louis and Meriel had often traveled as Mr. and Mrs. Louis Capet, emigrés

---

37 A type of portable writing-desk, with compartments for writing paper and the like.

who had fled Napoleonic France for the relative peace and safety of the New World, and it was under that name that the money at Nussman's Bank had been left for them. But Wessex was forced to conclude that Louis had not received the money, and within a few days of his arrival in Baltimore, Mr. Nussman was dead and Louis vanished.

He turned to the second trunk. Women's clothes, undoubtedly Meriel's, but the diary he had expected to find was not here.

"Here's a pretty puzzle," he said aloud. Where were Meriel and Sarah? If the villain who had seized Louis had taken Meriel as well, why had he delayed long enough for her to write for help? Why had he left their belongings behind for Sarah to discover? And if Sarah had found their possessions but not their persons, what had she found afterward that caused her to vanish in turn?

"I have too many questions and not enough answers," he said aloud, rising to his feet with a sigh. "Atheling, you may distribute these items to the deserving poor, and do something with the trunks as well. We will retain Her Grace's possessions against her return."

"Very good, Your Grace."

Point: Sarah had been in Baltimore within the last six weeks, but for no more than three days.

Point: she had found Meriel's lodgings, but the evidence was against her having found the girl herself.

Point: after that—with or without Meriel, but certainly without Louis—she had vanished herself.

Where? And most of all, *why?*

8

The Man Who Came to Dinner
(Baltimore, September 1807)

T̶he following evening, at eight of the clock, His Grace presented himself at the Governor's Palace. The day had been spent in
frustrations large and small.

His first need had been for faster transportation than a borrowed
carriage. The horses at the local stables—for Wessex had not been
able to bring Hirondel with him on the long sea voyage—were found
wanting, and so Wessex had taken one of them to pay a call on Mr.
Bulford, regarding his hunter-hack. Mr. Bulford's Further was an
enormous bay with a mouth like iron and a stubborn and rebellious
spirit, but he was also a well-formed beast whose deep chest and
powerful haunches spoke of considerable stamina. Wessex bought
him at once for very little more than he was actually worth and rode
him back to the stables, leading his hired horse.

Once mounted, he went to the docks to deal further with the
wreck of the *Day-dream*. The investigation had been unable to establish any cause for the fire, which did not surprise the Duke. He
was also able to discover that Sarah—or at least a woman masquer-

ading as the Duchess of Wessex—had arrived about a month ago in company with a tall, dark-haired gentleman on the mail packet from Boston. The gentleman had boarded a Dutchman bound for Spanish Florida, and the lady had gone into the city and not returned.

By then it was nearly noon, and Wessex repaired to a nearby tavern—which rejoiced in the cryptic identification The Gun and Cameras—for a noonday meal. He had not yet been served when a seafaring man came and sat down, uninvited, at his table.

Wessex tensed, fearing another confrontation with the White Tower. The man had a rough, almost piratical look to him. His eyes were hazel, and he had a pronounced scar on his chin.

"I'm Pendray. My ship is the *Jahrtausendfeier Falke*. The word in the port is that you're looking for the Duchess of Wessex."

Pendray told his story quickly and to the point. He knew nothing of the Duchess, only that in the spring a woman had come to him asking that a letter be delivered to her.

"I took it—aye, and delivered it, too. T'was the least I could do for a countrywoman." His description matched Meriel's closely, and Wessex recalled that the Highcleres held land in Cornwall, and that Meriel had been raised there.

"Did the Duchess come, then? The maidy thought she would," Pendray said.

"She did. But as for what happened then—" Wessex stopped abruptly.

"It was your ship as burned in the harbor yesterday, was it? You could see the blaze two miles out to sea. Aye, and the maidy did look as if she were being hunted by ghosts. There was that iron in her soul," Pendray said consideringly.

"Whoever is hunting her will find me hunting them," Wessex said mildly.

"Then good luck to you, me lord," Pendray said, rising to his feet. "I've done what I came to."

Wessex accomplished little more before he retired, in a black and dangerous mood, to dress for dinner. Atheling still had not found the girl who had served Sarah, but the inn's servants had been happy to gossip, and so Atheling knew that Her Grace of Wessex had vanished between sundown and sunrise, and that her room had been locked from within.

"You're sure of that?" Wessex demanded.

"It is an article of faith below stairs," Atheling answered reprovingly. "Beyond that, Your Grace, I could not venture to speculate. But I have taken it upon myself to examine the rooms in which Her Grace was lodged, and the lock of the door has indeed been replaced within the month, I should say, which would be consistent with the aftermath of some individual breaking down the door."

The broken lock would not be a key-lock, of course, but a drawbolt such as was on the door of Wessex' own rooms. The door could not be locked if the occupant were absent, but when one traveled with servants such a lack was of little moment.

Wessex wished with all his heart that he and Koscuisko were working together on this. His partner had many strange interests, and magic was among them. He could at least have ruled out the possibility that Sarah had been removed from her rooms by some unnatural agency.

"Well, there's a pretty puzzle," Wessex grumbled.

The Governor's Palace was a tiny scrap of England transported to an alien land. Though it had been begun barely a hundred years ago, uncounted craftsmen had labored to give stone and timber, glass and plaster, all the might and power of the Crown itself.

Wessex's arrival had been made the excuse for a gala, and the Duke was resigned to a tedious social evening of the sort he despised. There was the faint enlivening possibility that those responsible for the *Day-dream*'s burning would attempt to murder him again, or that Lord Q might send further agents to entertain him. Though he knew it was childish, Wessex hoped that either or both possibilities would obtain. Otherwise, the only prospect before him was a toweringly dull evening which he must spend doing the pretty instead of searching for his wife.

❖   ❖   ❖

The current Governor of Maryland was Caleb Mandragore, Lord Chesapeake. The Earl, who was born in New Albion and educated at Oxford, had been chosen for his stolid unimaginativeness and unswerving loyalty to the Crown. It was possible, King Henry had once confided to Wessex, to predict what Lord Chesapeake would do in every possible situation, and therein lay the Earl's value. When men like Burr and Wilkinson planned new configurations of power in New Albion, Chesapeake stood unswervingly for the Crown's interests, no matter how much he personally stood to gain by a weakening of ties to the mother country. Rebellion, or even insubordination, would never occur to him.

Wessex arrived at Mandragore House a little before the hour. The drawing-room was already filled with guests, the cream of County society, but as he had rather expected, Wessex was ushered up to the first floor and into Chesapeake's library.

"Good heavens—is that what they are wearing in London these days?" Chesapeake asked, as soon as initial pleasantries had been exchanged. He raised a quizzing-glass to his eye and inspected Wessex's toilette critically.

Both men wore the silk stockings, knee breeches, and tailcoats that Fashion demanded for evening, but where Chesapeake's substantial personage was upholstered in an ice-blue satin brocade, with wig to match, Wessex wore his own hair, and a soberly immaculate black broadcloth. His cravat was snowy white, fixed in place by a pearl hardly less immaculate, and his waistcoat was of unembroidered oyster-colored satin, as plain as the buttons on his coat. Save for a single elegant fob and his pearl cravat-pin, the only jewelry Wessex wore was his ducal signet.

"It is what some men wear," Wessex admitted. "Prince Jamie was ever one to lead the style, though of course one suspects his valet, Brummell, of being its true instigator."

"Hem. Well! Could I help Your Grace to a glass of sherry before dinner? It's the last of the Spanish I laid down last year, and when I shall be able to obtain more, I cannot say. Curse this foolish war—it makes life intolerable, I tell you!"

"So I understand," Wessex murmured amiably, and suffered himself to be helped to a glass of what even he had to admit was a quite tolerable sherry. Now that Spain had declared for Napoleon—and, more to the point, now that d'Charenton had the Port of Nouvelle-Orléans in a stranglehold—the clandestine trade between Louisianne and New Albion, to which King Henry and his ministers had turned a forgiving eye, would cease.

Wessex forced himself to engage in idle chit-chat, until at last the Governor brought himself to broach his reason for this private interview.

"So, Your Grace. We rarely see men of your caliber travel to the New World on pleasure. How unfortunate that the letter announcing your visit went astray, for we are ill-prepared to greet so illustrious a visitor. I am sorry as well to hear that your visit has come at so high a price."

"I am sure I shall easily be able to replace the ship, my lord. But I am afraid my visit to your beautiful country is not entirely a matter of pleasure. In fact, it was arranged in some haste."

"Ah, yes. The young woman who paid a call on me, not three weeks past."

"My wife," Wessex said, in tones that brooked no further discussion of the matter.

"Naturally I did all that I could to help her," the Earl said, shifting his course slightly at this new intelligence. "It isn't pleasant to think of Baltimore as a place from which people simply . . . disappear."

"Perhaps you could tell me precisely what she was looking for?" Wessex asked, his tone once again agreeable, and Lord Chesapeake was happy to oblige.

"She was seeking news of a young woman, who had lately been a resident of one of the less-reputable lodging houses of our fair city. She could not provide a name, but she did sketch a very fair likeness."

The Earl took a curl of parchment from the tea-chest at his elbow and passed it over to Wessex. The Duke gazed down at what was indeed a very fair likeness of Meriel Highclere-Capet, done in Sarah's hand.

"I know the girl. She is the daughter of the Earl of Ripon, a young friend of Her Grace. We had feared Lady Meriel found herself prey of an . . . unscrupulous adventurer." Wessex felt little guilt in slanging Louis' character so, for he believed that the young King was in all probability dead. If news of him had not surfaced in the four months since his vanishment, there was scant other conclusion for a suspicious political to draw.

"Then I am sorry I could not be of more help. No such person has come to the attention of the authorities in Baltimore or the surrounding districts, nor has a body which answers such a description gone unclaimed. I offered to send to New York and Boston for news, but Her Grace was certain Lady Meriel was in Baltimore."

"And so was I. But perhaps she has left," Wessex suggested idly, for it would never do to disclose how ardent his interest in the matter was.

"If she went by ship, there will be a record of it."

If she traveled under her own name—or her own will, Wessex thought grimly. "Could she have gone by road?"

"A woman traveling alone?" the Earl scoffed. "My dear Duke, outside the city there are no roads to speak of, and the city is surrounded by native peoples who act as if they own the place! Unless she went to the Indians, she will have gone by water, mark me on this."

"I suppose you are right," Wessex said reluctantly. It seemed that Lady Meriel's trail was as cold and untraceable as her husband's.

"Will Her Grace be joining us this evening, Your Grace?" the Earl asked.

Wessex hesitated, fuming inwardly about being caught in so neat a snare. "Indeed, I am certain she would, did I know where she was. But it seems she has followed Lady Meriel into oblivion. It is awkward of you, my dear Chesapeake, to misplace so many young ladies so cavalierly. I should look into the matter, were I you," Wessex said, neatly turning the admission into a mild barb.

The Earl set an excellent table, and populated it with the cream of Baltimore society, including several samples of the native aristocracy, who wore silk and egret feathers as easily as their European counterparts.

Wessex conversed easily on the news from England, and with only a fraction of his attention on his dinner partner. The Earl had said that no one left Baltimore overland save by the help of the native population, and Sarah had claimed ties to one of the local tribes, Wessex remembered. Would she have gone to them after conventional methods of discovering her friend's whereabouts had failed?

At the same time, the part of his mind that was a trained political was busy, putting all the tit-bits of news he had gained into some coherent mosaic. D'Charenton's harsh rule would create even more unrest along the southern border, unrest the more radical factions in New Albion would be quick to capitalize upon.

But he cared little while Sarah was among the missing. Wessex realized with a distant incredulous amusement that he was prepared to consign the entire chessboard of New World politics to the devil if he could only guarantee his wife's safety.

It was a lowering realization, but it did not keep him from maneuvering to gain a private word with the Cree gentleman who had been seated opposite him at dinner.

At the conclusion of the meal, Lady Chesapeake had gathered up the ladies, who retired to the parlor and left the gentlemen to Stilton, port, and walnuts. The talk instantly became freer, and the darker aspects of the Nouvelle-Orléans situation were discussed.

The port had always had a reputation for the more unsavory forms of magic, and d'Charenton's reputation had preceded him. The men gathered about the table feared worse than a revolt of natives or freedmen. They feared the same dark forces with which the Tudors had swept the Plantagenets from the throne of England four centuries before.

Wessex played only a superficial part in the discussion, instead arranging to place himself beside the Cree merchant whose presence he had marked over dinner.

Sir White Badger wore his hair long, after Native fashion, but in every other way he appeared to be a cultured European gentleman, his English entirely without a trace of the regrettable Colonial accent. Wessex had gathered from the table talk that White Badger was in trade, his knighthood a recognition of the substantial revenue his activities had produced.

"I wonder if I might have a word with you, Sir White Badger?"

"To speak frankly, Your Grace, I was hoping for the same, but I fear this is not the place. Do you know the Cree village to the west of town, along the river?"

"I can find it," Wessex said shortly.

"Then come this evening after you leave here," White Badger said. "I believe I have news for you. A letter."

The courthouse clock was tolling half-past one as Wessex's hired coach rolled away from Mandragore House.

If this were a trap, he would be walking into it all too easily, he knew. But the opposition had no markers upon the table, and thus his own role was that of rainmaker. The Native population took little interest in affairs outside their own land: it was unlikely that White Badger were acting as a French agent, or even as an English one.

No, Wessex decided. The worst he could expect was a small ambush from Thomas Wren or his confederates.

A quick interlude at the Royal Baltimore allowed Wessex to change from his dinner dress into riding clothes, and to arm himself with a variety of ingenious devices against future trouble. By the time he was dressed, Atheling had obtained Further from the livery, and by two of the clock Wessex was riding toward the Cree village. It was a symptom of his clandestine existence that it had never occurred to him to question the need for meeting in the hours of darkness.

The road to the village skirted the woods. It was broad and well-marked with whitewashed stones along its edge, and thus easy to follow even in the darkness—which was just as well, as the big bay did not like being roused on a fool's errand in the middle of the night, and made his displeasure known. Wessex had to fight to hold him on the road and keep him to a steady pace, and to his annoyance found himself using both whip and spur constantly as the hunter sulked and grumbled about his work.

The night was quiet, its cool a welcome relief from the late summer's daytime heat, and only the distant barking of an occasional dog interrupted the silence. When the road turned into the woods, Further slowed, picking his way carefully along the dark road. Here

Wessex dared not goad him on over an unfamiliar track, and resigned himself to a snail's pace, but almost at once he saw a glimmer of light ahead. Within a few moments he could see it clearly: a lantern hanging upon the porch of one of the small cottages on the outskirts of the Cree village.

On a previous New World sojourn, Wessex and Koscuisko had traveled with the citizens of New Albion, and so he was familiar with the Native villages, their architecture an amalgam of traditional and European styles. He found his way to White Badger's doorstep easily, dismounting and tying Further to the railing. He took his pistol from his saddlebags, and slipped it into a coat pocket before stepping up onto the porch. From within the small house he could see the spark of a candle-flame, and the door stood open.

"Come in, Your Grace," White Badger said.

Wessex entered. In contrast to its exterior, the inside of the cottage was wholly Cree. The walls were hung with shields and painted furs, and chests and wrapped bundles lined the walls. His host was seated on a wolfskin, facing the door, his evening clothes in sharp contrast to his surroundings. Wessex entered and sat beside him, careful to keep both the door and the cottage's windows in sight.

"I do not think you would care for the black drink of my people, but I am prepared to offer you wine or brandy, Your Grace," the Cree nobleman said.

"You are very kind," Wessex said. "A glass of brandy would be most welcome."

His host produced a familiar squat green bottle, and poured a generous libation into two gold-washed silver cups. Both men drank in silence.

"You've come looking for the Duchess of Wessex," White Badger observed at last.

"Yes. I was wondering if she might have come to you."

"Say, rather, that we came to her, for an elder cousin came from the Smoking Mountains following a vision sent to her by spirits. The Daughter-of-the-Wind told us an Englishwoman would soon come to prove the truth of her words."

White Badger watched Wessex closely for signs of incredulity, but Wessex was used to the Native notion of following omens found in dreams, and said nothing. Other matters concerned him. The Sahoya was the spiritual leader of a tribal confederacy several hundred miles to the west of Baltimore. What possible business could she have with Sarah?

"The Sahoya told us a woman who was Cree and not-Cree would be sent to us by Grandfather Bear, and that we should aid her to aid ourselves. And such a woman did come."

"Sarah," Wessex said.

"So she named herself. And what the Sahoya said was true, for Her Grace was no stranger to our ways. She sought her friends who were missing, and the Sahoya sought them with powerful medicine. What they did together I do not know, but they and Meets-The-Dawn, the son of the chief, went away from here at the full of the last moon, heading southward. She left a letter, but the chief was afraid of what it might say to the English, and so ordered it burned unread."

For a moment, that disappointment overwhelmed the other information Wessex had been given, but then a lifetime of discipline reasserted itself. The moon had been nearly full tonight. Wherever Sarah was, Wessex was nearly a month behind her.

"I need to find them," Wessex said.

White Badger shrugged eloquently, palms outspread.

"If you didn't mean to tell me where she is, why tell me this much?" Wessex asked, holding his formidable temper in check with an effort.

"For the same reason the chief burned her letter. So that you would leave the matter alone. Her Grace is a woman of power, and if you come to the Governor demanding that he find her among the People, the Governor will send for troops to do as you ask. And the People will fear that the Earl means to use the troops to drive them from their land, as was done in the past when your ships first came. I hoped that if you knew that Her Grace acts upon her own interest and of her own free will, you would allow her to do so in peace."

There was a delicate balance between European interests and Native ones in New Albion, Wessex knew, for while the Crown saw its colony as a ready market for European goods, to be exchanged for the raw materials of this lush and fertile land, others saw it as a new homeland . . . a homeland whose present occupants must be brushed aside.

"And do you truly think that I will leave the matter at that? If you do not know where the Sahoya has taken her, others here must," Wessex said.

"Will you meddle in the affairs of the People? The White King across the water has said his followers will leave us to do as we would," White Badger said.

"Not with my wife." Wessex sighed and stretched. "Tell me where she is bound, and I will go there without alarming Governor Lord Chesapeake, I promise you. Refuse me, and make me your enemy. And if I too disappear, there will be more trouble than you can easily imagine," he added for his sharp ears had heard the stealthy sound of approaching footsteps outside the cottage.

"Not if you come to Nouvelle-Orléans with me," Illya Koscuisko said from behind him. "Now do be a good fellow, Wessex, and keep your hands where young Wren and I can see them."

Wessex looked over his shoulder. Koscuisko was holding a pistol on him. "There's a back door, you know," Wessex's partner said conversationally. "Do come in, Mr. Wren. You're frightening the horses."

Thomas Wren stepped through the front door. The young field agent's face bore the marks of the battering Wessex had given him yesterday, and his face was drawn and white with tension. Wessex only hoped the rifle he held wouldn't go off unexpectedly.

"I thought you had already left," Wessex said to his partner.

"I so hate to travel alone," Koscuisko said. "So I've been following you about. If Lady Wessex is missing, I think you might have mentioned the fact. I should certainly like to help you find her."

"Then go away," Wessex advised him.

"Alas." Koscuisko shook his head, his face unwontedly grave. "She isn't here, Rupert. I've already spoken to the sachem and to MacGillivray. None of them knows where they went—only that the Sahoya took provisions for a long journey, and MacGillivray thinks she meant to go to Louisianne."

"Then I'll follow them," Wessex said stubbornly. "She's only a month ahead of us—I will catch up to her before she reaches the city, and—"

"Lady Wessex can take care of herself," Koscuisko said. "Which is more than I can say for you, my fine fellow. You'll never travel as fast as the Natives can. But I'm headed there anyway. Come along to Nouvelle-Orléans and we can ask d'Charenton to confide in us. Who knows what he might know? And perhaps we'll find Sarah there before trouble does."

Wessex shook his head.

"I do wish you weren't going to be difficult," Koscuisko said mournfully. "But we'd thought you would be."

A flare of warning coursed through Wessex, and he reached for his pistol. Neither of the White Tower agents fired or even tried to seek cover. Why not?

His fingers closed clumsily over the pistol, then opened again. The weapon fell to the ground, the powder spilling from its pan in a silvery rill.

"Drugged," Wessex said. The words came out slurred, and his vision began to darken.

"All in all the safest thing, as I'm sure you'd agree in other circumstances," he heard Koscuisko say.

Wessex lunged to his feet—and fell, instead, into oblivion and the mocking laughter of his own failure.

He awoke with a confused memory of an uncomfortable journey by horseback. The air around him stank of kerosene and raw spirits— which did nothing for his headache—and there was a dull rhythmic sound in the background that Wessex was wholly at a loss to account for. The deck beneath him vibrated.

He sighed, and sat up. As he'd expected, he was chained hand and foot. It was just dawn—he was outdoors, on the water, under a canopy erected upon the deck of a boat. Koscuisko was sitting on one of Wessex's trunks, watching him expressionlessly.

But Wessex lost all interest in what he intended to say to his partner when he got a good look at his surroundings, for what Wessex saw before him was one of the odder apparitions of his career.

He lay upon the afterdeck of a low open boat. There was a small building amidships, and through its open doorway Wessex could see the open flames of a furnace and hear it being rhythmically stoked. Above that noise was a monotonous mechanical clattering. Black coal-smoke belched from a smokestack above, raining soot and smuts down on the water behind, and on both sides of the ship, water wheels higher than a man turned round and round, forcing the ship forward through the water.

"You've put a steam engine on a boat," Wessex said in disbelief. Steam engines had been known since the 'seventies[38] and the first attempt to adapt them to marine navigation had been made a few years ago,[39] but he'd had no idea that the technology had progressed so far.

"Actually, our Bobs did that," Koscuisko said modestly. "But this will be our first extensive trial. Only think: depending on the number of portages we need to make, we should be in Nouvelle-Orléans in less than two weeks. We can bring the *Royal Henry* down the Mississippi and anchor her upriver of the city. When it's time to go, anyone chasing us will be fighting the current, but we'll have the power of steam to carry us on the wings of eagles!"

"I think you're mixing your metaphors," Wessex said mildly. "Oughtn't it to be 'on the backs of dolphins'?" His voice was hoarse with the aftereffect of the drugging he'd received, but the news Koscuisko had conveyed lightened his spirits. If they arrived in Nouvelle-Orléans within a fortnight, there was every possibility he might arrive in time to head Sarah off, always supposing that were truly her destination. "I think I shall have you blackballed from your clubs for this."

"They were getting to be a bore anyway," Koscuisko answered lightly. "Have some coffee." He held out a large leather-covered flask.

"No tricks this time?" Wessex asked.

"I wouldn't dare. No, in a few more miles the chains come off as well. I won't insult you by asking for your parole, of course."

---

38. 1774
39. 1802

"Of course," Wessex grinned wolfishly. The flask was warm between his hands, and he drank appreciatively. Then he lay back and regarded the river through half-closed eyes, laying his plans.

Sarah, The Daughter-of-the-Wind, and the young warrior Meets-The-Dawn traveled west and south, through a beautiful unspoiled land that had barely felt the touch of the European conquest. The untrammeled landscape beckoned to her as the manicured estates of England never had. This was the heritage she had been born to take up.

Why had she not gone to her Cree kinfolk when she first lost her parents, instead of allowing her cousin Masham to co-opt her as an unpaid servant? Her Cree relatives would have made a place for her among them—she might even now be happily tending her first-born, instead of wandering the wilderness on a hopeless quest. She could have been happy with Meets-The-Dawn.

The realization brought Sarah no comfort, only a nagging sense of discontent. The lack of a child to bless her marriage troubled Sarah deeply, though she and Wessex had not spoken of it. He seemed content that his titles and dignities should pass elsewhere—well, so was she, but she wanted a child for itself, not as an heir to the Dukedom. A marriage without children was a lonely one, no matter how much its partners loved one another.

And she did love Wessex, impossible though he often was. Though she was saddened by the loss of what might have been between her and Meets-The-Dawn, it was a theoretical regret only. She did not mean to pursue a romance with him, though the young Cree warrior had given her clear indication of his interest. And who would know what she did, out here in the wilderness?

I will know, Sarah told herself firmly.

"We are entering Numakiki lands," The Daughter-of-the-Wind announced one morning. "We must go carefully, for the omens are potent, yet they are hard to read."

"Who are the Numakiki?" Sarah asked, her hands busy with the familiar morning tasks. The fire must be fed, so that their morning porridge could be boiled, and so there would be embers to carry in a clay jug through the day—simple tasks such as any hunter might perform, and Sarah did them without thinking.

"They are a strange people who came from the south in the long ago. Their own storytellers say they came from the land of the sunrise, and were sent away because their ancestors performed a great evil. When we first saw them, we thought they were sick, or cursed, for their hair and skin and eyes had no color at all." The Sahoya smiled wickedly, relishing the joke. "Like you, Sarah, and the other English."

"The Numakiki are English?" Sarah said, still more confused.

"No," The Daughter-of-the-Wind answered. "The Numakiki are the Numakiki. Their name in Sioux is 'Mandan,' which means 'people.' They worship an invisible wind that looks into men's souls to punish or reward, so they say, and they guard their privacy fiercely, though they maintain trade with the Arikara Sioux and a few other tribes to the south such as the Choctaw and Natchez. We will be fortunate to cross their lands without being seen."

But luck did not seem to be a thing in very great supply this day. Before the sun was very much higher, Sarah became certain they were being followed.

Their path had led them to the bank of a great river, which the Sahoya had said they could follow for many miles. Sarah knew that rivers took the place of roads here in the wilderness, and that they were a natural pathway for trading posts and settlements. But Sarah did not know if traders had even been this far west, for New Albion seemed very much a land that had been left in the hands of its original owners.

"We are hunted."

Meets-The-Dawn spoke softly, for her ears alone. His watchful obsidian eyes flickered right, then left, indicating the presence of their stalkers. The Daughter-of-the-Wind strode on ahead, serenely confident that whatever danger they courted would not touch her. Though Sarah admired the Creek shaman, she had to admit, if only to herself, that she didn't *like* her very much.

"I know," she whispered back. "Perhaps they are only curious.

When they see that we mean no harm, they will leave us in peace."

"May it be so," Meets-The-Dawn answered soberly.

They walked south, in sight of the great river, for several hours.

"This is not right," the Sahoya said, stopping. She gestured toward the horizon.

"What is it?" Sarah asked, and then she smelled it for herself. Smoke.

"There is a settlement near her," she said slowly.

"A settlement where none should be, unless I have led us far wrong," the Sahoya answered. "I fear it is the city of the Numakiki. I had meant to bring us to the river many miles downstream from it, but I fear now that we are harried to its very gates, as the hunter drives the game."

"But we have done no harm," Sarah said. "All we ask is safe passage across their realm."

"And perhaps we shall receive it," the Sahoya answered. "I have trusted the spirits to guide us upon our path," she said, sounding faintly dismayed, "and they have led us to this."

"There is an expression among the English," Sarah answered. "It is 'play the hand you are dealt.' Perhaps we are meant to meet with the Numakiki and gain wisdom from them."

The Sahoya turned away and walked on without speaking, her silence eloquent of disbelief.

When they had walked only a little further, Sarah understood the reason for the other woman's silence. Stretching before her, on a low island in the center of the swift-moving current, was a city the like of which Sarah could not have imagined. It was larger than any Indian village she had ever heard tell of, with housing for hundreds, even thousands, of people within its vast palisades. It was as if an Egyptian temple, or a medieval castle, or some mad conflation of the two, had been transported to the depths of this uncharted land.

"What is this place?" Sarah asked, stopping. "Who are these people?"

"Sorcerers . . . madmen . . . I know not. But without their goodwill, we will travel no farther, Sarah," the Sahoya answered.

Even from here, the small party could see the watchmen on the tall stone towers that edged the city—and more to the point, the watchmen could see them. Sarah blinked, as a series of bright flashes came from the nearest tower.

"They are using a heliograph!" she exclaimed.

"They signal the warriors who pursue us," the Sahoya said, discontent in her voice.

A few moments later, the men following Sarah and her companions showed themselves. There were twelve of them, all tall men armed with round bark-covered shields and long spears. Many of them had light hair and pale eyes. Their leader, who wore a curious round cap of painted leather that extended in back all the way over his shoulders, advanced and spread his hands in a gesture of friendship, bowing slightly and speaking words that were incomprehensible to the travelers.

The Sahoya copied his movements, speaking first in her own tongue, then in Cree, and at last in English, but it was plain that he understood her as little as she did him. Sarah spoke to them in French with no better luck.

The warrior band—an honor guard if not an execution party—surrounded the travelers and moved on down the river. Sarah and her companions had little choice but to accompany them, and soon they were in sight of their destination.

A raft lay beached on their side of the river. It was made of unpeeled logs decked with smooth-sanded boards. Two ropes of braided leather stretched from two stout poles outside the palisades to a matching set of poles driven deep into the clay of the bank, forming the railings of a bridge without a floor. Another Numakiki stood beside the raft, and to Sarah's astonishment, he wore a sword girded about his waist—not a rapier such as Wessex often wore, but a broad flat sword such as knights in fairy tales carried. When he saw them, he began making the raft ready for the crossing, flinging carved wooden hooks over the leather ropes and setting the butt-ends of the shafts into holes drilled in the raft.

When all the passengers were aboard, the sword-bearer pushed off from the shore with a long birchwood pole. Two of the warriors on either side grasped the braided ropes, and by a combination of pulling and poling, the raft traversed the swift-running river safely.

They were met upon the island side by another delegation of

sword-bearing Numakiki. Up close, the stone towers were even more spectacular than they were from a distance, the huge blocks of native granite polished as smooth as river stones and fit together almost without a visible seam.

"What do you suppose they want with us?" Sarah asked. The Daughter-of-the-Wind shook her head, as baffled as Sarah.

They were led up the road to the gates of the stockade, and waited outside as the gates were drawn open smoothly by an ingenious mechanism of ropes and pulleys. As the gates swung open, the travelers were greeted with an amazing vista—a vast medieval city built entirely out of stone. Sarah could see that Meets-The-Dawn and the Sahoya were as stunned as she, for none of them had ever seen anything to match this. Even London, with its many imposing public buildings, looked positively ramshackle in contrast with this cyclopean city.

The city seemed to be organized around an open central space, and as they were led toward it, Sarah could see that the central square was dominated by an enormous flat-topped pyramid. A slender figure in a long white robe stood at the top. Sarah frowned in disbelief. Despite all possibility, there was something familiar about that figure. . . .

"*Sarah!*" Meriel cried. She ran down the steps of the pyramid, black hair streaming behind her, and flung herself into Sarah's arms. "How strange you look! I took you for an Indian at first, dressed like that, but it *is* you!"

Surprised and delighted to see her friend again, Sarah held her close, startled out of her childhood stoicism. "Meriel! What— How—"

Meriel stepped away from her, gesturing emphatically to the warriors surrounding the travelers and speaking rapidly in the Numakiki tongue. Sarah regarded her friend in wonder. Meriel was wearing a long white sleeveless robe of native homespun, with a scarlet leather cloak about her shoulders. Her hair was held back with a thin gold fillet, and about her throat she wore a crudely fashioned golden cross.

"They won't harm you," Meriel told Sarah after a moment. "I have told them that you are of the Book—but who are your friends?"

"You can *talk* to them?" Sarah asked in surprise. Meriel had certainly changed from the shy little mouse Sarah had known two years before, the sheltered young noblewoman desperate to escape her uncle's kingmaking ambitions.

"Of course." Meriel seemed confused by Sarah's bewilderment. "They're speaking Latin."

"I was terribly afraid until I realized that was what it was," Meriel told them later. "I know that many who discover their city are executed—that might well have been my fate had I not realized that I knew their tongue," Meriel admitted.

The travelers had been lodged in a stone guest house near the great pyramid, and feasted lavishly by an old man Meriel named the "Prester," or chief. With Meriel to translate for them, matters had become much more friendly, though their weapons and possessions had still been taken from them, and Sarah mourned the loss of her Baker rifle.

While the party had so far been treated as honored guests, Sarah knew the difference between that and the hospitality that she expected to encounter in any Native settlement.

"But how did you get here?" Sarah asked. "I came to Baltimore to find you—and then when you were gone, I thought you must have gone to Nouvelle-Orléans to look for Louis, and so I followed you there—or I thought to." *And why did you go, if you were not going in search of him?*

"Has there been any word of him?" Meriel asked quickly, and Sarah saw that the younger woman's eyes bore the haunted expression of too many bleak nights filled with sleeplessness and worry. She shook her head sadly and watched the hope in Meriel's eyes dim.

"He is in God's hands, then," Meriel said softly. "As for me, I . . . came here for other reasons. But I must go to Nouvelle-Orléans as soon as I can arrange to leave. I have an . . . appointment there."

"You must tell us your story, Lady Meriel," The Daughter-of-the-Wind said courteously.

"I will tell you what I can," Meriel answered deliberately.

✸   ✸   ✸

Their Latin was so debased by the years, even centuries, of their isolation that it had taken Meriel weeks to realize that this was the language they spoke. At first, her captors had understood her halting Church Latin as little as she had understood their curious hybrid tongue, but slowly her ear had become accustomed to their speech. On the second day of her captivity, the Prester had returned her rosary to her, and stayed to listen to her prayers. From that had come her freedom, for she later learned that rosaries were part of the treasure they guarded, though the Numakiki had long since forgotten their use.

It was the Prester, Shining Spear, who had shown her the Numakiki treasure rooms, filled with gold and gemstones—of European manufacture—enough to ransom a hundred kings. What quirk of fate had brought that royal treasury here, Meriel did not know, but she had told Shining Spear all that she knew of the artifacts he guarded as steadfastly as had his fathers before him, and of the lands from which they had come. Though she had asked, no one among the priesthood recalled where they had come from before they had settled here, or how they had come to have such riches in their possession.

With the Prester's support, her life in the Numakiki city had become much easier. After her liberation, she had worked as a servant in the temple along with the highborn Numakiki maidens. With them, she attended the ceremony with which the ancient Prester greeted each dawn, recognizing with sorrow and horror the blurred remains of God's own Holy Mass, worn away to hocus-pocus by the passing of centuries. Unable to keep silent, she had spoken to the old priest of the True Faith of which his own ritual was only a dim copy, but Meriel was no priest, and there was little of the Greater Mysteries that she was able to teach the old man, though she found in him a friend, a wise and curious mind who delighted in learning.

At last, trusting greatly, she had even confided the detail of her vision to him—how she had been summoned by angels, led into this wilderness to find the Grail and to take it from its guardians.

But though Shining Spear had believed Meriel, First Sword—

the younger of the two priests she had met upon her arrival here in the city—had not. First Sword steadfastly refused to even consider releasing the Grail into her hands, claiming that her visions were a trick to rob the Numakiki of its wealth. And in the end, the matter was not left to be settled by faith, but by a show of political strength. First Sword would not give up his treasure, and by his decree Meriel would live out her days a servant of the Numakiki.

She had prayed for guidance, and when Sarah had arrived, it had seemed to Meriel that her prayers were answered. But after the first shock of cheer at being reunited with her friend, Meriel was forced to admit that Sarah's arrival made little difference to her plight. She was a powerless captive here, her quest at a standstill.

And so, when she told the others her tale, there was much she omitted. She told them nothing of angels summoning her into the wilderness. And though she spoke of hoarded treasure, she did not mention the Grail.

They spoke until very late, with Meriel purposely delaying until the curfew gongs tolled through the city. One of the reasons she had been allowed to go off with her friends was so she could question them and report all she learned to First Sword before he met with them himself. The Numakiki sub-Prester liked to seem omnipotent, and for once his vanity and arrogance had worked to Meriel's advantage. But she had won a small delay, nothing more. It was frighteningly likely that tomorrow First Sword would decide that Sarah, the haughty Creek princess, and the Cree warrior represented a threat to his power, and their heads would go to join those of other enemies that had hung upon the gates of the city.

Somehow she must prevent that. And get the Cup away from him before she had to explain somehow to Sarah that she would not leave without it.

As always, when she returned from outside, Meriel went first to the Grail.

It was as luminous as ever in the last rays of the fading evening light. Men had fought and died to possess it, empires had risen and fallen because of it, but the wealth with which men had ornamented it only underscored the fact that the heart of its mystery was a fundamental simplicity, the beauty of a thing crafted for use by the need to which it must be put.

"You will not have it, Green Stone."

Meriel jumped, hearing First Sword's voice speak her Numakiki name. She turned to face him.

First Sword stood in a pool of shadow. The rushlights that illuminated the sanctuary burnished the highlights of his coppery skin, leaving his eyes in shadow.

"It is not for myself that I ask it, but for God," Meriel reminded him.

"Who is this 'God' of yours, that he demands our treasure? When it no longer resides among the People, then the People will pass away, so does the ancient wisdom teach us. Is that the revenge for which you hunger?"

"I do not want revenge," Meriel said wearily. She longed to ask after Shining Spear, for she knew that the old priest kept the dawn and sunset vigil over the Cup, but she would not give First Sword that satisfaction.

"You want to take the Cup away," he repeated.

"I seek to do what God commands," Meriel answered resolutely.

"And your friends? These spies you have brought upon us? Do not bother to tell me what they have said to you today, for I will not believe it."

"If you harm them, First Sword, you will gain powerful enemies among the Nations," Meriel warned despairingly.

First Sword laughed. "No one will know. Enjoy your time with them—and with us—Green Stone. Both grow short."

The Sanctuary was wholly lit by lamplight now, and First Sword turned and strode away.

He will not listen! Meriel felt like stamping her foot in despair, but the Red Cross Medicine Society guards still watched over the Grail, standing motionless in their niches as if they were carved of stone. At last she sighed and turned away, her worst fears confirmed. Her friends' arrival would be all the pretext First Sword needed to eliminate what he had always seen as a threat to his power, the stranger and her friendship with Shining Spear.

Though at this time of day Meriel should have gone directly to the Young Women's sleeping room, she went instead to Shining Spear's rooms, still worried at his absence. Bright lamplight showed from beneath the door, and Meriel could hear the murmuring of women's voices within.

The guards had become used to her comings and goings here, and so admitted her without protest. Meriel pushed open the door and went inside.

Shining Spear lay upon his bed, two of his daughters with him. Meriel let out a soft cry of dismay, and the wise old man's eyes opened. He held out his hand.

"Come here, Green Stone, and tell these foolish girls that I am well enough to keep my vigil," he said.

Meriel came and knelt beside the bed. "Of that there is no doubt, Grandfather, but the time of the vigil has passed."

"Did First Sword do what must be done?" the old man asked.

"He did," Meriel answered. She would have said so even if it were not true, for there was an undertone of grey in the old man's skin, and his breathing was labored.

Shining Spear was the oldest man Meriel had seen among the Numakiki, and Meriel did not doubt that much of the reason he had lived so long was to spite First Sword, who was eager to assume the full dignities of Prester. But even the strongest will must bow in the end to the dictates of the body. Last month—yesterday—this morning—Shining Spear had been a frail old man. Tonight, he was a dying one.

Meriel clasped his hand in her own. It was cold and dry.

"Leave him alone, foreign woman!" Gold Hands shook her by the shoulder, jerking her backward, and White Knife raised Shining Spear up to drink from a small wooden bowl. Meriel caught the scent of the bitter herbs used as a purgative by the Numakiki, and doubted that whatever medicine White Knife was giving Shining Spear would help him very much.

But the color returned to his face after he drank, and Shining Spear was strong enough to send his daughters from the room. They went, casting baleful looks over their shoulders at Meriel.

"And so, Green Stone. It looks as if I will soon see with eyes of my own the truth of what you have told me."

"I hope you will," Meriel said, tears welling up in her eyes. "And perhaps this is only a passing sickness, and you will live for many years yet." She reached into her robe and withdrew the one possession the Numakiki had not taken from her—her precious rosary. She placed the crucifix in his hand and wound the prayer beads about his wrist. "But I must tell you that I will be leaving you soon. My friends have come today, in search of me, so . . ."

"You are a very bad liar, Green Stone," the old man told her gravely. "First Sword is jealous and proud. He will release nothing that his hand has taken up. In a time of change, he will stand like the hundred years' oak which does not bend before the storm. When he falls, as he must, many will fall with him."

"I know," Meriel whispered, bowing her head.

"You must escape," Shining Spear said. "You and your friends. It can be done. My guards are loyal to me, not to First Sword. They will take you down the river, tonight—"

"I cannot go without the Grail," Meriel said miserably. "I cannot." The prospect of her death made her tremble in fear, but she could not abandon her promise to God.

The old man's eyes closed in defeat. "Then the Great Spirit must save you, Green Stone, for I cannot. Send my daughters to me. I will sleep now."

The moon had risen, granting its pale illumination to the night. Fireflies danced in the air outside, and the sound of the river underlay the calls of frogs and the cries of owls and other night hunters. As the moonlight crept across the dormitory wall, Meriel lay sleepless. She had been faced with an impossible problem before, but now it was a problem with a time-limit. The moment Shining Spear died— and despite her brave words, that time would come soon—First Sword would become Prester, and Meriel had no doubt he would execute the four of them. From what the Creek woman had said, war would surely follow, but First Sword would not care about that. He was not a peaceable man.

Try as she might, Meriel could not imagine any solution that allowed her both to achieve the Grail, and to allow the four of them to escape. In all the time she had been here, she had never so much as touched the blessed Cup. There was no way at all that she could carry it from the temple and out of the city undetected.

Why did You lie to me? If you meant me to come here to die, I would have come—but You brought me here, and Sarah followed me, and it is all for nothing!

Still, there was no answer.

"So the Numakiki are white men who came here long ago," The Daughter-of-the-Wind said, when Meriel had left. The priest-guards had also left them, barring them in for the night. The window was covered by a stout lattice—enough to discourage escape, for the sound one made getting through it would surely bring guards. The Creek sachem frowned for a moment, considering matters further. "This explains much, considering that they are all mad. But I think your friend is mad as well, Sarah, for she says she still wishes to go to Nouvelle-Orléans, even though you have found her."

"I think she believes that her husband may be there," Sarah said slowly, for there was much about Meriel's tale that still puzzled her. Meriel had spoken much of her adventures and little of the reason for them, and so Sarah was not quite sure why Meriel had left Baltimore in the first place, for it was obviously not to go in search of Louis.

"The news from there is very bad," the Sahoya said, for the travelers had shared news and gossip along the road. "The French Emperor's new ruler is an evil man. It is said that the rivers run with blood because of him, and the spirits of the earth flee his shadow. He calls devils to walk beside him."

"What nonsense!" Sarah said roundly, nettled at this lurid reflection of her own formless fears.

"I do not think so, Sarah. Louisianne has always been a bad friend to the People, enslaving us when it could. She brings men from all over the earth to toil and die for her. I think the French

Governor would enslave devils if he could, and so he has," The Daughter-of-the-Wind said.

"Rumors," Sarah said stoutly. "And I, for one, will wait until I get there to decide whether they are true or not."

"So you will still go south?" the Sahoya asked.

"If—when!—we get out of here," Sarah answered.

"Have you a plan?" Meets-The-Dawn asked, his voice low.

"Not yet," Sarah admitted. "I wish Meriel had told me the whole of her news—she is holding something back. I can feel it."

"Perhaps she thinks—as do I—that to talk of ransom is a soothing story for children," Meets-The-Dawn said, with an angry glance toward the Sahoya. The Creek shaman regarded him coldly, still certain that her rank would protect her and that she could send word to her people through the Numakiki's trading partners.

"There is something here that does not make any sense," Sarah persisted. "If Meriel did not come in search of her husband, what *did* she come looking for? And for that matter, I would dearly love to know how it is that the Numakiki speak Latin, and no tongue of the People!"

"Latin is the tongue of the Black Robes who come with the French to bring us the White Christ Religion," Meets-The-Dawn offered, sounding as puzzled as Sarah. "But the Numakiki do not trade with the French."

But their speculations could gain them nothing, nor was there any real possibility of escape from the place in which they were held, and so at last Sarah and her companions slept . . . to be awakened, just before dawn, by a rumbling that shook their prison as the fox shakes a fat rabbit.

Meriel sprang upright at the first tremor. She recognized it for an earthquake, such as she had experienced while in Spain, but this one was of a much greater intensity.[40] Meriel was already on her feet,

---

40. The New Madrid Quake, which struck on December 16th, 1811, at 2:30 A.M., was the first of three major quakes—Richter 8 or above—to strike The

running for the door across a floor that danced beneath her feet as the other maidens, awakening around her, began to scream.

This is my chance. Her own thought, yet one seemingly come from outside as much as the angel's voice had. It was a chance that was no chance at all, yet she could see no other way. If nothing else, she could get out of the temple during this confusion to warn Sarah and the others of what would happen when Shining Spear died.

She reached the doors of the dormitory only an instant before the others. The polished wood gave beneath her hand, for they had been left unlatched to allow Gold Hands and White Knife to come and go, Meriel guessed. The Red Cross Knights were nowhere in sight, and the vigil lamps had spilled upon the floor, where the burning tallow gave off choking clouds of smoke. Another jolt, more powerful than the preceding ones, nearly knocked her from her feet. She coughed, and realized the air was full of dust, and more smoke than the spilled lamps could account for. Beneath her feet, the floor shook again, with a frightening rolling motion like the deck of a ship in a storm, and she could hear the grinding of the stones in the walls around her as they grated against one another like giant's teeth. The corridor was filled with people rushing toward escape or rescue. Someone shoved her from behind and she fell, rolling quickly toward the wall to protect herself. Using it as a support, she clambered to her feet again. In the distance, the war-horns bawled their warning across the water.

Meriel hesitated. Some great disaster had struck, this much she knew. It might provide the chance for her to escape with the Grail and free her friends as well—with her black hair and sun-bronzed

---

New Madrid Fault Area in less than three months. The New Madrid Quake rang church bells as far away as Boston, made the Mississippi flow backward, and affected an area that stretched from Kansas to West Virginia, from Michigan to Louisiana. On January 23rd and February 13th, tremors of similar intensity to the first struck an already ravaged area. While the earthquake of 1807 that I describe here is not recorded by history, it is an entirely possible event.

Interestingly, the Shawnee chief Tecumseh is said to have predicted the New Madrid Quake, down to the day of its occurrence, years in advance.

skin, Meriel could easily pass as one of them, and nobody would notice her in the confusion. Yet she could not abandon Shining Spear without knowing what had happened to him.

The Men's Side was in darkness, though the indigo pre-dawn sky showed through the slits in the walls. Meriel found a basket of torches and lit one by the guttering blue flame of a spilled rushlight. The torch's flame turned the haze of smoke white—the temple itself might be stone, but there were many things inside it which could burn.

There were no guards watching before his door, and when Meriel entered, at first she thought the chamber empty, then she saw Shining Spear still lying upon his bed. She set the torch into a wall bracket and knelt beside him, and only then did she see the slow rise and fall of his chest, and the green gleam beneath his sleeping furs. Hardly daring to believe her eyes, Meriel turned back a fold of the blanket.

The Grail was here.

"It is said . . . that the cup gives eternal life, if one knows its secret. Gold Hands brought it to me, but her magic was not strong enough," Shining Spear said, his voice frail.

"I am sorry," Meriel said. "There is nothing I can do. The Grail is a medicine not for earthly bodies, but for souls."

With an effort, Shining Spear reached out and grasped Meriel's wrist. Carrying her hand forward, he placed it upon the Grail.

She had always thought, when the moment she first touched it came, that there would be a great shock of holiness, some numinous epiphany like her vision in the church in Baltimore. But all she felt was the sensation of warm stone beneath her fingers.

"Take . . . take the cup, Green Stone. Fulfill your destiny. I am still Prester. While I live, my will is law, and I say this. Take the cup."

Weeping, Meriel crossed herself, and kissed Shining Spear upon the forehead. Then she got to her feet and wrapped the Grail carefully in her blanket. When she looked at Shining Spear again, his eyes were closed, his face peaceful in death. Cradling her precious burden in her arms, Meriel hurried from the room.

She did not know how long it took her to reach the front of the temple, for many of the passageways were blocked by spilled goods, and in some, roof or walls sagged frighteningly, ready to collapse completely. As she neared the entrance she could hear the wailing of the people outside, but she was not prepared for the sight that greeted her.

The Numakiki city had been smashed, as if the earth upon which it stood was a blanket rumpled by a fractious child. Two of the towers had fallen, pulling the log palisade down with them, and half the island had simply been sheared away, flooding much of the city. Hundreds must have died at once, and the survivors flocked toward the temple, crying out for help.

They are dead—Sarah and the others are dead, Meriel thought sorrowfully, looking over the devastation. And her own way of escape from the city was blocked—she'd thought of stealing a canoe, or even of swimming, but the river was more turbulent than she had ever seen it—angry and brown, its surface rippling with foam.

First Sword had survived, and was standing a few steps up from the bottom trying to calm the people. *And soon he will say that the Great Spirit has sent the earthquake because he is displeased at the strangers in their midst—as if an execution could improve matters!*

She clutched the blanket-wrapped bundle of the Grail tightly. The priests who had instructed her had told her always that God was not to be bargained with as if He were a heavenly tradesman, but she could not keep herself from thinking: *I will do all I can, but You must help me.*

There was a way.

Reluctantly Meriel turned back the way she had come, into the labyrinth of the temple.

Sarah awakened sharply as Meets-The-Dawn shook her. She wasn't sure why: it was just before sunrise, and all was silent in the Numakiki city. Even the dogs were still.

When he was sure she was awake, Meets-The-Dawn turned to the Sahoya, but before he could rouse her, the ground began to shake as violently as a horse trying to dislodge summer blackflies. Sarah cried out in surprise. She struggled to her knees, gazing about herself wildly, but she could see little in the dimness. Beneath her the ground rolled like the deck of a ship, and the silence of the dawn was broken by screams and clamor as the Numakiki city awoke to bedlam.

At last the shaking stopped. The Daughter-of-the-Wind was at the door, but it was barred from without. Sarah glanced toward the window. Between them they could get the lattice off, and in the confusion the sound would not be heard. She scrambled over the bedding and began shoving at it. The peeled willow wands creaked, but held firm.

Then Meets-The-Dawn joined his strength to hers. There was a splintering sound, and the bars over the window sagged free.

Meets-The-Dawn was first through the window, and Sarah slithered quickly after him, followed by the Sahoya. The back of the so-called Guest House gave on a narrow alleyway. At the moment it was deserted. There was a faint scent of smoke in the air.

"What has happened?" The Daughter-of-the-Wind demanded. She struggled through the window, and Sarah helped her to the ground.

"What is called an earth-quake, I think," Sarah said. "I have heard they can be very powerful."

"So the earth-folk aid us," Meets-The-Dawn said slowly. "That is well. I should not like to be their enemy."

Sarah was thinking furiously. Meriel had told them that she slept in the temple at the center of the city. Could Sarah get there, find Meriel, and escape in the confusion?

"Go—find us some way off this island—I will find you!" Sarah promised the others recklessly. "And if I do not, then I thank you for helping me as you have."

"I will go with you," Meets-The-Dawn said, but the Sahoya held him back, saying, "One will travel faster than two, and I will need your strong arm."

Sarah ran through the maze of alleyways and damaged buildings. The streets were flooded, and all around her the devastation was more terrible than anything she had seen outside her visions. Fire had taken possession of those parts of the city which were above water, and the sky was filled with smoke.

She had a good sense of direction, so while Sarah was not lost, precisely, she found herself going in circles trying to find an un-blocked way to reach her destination. From the numbers of people in the streets, Sarah realized that many of the folk were fleeing the city, and she wondered if her decision to look for Meriel had been a foolish one. What if Meriel were already dead—or looking for her as well? They might both wander the city until they were recaptured.

As the sun rose higher, Sarah won free onto an unblocked thor-oughfare. She was still a great distance from the center of the city, and realized she had little hope of reaching Meriel, even if her friend *had* remained within the temple. A part of her found a certain gal-lows humor in the fact that she had sailed to America armed in all the panoply of might that could be wielded by the Duchess of Wes-sex, only to discover herself in a situation in which such exalted rank counted for nothing.

Sarah knew she was running out of time. She must escape herself while she still could, but her hardy conscience stubbornly rebelled against such prudence. She had come in search of Meriel, and she would not leave her. If she could do nothing else useful, she could find the others and urge them to escape without her, then hide nearby and await another chance to escape with Meriel.

But the need to avoid recapture became ever more urgent as the people began to recover their senses, and to her great frustration, Sarah found herself dodging back toward the prison-house near the gates of the city. She ducked into a doorway as six warrior-priests marched by. They wore the short kilts and red-painted crosses Sarah had seen before, and their presence was a sign that order was re-turning to the city. She had tarried too long.

Just then she saw a flash of green, brilliant as noonday sun on a mirror, from the alleyway across the street. Though Sarah stared in that direction intently she could see nothing that might cause it, but when she looked away, the flash came again. Determined to solve this mystery, Sarah waited for an opening, then fleeted across the wide avenue into the alley beyond.

There was nothing there.

But the flash came again, this time from a rooftop several hundred yards beyond, and once again Sarah followed it. Time and again she resolved to give up the fruitless chase, but the conviction grew in her, somehow, that the green fire was a message meant for her eyes alone, leading her onward—but to what?

At last she stood in a space between two buildings—little more than a shambles, now—that faced what remained of the palisades that had surrounded the city. The wall's ancient architects had understood the necessities of defense, for there was a wide open space between the last building and the wall . . . or where the wall should have been.

The earthquake that had struck the city had twisted the stout pine logs like so many wooden toothpicks, leaving only a row of shattered stumps between Sarah and the river. And at the water's edge, she saw a flash of green.

When Shining Spear had shown Meriel the Numakiki treasure rooms weeks before, neither of them had imagined that she would have any use for its greatest secret: a tunnel that led from the city to a sheltered cove at the edge of the river. The tunnel offered no chance of escape, for the river was far too wide to swim, and too fast for even a strong swimmer, but it did offer a place to hide, and so Meriel took it.

She was lucky enough to have light to guide her, for a lantern was among the treasure—booty from some uncelebrated yet recent encounter between Europeans and the Numakiki—and a packet of Lucifers[41] was with it. She was able to easily strike a light. The tunnel was so low she had to go stooped over, and the timbers that shored it up were black with age and damp. Her footing was treacherous, for the floor of the tunnel was filled with water-rotted debris and the litter of the small animals that had made it their home. The small folded forms of bats, like strange leaves, clustered along the walls in

---

41. An early form of match, later called Lucifer matches to distinguish them from the so-called "self-lighting" match (similar to the modern wooden kitchen match).

places, and Meriel shuddered and closed her eyes, hoping the lantern-light would not disturb them.

Soon she could see daylight ahead and stopped to blow out the lantern. The passageway narrowed and lowered, until Meriel had to abandon the lantern and go forward on hands and knees, her precious burden awkwardly clutched to her stomach and her white robe girded immodestly high.

At last she reached the end, and peered out through a screen of bushes. The tunnel let out into a sort of cove, and a fan of sand spread out around the tunnel mouth. Above, the bank overhung the entrance sharply, so one would have to have keen eyes indeed even to see that there was a tunnel here, cut into the blue clay of the bank.

There was no one in sight, but the river itself was thick with debris, for the Numakiki had a habit of consigning to the river anything which they did not want, and were adding much to what it had taken from them this morning. Freedom—the far bank—was tantalizingly close, yet she had no way of reaching it.

Little as she wished to do so, Meriel knew she must wait for night to come again before venturing into the open air to investigate possible means of escape. She crept back from the entrance to the passage and sat with her arms wrapped around her knees, trying not to think of what she must do next.

Eventually she dozed, only to wake again as if she had been called. She gazed uncertainly toward the river, and her attention was caught by movement at the water's edge. She stared for a moment, doubting and fearing what she saw.

"Sarah . . . ?"

Sarah heard the hoarse whisper of her name just as she was about to turn back into the city in search of a hiding place. She stood, silent, and then it came again. She hurried forward, to where she had last seen the green spark.

Meriel crawled out from beneath the riverbank, muddy and signaling her frantically. Heedless of scratches, Sarah thrust her way through the scrim of bushes and found herself in a sort of den cut into the island's shore. The two young woman hugged each other tightly.

"I thought you must be lost—"

"I looked for you, but you were gone—"

"I was sure you were dead, but I hoped—"

Their stories were exchanged in hasty whispers. Meriel told Sarah about Shining Spear's death, and First Sword's intention to execute the foreign captives.

"Then I hope Meets-The-Dawn and the Sahoya got away safely," Sarah said somberly.

It was absurd—the two of them alone in the wilderness, in hiding from natives who would almost certainly execute them if they discovered their hiding place—but Sarah felt a surge of sudden optimism. If they escaped the Numakiki, they would be among friends all the way back to Baltimore.

"Tonight we will find some way to cross the river. And then we can go home. Wessex is sure to be in Baltimore by now, and I'm sure he can—"

"No, Sarah," Meriel said softly. "I must go to Nouvelle-Orléans. I told you that."

"Leaving aside 'how,'" Sarah said tartly, "can you not tell me *why*? It is hundreds of miles to Nouvelle-Orléans. There will be wolves, pirates—even if we escape the Numakiki—and—"

"I must go," Meriel said unhappily. "I must take this to Nouvelle-Orléans."

She drew a bundle Sarah had not noticed before onto her lap, and folded back a corner so tenderly that Sarah would not have been surprised to see a child nestled there. Instead, it was the most fabulous cup she had ever seen, its stem a golden jeweled falcon and its bowl carved of jade, or emerald. . . .

"My goodness," she said inadequately. "And you have to take that to Nouvelle-Orléans? We'll be lucky not to be robbed before we've gone ten feet."

"Will you help me, Sarah?" Meriel begged.

"I suppose I must," Sarah said helplessly. If the cup was the source of the green fire that had led her to Meriel, it must be magic, and Sarah had learned to treat magic with serious respect. "For now that I come to consider it, going to Nouvelle-Orléans and being shot as a spy will be far more comfortable than returning to Baltimore and explaining to Wessex just what it is I have been doing here and why I did not wait for him to arrive before I did it. Though I must say, if you brought that with you, you have had the luck of the fiend to get this far."

Fiendish or otherwise, their luck held good. In the twilight of a long and uncomfortable day, Sarah and Meriel crept down to the water's edge. The river had calmed somewhat, and they must try to swim across, despite the residual turbulence. There was no choice. The current would carry them miles downstream, but if they were lucky, it would not drown them before they could reach the far side. They could not chance trying to steal a raft or a canoe, even if there were any left. It was this, or go to surrender themselves to First Sword. And they must go now, while there was still enough light by which to choose their landing.

At least we both can swim, Sarah thought hopefully. *And at least the Numakiki have other things to worry about at the moment. If we're lucky, they may even think we're dead.*

"Come on," Meriel whispered. Moving in a a crouch, still clutching the blanket-wrapped cup, she pressed through the trees and scurried down to the water. Sarah could see her lips moving in silent prayer.

Then, as Meriel reached the water and began to wade out, Sarah stared in amazement. What she could only describe as ripples of calm began to spread outward from Meriel. Silence descended as the rushing of the river, its sound almost unheard through long familiarity, dimmed and then hushed entirely. It was a miracle—there was no other word for it.

Sarah scrambled out of the cave after her friend, astonishment and curiosity making her reckless. As far as she could see in either direction, upriver and down, the river was as smooth and quiet as an English millpond.

The Numakiki saw it too, for there were shouts from the remains of the wall, and Sarah heard a thrown stone plash into the river. The sound galvanized her, and she waded quickly into the water after Meriel. The shouts from behind them grew louder, and soon someone would swim out after them. Sarah had seen no bows among her captors, but a well-thrown spear would be just as deadly.

Sarah was a strong swimmer, and unencumbered, and the river's stillness was no illusion—aside from its temperature, cold even now, this was no more hazardous than taking the waters at Bath. At intervals she reached down with her toes, and after what seemed an eternity, felt them brush the river bottom.

"Take my hand!" Meriel gasped. Though she was not a strong swimmer, she had hung back from the shore, obviously waiting for Sarah. "Take my hand! We must walk from the river together, or I know not what will happen!"

Sarah glanced behind her. The gap in the palisades was filled with torches, and just rounding the end of the island, she saw the sharklike shape of a canoe, followed quickly by a second one. They would reach them in scant minutes. She grabbed Meriel's arm and dragged her toward the land.

In the shallows, Meriel stumbled and fell to her knees. The cup fell from her hands to the bank, and she cried out.

As if in echo of her cry, there was a loud booming sound, followed by a roar that was like no sound Sarah had ever heard before. In an instant, the river became a foaming mass of white, shining ghostlike in the gloaming. It was as if the fury deferred in their crossing had been added to the river's normal flow, and the result was a maelstrom that swept the canoes downriver faster than a horse could gallop, tumbling them through the sudden rapids like driftwood.

"Dear God," Sarah whispered, stunned and staring.

Meriel pulled herself to her feet and picked up the cup again. Cradling it in one arm, she wrung out the sodden blanket as best she could and wrapped her treasure again.

"Come," she said, and Sarah could hear that her voice was thick with tears. "I do not think they will follow us now."

9

Life on the Mississippi
(Nouvelle-Orléans, October 1807)

Except for one brief portage to reach the Ohio River, the entire journey into Louisianne had been accomplished via Robert Fulton's peculiar invention, and with all the speed that Illya Koscuisko had promised. It had been a covert passage by no stretch of the imagination, for both the Mississippi and the Ohio were heavily-trafficked rivers, even in these days of French embargo, and the *Royal Henry* was the target of catcalls and profane questions from the flatboatmen at her every sighting. Fortunately, she was also armed, with fore and aft guns, and between that and a superior turn of speed was able to show her heels to the several bands of river pirates they encountered.

Though the crew of eight which tended to the *Royal Henry*'s needs were all employed by the White Tower, they undoubtedly believed that their master was some such veiling organization as the Royal Society for the Advancement of Scientific Thought or the Wanderer's Club. In any event, they did not treat Wessex as though he were under a cloud of any sort, and in other circumstances, Wessex might have used such inattention as the foundation of an escape attempt, but in this case he was honest enough to admit that Koscuisko had been correct. Sarah was no longer in Baltimore, and from what little he had learned, Wessex might as well seek her in Nouvelle-Orléans as anywhere else.

At least, so, long as he was not called upon to murder the Duc d'Charenton. He had not raised his doubts upon the subject of the political assassination with Koscuisko again, but it was much in his thoughts. To kill a man—especially an important, well-protected diabolist such as d'Charenton—(who, in Wessex's private opinion, had badly needed killing for many years) was a matter that called for careful planning and a delicacy of approach in addition to the necessary Royal blood. Nothing in Wessex's hypothetical notions of how to proceed with such a matter included the concept of arriving on the spot in a highly-conspicuous, fabulously unique, exquisitely noisy steam-driven riverboat.

Gossip about this strange river chimera preceded them, and by the time they reached the Upper Delta it had become routine for *Royal Henry* to encounter curious onlookers standing along the levees that gave the Louisianne plantations their slim protection against Old Man Mississippi's recurrent floods. The landscape they passed through had become one of live oak trees dripping with Spanish moss. Beyond the trees was the ghost-haunted bayou country, where reptiles larger than a man—and less natural things—waited to prey upon the unwary.

"I hope you are not anticipating a clandestine entry into the Port?" Wessex asked his partner one afternoon. It was unreasonable to think that d'Charenton would not be as well informed as the citizenry along the river and be awaiting the steamboat's arrival with interest. They were now only a few days at most from the city.

"Oh, the *Royal Henry* will go to ground and vanish before we reach the city," Koscuisko answered airily. "The captain and his men can have her in pieces in half a day—"

"If she does not explode first," Wessex reminded him, for the steam engine was a volatile thing whose boiler had threatened them with instant annihilation a number of times already.

"—one way or another," Koscuisko amended with a smile. "From our last anchorage it is but a few hours to a plantation house that I know of, whose master, if not precisely a Free Acadian, is no lover of Imperial France."

"And what the devil," Wessex demanded waspishly, "is a Free Acadian?"

"You haven't paid attention to your briefing book," his companion chided reprovingly. "The Free Acadian Liberation Front is the organization that wants Louisianne to be independent of Imperial rule. Their notion for government is a sort of Parliament, with a Prime Minister but no King. The Sons of the Sun, on the other hand, demand a King and no Parliament, though they're equally against Napoleon. The Creole Freedom Party wishes to return Louisianne to the flag of Spain and throw out the French *and* the Acadians, which is only a thought awkward since Spain has declared for Napoleon and has a Bonaparte bottom on her throne. The Franco-Albion Alliance wishes to see Louisianne become a part of New Albion while retaining its autonomy, and I assure you I have no more idea than they do how this marriage of ice and fire is to be accomplished."

Wessex raised an eyebrow, but said nothing.

"There are, of course, other factions, such as Monsieur Lafitte's notion that *he* shall rule the Gulf as a sort of anarcho-pirate kingdom, and Mr. Burr's notion that he and Mr. Jackson shall divide it between them. To these last, His Majesty is particularly opposed, of course, but as for the rest—" here Koscuisko shrugged, in flamboyant detachment, "—I suppose one revolution is as good as another, when one comes right down to it."

"No revolution is better than any," Wessex said somberly. "A revolution is a bloody thing, demanding payment in thousands of lives."

"Would you have France control the Gulf?" Koscuisko asked bluntly.

"She won't control it for long, if d'Charenton is up to his usual starts, whether England does anything or not," Wessex pointed out reasonably. "So I don't see why it is our business to interfere."

"Because France is a slave nation, and England is not," Koscuisko answered, "and that alone will mean war in the end, unless someone heads it off. And if—as has been true in the past—d'Charenton can call upon powerful occult allies, who is to say that he might not hold Louisianne in defiance of all reasonable expectations?"

"Because," Wessex said patiently, "the Duc d'Charenton would drive the Devil himself to drink on short acquaintance. He will unite every faction in Louisianne against him, if he has not done so already."

"And if he has in his possession the true King of France?" Koscuisko asked quietly.

Wessex was once more puzzled as to how much Koscuisko actually knew of the matter that had brought Wessex to the New World—not Sarah's disappearance, but Louis and Meriel's. There was no safe way to find out, and so the Duke turned away and silently watched the river.

All that day the *Royal Henry* stayed close to the bank of the river looking for a navigable tributary. At last she found one and turned up it, the relentless chugging of her engine suddenly louder among the trees. A shadowy darkness descended almost at once, and glancing toward the stern, Wessex could barely see the bright surface of the river through a gap in the trees.

At the bow a crewman with a pole took soundings, calling back the depths in a peculiar patois native to the river. Herons lumbered awkwardly out of their path, and alligators—the crocodile's New World cousin—slid malevolently into the water as they passed. The air turned oppressively humid, filled with the smells of mud and decay.

At last the stream was too shallow for them to advance farther. The engineer bled pressure from the boiler. The engine stopped, and in the sudden silence, they could hear crashing sounds as other, heavier, animals fled the steamboat's noisy intrusion.

The boat settled into the mud.

"And now?" Wessex asked dubiously, regarding the swamp that surrounded them. While it was true that less than half a mile in any direction might take them onto one of the great plantations that edged the river, a wrong turn could immure them in this soggy wilderness forever.

"We go back the way we came," Koscuisko said gaily. "It is a metaphor for life itself, my friend."

By late afternoon the crew had deployed the skiff that the steamboat carried and loaded the two politicals' luggage upon it. One of the ship's crew went with them as steersman and guide, and Wessex and Koscuisko poled the boat back into the river shallows. Even in October, the climate was tropical, and Wessex found himself regretting his dashing plumed tricorn *a la militaire.* His coat reposed atop his luggage, as did his partner's, for the line that style demanded was far too confining to permit of physical labor.

They were careful to stay out of the current—without the mechanical intercession of the riverboat, it became clear to Wessex how dangerous the river could be—and within a few minutes, had drifted downriver to their destination.

It was a loading dock such as Wessex had seen elsewhere along the river—a structure at which the flatboats could anchor, and from which cargo could be loaded for transportation farther downriver. A young Negro child was sitting on the end of the dock, dabbling at the water with a peeled willow wand. In Wessex's youth, the fashion had been to keep such children as pages, garbed in fantastically ornate livery, turbaned and jeweled until they resembled Indian potentates. In contrast, this child was barefoot and half-naked, his only clothing a pair of cut-down trousers that ended raggedly at the knee.

When the boy saw them, he leapt to his feet animatedly. "Is yo de gemmun fo' de *baas*?" the child called in a patois so thick Wessex could barely make it out.

The boatman threw him a line, and the child hurried to make it fast as Wessex and Koscuisko held the boat from drifting. Their trunks were quickly transferred from the boat to the dock, and almost before the two of them had stepped from the boat to the land, the boatman was polling his craft back upstream. Wessex shrugged quickly into his snuff-colored coat and adjusted his hat. Koscuisko, hatless, took even more time to adjust his own, macaroni-inspired[42] garment to his satisfaction.

---

42. Which is to say, dandified. The macaronis—immortalized in the song "Yankee

"Ah ter shows yo to de big house," the child announced importantly. "*Baas* Baronner, he waitin' fo' yo'." The boy danced off, looking back at the guests impatiently.

"And this, one supposes, passes for secrecy in this country?" Wessex drawled.

"Ah, well, it hardly matters what anyone sees. It's what they think they've seen that's to the point," Koscuisko answered philosophically.

The two men climbed the steep switchback to a broad path overhung with weeping willows, the journey causing Wessex to regret his coat. A sweep of immaculate emerald lawn swept down to the edge of the bluff, and at the top of the gentle slope lay their destination, a sprawling three-story mansion built in the grand style of the plantation aristocracy. Its architecture resembled that of the Caribbean, with open galleries of ornate ironwork incorporated into each floor to catch any breeze that blew. The lacy white ironwork against the pale blue background of the painted plaster walls gave the house a grand, if baroque, aspect, and that the several outbuildings typical of a southern plantation were each painted in a different pastel color only intensified the effect.

"I think it would have been worth the journey, if only to see this," Wessex murmured in awe.

"Philistine," his companion answered.

Their young guide, meanwhile, had deserted them to run ahead, shrieking news of their arrival. Wessex and Koscuisko followed more leisurely. As they approached the veranda, a man who could only be their host strolled out to greet them. He was immaculately dressed in the flamboyant Creole style of the native *Orléannais,* and his smooth dark skin bespoke his African ancestry. For a moment Wessex was startled, then recalled that the peculiar institution of slavery as practiced by the Louisiannes allowed not only for the existence of free people of color, but for such people to be slaveholders as well.

Doodle"—were those who dressed somewhere beyond the cutting edge of fashion, known particularly for their exaggerated lapels, high collar-points, and (naturally) plumed hats.

"Welcome to The Clouds. I'm Rhettler Baronner, your host. I hope you had a pleasant journey down the river?" His French was impeccably Parisian, save for a faint flat drawl which suggested its New World origins. Without seeming to hurry, Baronner ushered his guests quickly inside, away from the inquisitive eyes of the servants. Wessex tucked his hat beneath his arm and followed.

The Clouds was as opulent as an oriental palace, its interior a strange mixture of concession to the tropical climate and adherence to notions of European elegance. The broad, cypress-planked floors were covered with brilliantly-colored oriental rugs, and the sideboards were filled with displays of silver and glittering crystal.

Baronner brought them to a handsome room on the first floor. Large French windows stood open on two sides of the room, leading out onto the veranda, and the river was plainly visible above the trees. An ornate *chinoiserie* desk stood in the middle of the room, its every surface lacquered and gilded, and there was a large painted screen in one corner of the room.

"Please, gentlemen, make yourselves comfortable. Your rooms will be ready shortly. In the meantime, would you care for some refreshment?"

Without waiting for an answer, Baronner reached for the bell-pull that hung beside the door and rang it sharply. Within a short time a handsome young Negress entered carrying a silver tray upon which was a bowl of ice, a bowl of fresh mint, several cones of white sugar, and a decanter of whiskey. She set the tray upon the desk and departed, and then for several minutes there was nothing but silence as Barroner industriously combined the ingredients, presenting the result to each of the visitors in a silver cup.

"It's called a julep. It's a local specialty, said to cure everything from lumbago to yellow jack. It's a bit late in the year for them, but I thought you being from up North, you could use something to take the edge off our weather."

Wessex sipped gingerly at the freezing fiery concoction, but found it surprisingly palatable. Across from him, he saw Koscuisko coming to the same conclusion rather more quickly, but then, the Pole's capacity for spirits was a notorious one.

"You have a beautiful home," Wessex said, in an idle tone.

"Thank you." Baronner smiled, seating himself across from the two men. "I'm a gambler by profession. I won The Clouds at a game of cards and decided to keep it—the atmosphere in Nouvelle-Orléans is decidedly unhealthy these days, and anyone who can take to the country has done so."

"What can you tell us about d'Charenton?" Koscuisko asked, leaning forward.

Baronner raised his hands in a gesture of denial. "I'm a peaceable man. I don't take sides, and I don't inquire into other people's business. From time to time, I entertain guests who find it convenient to have a place to meet where no one will notice them, but that's as far as I go."

Wessex said nothing. It had been obvious from the moment he had not asked their names that Baronner was running The Clouds as a sort of accommodation house . . . but in that case, who was it that Koscuisko had come here to meet, if it was not Baronner?

"That much being agreed to," Koscuisko responded glibly, "what *is* going on in the city these days?"

Baronner shrugged, looking suddenly tired. "General Victor's troops patrol the streets, he drills the citizen-militia and recruits constantly. Admiral Bonaparte's ships patrol the Gulf and the mouth of the river, chasing ghosts and Lafitte's ships in equal measure. But neither force can be everywhere at once." He shrugged, a gesture very French. "The city is very . . . quiet . . . these days. People tend to vanish suddenly and permanently." Baronner hesitated, on the verge of saying more, then obviously changed his mind. "But what can one expect of people little better than Yankees and Kaintocks?" He smiled, with the easy charm of the gambler.

"Kaintocks?" Wessex asked, unfamiliar with the term.

"The wild men of the river . . . at least, in the days when Albionese goods were passing through the port. They would take their pay on the docks, and then drink and brawl through the city until it was all spent. But Governor d'Charenton has closed down The Swamp—that was the name of their particular district—and burned its shanties to the ground. As I have said, Nouvelle-Orléans is very quiet these days."

Wessex glanced at his partner. He knew Koscuisko well enough to know that Baronner's news did not make good hearing for the ex-hussar.

"Perhaps it will not be quiet for too much longer," Koscuisko offered politely.

For a moment it almost seemed that Baronner was going to cross himself. Instead, he got to his feet. "Gentlemen, I am desolated to announce that the press of business forces me to abandon you until dinnertime. Please ring for whatever you might need—we keep civilized hours here; dinner will be at 8:30." He bowed—the short abrupt gesture of the Continental—and strode from the room.

" 'Nouvelle-Orléans is very quiet these days,' " Wessex quoted mockingly in English. "Perhaps we can just go home, in that case."

"Without doubt," Koscuisko said sourly, gazing off into the distance with an unwontedly somber expression.

"And all things considered, I don't wish to be vulgarly inquisitive, my dear fellow, but who are you this week? And come to it, who am I? I don't imagine the Duke of Wessex will be entirely welcome in these precincts. He is *un Anglais*—or so I have heard," Wessex added in French.

"Without a doubt, of the most English," Koscuisko answered, switching easily to French as well. "I have the honor to present to you Count Jerzy Aleksander Kouryagin, special attaché to the Tsar—on detached and very special service."

"Russia not yet being an ally of France, for all Talleyrand's blandishments, but still both skittish and highly courted, especially since the Danish alliance," Wessex footnoted. "And I suppose I must be M'sieur le Chevalier de Reynard once more, neither too Republican, nor too Royalist, but certainly not English."

"Very much like Louisianne," Koscuisko supplied. "And though the identity is a trifle blown upon in Paris, that will hardly matter here. A good choice. But for now, I leave you as well. I believe I shall take a walk about the grounds to stretch my legs. I trust you will do nothing to distress our host?"

"Certainly not," Wessex said, stepping over to the table to pour more whiskey into his cup. He eyed the makings of the julep and shuddered inwardly. One had been sufficient. Leave it to the French to serve their drinks so barbarously cold. "I shall be a very pattern-card of virtue."

But as soon as Koscuisko had left—Wessex did not doubt he was heading for a particular and long-planned rendezvous—the Duke moved to the edge of the window and peered out. As he had suspected, a few moments later Koscuisko appeared. The man had stopped by his luggage (which had been delivered to the house by this time) to add a polished high-crowned beaver and his customary walking-stick to his ensemble, and strolled across the lawn, an idle man of fashion, with barely a glance up at the windows. Wessex made sure Koscuisko did not see him, and waited until Koscuisko had disappeared beyond the edge of the trees, then checked his watch.

It was just rising six, and despite his airy badinage of a few moments earlier, he had no intention of allying himself, even by inaction, with whatever plans his sometime partner had. That meant departing at once, before he could be further entangled in Koscuisko's schemes. As long as he oriented himself upon the river, he could not fail to reach Nouvelle-Orléans eventually.

But for now, he must move quickly. He crossed to the door and listened. Hearing nothing, he opened it slowly and stepped into the hallway. A quick search of the rooms on this level located his luggage, and Wessex risked a stop to accouter himself. While it was true he had not done his own packing for this jaunt back in Baltimore, Koscuisko knew what was needed as well as did he, and on the voyage south Wessex had determined that his potential needs had been as well supplied as if he were in fact here in his official capacity.

Money, in the form of impeccable gold napoleons, went into the hollow heels of his boots as well as into his wallet. His knives and pistols took their accustomed places in his coat. His rapier and sword-cane—here Wessex hesitated, then chose the rapier, as the heavier and slightly more reliable weapon. He had no identity papers, but those would be relatively uncommon in a port the size of Nouvelle-Orléans, and easy enough to acquire in any case.

What he would do when he reached the city, Wessex had not yet decided.

❖   ❖   ❖

It is a matter more difficult than perhaps it first seems to make one's clandestine egress from an unfamiliar country house in the early evening, but His Grace the Duke of Wessex had a great deal of practice at this obscure art, and gained the front steps without incident. It was to Mr. Baronner's advantage to hold himself insensible of the comings and goings of his guests, and so Wessex was not terribly concerned about being accosted by his host. While Koscuisko had been heading in entirely the opposite direction, Wessex had no faith in his remaining absent, and so speed was of the essence.

A long broad avenue stretched from the front door to the distant iron gates—a distance, Wessex estimated, of over a mile. Beyond the gates Wessex could see a road which would be his eventual, but not immediate, destination. He began walking away from the house at an angle, briskly, but not as if here were running away.

The plantations of the New World had much in common with the great country houses of the old. Each was as much a small village as a single domicile, with outbuildings scattered about its grounds. Moving without haste, Wessex found one that suited his needs. He opened the door and stepped inside.

Not all plantations had ice-houses, but Baronner had served them ice with their juleps, and so Wessex had known to look for one. In winter, ice would be harvested from shallow ponds and even from the river itself, cut into chunks and stored between layers of burlap and sawdust for later use. Wessex seated himself upon the shelf that ran around three sides of the room and felt the marblelike chill sink through his trousers. After the muggy heat of the day, the cool of the ice-house was particularly welcome, though it would be an uncomfortable place to remain for very long.

It was not necessary to have a hidingplace that would be safe from an earnest search, for Koscuisko could not search for him without admitting to their host that Wessex's absence was not an expected and deliberate thing—a confession which would undoubtedly cause the already-skittish Baronner to withdraw his assistance. All Wessex need do was wait here long enough for full dark to cloak his movements and then take to the road. He could borrow or even steal a horse at the next plantation he passed.

And then . . . ?

In Nouvelle-Orléans, he would have all the advantages of a great urban center at his disposal. Wessex backed himself to bluff his way both into and out of the local White Tower listening post, if need be; he would certainly be able to discover if Sarah, or Louis, or even Meriel, were there, and lay his plans accordingly. As for d'Charenton, at the moment Wessex was minded to let him alone, so long as their paths did not cross. D'Charenton was France's problem. Let France deal with him.

And as for Bonaparte's quest for the Hallows . . . well, even assuming they *did* exist (a point upon which Wessex was doubtful), if the Corsican could master them all, who was to say he didn't deserve the laurels of victory?

It was an idea he would never have entertained five years ago, or even two, but more and more these days, Wessex was being forced to the conclusion that he must withdraw entirely from the Shadow Game. It seemed he was developing an inconvenient sense of ethics, a fatal thing for a spy. With a faint sense of relief, Wessex realized that he would be glad to leave the chessboard of Europe to other players and retire into public life.

If he were allowed to.

If Sarah were still alive.

Not for the first time, the specter that had haunted his every hour since his return to England thrust its way into the forefront of his consciousness. Sarah might be dead even now. Six weeks had passed since anyone whom Wessex had talked to had seen her alive. Those forces that had so easily swept Louis up in their net might have taken her as well, with the same casual malice.

If that were so—

Let it not be so. Awkwardly and painfully, Wessex petitioned the Power that he had not entreated since the day his father had vanished forever into France. *Let it not be so.*

For if it were, Wessex need have no further fear of making old bones.

❖   ❖   ❖

Illya Koscuisko strolled, quickly but without haste, in the direction of the slave quarters. He had been told in Baltimore to make himself available for a briefing from a local contact who would wait for him at The Clouds. His man would find him—if he did not, Illya was to try at the same time each evening for the next three days, after which he was to go on—alone—as best he could.

Dead or in London. The orders Paris Station had passed him about his partner still ran, loath though Illya was to consider the fact. While he was in London delivering Rutledge, he had been briefed in place of Wessex for the d'Charenton matter, but he had been sent to assess the situation in Louisianne, not to act upon it. London still wanted Wessex to pull the trigger, for the Duke had experience in executing sorcerers and could do it in safety. That Wessex should be traveling to New Albion on business of his own instead of going to ground, or that Illya should have disregarded his orders far enough to first follow, then kidnap, the Duke, was something Misbourne had probably not contemplated.

"Probably" is not "certainly," Illya reminded himself. It was entirely possible that Wessex was even now sailing under secret orders of his own, and that the search for his missing Duchess was merely a cover story. Stranger things had happened in playing out the Shadow Game, but somehow Illya doubted that this was the case, this time. He had known Wessex a long time, but the cool, imperturbably indifferent political he had known existed no longer. That man had vanished like morning frost under the glow of Roxbury's sun, and the Wessex who remained cared passionately about too many things. The English, Illya told himself wisely, were not made for passion, and he feared its effects on his friend.

He'd hoped he could tempt Wessex back to the Game by bringing him along to Nouvelle-Orléans. If he could not do that, at least he could keep him safe from capture and execution by another of the White Tower's agents. If not for Wessex's intervention, Illya himself would have been dead long ago, and Illya longed to return the favor.

Still, it would have been easier if the two of them could have been open with each other as of old. Not only was Illya not entirely certain Sarah was missing—though, given Wessex's half-mad behavior, he was inclined to credit her voyage and disappearance—he could not imagine what reason had brought her to the New World in the first place, assuming she had indeed come. Wessex presumably knew, but had not confided in him.

Illya shook his head regretfully. The only thing more stubborn than an Englishman was an Englishman in love, and Illya felt he recognized the symptoms.

His peregrinations had brought him across the wide lawn and its pastel outbuildings, through a stand of cypress, and into another world entirely.

Here rows on rows of tiny shanties of unpainted wood stood huddled together. Some had small gardens beside them, others only the broom-scrubbed dust of a Louisianne dooryard. In the pale dust, children too young to work played elaborate games with twigs and pebbles for toys. The field laborers, men and women alike in garments of shapeless canvas, walked slowly through the late-afternoon sunshine in the direction of the communal kitchen in which their evening meal was being prepared. Some glanced at him curiously as they passed, but most kept their eyes downcast and averted.

This was the *barracoon,* the habitation of the human property whose ownership was permitted by the infamous Black Code[43] of Louisianne.

Slavery was a difficult notion for Illya to comprehend. The soldiers of every army in the world were worse fed and worse treated than the slaves of a Louisianne plantation, but they were still free. The servants of every noble house, the serfs of Illya's homeland, impoverished and exploited as they were, still possessed that elusive quality of freedom that these people did not. It was—his mind scrabbled for some comparison—like a soup without salt. There was no

---

43. The *Code Noir,* or Black Code, was written by the Superior Council of New Orleans in 1724, primarily to govern the conduct of the blacks in Louisiana. While it admits of the possibility of manumission, its penalties are some of the harshest found in the New World.

difference that could be seen between the free and the unfree, but there was a difference nonetheless.

"*Baas*—is it true?"

Illya stopped. The woman who had served them in Baronner's library stood in the doorway of one of the cabins. It had no door, only a length of faded calico hung over the entrance that the woman held back with one hand, ready to retreat into the poor shelter of her home at any moment.

Illya took a step closer. "Is what true?" he asked, his voice as low as her own.

"You've come from *faraway*—" her voice made the phrase into one word, as perhaps it was in her mind "—and we hear—is it true what the English say, that they make a law that nobody can own anybody no more?"

Her eyes were wide with both hope and fear. She was risking much in even speaking to him. His displeasure could get her killed. Under the law, her life was worth nothing more than an arbitrary amount of money. Under law he might kill her, but he could not murder her any more than he could murder a fish, or a bird.

"Yes," Illya told her in a low voice. "It is true. No Englishman may own a slave, and any slave who reaches English soil is free."

"Free. . . ." the woman whispered.

"It is called Wilberforce's Anti-Slavery Bill. It has been law since March of this year—law in New Albion and Prince Rupert's Land both. If you can get North, you will be free," Illya told her.

"They kill you if you run," the woman said flatly, the animation suddenly fading from her face. She dropped the curtain and retreated, and Illya found himself staring at a blank expanse of fabric.

He shook his head, suddenly angry with himself. What right did he have to fill the girl's head with unattainable dreams? He did her no favor by doing so. He turned away and walked on.

At last he reached the edge of the slave cabins, and was standing on the edge of a verdant and tangled patch of primal Louisianne. Even this late in the year, the land was as lush as the dreams of an opium eater, a labyrinth of trees and vines and pools of black water.

"So, *Anglais*, you 'ave kep' our *rendezvous*, hahn?" an oddly hollow voice asked in heavily-accented English.

"I am not English," Illya replied, also in that language. He turned slowly toward his interrogator.

The man facing him was dressed like any Orléannaise lordling, but his face was concealed by an elaborate mask of gilded and painted leather such as revelers wore at Carnivale. Illya recognized the mask as that of Momus, the Greek deity of mockery and misrule[44] who had become the patron of the wild celebrations that signified the beginning of Lent. It was the mask which distorted his voice and made him impossible to recognize, but Illya had a sudden notion that the masked man recognized *him,* for he took a step backward and raised a hand, as if to ward off a blow.

"No," he said. "You are no' *Anglais,* and dat de trut'. But I was tol' an Englishman would come."

"Plans have changed. Are you Momus?"

"If you are Janus, den I am dat ol' man of de moon, me." It was the sign Illya had been told to expect back in London.

"The moon brings lunacy," he answered, giving the proper countersign.

"It is a crazy worl' we live in, *n'est-ce pas?*"

Sign, countersign, and confirmation. They could proceed.

"What do you have for me?" Illya asked. All he knew was that "Momus" was a well-placed local who had been feeding information about d'Charenton to Lord Q of the White Tower for months. Illya hoped the man would be able to tell him something fresh about the local situation.

"De news is no' good, *cher.* Gove'nor 'Charenton is a fien' out of hell. He worship de Black One in de cryp' under de Cat'edral de Sain' Louie. He mean to mak' hisself King here in de New Worl', an' have de power of de anoint' King, him, lak' de ol' Kings in de Ol' Worl'."

The power of the anointed kings, the kings of the land, came from the sacred marriage with the land. Henry had made it upon his accession, and Prince Jamie would make it in turn. Illya's own father

---

44. At least, according to Hesiod. Momus, son of Nyx, was the Greek deity of mockery and scorn, as well as the patron of writers and poets. He was the only god to be permanently banished from Olympus.

had pledged to the land, for he had been of noble blood. It was access to this power which Napoleon had lost by executing the old king, for the Revolution had destroyed any who might have helped him reconstruct the ancient ritual, and the land would never accept a regicide.

"D'Charenton means to make himself king?" Illya said. "Of *this* land?" But what, if anything, did this have to do with what Talleyrand had sent d'Charenton to do?

"I know—I 'ave tol' him, me, dat dis will no' work. But 'e say, dat *diable*, dat he get de *Voudou Magnian* to speak for him to de lan' spirits, an he will mak' de sacrifice which will work wit'out fail."

"When will he make the sacrifice? Where?"

"In de Congo, on de Day of de Dead. But Jean 'ave de *cher p'tit* safe in Gran' Terre. 'Charenton wan' him fo' de deat', an' he mak de bargain wid Jean dat he will ransom him an' let de pirates go free, but Jean, he wan' to rule Louisianne, an' he t'ink he kill 'Charenton instead, so dey fence, lak two ol' bull gator."

The complicated plot, delivered in this garbled and native patois, was starting to make Illya's head spin. But there was one thing he was clear upon. D'Charenton meant to sacrifice a human being to gain his power over the land, and there was only one sacrifice which could bestow it upon him—or upon any man—now.

Louis. The lost Dauphin, now king in exile.

Suddenly Wessex's actions became terribly clear. At the end of their last mission to France, Wessex had let King Louis go. Louis' uncle, the Abbé de Condé, had married him to Lady Meriel before they had disappeared, obviously heading for the only place on earth in which they might be safe: the New World. Somehow d'Charenton had tracked them here. He had schemed to gain the governorship of Louisianne in order to have a stronghold from which to act. The talk of Hallows with which he had deceived Tallyrand must be no more than a smoke-screen over d'Charenton's true ambitions.

But somehow the young lovers had managed to get word of their plight to the Duchess. The Duchess had come to the New World to aid them, Wessex being elsewhere, and Wessex had followed her. No wonder he had been seeking Sarah in Baltimore so desperately, if he knew she was embroiled in d'Charenton's plot!

"This," he said inadequately, "is very bad."

"I mus' go," "Momus" said, taking a step backward.

"Wait!" Illya said. "You must tell me—"

But "Momus" was gone. He had vanished right before Illya's eyes, fading into the twilight swamp as though he were a creature born of the mist itself.

Charles Corday hurried through the bayou toward the river road where Remy Thibodeaux waited with his horse. The mask of Momus was clutched in his hand, and he cursed his evil luck roundly.

The thrice-damned *Anglais* had sent him one of the two men who might recognize "Gambit" Corday on sight, and if the mad hussar was here, could the icewater *Duc de Anglais* be far absent? If they realized Momus' true identity, they would doubt his motives, and Gambit had never been so passionately sincere in his life.

D'Charenton and Lafitte—his beloved Louisianne was truly caught between the devil and the deep blue sea. Each wanted to rule here as king, and between them they would tear *la belle Louisianne* to pieces, and the scraps to be licked up by English dogs who would drive Gambit's people from their homes once more. Between them they would kill the only man who could rule his poor homeland with the consent of all her people.

He reached the road. Thibodeaux stood holding the horse's head, a lantern in his free hand. Moths swirled about it like smoke. Corday had to ride all the way back into the city tonight to dance attendance upon d'Charenton so that his afternoon's errand would not be suspected, and afterward, he had an appointment outside of town—one that he dared not miss, for it was to crown Sanité Dédé's successor as *la Reine de Voudou*.

"It go well, hahn?" Thibodeaux asked, holding the stirrup so Corday could mount.

The Acadian assassin merely groaned. "Tib, it could no' go more bad if it try wid bot' han's for a week."

*　　*　　*

Had he known Gambit's sentiments, Illya Koscuisko would have echoed them fervently. He stood in one of the first-floor bedrooms of The Clouds gazing around himself. He had already searched all the other rooms on this floor, but the items missing from Wessex's trunk told the story with an economical eloquence that left Illya no need to conduct a search.

The damned cold-blooded Englishman was gone.

Just when I have the one piece of information that could bind our interests irrevocably together, Illya thought, sitting down on the bed. His hat tipped forward, and he grabbed it and flung it savagely across the room, the gesture doing little to relieve his feelings.

Wessex had done a moonlight flit. He might be anywhere by now—and to raise the view halloo for him would spook Baronner mightily, losing Illya his vital base of operations.

No. He had to let Wessex run, and hope the Duke didn't end with his hide nailed to the door by some overeager lamplighter. Meanwhile, he had to find out where Grand Terre was, get some reliable maps, and somehow infiltrate it, preferably within the next day or so. Once he had Louis—and whoever else Lafitte was holding—safe, he could try to stop the rest of d'Charenton's ceremony.

Providing, of course, he could figure out what his contact meant by its taking place in the Congo on the Day of the Dead.

And before he did any of those things, he had to dress for dinner and think up some plausible tale to account for Wessex's absence. Swearing softly to himself in French—a good language for swearing—Illya drew off his gloves and began to unknot his cravat.

The night was thoroughly established, melodious with the nightsounds of frogs and owls, when Wessex crept circumspectly from his refuge. The Clouds was ablaze with light, every window filled with a profligacy of candles, their light casting squares of green brightness upon the dark-shadowed lawn. The servants were in their cabins, or serving in the great house. There would be no one to see him go.

Moving quickly and quietly, Wessex made his escape. The road was smooth and broad, the product of that same enslaved labor that

created so much of the elegance of Louisianne. Even without much
light—for the moon was waning, and would be full dark in a few
days—progress along the broad smooth road was easy. For a mile or
so directly along The Clouds' frontage, the surface was white sand,
imported from some unimaginable distance. Afterward, the road re-
verted to the red clay of Louisianne, but it was still obviously a well-
traveled thoroughfare of far better quality than anything England
could boast.

*We shall see how long this endures once Louisianne no longer
has slaves to toil for her,* Wessex thought to himself. He had seen
no sign of the unrest that Misbourne had predicted once news of
the Anti-Slavery Bill had been disseminated, but was willing to con-
cede that he simply had not looked in the right places. It was unimaginable that men would wish to remain slaves with freedom so
close, or that the Louisiannes, who considered their slaves property,
not men, would stand by tamely and watch them run off.

His meditations came to an abrupt halt when he saw a light
twinkling in the far distance. Wessex headed toward it, careful to
keep to the road. Distances could be deceptive in the dark, and he
had no desire to find himself chasing will-o'-the-wisps all night.

But the light proved more elusive than it had first seemed, and
the Duke was just about to abandon his search for its source when
the sound of the drums began.

The sound was muffled by the trees—which was why he had not
heard it until now—and at first he thought his ears were playing
tricks on him, but as he drew level with the light the sounds came
to him plainly. Two drums, perhaps three, their deep voices weaving
a complex pattern around each other. It became stronger as he listened to it, as if his hearing were attuning itself to the call of the
drums, and beneath the pagan cadence Wessex fancied he could
sense the same desperate tide of blood-fever that had driven the
mobile in the days of the Terror.

He was not sure what this might be, but he would rather investigate it than leave an unexplored mystery at his back. When he drew
level with the flickering light, Wessex turned off the road and started
toward it.

❋   ❋   ❋

As he drew closer, he saw that it was not one light, but two—two large bonfires set out here in the middle of the swamp. They were set as far apart as might constitute the size of a large room, forty feet or so, and the space between them was bare of vegetation, beaten down as though it were often used as a dancing-floor. There were almost sixty people gathered here between the heat of the two fires—the women with their heads covered by calico tignons[45] the men with a sort of white scarf tied about their brows. Their clothing varied from the rags of the field slaves to the elegant French confections of the notorious *placées,* the "serpent-women" of Nouvelle-Orléans,[46] and as Wessex continued to observe, he realized that some of those he had taken for octoroons were in fact Creoles or French.

The drumming Wessex had heard came from an enormous drum laid on its side. A young Negro sat astride it, drumming with two sticks upon the painted sheepskin head between his knees. On either side of the enormous cylinder sat a man and a woman, beating on the drum's wooden ribs with what looked like the leg bones of some large animal.

At the far side of the clearing, directly opposite Wessex's concealed position, a long table had been set up. At one end of the table stood a black cat, and at the other end, a white one. Between the two cats were a sort of tree or bush in a small pot, a couple of calabashes[47] and a statue about three feet high. It was shaped after

---

45. One of the provisions of the Black Code was that the women of color, especially the *placées,* must have their heads covered by a scarf at all times. This measure, originally designed to render the "serpent-women" less attractive, resulted in the ornate and elaborate tignons worn by all black women of New Orleans, whether slave or free.

46. The *placées,* the free women of color who were the mothers of the second families of some of the most respected members of New Orleans aristocracy, were known as "serpent-women" by the embittered wives of their paramours. Some say it is because they boasted of tracing their lineage all the way back to Melusine, the serpent-tailed fay who founded the dynasty of the Angevin kings.

47. A gourd which, when dried, can be used as a storage container, a cup, or a rattle.

the fashion of one of the saint's statues the Catholics used, but it wore bright cloth garments—lovingly embroidered and beaded with cryptic symbols—and its face and hands were coal-black. Around its neck the statue wore an elaborate necklace of animal bones and teeth.

It took Wessex several minutes of watching to determine that the cats were both stuffed, and while his attention was elsewhere, the drummers stopped.

The silence that followed was absolute. The drummer walked toward the table, reached out toward the doll, and—Wessex could not see precisely how, for the two fires gave scant illumination—suddenly there was an enormous snake coiled about his hand and forearm. As he brandished the serpent, a young woman—Creole or octoroon, Wessex could not decide—strode forth from among the worshippers and began to dance with the young man and the snake in a complete and surreal silence.

Wessex was not-at-all certain of the import of what he was seeing. It did not seem to have any of the hallmarks of d'Charenton's brand of diabolism, for there were no Christian symbols present to be degraded. It seemed in fact to be a sort of cousin to the English witch-cult, practiced by the slaves—inevitable, for though Louisiana was a Catholic land, the Black Code forbid the teaching of Christianity to the slaves as well as forbidding them to practice the religions of their birthplace.

In any event, what went on here was nothing to do with him, for the simple reason that Wessex could see no way to turn it to his purpose. He would wait until the covering sound of the drums resumed, and then make his escape.

But as he waited, he could not help but watch.

Now the man was passing the serpent over the heads and bodies of the gathered worshippers while the woman spun in a strange sensual dance of her own. She had in her hand one of the calabashes from the makeshift altar and Wessex could see drops of a pale liquid sparkle in the firelight as she showered the calabash's contents upon the assembly as she danced. The weight of expectation was almost palpable, and occasionally, now, sharp cries of anticipation would break forth from the waiting congregation.

He had been wrong to wait. Better to go now and risk detection than to stay and face what was so obviously being summoned here. With difficulty, Wessex drew his eyes away from the scene and looked back the way he had come. The bayou night seemed much darker now, and he blinked, trying to clear his eyes of the fire-dazzle. He had the worrying sense that he had watched the ritual much longer than he knew, and had somehow allowed himself to become enchanted by it.

And as he moved, one of the shadows moved with him.

Wessex stopped, sensing danger, and then sprang in the direction of the road, seeking to outrace whatever guardian he had disturbed. Behind him, the drums commenced once more with renewed fury. For a few moments the Duke led his pursuer on a wild chase through the trees, until at last he reached a clearing he remembered seeing on his way into the bayou. He stopped, turning to face his attacker.

There was no one there.

For an instant, Wessex wondered if either his eyes or his nerves had played him false. But no. There *had* been a watcher, though it seemed now to have fled. Or if it were some sort of spirit, perhaps he had left the area it was set to guard. He took a moment to re-orient himself, and then began walking quickly and cautiously toward the road again.

But for all his care, he never reached it.

10

A Glorious Thing to Be a Pirate King
(Nouvelle-Orléans and Barataria, October 1807)

If he were not being driven nearly mad with worry, Louis reflected, his life here would be a very comfortable one.

He had spent the summer as the personal captive of Jean Lafitte, scourge of the Gulf. Grand Terre—or as it was as often styled, Barataria—was some sixty miles south of Nouvelle-Orléans, on the islands of Grand Terre and Grand Isle. No pilot who did not know the waters well could navigate the channel that led to the pirate city. It had been a continuous base for smugglers and pirates for over a century—Blackbeard himself had once taken refuge here.

Before Lafitte had taken it over, Barataria had been as wretched a hive of scum and villainy as the world could boast: under Lafitte's iron generalship, there was rule . . . of a sort.

I suppose I ought to be grateful for small favors, Louis thought gloomily. Certainly his circumstances had much improved from those that had obtained when he had awakened in the hold of the *Merchant's Luck.* Now he ate from china and crystal and slept between linens and silks. The library and the music room of Lafitte's grand mansion Chandeleur were both open to him, and when the *Pride of Barataria* was in port, he could often count on a game of chess with her master. Lafitte was an excellent and ruthless player, and Louis' own game had improved under Lafitte's harsh tutelage.

But this comfort and ease would last only until Lafitte found a buyer for him, for Louis was as much property as the chests of looted plunder that crowded the warehouses of Barataria, or the Africans smuggled in from the Sugar Islands, whose clandestine resale made such a large part of Lafitte's trade.

Louis supposed he ought to hold himself fortunate that Lafitte was not even considering England or France as a buyer, for in either case, Louis would already have been delivered up to a lifetime—short or long—in a cage. The Emperor Napoleon would execute him. King Henry would use him as a stick with which to beat the Grande Alliance. Either life would be as unsatisfactory as the underground existence he had fled in France.

However—and as the moment grew closer, Louis grew less philosophical about it—the idea of being delivered up to d'Charenton's mad lusts held even less charm than a full-dress execution[48] under the gentle auspices of Imperial France. They were very well informed here in Barataria, and Lafitte saw no reason to keep the news of what Nouvelle-Orléans had become from his captive's ears, so Louis was entirely aware of the fact that d'Charenton wanted him ardently and Lafitte was willing to supply him—or so he wished d'Charenton to believe. For the past several months, delicate negotiations between the Imperial Governor and the Pirate King had been taking place, though Lafitte was in no hurry to conclude them. Lafitte wanted more than the fleeting and untrustworthy gratitude of the Imperial Governor. Lafitte wanted to rule Louisianne in

---

48. Hanged, which is to say partially strangled on the gibbet; drawn—the intestines pulled out through a slit below the navel and then burnt before the victim's eyes; and quartered—each limb tied to the tail of a horse, and the four horses lashed to go in opposite directions. (This usually dislocates the joints, but the actual quartering is accomplished with an axe or saw.) The last full-dress execution for treason took place April 9, 1747, and the penalty was not abolished in England until 1821.

d'Charenton's place, and d'Charenton knew it. Only the utter unassailability of Grand Terre had protected him this long.

Louis stared moodily out through the library windows. Across the channel that separated Grand Terre from the mainland, a grove of cypress festooned with moss stood like silent bearded Druids. There was a flash of white as some bird Louis could not identify took wing, and the slanting late-afternoon light of autumn gave everything a honeyed glow.

Outside that window was everything Louis had once thought he ever wanted—the mystery and romance of the New World, the grace and culture of Royal France—the best of both worlds, here commingled and awaiting him.

He might as well have longed for the gardens of the Moon. Lafitte let Louis have free run of Chandeleur not because he was trusted . . . but because he was very well guarded. He got to his feet and walked over to the French doors. He reached for the handle.

"Don't." Robie spoke from his position by the fireplace.

The Dane was still dressed as he had been on the deck of the *Pride of Barataria*, all the way down to the pistol stuck through his blue silk sash. The only difference, perhaps, was that the moleskin breeches and calico shirt were clean and free of salt and oil, and that he wore a festive red ribbon at the end of his long cream-colored braid.

"Or you'll shoot me?" Louis asked, without turning. Ridiculous to have this clutch of fear from a boy so many years his junior, but the Dane was merciless.

"I won't have to," Robie said, sounding bored. "I have a knife, Frenchman. I'll nail your hand to the door."

"Captain Lafitte would not like it if I bled all over his woodwork," Louis said, striving for lightness. The boy terrified him, most of all because nothing in the universe seemed to frighten Robie.

"Wouldn't be the first time." The young pirate was unimpressed. "It comes out with a good scrubbing and another coat of paint."

Defeated—even in the small battle of getting the last word— Louis turned around.

Robie leaned against the edge of the pink marble fireplace, carved with nymphs and Tritons, that Lafitte had liberated from God knew where. His china-blue eyes were hooded, his expression sullen, but in all the weeks he'd been here, Louis had never once seen Robie smile. Robie did not want to be here, away from the *Pride of Barataria,* and blamed Louis for his presence on land. It made him an ill-tempered jailer.

"Do you want to go for a walk?" Louis asked at last. Within limits, he was also allowed the liberty of Chandeleur's grounds. No sane or prudent man would want to go down into Barataria itself with anything less than a brigade of guards, and Louis didn't think the exercise was worth it. In Barataria, he was just as likely to be killed by someone who didn't know who he was.

"Not today," Robie said. "The *Pride* got back first thing this morning, and Bos's going to be having visitors." "Bos" was the title that had been conferred on Lafitte by his felonious subjects.

"What visitors?" Louis asked. Robie just shrugged. Few things, so Louis had found, interested the boy particularly. Not reading, not music, and certainly not answering Louis' questions.

But there was little else to do with his time but ask them.

"Will Captain Lafitte be bringing his guests to dinner?"

A shrug.

"Will he be dining at home?"

Another shrug.

"Do you know that your hair's on fire?"

Robie snorted dourly. "You're getting bored, Frenchman. That's bad luck. You might get careless."

"I have you to defend me from such a fate," Louis answered irritably. He could bear the library no longer, and left the room.

Robie lounged after him, the boy's bare feet soundless on the wide-planked cypress floors of the great mansion. Louis did not have to look back to know he was there, for Robie was *always* there, as constant as his own shadow. He wandered aimlessly through the rooms, amazed as always that every stick of furniture, every candlestick and cream-pot he saw, had been pirate plunder. Lafitte might claim letters of marque from Cartagena or Spain or the Queen of the Gypsies, for all Louis cared—the man was a common pirate.

But such a successful one. . . .

That, Louis reminded himself, *is because he is both clever and ruthless. And if you wish to escape him and see Meriel again, you must be at least as clever, if not as ruthless.*

Dinnertime came and went without Lafitte, and Robie was in a worse—therefore more silent—mood than usual. Louis took that as his excuse to retire early, and went up to his room. Robie did not follow him inside. There was no need. The windows were covered with ornamental but still quite functional bars, and the room was searched every morning for anything Louis might have smuggled into it.

Not for the first time, Louis wished Sarah Cunningham were here with him, for with that resourceful lady's help he had managed to escape a trap far more intractable than this. But the one spark of hope he allowed himself to cherish was that Meriel had appealed for aid to Sarah, and that Sarah was with her. If Sarah were with Meriel, then Louis' wife was protected and safe. But he could expect no such intervention for himself.

Dejected, he flung himself down onto the bed, only to hear the unmistakable crackle of parchment when he did. Investigating the source, he found a message slipped beneath his counterpane.

Fear not, he read. The message was written in good Church Latin, a language even those pirates who could read were unlikely to know, the small words cramped together at the center of a large piece of brown parchment. *Help is at hand.*

It was unsigned, of course, but such messages often were. Louis crumpled it in his fist, and as he did so, he caught a faint scent of lemon. Frowning, he sniffed at the note. The scent was stronger.

Louis had been raised among conspirators, and his earliest memories were of secret messages exchanged by candlelight. The scent kindled old memories, and he rummaged about his rooms for a candle and some matches. Since the only thing he could do with them would be to set his rooms on fire, there was no reason not to allow him to have them.

With only a little work, he managed to light the candle, and then held the parchment up to the heat of the flame. As he had half hoped, more writing appeared, the pale brown letters written in Latin and lemon juice darkening with the heat.

Tonight when the stairwell clock strikes midnight, go to the door of your room. It will be unlocked. You must leave the house, and go to the small boat landing on the north side of Grand Terre, the one near the warehouse docks. Do not let anyone see you. I will come to you there and take you to a place of safety. Do not fear to be betrayed, for you will recognize me and know me without doubt for a friend. Burn this.

Louis instantly did as the note commanded, throwing the burning scrap of paper into the hearth and then scrubbing the ashes into dust. Undoubtedly someone would know something had been burnt here, but not before tomorrow morning—and by then, if the anonymous writer told the truth, Louis would be far from here.

He shook his head, suspicious by long habit and unable to believe his good fortune. It might be a trick—but why would Lafitte bother to trick him into anything? He was already wholly within the pirate chieftain's power. Lafitte needed no excuse to kill him, and no reason. He could do as he liked.

And there was the matter of the door. If it was not unlocked, the matter ended there.

Ah, but if it was. . . .

If it were open, and this turned out to be a long involved masquerade, he would be no worse off than he would be if Lafitte used him to bait d'Charenton into a trap. He had been too long a playing-piece not to have developed a certain detachment from his own life. When the last chime of the long-case clock echoed into silence, Louis rose, fully-dressed, from the bed, and tip-toed toward the door, shoes in hand. He tested the latch. The knob turned without impediment. He eased the door open.

The landing was empty and dark. There was no sign of Robie. Louis eased out into the corridor. Still no one. His spirits began to rise. Perhaps this would end happily.

Louis walked cautiously down the stairs, staying close to the edges of the treads to keep them from creaking. He crossed the broad marble floor of the foyer to the front door, moving carefully in the near darkness. It, too, was unlocked. Louis swung the door open the barest amount necessary for him to escape, and closed it again.

His eyes, adjusted to the lack of light inside, found the midnight world bright. He stopped to slip his shoes on at the gate, and walked quickly toward the north docks.

This was the most dangerous part of his escape, for he would be skirting the pirate-town, Barataria, itself. While Lafitte's personal charisma imposed a sort of draconian law upon the town and peace upon the grounds of Chandeleur itself, Barataria was a lawless, anarchic place whose bars, brothels, and gaming hells never closed. If Louis were caught there, not even the invocation of Lafitte's name could save him from the pirates' murderous whimsy.

As Louis came closer to the town, he heard snatches of music and the sound of breaking glass. The overpoweringly sweet scent of the lethal cane liquor brewed here filled the air, along with the constant smell of woodsmoke. Despite the blackout curtains that were supposed to hang over every window, the town blazed with light, making it easy for Louis to find his way. He stayed out of the light as much as he could, taking to the brush a couple of times to avoid parties of revelers.

The way they lived was foolish and strange, Louis reflected. Men took to piracy in order to gain wealth, and as soon as they obtained it they wasted it away in empty diversion. All their hard-earned gold went to fatten the purses of tavern-keepers, fences, and madams, and the pirate had no other choice but to return to his dangerous profession.

Soon the warehouses were in sight. They were padlocked at night, but not guarded—for all their bloodthirsty ways, there was a curious honor among pirates. Louis moved more carefully now, groping his way through the dark with only the light of the moon to guide him. A lone lantern hung at the end of the dock, and by its light, Louis could see a dark cloaked figure, standing as still and as awesome as Death himself.

Was *this* the man he was supposed to trust? Louis stopped, confused.

As he hesitated, the man at the end of the pier flung back his hood and lifted the lantern, holding it so that its light fell full upon his face.

Louis stared for a long moment, until memory awoke. This was the partner of the Duke of Wessex, the Polish hussar who had been with him during the escape at the chateau. As much as he trusted anyone, Louis knew he could trust Illya Koscuisko. He started forward, his hand raised in greeting.

Koscuisko turned to hang the lantern back on its hook.

Suddenly there was a thunderous rattle from behind both of them, as the door of the warehouse rolled open. The dock was flooded with light, revealing Louis, Koscuisko, and the small boat in which he had obviously planned to effect their escape in its merciless glare.

Louis whirled, squinting into the light.

"Hi," Robie said, leveling his pistol. "Missed me?"

Behind him stood Lafitte, one hand resting negligently upon the sabre at his hip, with four bully-bravos at his beck. The pirate king was dressed immaculately in buff-and-indigo evening dress, the red ribbon of an order he was probably not entitled to crossing his broad muscular chest. His thick dark hair was caught back in a blue velvet ribbon, and the heavy gold rings in his ears glittered. He wore diamonds from his cravat-pin to his slipper-buckles, and looked ornate and dangerous.

A trap? Looking at Koscuisko's face, Louis knew that the escape attempt had been genuine on Koscuisko's part, at least.

"I am master of all that takes place in Barataria," Lafitte said, smiling dangerously. "And now I am master of both of you."

"If it please the king," Koscuisko's voice rang out, steady and unafraid, "I should like to open negotiations for my life and my freedom."

Lafitte admired audacity; this Louis knew from experience. Koscuisko was playing his hand entirely right.

"Kill them both," Robie suggested hopefully.

Lafitte draped an arm about his protége's shoulders. "My dear boy, when will you learn to savor your pleasures in the proper order? First we will allow our impetuous friend to charm us with his foolishness, *then* we shall kill him. All things in their season, you know."

"I am not so foolish as all that," Koscuisko said, coming up to stand beside Louis. "I am, after all, authorized to treat with you as a sovereign power on behalf of King Henry of England. I can show you papers to that effect, if you won't shoot me."

"Forged," Robie said contemptuously.

"Perhaps," Lafitte said. "But as a privateer, I am a believer in a free market economy. We will allow M'sieur—or is it Mister . . . ?"

"It is, in fact, neither," Koscuisko answered. "I am Count Jerzy Illyavich Koscuisko, of His Majesty's Royal Mounted Hussars"—he bowed stiffly from the waist, bringing his heels together with a sharp click;—"and I think you will find that our interests can lead to mutually beneficial ends."

An hour later, Lafitte and his principal captains, René Béluche and Dominique You—both expatriate from the *Grande Armée*—sat across the long mahogany table from Koscuisko and Louis in Lafitte's private sanctum.

Louis had only seen this room once before. The chamber had no windows, and the walls were hung with red silk damask and set with mirrors. The floor was an elaborate mosaic of black and white tiles, set in a swirling pattern, and the ceiling was a jigsaw of mirrors that reflected back the light from the ornate brass and crystal chandelier and the sconces on the walls.

It was a room in which it would be very difficult to keep secrets, for the mirrors ensured that every side of every person there was visible at all times, and the lack of windows or vents made eavesdropping impossible. In this room there was no day or night, summer or winter.

"I'm not happy with you," Robie breathed in Louis' ear.

In the mirror behind Lafitte, Louis could see the reflection of himself and the young pirate who leaned over him. Robie had dragged one of the chairs over beside the door, but he hadn't seated himself, preferring instead to prowl the room like a panther with a toothache.

"I would rather not be here myself," Louis answered in a low voice. Robie gave an irritated snort and moved away.

"So, M'sieur le Comte. You affect to treat with me on behalf of England. You even show me papers—" here Lafitte gestured to the documents Koscuisko had produced, lying in a disorderly heap in the middle of the table "—that indicate you are indeed a clandestine envoy of the English King, with the ability to discuss treaty terms in his name. But it occurs to me to inquire what terms you think I might find of interest?"

"You do, indeed, have your kingdom here, Captain Lafitte. But it is threatened now by d'Charenton, and I think it will be more threatened every year. The *Albionaise* threaten you to the north and east, and though Spain is presently Louisianne's ally through her ties with France, that, too, might change, and then you would find yourself surrounded by enemies. And as you know, England is at war with France—and thus, with you."

"So I had heard," Lafitte answered with grave majesty. "And do you propose to end that war?"

"England proposes to end that war by winning it, and parading the tyrant Napoleon through the streets of his capital in chains," Koscuisko said, and for the first time, Louis heard a flash of true emotion in his words. "Meanwhile, she wishes economic stability restored here in the New World, by denying France access to its storehouse of wealth."

"You propose, in short, to make Louisianne another English province," Béluche said.

"King Henry proposes to make Louisianne an independent country allied to England," Koscuisko corrected him gently. "The only question that remains is—who is to rule it?"

"Not the only question," Lafitte answered, leaning forward. But Koscuisko had his attention. Louis could see it.

"Indeed. King Henry has one or two trifling requests to make of his new ally. Painless ones, of course."

"Of course," Lafitte answered, grinning wolfishly.

"King Henry would require that *Albionaise* goods move through the Port at no higher tariff than is imposed upon French or Spanish goods. And, of course, he would need the signature of the new ruler on Wilberforce's Pact."

"How will the plantations survive without slavery?" Lafitte asked.

"By paying their workers a living wage, just as the *Albionaise* planters now do. English mills will take all the cotton you can ship, as well as coffee, flax, and indigo at fair market prices. When the war is over, Continental markets will be open as well, and the Port of Nouvelle-Orléans is centrally located for both riverine and oceanic commerce. Your people will not starve."

"You paint a rosy picture of our future, M'sieur. But to do as you say means rebellion against a powerful Empire. Why should we turn against the Master of Europe? Why should Louisianne not simply remain loyal to France under her new master?"

"Because if the Corsican or his black dog, Talleyrand, has promised you Louisianne in exchange for fealty, I must tell you that Napoleon does not keep his promises. My country[49] has some experience of this, Captain; you must learn from our mistakes. By all reports you are a clever man—too clever to be taken in by this upstart Emperor. You need not trust the English King overmuch either, if Louisianne is master of her own fate. You can make your own way, in a wealthy country at peace with its neighbors, and with powerful friends in Europe."

"It is my experience, M'sieur le Comte, that those who revolt find themselves quickly without friends of any sort." Lafayette obviously considered the discussion at an end, but Koscuisko had not yet admitted defeat.

"This would not be the case . . . if Louisianne were in fact the true heir to Bourbon France," Koscuisko said, with an apologetic sideways glance toward Louis. "I am sorry, Louis. There is no other way."

So. In the end it comes to this. A great weariness settled over Louis. He had tried his utmost to outrun this fate, but it seemed it was to be his in the end.

"So *le pauvre petit* is who d'Charenton's dogs said he was? The King?" Strangely, there was a note of hope in Lafitte's voice, and his

---

49. Poland was partitioned out of existence in 1795 by Russia, Prussia, and Austria. The majority of the Poles fought for Napoleon in the vain hope that he would, as he promised, restore their country's independence. Of course, Napoleon never seriously considered doing so.

two generals leaned forward, gazing thunderstruck at Louis. Obviously, this was not news Lafitte had shared with them.

Koscuisko looked at Louis.

"I am my father's son," Louis said. "I am Louis-Charles de France, of the House of Bourbon."

"Oh, *terrific*," Robie said, from his post beside the door.

"Proof?" Lafitte said, almost reluctantly.

"Will you really need it?" Koscuisko asked.

"There is proof. Papers . . . depositions . . . jewels," Louis said. "The Abbé de Condé, my uncle, has them in safe keeping—he thought that—someday—I would wish to regain my throne. I can send for them, if I must. But the good Koscuisko is right. You don't need proof. Only a convincing figurehead." His voice was bitter.

"So. The little king does not wish to rule?" Lafitte asked archly.

"They killed my family." Louis looked straight into Lafitte's eyes. "They murdered my mother, my father, my sister . . . everyone I had ever known. Good people, blameless people, slaughtered like animals—and for what? For an *idea*. No, I don't want your damned blood-soaked crown. I swore I'd see its people in Hell before I ever took back the crown of France."

"Ah, but Your Majesty. The crown of Louisianne is a very different thing than that of France. In this New World we can build a new nation, out of the best of the old world and the best of our own hearts. Not a nation of Frenchmen or Spaniards, but a nation of free men, ruled by the best among them."

"A meritocracy needs no king," Louis reminded Lafitte sullenly.

"But a king needs counselors and ministers. And if any man may aspire to guide the King, will not the King be the best of them all?"

Louis smiled reluctantly, beguiled against his will by Lafitte's charisma. "In a kingdom where all men are welcome, and no man is a slave?"

"If it must be," Lafitte said, with a pretty show of capitulation on a point he must have known he would lose anyway. "No man is a slave aboard a privateer, and I think the law of the ocean should hold on land as well. But I regret. . . ." he paused, fixing both his captives with his burning black gaze, "that I cannot unilaterally agree to your pleasant proposal. I have allies who would be dismayed if I did not consult them. And I have yet to see what part England would play in this grand revolution. Will she send ships? Men?"

"If it must be accomplished by force, I will have nothing to do with it," Louis said quickly. "If Louisianne must be taken by force, you must look elsewhere for your puppet king."

"It is plain you do not know the present state of affairs in the city, *mon petit,* if you think you would be seen as anything but a savior. But come, M'sieur le Comte, it is time for some serious, as the English say, horse-trading. When I know what you have to offer us—in full detail—then I will consult my allies."

Wessex returned to consciousness reluctantly. As his senses returned, he continued to feign unconsciousness, while gaining all the information about his surroundings that he could.

It was day. He could feel the sun on his face, and the breeze that ruffled his hair suggested that he was outdoors. His arms were stretched behind him, tied, perhaps, about the trunk of a tree. Wessex tugged at his wrists and discovered himself securely bound. The back of his head ached burningly, mute testimony to its meeting with an immovable object somewhere there in the darkness of the swamp, and his feet were bare.

Never use magic where a bludgeon will do, one of his tutors had once told him in the long-ago, and it seemed that adherence to that particular piece of advice was universal. Certainly his captors had taken it to heart. Whoever they were.

Escape would be no quick and easy matter, and his struggles would undoubtedly be noticed long before he had freed himself. There was nothing more to be gained from shamming sleep, and so Wessex opened his eyes.

He was sitting on the ground against a tree somewhere deep in the bayou west of Lake Pontchartrain, on one of the natural levees this area abounded in. His coat, vest, hat, sword, and boots were gone, and with them his store of weapons. Off to his left, he could see a stretch of open water, its surface mirror-still. Enormous trees grew up out of the water as if they were the tent-poles of heaven.

Escape from this place would be impossible without a boat . . . and a map.

As his senses cleared further, he could hear sounds behind him; the normal clatter of a small enclave or encampment of perhaps twenty people. Wessex spared a moment to hope that he had become the prey of ordinary smugglers or outlaws. He would back himself to talk his way out of such a situation alive. If, on the other hand, these people were connected with the dancers he'd seen in the bad-lands last night . . .

"Hello, scrawny li'l w'ite man," a deep voice boomed. Its owner walked into his line of vision, and Wessex was hard-pressed not to show his astonishment.

It was a woman—a coal-black woman nearly seven feet tall, mus-cled like a young bull. Her skin was the true ink-black of the pure-blooded African strain and her white tignon was festooned with a cluster of bright red turkey-feathers. She wore a man's red flannel shirt and a necklace of amber beads that hung down past her waist. Her blue broadcloth skirt was hitched up almost to her knees, and her enormous feet were bare. Gold bracelets sparkled on her wrists and she wore immense gold rings in her ears, and when she smiled, she exposed teeth as white and strong as a wolf's.

"I be Annie Chris'mas, de na'chural dau'tah ob de typhoon an de lightnin'-quake. I kin out-fight, out-drink, and out-work any man on de Rivah, an' alla my chirruns is kings an' queens. I kin see sper-ruts an' ha'ants an' I know where de mandrake an' de nigh'shade grow. Alligator fear me, copperhead fear me, an' you do well to fear me, l'il w'ite man, c'oz I wring you' neck lak a chicken an' pop you in my iron pot to cook, I do'an lak what you say to me."[50]

---

50. Annie Christmas is a real unreal person, though she may have been inspired by a real woman. Curiously, she appears in both white and black folktales; in one, as a riverboatwoman who could outdrink, outwork, and outfight any man on the river. Her black incarnation is considerably more fabulous, granting her twelve coal-black sons born at a single birth, and a celebrated funeral involving a black hearse with black horses, and a black barge which floated her body out to sea, never to be seen again. For the purposes of this book, I have conflated Annie Christmas's two aspects into one character.

Wessex regarded her imperturbably from his position of submission. "Good afternoon, Mrs. Christmas. I am the Duke of Wessex. Perhaps you would be good enough to untie me, so that we might converse in a civilized fashion?"

The gigantic Negress threw back her head and roared with laughter. "I be Annie Chris'mas, Dook, not her Missus—ain' nobody on de Rivah do'an know me an' mine. But 'cep'n you, mebbe. Dat'll change, w'ite boy, before you sees Jesus."

The immense Amazon folded her arms and regarded Wessex through heavy-lidded eyes. So might a tigress turned human mercilessly regard her prey.

"W'at you doin' on de bayou, w'ite boy?" she asked. "W'at you doin' spyin' on us?"

Wessex had never felt himself at quite so much of a disadvantage. Obviously the woman wanted to make sure of him, and Wessex had no idea of how much she already knew, or even in which direction her interests lay. He had no recourse but to stick close to the truth and make a great play of his innocence.

"I am a guest at one of the houses near here. I went out for an evening stroll and lost my way, then I heard the drums. Believe me, I had no desire to trespass on any of your local . . . observances."

"*Voudou Magnian* be de judge o' dat, Dook. He be callin' you to him, wif de gris-gris we put agains' our enemies. Hey you! Caesar! Remy! You come 'long now."

At Annie's shout, two well-muscled swamp-rats, one white, one black, appeared. Wessex noted, with a faint pang of distress, that one of them was holding a long coil of rope.

"Remy, you get dat rope up ovah a branch. We string him up a li'l, den we ax him again."

Remy grinned widely at the thought, but the one called Caesar looked troubled.

"Dis a real fancy w'ite man, Annie. Maybe dey pay down in de Town to gets him back. When Cha—I mean Momus—gets back, we coulds ax him."

"Maybe an' maybe! An' maybe he a spy fo' dat black snake in de City! I'se ketched him, I gets ter kills him. He doan be tellin' nobody nothin' den."

Caesar moved around behind the tree to cut the ropes which bound Wessex, while Remy turned away, hefting the coil of rope in his hands.

From an impartial point of view, Wessex did have to admit that Annie Christmas' approach had the virtues of caution and simplicity, little though it recommended itself to him just at this moment. Once his hands were freed, Wessex thrust himself to his feet, thinking of nothing but seizing whatever opportunity Fortune presented to escape. To his surprise, neither Caesar nor Remy tried to stop him. Remy glanced casually over his shoulder, saw Wessex free, and went back to his attempts to sling the rope over a sturdy branch, as Annie Christmas came forward in a wrestler's crouch, her enormous muscled arms outstretched.

"Come on, Dook," she crooned. "Dance wid Annie."

In that moment Wessex decided that taking his chances with the alligators and swimming for it would be a better choice than wrestling this black Amazon, but it was not one he was allowed to make. With lightning quickness Annie rushed forward.

Wessex struck first, a blow that would have stunned a man and felled an ordinary woman. Annie grunted as his fist struck her, but then seized him by the arm and pulled him toward her. Wessex lashed out with his stockinged feet—desperate to do anything rather than be enfolded in that destructive grip—but he might as well have been a child, for all the reaction Annie Christmas showed to his blows. She crushed him against her in a brutal embrace.

"Doan wants ter hurts you, w'ite boy. Annie wants you ter stay nice an pretty fo' de hangin'."

Wessex struggled for air and could not breathe. The world went grey about him, and slowly, without conscious volition, he ceased to struggle. He was still aware, but the world seemed far away and unimportant. In that moment, Annie spun him around in her grasp, holding him with his arms twisted up behind him as Wessex gasped for breath. His feet did not touch the ground as she walked over to the place she had chosen.

"Get to it, Remy, yo' lazy scoun'rel. An you, Caesar, you keep hol' o' dat tail o' rope."

Wessex felt the rope settle around his neck, but before he could react, he was pulled from his feet by the noose about his throat. He grabbed it—Annie had neglected to tie his hands behind him—and tried to ease the pressure about his throat, but the noose was made, not as a proper hangman's noose, but as a slipknot, and it had pulled tight, choking him. As Annie took over the rope, Wessex was hauled twenty feet into the air, still laboring to force his fingers between the rope and his throat.

"Annie Christmas! What you doin' dere, girl?"

Dimly, against the thundering of blood through his veins, Wessex heard the outraged bellow. Suddenly the rope went slack, and Wessex plunged to the ground to land with a jarring thud. Half-strangled, he rolled to his knees and worried the rope over his head, flinging it as far from him as he could. Then he could do nothing other than drag the breath into burning lungs for a few moments.

"Oh, dis jus' keep gettin' better an' better," a familiar voice said mournfully from above him.

Wessex looked up and met Gambit Corday's eyes.

The volatile Acadian who had spared his life once before looked as if he had aged twenty years, not two, since the last time Wessex had seen him. Charles Corday had been an assassin in the pay of France, and had dressed like an apprentice ratcatcher. Now he dressed in the first stare of fashion, from his bottle-green wasp-waisted coat to his striped silk waistcoat and white-topped high-heeled riding boots.

"What you doin' here, cher?" Corday asked.

"Taking the air," Wessex answered. His voice was a rasp, and he coughed with the effort of speech.

Corday reached out a hand to him, and with its help, Wessex gained his feet.

"Girl, what you got to say for yo'self?" Corday demanded of Annie. Her former compatriots were nowhere to be seen, and Corday seemed completely unafraid of the enormous woman.

"We foun' him at de *Voudou Magnian*, an he din't give no good account of hisse'f," Annie said. "So I t'inks I string him up a li'l."

Corday gazed from Annie to Wessex, obviously unable to decide whether to laugh or cry. "Well, dat a good t'ought, *p'tit*. But I know dis man, an' he doan be talkin' to jus' anybody who romance him, no. I take him along an' hear what he have to say, eh?"

With an arm about Wessex's shoulders—as much as a show of
favor as for support—Corday turned him and walked toward the
encampment whose presence Wessex had only guessed at. It was an
interesting sight—a jumble of tents and shanties, all carefully cam-
ouflaged to be invisible from any distance, and the tent that Corday
chose as their destination was seen to be uncommonly well appointed
once Wessex gained its interior. It looked, in fact, remarkably like
the tent of a field commander, including the detailed map pinned to
the center of the table. Wessex glanced at it—it was a map of
Nouvelle-Orléans and the surrounding plantations, and there were
colored pins and flags studding its surface.

"Here. Drink dis." Corday shoved a glass of whiskey into Wessex's hand. The Duke drank gratefully, coughing this time only a
little. He handed the glass back to Corday and seated himself in a
chair.

"I'm surprise' your partner didn't rescue you. Though I don' t'ink
a bullet could kill Annie. She tough, her."

Corday's English improved as he regained his composure, but
his casual reference to Koscuisko did little to quiet Wessex's nerves.

"Your fortunes, at least, seem to have improved since I saw you
last," Wessex said, nodding toward Corday's coat.

"Hahn. Dis t'ing," Corday said in disgust. "I 'ave move up in de
worl' since I see you last, Your Grace. I am now de Governor of
Nouvelle-Orléans' private secretary, me."

"You?" Wessex said, unable to conceal his surprise.

Corday made a rueful face and pushed his unruly auburn hair
out of his eyes. "De Black Pope mak' me do dis, so he t'ink. 'Charenton, devil damn him to hell, t'ink I just—" Corday spread his
hands, at a loss for the proper word. "—nobody. So he use me for
his plans, an' tak me into his confidence, him, an' I t'ink my soul
nevair be clean again."

"You're the last person I'd expect to hear talking about a clean
soul, Corday," Wessex mocked. "How many men have you killed?"

"No' so many more den you, Your Grace." Gambit flung himself
into a chair with untidy grace, pouring himself a generous measure
of the whiskey before pushing the bottle toward his guest. "So. Ask

me w'at dat white spider's plans are, you. Dat why you follow me here from de Clouds, hahn? I should 'ave known you would be close by. But you are a fool to follow de drums, cher, and dat's de trut'."

Obviously Corday believed that he and Koscuisko were working together, and that he had fallen prey to some terribly clever plan of theirs. Wessex had no desire to disabuse him of this error.

"So you are working for the White Tower these days, Corday? It's a dangerous double game," Wessex said. The compassion in his voice was feigned, but there was real pity behind it, for a man who had worked closely with the Duc d'Charenton for so many months.

"No' for de Wite Tower, Your Grace. I do dis for La Belle Louisianne." Corday drank the whiskey down as if it were well-water, and after a moment he seemed to breathe easier.

"You wonder why Bonaparte send 'Charenton here, you—but us, we wonder why 'Charenton come, eh? W'at is it here dat he want so bad? Den we figure, he lookin' for de King—de true King. Only dat ain't it. Or not all of it."

"Louis," Wessex said. But Corday did not seem to hear.

"So I come wid him. Talleyran', he t'ink I wan' to come because I get de chance to settle old scores, hahn? But I got no old scores to settle, me, excep' wid France an' Englan'. La Belle Louisianne mus' be free, an' we mus' be free to stay wid her."

"The Acadians," Wessex said, realization dawning. "You're working for the Free Acadians."

"W'at you t'ink, I do dis for my healt'?" Corday demanded crossly. "No. All dis time, nobody can agree w'at to do, but if we 'ave de true King, we form an alliance an' t'row de Tyran' out. Cajun, Creole, Frenchman, Baratarian, dere's lan' enough here for all to live free."

Almost a century ago Acadia, a French colony on the coast of Prince Rupert's Land, had passed from French into English hands. The French inhabitants had been dispossessed by the Scots settlers, and forced from their homeland south into French-held Louisianne. Wessex knew that the Acadians still mourned their lost homeland. That loss would make them even more unwilling to be dispossessed again. Wessex smiled thinly. Here was a feast of information, though gaining it had obviously cost Corday dearly. Yet though Wessex was willing to bet Corday was telling all he knew, Corday had mentioned only Louis Capet, and not the Grail.

"True—if you can find Louis, and if Louisianne will rise up in support of him. But revolution is a tricky business, as the French have learned to their cost."

Corday groaned, holding his head and resting his elbows on the table. "It all come to bits, Your Grace. 'Charenton want de true King, an' he t'ink he can get him. But he wan' him dead, him—he got some crazy notion he can be king here, an' rule over de lan'. An' dere somet'in' else he won' tell me, eh? Somet'in' he plannin' fo' All Souls Eve."

"October 31." The eve of All Souls Day was supposed to be one of the two great nights of power in the year—but did the Old World's rules of magic hold true in the new?

"Somet'in' big. Somet'in' he t'ink even I do'an put up wid, me," Corday said bitterly.

Wessex shot Corday an appraising glance. He'd always known the Acadian as a cool emotionless killer, technically expert and un-involved—not a political, but a dependable assassin. For years, Corday had eliminated the enemies of Imperial France as passionlessly as a skilled gardener pruned his garden, making his kill and then vanishing like smoke. That he'd been caught at Mooncoign two years ago had been due to a stroke of unexpected fortune for England, not the result of Corday's lack of skill. Despite rigorous questioning afterward by the White Tower, Corday had given up none of his secrets, and an exchange of hostages must have been arranged, for Wessex had next encountered Corday in Denmark.

But in Denmark, Corday had not been working for France's interests, but—Wessex now realized—Louisianne's.

"This is why you did it, isn't it?" Wessex said quietly. "It was all for this."

Corday shook his head, protesting the necessity even as he confirmed Wessex's guess.

"He knew, de Black Pope. Allus playin' bot' side agains' de middle. He been plannin' t'ings so Louisianne rise up an' cas' dat tyran' out; so he have de rat-hole to slide into if de Gran' Alliance win. But if he do dat, what happen to de Aca'juns, eh? Dis our homeland now,

an' we doan be movin' again, *cher*, no." Corday poured himself another glass of whiskey. It was his third, but the Acadian didn't seem
in the least impaired, only now his hand had stopped shaking when
he poured.

"So Talleyrand sent you to Louisianne, knowing you would do
all you could to topple d'Charenton and save him the trouble since
you wanted Louisianne for your own. But what he didn't know was
that you weren't working alone," Wessex said, as the last piece of the
puzzle fell into place in his mind.

"Nevair. From de firs', I work for Acadia. What do we care if I
kill Englishmen, hahn? But den, we hear dat de Los' King is alive."

"And you hoped that he would depose Napoleon, uniting Louisianne and France before the Bourbon throne once more."

"But he vanish again," Corday said with a sad smile. "An' de
Corsican give us 'Charenton."

"A blessing in disguise," Wessex pointed out, "as his presence
will unite those who wish a free and independent Louisianne as nothing else would."

"But we 'ave no leader. Dere is no one anyone can agree on to
lead us but de Bourbon heir, an' Triton 'ave him. Bein' united do'an
do us any good if 'Charenton kill us all firs'. So now I 'ave said
enough. Now is de time for you to talk, Your Grace. Tell me w'at
de W'ite Tower will do for La Belle Louisianne, an' what she want'
in return. If you 'ave brought us a *sorcier* to deal wid 'Charenton, I
'ave not seen him, me."

So Louis was dead, for Corday's remark about Triton surely
meant that the boy had drowned. Wessex put the thought aside,
another thing he would not think about until he reached a less-
volatile refuge. For now, he pondered the other things Corday had
told him. That Corday was willing to stand his ally at the moment
was unexpected *lagniappe,* as the Acadians would have it.

"I'm afraid you will have to apply to the good Koscuisko for your
particulars, Corday," Wessex lied suavely. "They are not a part of
why I came here. I have urgent business in Nouvelle-Orléans."

There was a long moment while Corday decided whether to accept this. But in the end he did, because like it or not, Corday
courted England precisely because he did *not* want Louisianne to

become another part of New Albion. Corday would do whatever he must to keep his people from being cast out of their homeland a second time, and Wessex found a grudging sort of respect for the Acadian's devotion, if not his methods.

"I mus' be back dere by noon tomorrow," Corday said, and the lines of pain about his mouth deepened at the thought. "I tak' you den, so you do'an catch Annie's eye again, neh? 'Charenton t'inks I 'ave a *cher-amie* on one of de plantations here."

"The Clouds, I presume?" Wessex asked.

Corday nodded. A mythical sweetheart was a good cover for Corday's frequent journeys into the bayou, and the enigmatic Rhettler Baronner could undoubtedly be called upon to endorse any alibis that might be needed.

"But for now, Your Grace, we got to get you prettied up, hahn?" Corday said, with a ghost of his past gay recklessness. "You frighten de ladies, *cher*, you go into Town lookin' like dat."

Corday was as good as his word, providing Wessex with dinner, a bed, and fresh clothes. He had even managed to recover a few of Wessex's personal effects from the others in the camp, so the Duke rejoiced in the possession of his own boots—their secret freight of gold doubloons still concealed—and his rapier.

But the rest—his knives and pistols, his compass, his garotte, and his incidental jewelry, were gone. Such losses happened in the field, and Wessex held them to be of little account. It was enough for the moment that he was shaved and dressed and out of the hands of the homicidal giantess Annie Christmas.

Good manners dictated that he not try to see more of his hosts than absolutely necessary, so Wessex remained inside the tent. Corday brought him dinner—a spicy local stew he called *jambalaya*,[51]

---

51. Since no book set in New Orleans is complete without a discussion of the food, I should mention here that there are as many recipes for jambalaya (a cousin of the Spanish dish *paella*) as there are Orleannais. A good selection can be found at http://www.gumbopages.com/food/jambalaya.html

Bon appetit!

which seemed to Wessex to consist mainly of sausage and fire—but did not eat himself. He had finished the first bottle of whiskey earlier and was halfway through the second, still without its seeming to have any particular effect upon him.

"Is it so bad?" Wessex asked at last. If it was compassion that motivated him, it was the detached compassion of a craftsman for his tools. Corday was his passport out of here, as well as a vital link in the Rebellion's plans. He could not be allowed to destroy himself now.

"I 'ave seen evil." Corday spoke in the local French patois he must have learned as a child, his voice so low that Wessex had to strain to hear him. Corday did not meet the Duke's eyes as he spoke, but gazed off into nothingness as if he saw visions there. "I 'ave seen monsters—an' done dere work, too. I 'ave killed innocent men. I 'ave killed women, me. But I did not *play* wit' dem!" The last words came out in a strained whisper, as if Corday had finally mustered up the courage to speak of unspeakable things.

"Charenton, he is *un amateur*—an amateur. It is all for fun, what he does, for sport. Dey die, cher, to amuse him, an' he try . . . he try to make ot'ers like himself. Children. De Mam'selle Delphine. . . ." Corday stopped speaking abruptly, his voice catching on something suspiciously like a sob. After a long pause, he spoke again. "If I could, I would kill him myself, me. But I canno' risk de lives of de ones who follow me. I will no' give anyone to him in dis life or de nex'."

It was the ultimate dilemma of the deep cover agent. How did one keep his soul safe while presenting an acquiescent face and a studied mask to all manner of horrors? Wessex knew of, and had known, men and women who had been forced by the highest sort of altruism to do things against which they rebelled as much as Corday did against being made d'Charenton's *intime*. The effort destroyed them all if they left escape from their double role too late.

"No," Wessex said. "You won't have to." A decision he couldn't remember having made presented itself to him with the inevitability of the only clear choice. D'Charenton would have the answers that Wessex sought, and so Wessex must seek him out to discover where

Meriel and Sarah were. Killing him would be act of virtue. "Don't worry, Gambit. This death's on me."

And more than ever before, Wessex was determined that it would be his farewell performance on the chessboard of the Shadow Game.

11

The Shortest Way to Hades
(Nouvelle-Orléans and Vicinity, October 1807)

The deliberations at Chandeleur went on for another couple of hours, but they were now between Lafitte and his pirate captains. Illya and Louis were left to their own devices elsewhere in the house, with Robie in attendance.

"So, you will make a king of me yet," Louis said. He was striving for a light tone, but he could not conceal the bitterness in his voice. Lafitte might try to make it all seem like an exciting social experiment, but his flattery could not disguise the fact that these were the same gilded shackles that Louis had fought against all his life.

"For what it's worth, I'm sorry," Illya said. "This seems to be my month for persuading people to do things against their better judgment. But I don't see any other way out. Do you? You are the one thing all the factions can unite behind—the True King."

"A king must be trained in kingship. He must . . . know the land, and all its people. I know nothing of those things," Louis pointed out. He could remember no other life than that of a pawn in hiding— a poor beginning, he thought, for kingship.

"I don't think they will matter for the sort of thing Lafitte has in mind," Koscuisko said absently. "The important thing is—can you kill a man?"

Louis stared at Koscuisko in astonishment. Behind him, he heard Robie snort derisively.

"I . . . you want me to kill Lafitte?"

Koscuisko shook his head quickly. "Not him. Someone has to kill the Imperial Governor, you see, and the fellow who was supposed to do it has turned up missing. Very awkward, but what would you? And d'Charenton is a sorcerer, so . . ."

"So only an aristocrat or a prince of the Church can slay him without harm," Louis finished. "Ah, well. At one point I was to have taken Holy Orders, so I suppose. . . ."

"Killing a man isn't hard," Robie said contemptuously. "Half the men and two-thirds of the women in Barataria would do it for a dixie[52] and a bottle of rum, and they wouldn't much care if they died of it."

"If it were that alone, it would be a simple matter," Koscuisko said. "But there is a power in *l'art magie,* and especially in diabolism, which does not die with its wielder. It strikes back at the slayer of an adept, but unfortunately, that is not all it does. It . . . well, it takes on a separate life."

"A *duppy,*" Robie breathed, and for the first time Louis saw actual fear in his eyes. Sailors were a notoriously superstitious lot, and feared the spirit world far more than their land-dwelling counterparts did.

"Yes, if you like. It has much the aspect of a ghost, a sort of artificial elemental. And I should not wish to free that which has been bred in d'Charenton's soul to walk free of the bonds of flesh, not even if I were to put an ocean between us. So he must be killed by a man who is more than a man; one of royal blood."

Louis swallowed. He had assisted at more than one exorcism

---

52. A ten-dollar bill in circulation in New Orleans in 1807. The one in our world was printed in English and French. In French, the word for ten is *dix,* thus the note became known as a "dixie." The name became transferred to the city, and eventually, via the song, to the entire American South.

while living beneath his uncle's roof, and knew the truth in Koscuisko's words. But though he had been a hunted prize all his life, he had never killed a man—certainly he had not executed one in cold blood. He wasn't sure he could.

His face must have showed his thoughts, for Robie turned away from him in disgust.

"What about you? You could do it yourself—or is that business of you being a count just another taradiddle?" Robie asked contemptuously, turning to Koscuisko.

"In Poland we elect our kings. Our relationship to the land-spirits which confer royalty is not . . . sufficiently similar to what is done in the West for me to be certain that I could kill him effectively," Koscuisko said, unembarrassed by the admission. "And I think the stakes are too high in this case to risk the experiment."

"I will do what you ask of me," Louis said. "If I can." He thought—not for the first time—of Meriel, and wondered if Koscuisko had any news of her. Not knowing what had become of his wife was a constant dull grief—and one he would not parade before Robie or any of the other pirates. His questions could wait until he had some privacy in which to ask them.

As the sky began to lighten, a servant came to bid them come to breakfast. They followed her into the dining room. The sideboard was lavishly laden with covered silver chafing dishes—the sight of them, if not the hour at which they were presented, was familiar to Louis. The three of them were the only diners, apparently.

"The condemned man?" Koscuisko offered, gesturing toward the table.

"I suppose we should eat while we can," Louis answered. Robie was already filling a plate, ignoring them both.

Lafitte entered as they were finishing breakfast.

"And now, the preliminaries being accomplished, it is time for M'sieur le Comte *et moi* to pay a social call upon my brothers in this great adventure. I am desolate not to be able to include you, *mon pauvre petit,* but it is much better for us all if you remain safe and well here in my little snuggery."

"So I am to go back to my kennel?" Louis asked, with an acid punctilio Illya had not heard from him before.

"Until I call for you," Lafitte answered, meeting his eyes. There was a silent clash of wills—king-regnant and king-to-be—that made Illya hold his breath, but Louis capitulated, as he must.

"Then I will be in my room, catching up on my sleep. Come, Robie. You would not wish to misplace me again." Louis pushed himself to his feet and walked quickly from the room. Robie, who had not finished eating, flung down his fork and hurriedly followed.

"Perhaps someday you will tell me how you overpowered my young watchdog long enough to lock him in the cellar," Lafitte said to Illya when the others were gone.

"I am saving that story to beguile a long dull evening," Illya answered gravely. "Is it too forward of me to ask where we are going?" he added, after a pause.

"To visit an acquaintance of mine who will know better than I how things stand in Nouvelle-Orléans. And to present King Henry's gracious proposal to him, so that he may make it known in the proper quarters."

"After which Louis and I go free?" Illya suggested.

"After which, we determine when we will strike," Lafitte corrected him silkily. "Once Louis is crowned, and Louisianne liberated, we will see."

There was a proverb about riding a tiger, and though Illya could not remember its precise wording, he knew that tiger-riding wasn't considered a gateway to a long and healthy life. Unfortunately, he had no choice. Having been forced to make his offer of England's support to Lafitte instead of to Momus' people, he must take what came.

And hope he returned alive from riding the tiger.

The first part of their journey was accomplished aboard the *Pride of Barataria,* which today flew the colors of Imperial France and kept a sharp watch out for any of the ships of Bonaparte's navy. Though the little fleet could not be everywhere, Admiral Bonaparte's patrols had cut severely into the privateer activity in the Gulf, or so Illya gathered from the talk among the sailors on deck. After an hour or so under sail, the *Pride* put in at a sheltered inlet, and Illya, Lafitte, and four crewmen proceeded by ship's boat into the bayou.

It was eerily quiet, for once they were off the open water, the enormous cypress trees with their freight of hanging moss tended to muffle sounds. Distances were deceptive here; Illya was willing to bet that he was not more than ten miles from The Clouds, though the landscape seemed that of another world entirely.

"If Momus is not there, he can be sent for. I know of no other way to reach him. If he wants me, he goes to a certain shop in Royal Street and leaves a message for me to meet him. If I want him, I go to a certain fishing camp on the levee that is a refuge from Imperial justice. It is a game for boys. He is Momus. I am Triton. It amuses—and perhaps it is a safer thing than to have our names run free to reach d'Charenton's ears."

"Do you know who Momus is?" Illya said, unable to keep the shock from his voice.

"Of course not. He wears a mask, as do I," Lafitte spoke as to a backward child. "You have met him, I think. Do you?"

Illya did not answer.

The new day's beginning made the horrors and excesses of the old seem faintly unreal. Wessex rose at an early hour, dressed, and shaved himself once more with Corday's razors. A young mulatto girl brought him strong chicory-laced coffee and a plate of hot fragrant beignets.

As he ate, he became aware of a sudden undercurrent of excitement running through the camp. It was not the sudden shouting of men under attack—had he heard that, Wessex would have taken his chances on a lone escape. It was more as if some sudden news had come, and a moment later Corday entered the tent to confirm Wessex' guess.

"Bad news, Your Grace. We do no' depar' at once, eh? Triton is comin' to call—an' he would no' do dat if dere were no' somet'ing importan' he 'ad to say to me, hahn? So we mus' wait until he comes."

"Triton has the Bourbon heir." When Corday had said that last night, Wessex had assumed he meant that Louis was dead. But if it were only a code-name. . . .

"Triton is a man? You mean King Louis is alive?" Wessex asked incredulously.

Corday stared at him, looking faintly surprised that Wessex had ever thought otherwise. "Of course. He 'as been hostage in Barataria since de spring, de Young King. But Lafitte will no' give him up for asking, eh, an' I canno' take him. But I console myself, me, dat if I canno' take him from dere, 'Charenton canno' do so eit'er. De two o' dem 'ave bargain' for mont's, an' so long as dey do, de Young King is safe."

"If d'Charenton sent one dispatch to France with this information, Napoleon would send a fleet that even the King of the Gulf could not turn aside," Wessex pointed out.

"He will no' do dat. He wan' de Young King for himse'f. De Black Pope no' like dat, if he knew," Corday said with a ghost of his old playfulness. "But who will tell him, eh? Not I."

So one of Talleyrand's blades had finally turned and cut his hand. Wessex could not entirely suppress a smile at the thought. Corday was Talleyrand's creature no longer. He flew free of his master's hand at last, playing his own game for his own reasons, and Wessex was surprised to find how much he envied him.

"Very well. We wait. I've never met a god of the sea before."

An hour later Triton and his delegation entered the camp.

For this meeting, oddly enough, Corday donned a mask. It was of gilded leather, and covered his face completely, giving his voice a spectral echo. He offered Wessex a loo-mask of black silk: "You ne-vair know when you meet old frien's, Your Grace," and Wessex had put it on, tying the strings behind his head. A poor disguise, but unexpectedness was the best disguise of all.

Wessex walked out of the tent, following Corday. The other delegation was already on land—their leader, who must be supposed to be Triton, was wearing a mask of green silk that covered half his face. Its eyeholes were rimmed in gold embroidery, and the rest of his costume was of a piece with the mask—elaborate, dandified finery. Wessex supposed this must be one of Lafitte's high-ranked lieutenants. With him—suddenly Wessex was glad of the mask—was Illya Koscuisko.

This was an unwelcome surprise—and not for Wessex alone, to judge by the way Corday recoiled.

"I'm sorry not to be properly dressed for the occasion, but it didn't occur to me that I'd be needing a mask this long before Lent,[53]" Koscuisko said, seeing Corday and Wessex. "How nice to see you again, M'sieur Momus."

So Koscuisko had met Momus before? Interesting. It lent a certain unnecessary corroboration to Corday's tacit claim to be leader of the Free Acadians.

"Why 'ave you come?" Corday/Momus demanded unceremoniously of Triton.

"For the pleasure of your company," Triton responded, with a deep mocking bow. "And I suggest that you hear what I have to say in private."

Corday glanced around. There were half a dozen of his lieutenants watching with open interest, and more of his men gathered nearby, trying to watch without seeming to.

"Come wid me, den," he said, motioning toward his tent.

"Go back to the boat and wait for us," Triton told his sailors. "And if any of you is drunk when I return, he can resign himself to swimming home."

Without waiting to see how he was obeyed, Triton strode ahead to Corday's tent. Corday followed, but Wessex dropped back to walk beside Koscuisko. He knew a mask and a borrowed suit of clothes wouldn't deceive his partner for long, and could see no value in continuing the masquerade.

"As you see, I thought I'd look up old friends," he said in a low voice.

---

53. Illya is referring, of course, to Mardi Gras, also called Carnivale, or "farewell to the flesh," a festival of riotous self-indulgence (and masks) that marks the beginning of the forty days of Lenten abstinence which precedes Easter in the Catholic faith.

"How charming. Momus is Corday," Koscuisko answered without missing a beat.

"And Triton?"

"Lafitte."

"Does he have Louis?"

"Yes. And—" But Koscuisko could say no more, for they had reached the tent.

Momus and Triton were seated on either side of the long table, the map of Nouvelle-Orléans between them. As the symbol stood, so stood the reality. Lafitte could control the Gulf. Corday could rally the city. Neither man had the power to take or hold Louisianne alone.

Corday sat back and gestured to Lafitte to refresh himself. There were bottles of whiskey, rum, and brandy on the table, this last direct from French cellars.

"I 'ave not a great deal of time, Triton," Corday said. "I mus' be back in de city by noon."

"I have come to place a proposition before you," Lafitte said smoothly. "We shall throw off the yoke of France, free the slaves as the English do, and open the Port to English shipping."

Corday stared at him for a moment and then began to laugh, the sound echoing from the grimacing burnished mask he wore.

"Oh, cher, you are too kind, to come all dis way to cheer me so," he said at last. "Now, why 'ave you truly come?"

"Recently, I had the good fortune to entertain an emissary of King Henry of England," Lafitte said.

Corday started to look at Wessex, then stopped himself. He looked instead at Koscuisko, the mask impassive. "And?"

"Count Koscuisko suggests that the King will back Louisianne as an independent nation, providing only that we end slavery and open the Port to English goods. As a member of the Grande Alliance, we will be entitled to call upon England's help if the Emperor should decide to contest the issue."

"De people will fight," Corday warned.

"To keep d'Charenton? You surprise me. What we hear in Barataria is bad enough. The reality must be worse."

"Who will lead dis new Louisianne? Will Lafitte give up Louis to be her king?" Corday asked stubbornly. "De Sons o' de Sun deman' a king, an' de Acadians will accept one, so long as he does no' rule absolutely. De Creoles will accep' dat too, I t'ink, if dey are promised a say in t'ings."

"And what of Lafitte?" Triton asked archly. "What do you think he should get for giving up his rich prize?"

Sitting beside Corday, Wessex had the sudden notion that Corday knew very well who was behind the mask of Triton. These identities were a legal fiction between them, nothing more.

"He can 'ave a pardon for himself an' his men, lettairs of marque agains' France an' her allies, and to be Firs' Minister—if he can deliver de King alive. My people will agree to dis."

"It has taken you long enough to become reasonable," Triton said.

"I 'ave seen worse den pirates, *cher*. An' I do no' care who rules La Belle Louisianne, so long as Acadia remains a part of her. Yes. I will make dem accep' it."

"Do you think this can work?" Lafitte asked, and suddenly the artifice, the pretence, were gone from his voice. He leaned across the table and stared into his opposite's eyes.

Corday reached up and slipped the mask from his face, laying it down on the table.

"Yes, Jean. I t'ink it can work. Let me send messengers to de cells of de ot'er groups an' call a gen'ral meeting. Show dem de King, an' let him speak to dem. But it mus' be done soon. Before de t'irty-firs'. 'Charenton mus' be dead before he do what he will do den, and Louis mus' be ready to tak' his place."

Lafitte absently pulled off his green silk mask, and leaned forward, black eyes glittering. "Tell me."

If Corday's explanation was not precisely illuminating, it was clear on one point: that after d'Charenton performed his black Hallowmas ritual, it would no longer be possible to kill him.

"And how will we kill him now?" Lafitte said. "That has always been a troublesome point. For myself, I had meant to take him prisoner only."

"That matter is taken care of," Wessex said, laying his own mask upon the table. "I am the Duke of Wessex, related by blood to the King of England, and I will kill your sorcerer for you as I have killed others before him. For what it's worth, I also guarantee King Henry's terms. Neutrality or membership in the Grand Alliance as you please, but free shipping and an end to slavery in an independent Louis-ianne."

"Well," said Koscuisko, "nice to see you back on form, Wessex. Louis will be pleased."

"We are going to talk later," Wessex promised his friend mean-ingfully.

"I can get them into the city," Lafitte said of the two politicals. "I will bring the two of them and the King to the meeting. We can hold it at Dédé's—"

"She is dead. All de *Voudous* 'Charenton can fin', he tortures for de secret o' de *Voudou Magnian.*"

"What can he want with them?" Koscuisko asked, puzzled. "d'Charenton is a Satanist, not a witch."

"He wan' de power of de land itself, to be King in de old way, he say," Corday answered. Koscuisko shook his head, still puzzled.

"Then we will use the brickyard in Congo Square," Lafitte de-cided. "Tell them that. The brickyard, in three days' time."

"I hope your business in Nouvelle-Orléans was no' too urgen', Your Grace," Corday said, smiling engagingly at Wessex as he rose to his feet. A terrible burden seemed to have been lifted from his shoulders with Lafitte's commitment to the Rebellion, and for the first time he seemed like the Gambit Wessex knew of old.

"It can wait," Wessex said briefly. A revolution backed by the Governor's private secretary and abetted by the King of the Gulf was likely to be brief and bloodless, and he'd already made up his mind to kill d'Charenton.

"Then all is well," Corday said. "I will see you in Congo Square in t'ree days' time, Jean."

Their situation was grave, for they were alone and on foot in an implacable wilderness with nothing more than the clothing they stood up in. She did not know what had happened to Meets-The-Dawn or

The Daughter-of-the-Wind, whether they had escaped the ruined city or had died there. That Meriel had walked all this way from Baltimore in such a condition—and survived—was marvelous to Sarah, but Sarah could not bring herself to count on such fool's luck for her own survival.

The two of them slept the first night after their escape from the Numakiki in drifts of autumn leaves for warmth, and breakfasted upon raw fish tickled from the stream, for though Sarah could well have caught a rabbit in a snare of braided grass, without a knife she could not skin it, and without flint and steel there was no way to make a fire to cook it. Starting a fire with a fire-drill would take hours of tedious work, even if Sarah had been certain of how to make one.

But on the morning of the second day, Sarah awakened in the first light of dawn to see Meets-The-Dawn walking toward her, his hands spread in a gesture of peace.

He had a large bag at his hip, and slung across his back was a rifle in a fringed and beaded sheath. Obviously he had taken the time to loot the disordered city before escaping it.

"Meriel—look!" Sarah said, rousing her companion.

Meriel sat up, brushing her tangled hair back from her face and reaching instinctively for the falcon-cup. Sarah knew now that the thing was magic, but what more it was, Meriel wouldn't—or couldn't—say.

"*Wachiya*," Meets-The-Dawn said.

"*Wachiya*," Sarah answered gravely.

Meets-The-Dawn glanced toward Meriel, and it seemed to Sarah that there was a new assessment in his glance.

"When the waters stilled, the Daughter-of-the-Wind and I left the city in a canoe. We were swept to the far bank in the torrent that followed, and only now have we been able to cross the river and find you."

"I am grateful that you did," Sarah said feelingly. "Is the Sahoya with you?"

"Let us rest here a day, and I shall bring her. Then shall we decide together what shall be done. For you have found your friend and brought her out of her captivity, yet I feel your quest is not yet done."

"This is a good plan," Sarah said.

He slung a large bag down from his shoulder and set it at Sarah's feet, then disappeared abruptly as silently as he had come. Sarah stared after him, and so it was practical Meriel who pounced upon the bag and delved into its contents.

"Oh, Sarah—look! A comb! And bread—this must be from the city—and salt, and some knives, and a flint and steel—there is everything here!"

Sarah smiled to herself. How quickly one's notions of what was luxury could change.

"If there is flint and steel, we must gather wood and start a fire, for we will have guests for breakfast," she answered almost merrily.

As Meriel had gathered wood, Sarah had built a hearth of river stones and found a patch of wild onion before taking time out to order her hair and Meriel's into neat braids. Within the hour, Meets-The-Dawn had returned with the Sahoya and a string of fish from the river. This morning's breakfast was in great contrast to that of the previous day. Warm and full and in possession of a fine steel knife, Sarah felt much at peace with the world. If it were only possible to persuade Meriel to give up her mad plan of journeying to Louisianne, Sarah would be entirely content.

"Now that you have found your friend, where do you go?" the Sahoya asked pointedly, when the last of the fish had been eaten.

"I am going to Nouvelle-Orléans," Meriel announced, as though her decision had nothing to do with what any of the others might say.

Sarah stared helplessly at her friend for a moment. "Then I, too, am going to Nouvelle-Orléans," she answered lamely.

"The English are not welcome there," Meets-The-Dawn said, pointing out the obvious.

Sarah shrugged. It was hard to remember that this world considered her English, when she had grown up thinking of herself as an American.

"You bring magic to the French," the Sahoya said, pointing at the bundle that rested, even now, close by Meriel's side.

"Not to the French," Meriel said. "But I do bring it to Nouvelle-Orléans, because I must."

"Why?" Sarah demanded, unable to stop herself. "What about Louis? What can you possibly accomplish in Nouvelle-Orléans? And what is that . . . thing?" she finished inadequately.

Meriel gathered the bundle into her lap, cradling it protectively. "It is what I was sent from Baltimore to the Numakiki to find," she said simply. "And now I must bring it to Nouvelle-Orléans. I hope Louis will be there," she added, and for a moment Sarah saw tears well up in Meriel's green eyes, "but his fate is in God's hands. As is mine."

One of the Duke's favorite sayings was that it was folly to argue with an idealist, and Sarah supposed that Meriel might be lumped into that category. Unless Sarah were to hit her over the head and carry her back to Baltimore by force, there was no other course of action but to accompany her, for Sarah's stubborn sense of honor rebelled entirely against abandoning the friend she had come so far to find.

The Sahoya glanced at Meets-The-Dawn, and her face was unreadable. "And what will come of you bringing this magic, not to the French, but to Nouvelle-Orléans?" she asked Meriel.

"I don't know," Meriel said simply.

Quick as a striking weasel, the Sahoya grabbed for the bundle. She recoiled with a cry almost instantly, and the cup tumbled free.

It still seemed like an ordinary, if fantastically opulent, object, but at the same time it seemed more real than anything of the forest that surrounded them—and the Sahoya's fingers had been burned as if she had touched red-hot iron. Sarah reached gingerly for the cup at the same moment Meriel did, and her fingers closed on it first.

It did not burn her, but Sarah was suddenly filled with a strong sense that she wanted nothing to do with it. Somehow, to open her inner ears to the song this artifact sang would be to change her essential nature entirely. Yet Meriel handled it without trouble, and with every evidence of pleasure.

"This thing is no friend to the People," the Daughter-of-the-Wind said flatly, as if she were passing some terribly final judgment.

"If you allow it to do what it will, the future you saw for this land may come all the easier, Sarah of England."

Meriel stared at Sarah in puzzlement as she folded the cup back into her buckskin shawl.

"I will do all I can to stop that," Sarah said thinking of her vision of the terrible metal cities of the future. "But Meriel must also do as she feels is right. She is my friend, and I will help her."

"Then our ways walk together no longer," the Sahoya said. "And my aid to you is done. We will find a village from which we may go our separate ways."

"That would be best," Sarah said with reluctant fairness. "Where we are going is dangerous, and I do not want to draw the People into a quarrel between the French and the English."

"Wise words," the Sahoya answered grudgingly. "And I wish you safe journeying, both now and when we part. I will see to it that you are provided with all you need to travel safely."

Well, SHE certainly has a high opinion of herself! Sarah thought uncharitably. Nothing of those thoughts showed on her face as she thanked the Creek sachem for her kindness, for by her own lights, the Sahoya was being very generous in her offer of aid and protection. But it was equally true that none of the nations of the People would willingly involve themselves in a quarrel among the great European powers that fought for control of the land and its wealth.

"If it must be that our ways part, then I will leave Sarah with this last gift of the Numakiki," Meets-The-Dawn said, passing Sarah the rifle that lay on the ground at his side. "She walks in dangerous roads, and I would not abandon one of the People with no brother's gift to guard her back."

Sarah examined the rifle with interest. A slide and bolt on the side revealed that the weapon loaded from the breech, not the muzzle, unlike every other rifle Sarah had ever seen.[54] Still, it was clean and beautifully kept.

----

54. The breech-loading Farland rifle, invented by the Englishman James Farland and used during the Colonial Revolt (or War for Independence, depending on which side of the Atlantic you were on) was just as accurate and far more convenient than the Baker, which was a standard (for its day) muzzle-loading

Someone had lost a prized possession when Meets-The-Dawn had liberated this weapon. The bag of powder and shot that he handed her looked much like that which she had for her Baker, and she made no doubt this rifle would fire as well as the one she had lost.

"It is a handsome gift," Sarah said. "I am in your debt."

She knew what had motivated Meets-The-Dawn's gift to her. Among the People, a man who came courting would expect to woo his chosen lady with rich gifts. Though he could not expect to see her again, he courted Sarah as though she were a free woman.

Free! It was something she had longed for all the days of her life, and until now she had not really understood that it was a chimera, an illusion. There was no freedom, only service to one cause or another. No one who lived or thought or breathed could be free of the faculty of judgment, and in the act of judging came the choosing of sides.

She had always thought of Meriel as a timid little mouse, but Meriel was willing to risk great danger and even death for her faith. Sarah had long wondered if there were anything she herself would be willing to die for, and at last she had come to realize that there was: the cause that her father and her husband both fought for.

Justice. Justice, personified in the benign and constitutional rule of the rightful King. Without justice there could not be law, and without law and justice there was only chaos, in which brute strength ruled at its whim. She would dedicate her life to opposing that.

And so, despite the fact that she believed the Sahoya's warning, Sarah would help Meriel convey her burden to the City of Nouvelle-Orléans.

Their journey was swift now, as if unseen hands smoothed their way. Four days' travel downriver brought them to a village of friendly

---

weapon, allowing as it did for reloading from a prone or otherwise-concealed position. If its inventor had not died in 1776, the 95th Rifles would undoubtedly have been carrying Farlands, not Bakers.

Natchez, where the Sahoya invoked her people's trading agreements to gain for all of them everything they would need for their separate journeys. The Sahoya and Meets-The-Dawn headed north and east, toward English-held Transylvania, and Sarah and Meriel traveled downriver in style, on a passenger flatboat whose deck was nearly as big as that of the ship that had brought Sarah here from England.

No one would recognize either of them as English women in the native dress they now wore. Sarah wore buskins, fringed leggings, and a short buckskin tunic. Her blanket was rolled and slung across her back, and a bag of powder and shot hung at her hip. Her hair was oiled and tightly braided, and the braids wrapped for most of their length in thin-scraped doeskin, so that they hung stiffly at her back.

Meriel was dressed more modestly, in a calf-length tunic and high moccasins. She wore her red Numakiki cloak now, and carried her precious burden in a tightly-woven basket on her back. Her hair was oiled and braided as Sarah's was, her braids pulled forward to lie upon her breast, and she wore a cross carved of buffalo bone around her neck on an intricately-knotted thong, for some of the Natchez had been Christians, and she had been able to regain the symbol of her faith from them. From a distance, they looked like any young Native hunter and his woman, bound downriver on business.

And when they reached Nouvelle-Orléans . . . what then?

It was a question only Meriel could answer.

Soon it will be over. That thought was uppermost in Meriel's mind, for the dreams that guided her had begun again as soon as she and Sarah were on their way once more. Only this time her dreams were not of the Grail, but of the place to which she would bring it. In dreams she saw the towering gothic building which rose above the wood and brick structures around it—the Cathedral de Saint Louis in Nouvelle-Orléans, upon whose high altar she could lay her burden down at last.

Why had *she* been the one called upon to rescue the Holy Cup from the Numakiki, and why must she now bring it to Nouvelle-

Orléans? Meriel had prayed for answers and found none. All that was left to her was the glorious mystery of perfect obedience. It would have to be enough.

His horse was waiting for him as usual in the stable at The Clouds, and Corday rode back to town with a strangely unsettled mind. The masquerade he had devoted most of his adult life to was about to end. He should have felt gratitude and relief, especially after these last tense months of working both as d'Charenton's personal secretary and as the liaison between all the factions intriguing for Louisianne's freedom, but all he could feel was a sort of blank despair. *Nerves. Dat's all it is. De English Duke has said it: D'Charenton would dismay an angel.*

Fortunately, the aged voluptuary was unlikely to notice Corday's absence. More and more, these past weeks, d'Charenton had withdrawn into his pleasures and his arcane rituals, spending hours in the dungeons beneath the Cabildo and the Cathedral with Delphine McCarty and a succession of ever younger and more innocent victims.

But if he should suspect. . . .

Resolutely, Corday thrust the thought from his mind. He didn't dare to think such thoughts, lest they should call misfortune down upon him. He knew too much—the secret drops and passwords, the meeting places, and the names of enough of the conspirators to destroy the entire network. He was the weak link, the one whose loss could destroy them all, but there had been no other way. He was the one who had brought them all together, using intelligence gleaned from Talleyrand's files to find and recruit them, and so he'd had no choice but to know all their secrets.

Corday did not entirely trust the Black Pope not to betray him into d'Charenton's hands. But the plan was for Nouvelle-Orléans to be Talleyrand's bolt-hole against the hour of his master's misfortune, and Corday did not think Talleyrand would compromise that unless he stood to gain something he valued even more.

Corday had a nearly superstitious faith in the abilities of the Duke of Wessex. For years, Corday and Wessex had both been pawns on the same great chessboard, and Corday had done his best not to draw himself to Wessex's attention. When their paths had inevitably crossed, Corday had found his opponent, though English, to be gracious and honorable—and grace and honor were not qualities prized by the Shadow Game, the unending espionage between nations.

What coin was Wessex paid in, to hazard everything he was in the service of their contemptible profession? Corday knew he would never know the answer to that, but still he wondered. Did the English Duke yearn as he did for the day he could set aside the masquerade and walk openly in the sunlight once more? Or did he think, as Corday had for so long, that the day would never come?

As he neared the city, a mounted patrol of General Victor's soldiers stopped him and asked to see his papers. Corday showed them without surprise—such patrols were as much a part of the new regime as the evening curfew—and after a cursory check he rode on into the city. Corday had seen Napoleon's Paris and the great capitals of Europe. He had even seen London, called the Great Smoke by its inhabitants. Compared to these, Nouvelle-Orléans was a mere frontier town of plank and whitewash and wide unpaved streets, a Spanish-appearing city situated on the high ground between Lake Pontchartrain and the Mississippi River. But for Corday it was home, and thus more beautiful than its grander cousins.

It was afternoon when he arrived at the Cabildo. He was late returning, but d'Charenton would forgive him that if he had a suitably lurid account of himself to tender. D'Charenton pardoned the weaknesses of the flesh, thinking them peculiarly sacred, but he was exacting in the observances due himself, and so Corday did not tarry upon his arrival, nor stop to remove the dust of the road before presenting himself at the door of the Governor's private chambers.

"Charles Corday, to see His Excellency the Imperial Governor."

The soldiers at the door wore the ornate livery of the Governor's personal guard. Corday did not recognize them, but thought little of it. The requests to be transferred from the Governor's personal staff back to active duty were frequent.

One of the guards opened the door and Corday stepped inside.

D'Charenton was waiting for him, like a white spider in the depths of its web. He rose from behind his desk as Corday entered.

"Good afternoon, Charles. It's time we talked."

In that moment, Corday knew that things had gone terribly, unforgivably wrong.

The journey back to the *Pride of Barataria* had passed in a faintly awkward silence. Lafitte did not seem at all discommoded to be entertaining two English politicals—and in Wessex's case, a Duke—and Wessex knew better than to allow the pirate king to see any sign of division in his forces. Lafitte had gambled to make himself ruler of Louisianne, and now was settling for second best. That sort of change of heart needed to be closely watched, in case Lafitte was in fact playing an even more convoluted game of blackmail and betrayal.

So Wessex allowed Koscuisko to lead the conversation with a stream of aimless babble, and further allowed it to seem that his mind was occupied by his own part in the coming revolution, the execution of d'Charenton.

When they reached the ship, though, Lafitte seemed inclined to leave the two men to their own devices, so long as they stayed out of the way of the crew. Finding a secluded spot, Wessex resigned himself to his interrogation.

"You could have told me, you know," Koscuisko said mock-plaintively. "That you were running under sealed orders, I mean."

"You might have told me the real reason you'd been sent to Louisianne, come to that," Wessex pointed out. "Negotiating a peace treaty? Really, Illya."

"That was a divinely-inspired spur of the moment inspiration," Koscuisko answered. "My original plan had been to steal Louis from Lafitte and hide him at The Clouds."

"Baronner would have loved that. And then?"

"To see what our local contact—in this case, as it turns out, our old friend Gambit—could tell us about the lay of the land. To find out why d'Charenton really came here."

"That's a question I'd like to know the answer to myself," Wessex said broodingly. "Talleyrand sent him after the Grail—or so we believe—but Talleyrand didn't know Louis was here, I'll bet my life on that. And apparently d'Charenton has said nothing of the Grail to his most confidential secretary. How were you planning to destroy d'Charenton, by the way, if I hadn't turned up again?"

"In my usual splendid fashion—take him back to England and let someone else worry about it. But you think Lady Wessex may be in Nouvelle-Orléans? She was not in Barataria. I made sure of that," Koscuisko said, a note of apology in his voice.

"If Louis is here, why should not the others be here somewhere as well? Louisianne is as likely a place as any other, by now."

"It is possible that you may not find her," Koscuisko said, speaking delicately. "In Nouvelle-Orléans, or elsewhere."

Wessex turned fully to face his friend.

"No. It is not possible. Wherever Sarah is, I shall find her."

12

Assault upon a Queen

Louis awaited the return of Lafitte and Koscuisko impatiently, but not as impatiently as his companion. Robie was incapable of being still, it seemed. Throughout all the long day and into the evening he was constantly pacing, sitting down only to spring up again a moment later, rearranging the tol-lols and fantods in parlor and library until his constant activity bid fair to destroy what nerves Louis had left.

"Will you *stop* that?" he said at last, crossing the room to yank the paperweight from Robie's hand and slam it down on the shelf again.

Robie glared at him, pale china-blue eyes wide. "Oh ay, Your Majesty. Just as you say, Your Majesty. Is there anything else, Your Majesty?"

"Stop that. I'm no king," Louis said wearily.

"You were born one," Robie said, as if accusing Louis of some crime.

"I was born a Prince, and saw everyone I loved murdered by *la canaille* before I was nine years old. If that's enough to make me King, then I am King, but I don't notice it having made any difference yet. I am, after all, your prisoner."

"Jean's prisoner, not mine. I'd have fed you to the sharks when I found you. You're only trouble. You make him . . . dream too much."

So it was fear for his master that was behind Robie's foul temper.

"All men dream," Louis said gently. "He will be safe. Koscuisko is a good man."

"A good *English*man—or if not that, then working for the *Anglais*. Whose ships do you think we raid in the Gulf? The English King would hang Jean in chains if he caught him!" Robie said furiously.

"But he won't catch him, Robie. You heard Koscuisko. Lafitte is to be First Minister of the new Louisianne, and a trusted ally of England. And I will need him. Undoubtedly he knows more of how to rule a country than I do."

"Jean Lafitte is a great man!" Robie said belligerently. "He doesn't need you."

"There you are wrong," Louis said, becoming irritated beyond prudence at last. "I am the *imprimatur* of Royalty that will cloak his scandalous antecedents in the pall of respectability. A painted statue could do as much, but oh, I am *vital* to his success, I assure you!"

The two might have come to blows, save for the fact that Lafitte chose that moment to make his entrance.

"Put up your swords, *mes enfants!*" he said cheerfully. "My young Robie, you are out of temper. It is too long since you killed someone, eh? But there will be killing very soon—in judicious moderation, of course," he added, with a glance back at his two companions.

Louis looked past Lafitte to the men with him. One, he was relieved to see, was Koscuisko. The other was the Duke of Wessex. Louis' first thought was relief that he would not be called upon to be d'Charenton's executioner, for Wessex could surely perform that task. The second was that Wessex must surely have word of Meriel, for his Duchess and Louis' wife were close friends, and Meriel might well have sought out Lady Wessex after Louis' disappearance.

"Your Grace, I must have words with you," Louis said, coming over to the Duke.

"Louis. I'm sorry, I don't know where she is," Wessex said quietly.

Shocks quickly delivered were said to hurt less, but the blow was still painful. Louis bowed his head, steeling himself to accept it.

"A woman?" Lafitte had seemed wholly occupied with Robie, but his ears were sharp.

"My wife, Captain," Louis said evenly. "She was with me in Baltimore when I was taken, and I do not know what became of her."

Lafitte looked to Wessex.

"After Lady Meriel realized you were gone, she wrote to Lady Wessex of her plight. Naturally, Her Grace came as soon as she could. By the time I was able to follow, there was no trace to be found of either lady."

"*Sarah* is gone?" Louis said, bewildered. He could not imagine that anyone could easily vanquish the wondrous Duchess of Wessex. Wessex's face was expressionless, but his eyes were filled with a formidable resolution.

"It would help if we knew just how it was you came here," Koscuisko said. Louis shrugged.

"Captain Lafitte was kind enough to rescue me from a gentleman whose company had grown tedious—a certain Captain Franklyn of a ship called *Merchant's Luck*. I know no more than that. I was drugged when I went to the bank in Baltimore, I think, and awoke just as the *Luck* was being boarded."

Wessex turned his gaze on Lafitte. The pirate king was quick enough to understand the unspoken question.

"For my part, it was a day like any other. She flew a Dutch flag, but—*eh bien*—if we are not at war with the Dutch now, we may well be someday, and a prudent man takes his work where he finds it. The late Captain Franklyn said he acted for d'Charenton in the matter, but perhaps he was only trying to impress me." Though Lafitte kept his face grave, his eyes sparkled with a buccaneer's enjoyment.

"So d'Charenton's agents took Louis from Baltimore, but not his wife. Lady Meriel and Her Grace made their disappearance from Baltimore at a later date, either separately or together," Koscuisko said, summarizing matters.

"Perhaps d'Charenton will know." The words Wessex spoke were idle, but Louis shivered inwardly when he heard them. The Duke and the pirate were both what Louis knew he could never be— dangerous men. Men who could kill.

"And you shall certainly have an opportunity to ask him," Lafitte said, "but not before you have sampled what poor hospitality my Chandeleur can offer. We will make Frenchmen of you both, so that you can walk the streets of *La Belle Orléans* in safety. And to be sure of it, I will send my little Robie to Town to discover the freshest news. You see, *mon petit?*" he added, directing this last to Robie. "No imprisonment lasts forever."

"Free at last," Robie breathed in relief. "I'll go tonight. Don't do anything fun while I'm gone." The young pirate nearly ran from the room, his blond braid swinging behind him.

"Was it the hour? Was it the company?" Koscuisko asked plaintively.

"He's young," Lafitte said dismissively. "And has no love for great houses—even mine. His experiences in such have not been happy ones. But come. We are all comrades now in this great adventure, and there are many details for us to work out before the curtain rises upon the last act."

Robie stopped in Barataria proper long enough for a meal and to find someone who would row him across to the mainland. Grand Terre was two hours from Nouvelle-Orléans by coach, and it would be a long walk. He could have had one of Jean's horses, but a dock-rat coming into town on a blooded saddlehorse would cause talk. If he had to leave town in a hurry, all he had to do was take one of the horses from the smithy in St. Philip Street, for the smithy and everything it contained was only one of the false-front businesses that Lafitte owned in Nouvelle-Orléans.[55]

---

55. True in both worlds. In fact, by the beginning of 1813, Lafitte was supplying

❀   ❀   ❀

He walked through the night without fear, swinging a dark-lantern, for in addition to his knives and pistols, Robie wore several powerful *gris-gris* concealed in his clothes, and so had no fear either of ghosts or vaudois. His pistol would drive off a panther, and so long as he stayed away from still water, he had little to fear from Old Man Log, as the locals called the alligator.

He knew the sort of information that Jean was after, for he had collected it in a dozen towns in the Gulf and the Caribbean during their association. But as soon as he reached the city, he knew that this excursion would be not be like any other.

The sun was rising, driving the mist from the land, and the Crescent City—so called from the shape imposed upon it by its position between the river and the lake—was stirring to life. When he passed the Customs House the soldiers standing guard outside looked like painted toys, so rigid were they, and there was a mute unhappiness to this most flamboyant of cities that made Robie's hackles rise. There was something very wrong here, something that went far beyond the dissatisfaction the city felt in its new overlord, but it was in the French Market that Robie received his first real news.

The owner of Dulane's Coffee House was not willing to let Robie sit at a table like her regular patrons, but she was a kind woman who was willing to sell him a steaming fragrant bowl of coffee—black as hell and sweet as love, as the natives said—and allow him to loiter near the counter as he drank it. He'd had to use all the charm he'd learned from Jean to gain even that concession, for Dulane's catered to free persons of color, and Robie was far too fair to pass even as the lightest of octoroons. But none of the white establishments would have allowed him even this much license, for Nouvelle-Orléans was a city obsessed with one's station in life even more than it was with the color of one's skin, and Robie did not belong to either world: rich or poor, white or black.

---

most of the businesses in New Orleans with goods obtained through smuggling and piracy, and was well on his way to becoming a formidable commercial power in the city.

In better weather, the shop's patrons would sit outside, but it was almost November, and the shutters which made up the front of the coffee house had been closed and locked long since, driving Dulane's custom indoors. Robie didn't mind. It was easier to eavesdrop that way, and if few lingered at the tables at this hour, there were many who came to have a jug or bottle filled on the way to some early-morning rendezvous.

"They say the Duc will burn him. Ay! Such a beautiful young man, too."

Just now his attention was caught by a scrap of conversation flung out by a beautiful young Negress in a splendid green gown and elaborate tignon who had come to have her basket and bottle filled. Despite the opulence of her dress, Robie knew she was not one of the serpent-women. They would still be in their beds after the night's revels, nor did they rise before noon. This dazzling creature was at best a servant, clad in her mistress' castoffs and sent to buy breakfast for the household. *Funny, isn't it, how you can't tell slave from free by looking?* he thought sardonically. *Why, if I didn't know better, I'd say there wasn't any difference between them.*

"He will expect us to come and watch, which is worse," Madame Dulane was saying. "It passes understanding. If I discovered such a scandal so close to me, I would not make a present of it to the city, no."

"He wishes us all to know he is *très vigilant*, I suppose," the servant-girl answered. "But poor M'sieur Corday! It is a terrible way to die, the burning." Her transaction completed, the green-clad fair one went on her way in a swish of skirts.

"Have you not finished with that yet, you young felon?" Madame Dulaine asked Robie sharply.

"Yes, ma'am," Robie said meekly. He held out his empty bowl. "Is it true that Secretary Corday is to be burned?" he asked, as one hoping for gossip to prolong his stay.

"Tomorrow night." Madame was about to say more, when one of the French soldiers quartered on the town came into the shop. Robie and Madame Dulane both froze, identical expressions of wariness on their faces.

"Good morning, Madame." Outside the shop, the sound of hammering could be heard.

"Good morning, *Capitaine*. You are up early this fine morning."

"I come with bad news, Madame. All businesses in the city are to be closed until further notice by the order of His Excellency. The people are to remain in their homes."

Robie blinked, trying to disguise his shock. Such an order was unheard-of.

"But why? I will starve. And my patrons—"

"Go home, Madame Dulane." The captain's voice made it clear that there was no point in arguing. "Everyone must go. The Governor has issued a general order."

He turned toward Robie, but Robie had many years of practice in evading authority. He was already out the door before the captain had finished moving toward him.

All along Decatur Robie could see the soldiers closing down the market. Tempers flared high as the soldiers demanded that the vendors leave their stalls and shops—and merchandise—unattended, but Robie's attention was on the military waggon that stood in the street, surrounded by nervous soldiers.

It was filled with casks of gunpowder and coils of slow match, enough to blow up the entire street. Robie glanced from the waggon to the row of shops before heading up the street at a quick trot. An explosion here would do worse than just leave a large hole. Everything in sight was made out of wood.

And wood, Robie knew, *burned*.

Because it was important—or at least, because he knew Jean would think it was—Robie made a hurried tour of the rest of the city to see if things were as bad elsewhere. The streets were filled with soldiers who were reading out the Governor's General Order to the disbelieving populace. There were waggons on the fashionable uptown streets, too, though these were covered with tarpaulins, and Robie could not see what they contained.

He could guess, though.

Jean won't like this.

"You! Boy!" A soldier shouted behind him and Robie froze. He'd thought he was safe from detection, but he'd loitered too long.

"Sir?" Robie said meekly. One hand crept into his pocket, feeling through the slit he'd cut in the lining for the knife strapped to his leg. If he had to, he could slash the man's throat and run. If he had to.

"You're supposed to be at home—if you have a home. If you do not, the Governor can provide you one."

"No, sir. Yes, sir. I mean, thank you sir, but no. I have a home," Robie said quickly. The ragged appearance that would have served him so admirably in normal times worked against him now. He didn't look as if he belonged anywhere.

"Do you?" The soldier's eyes flared with suspicion.

"Yes, sir. Thank you, sir. I live on St. Philip, sir," Robie said, doing his best to imitate a terrified townie boy caught out on a lark.

"Then go there," the soldier said, aiming a blow at him that Robie dodged without thinking. He turned and ran.

They're burning Corday tomorrow night. That can't be good. And shutting down the city—that has to be worse. What do the soldiers want with all that gunpowder, as if I didn't know? Whatever it is, I don't want to be here when it happens....

Lafitte set an excellent table, and the oddly-assorted conspirators had lingered long over the port afterward, savoring what was to be their last respite before the revolution.

The Revolution . . . All his life, those words had only meant violence, betrayal, and death to the Duke of Wessex. The French Revolution had claimed his father, had catapulted him into the nightmare play of the Shadow Game, had been the one thing he had always fought to destroy. Now, against all expectation, he had become a revolutionary himself, pledged to kill once more, this time in the service of that bloodthirsty all-devouring goddess.

But this time would be the last.

Jean Lafitte sat at the head of the table, his eyes hooded like those of a contemplative cat. Wessex gazed across the table at the young man—so unready!—who would be king of a new and independent nation if their conspiracy prospered.

"Where is she?" Louis asked in despair.

Louis' anguished question roused him from his brooding.

"I don't know," Wessex said honestly. "But wherever she is, Sarah must be there also." And that was the truth, for good or ill.

"D'Charenton has her," Louis said, too caught up in his own fears to listen. The delicate crystal wineglass trembled between his fingers, and he tossed back its contents as if they were bitter medicine.

"No." Wessex was certain of that much. "Corday is his private secretary, and entirely in his confidence as far as I could gather. If your wife—or mine—were in d'Charenton's hands, Corday would have mentioned the fact, I believe."

"And none of the Brotherhood has taken them," Lafitte offered, putting a comforting hand over Louis' in an intimate gesture that Wessex found oddly reassuring. There were few men who could feign such compassion believably, if they meant harm to its subject. "I would have heard of it, believe me, *mon pauvre petit*. But I will make inquiries none the less. We will find your Queen. And now, I must go. There is much to do before my fleet sails."

The King of Barataria stood and took his leave.

Lafitte's labors would spell success or failure for the entire enterprise. If the captains of his unruly fleet could not keep Admiral Bonaparte's ships from coming to the relief of the city, the insurrection would fail.

"Queen." Louis recoiled from the word, as if this consequence of becoming King was one he had not thought of until now. He shook his head. "She should have been safe. I never should have allowed her to share my life. What a fool I was."

If you were, Louis, then so was I. Wessex did not say the words aloud.

It seemed he had barely slept when a hammering upon his door awoke Wessex. He sat up, instantly alert. The clock over the mantel said it was barely ten—far too early for them to depart. He rolled out of bed, his hand going at once to his sabre, before he went to the door.

"Wessex!" It was Koscuisko's voice. Wessex unbolted the door. His partner was as disheveled as he, standing in the doorway barefoot and swathed in a dressing gown of more than oriental splendor.

"What is it?" Wessex demanded. There was some faint noise from below, but not enough to explain Koscuisko's agitation.

"Robie's back. Corday's been arrested. And that's the good news."

"They're mining the city."

Robie lay sprawled upon the couch in the parlor. His face was grey with exhaustion and pain. Louis and Jean Lafitte were there, and Lafitte was cutting away the blue coat Robie wore. As he pulled it away the shocking redness of blood could be seen.

"Leave that," Robie said irritably. "It isn't important."

"It is if you die before telling us what you saw," Captain Lafitte said gently. "Come, drink a little brandy."

"I think I've killed the mare. I'm sorry, Jean. But I had to get here. It's bad. It's very bad." Robie took the cup in his good hand and drank.

"What happened?" Wessex had taken the time to make a rudimentary toilette and put on his boots. He entered the room holding his sabre in its sheath. Koscuisko had gone to see what he could do for the horse Robie had ridden here; as the boy said, he had forced her to the limit of her strength. "Who shot you?"

"Soldier at the gate. They're sealing the city. You can still get in through the cemetery, but the military gate is closed, and the one on the Esplanade." Lafitte gave him more brandy and water, and again Robie drank thirstily, his body trying to replace the blood it had lost.

"You said Corday was taken?" This was the worst news they could have gotten. D'Charenton could make a saint's statue confess to blasphemy, and Corday was already terrified of him. If he held out against the monster's persuasion for a day they would be blessed, but even that was not enough time.

"Let me—For God's sake, leave it, Jean!" Robie interrupted himself. Lafitte had cut away the shoulder of the coat and the shirt beneath, and Wessex could see the wound now. The ball had gone in beneath the shoulder blade, a bad wound. That the boy had ridden thirty miles after taking it was nothing short of a miracle.

"It is beyond my skill, I fear. I shall have to send for a doctor." Lafitte looked grim. Barataria was not the sort of place in which one found physicians of the Royal Society.

"I'll cut for the bullet, if you have the tools," Louis said abruptly. "The Abbé taught me a little of medicine. Enough to serve, I think." He was white-faced, but determined. Louis would have to probe for the ball to find and remove it, and the procedure killed nearly as many men as being shot did.

"Serve me right for not putting a knife through you when I had the chance," Robie said, with a painful smile. "Let me tell it once from the beginning, and then you can do as you like. It's as much as I'm good for."

In a faint but steady voice, Robie told everything he'd seen in Nouvelle-Orléans that morning—the shops being closed, the citizens being confined to their homes, the news he'd heard that Corday had been arrested, to be burned at the stake tomorrow night.

"I always told him he would live to be hanged," Lafitte said in an emotionless voice.

"And the soldiers are going around with casks of gunpowder. I think—I think they are mining the buildings, to blow them up, eh? They tried to arrest me, but I took a horse from the stable on St. Philip. There was no one at the smithy—I went there first. . . ." The last words came out in a slurred mumble, then Robie's head lolled to the side in exhausted unconsciousness.

Lafitte met Wessex's eyes.

"So. We have no choice but to hazard all upon one throw of the dice, *mon ami*. It is not the fight I would wish for, but it is the fight we have, *hein*?" Lafitte said.

"D'Charenton means to destroy the entire city—to burn it down around its people," Wessex said in disbelief.

"Burn down the city?" Koscuisko asked, entering from the terrace. There was blood on his hands and he looked grim. Wessex decided not to inquire after the fate of Robie's mount.

"Apparently this is that great dark ritual Corday said he was planning," Wessex said.

"But that's foolishness," Koscuisko protested. "Corday said that d'Charenton was trying to make the land marriage that the Kings make in order to bind himself to the land. But he can't do that by slaughtering everyone in the city—the Art Magickal just doesn't work the way d'Charenton fantasizes."

"The people will be just as dead," Lafitte said grimly. "And you will be king of nothing, eh, my Louis?"

"Not if we stop him," Louis said. He looked to Wessex.

"Illya and I will go to Nouvelle-Orléans at once. I may be able to find Corday and bring him out. I imagine I can certainly find d'Charenton," the Duke said grimly.

"The soldiers will shoot you down in the street," Lafitte said.

"I have some experience in moving about a city under martial law," the Duke answered.

"I will send a messenger to Momus'—Corday's—people," Lafitte said. "And I will take my fleet and meet Admiral Bonaparte at the mouth of the river. He will come when he sees the city burning, if he has not orders to come before. But before I do, *petit,* I will find for you the tools you require to save my young friend."

Lafitte went off to issue his orders, and Louis remained behind to tend to Robie, leaving Wessex and Koscuisko to make their own preparations to enter Nouvelle-Orléans.

Wessex must execute the sorcerer d'Charenton, but this time he had no blessed silver bullets nor rune-marked sabre to aid him as he had on other occasions. The shield of his rank and his bloodline would have to be enough to protect him from the death-curse of d'Charenton's blood.

He dressed with care from a selection of garments provided by his host: grey coat and breeches, a weskit of green linen embroidered with fine silver, a plumed beaver cockade. He oiled and honed his rapier, using a stone to bring its edge to ultimate sharpness. All he had to do was to deliver the killing blow, by any means at his disposal.

It would be for others to cut off d'Charenton's head, to bury his body in unhallowed ground, to take his heart and burn it before the altar of the church.

The pistols Lafitte provided were beautiful things, their barrels inlaid with red and green gold in a pattern of flowering pomegranates, their butts of ivory inlaid with sapphires and emeralds. Princely weapons, a pirate's plunder from one of the Spanish treasure ships. He cleaned them, debated with himself, and decided to charge them just before they reached the city—any earlier, and the powder would certainly shake from the pan as he rode. It would be best of all to charge them just before firing, but he might not have the luxury of so much time, and the chance that they would fire was better than nothing.

His riding boots had been polished by one of the servants to glassy brilliance. While he had been dressing, another servant had brought the documents that on any other occasion would have certainly allowed him and Koscuisko free passage through the city of Nouvelle-Orléans. They might be useless now, but again, any chance was better than none.

He wrapped a long sash of pale green silk about his waist and thrust the pistols through it, far enough to the sides that the drape of his coat would conceal them, then belted on his sabre. The enameled gold of its basket-hilt sparkled redly against the silk. It was an old weapon, something that was his own rather than a product of the White Tower artificers, one that he had called upon many times. He only hoped it would serve him as well as it had served his grandfather.

There was a knock at the door. He opened it to behold his partner.

Koscuisko was dressed as a priest, in a long black soutane that nearly brushed the ground.

"Impersonating a priest? Do you think that's wise?" Wessex asked mildly.

"It might gain us some small advantage," Koscuisko answered gently, holding his flat, wide-brimmed hat before him. He lifted it slightly, showing Wessex the pistol that lay beneath. "And it's always nice to be able to surprise people."

"Considering how much d'Charenton has surprised us thus far, it would be only kind to return the favor," Wessex agreed. "He may have given orders to execute all priests, you know."

"I do not think he will dare that until he is ready for his trap to close," Koscuisko said. "At most, I think he will be holding them prisoner, possibly in the Capuchin convent. If things work out as I hope, I can reach such prisoners and gain their aid to rally the populace against d'Charenton."

"If things work out," Wessex echoed. He did not need to say more. The situation in Nouvelle-Orléans was too volatile for any plans they made to survive their arrival. "At least we have two days to plan—today and tomorrow. He will burn Corday tomorrow evening, then conduct his ritual—whatever it might be—the following night. If he's still alive to do it."

"We'll hope he isn't," Koscuisko answered.

They reached the city late in the afternoon, making a wide circle about it to approach from the northwest. Their destination was an isolated house that had frequently provided their pirate host with a place to leave shipments bound for the merchants of the city. There they would be able to leave their horses and gain fresh news, for Rampart Street, as the name implied, was the northernmost stretch of the area surveyed for the city.

But when Wessex dismounted and knocked at the door of Lafitte's safe-house, there was no answer.

"Odd," he said aloud. He glanced at Koscuisko, who was as bemused as he.

"Perhaps they are hiding from the soldiers."

"Perhaps," Wessex agreed, and led his mount around behind house.

There the two men found the carriage house containing the carriage and its horses, a pen with a few chickens, and nothing more. They tried the house—the kitchen door was not locked—and found the rest of the house deserted. In the dining room, the dinner[56]

---

56. In the 18th and 19th centuries, the middle meal of the day.

service was laid, the meal on the plates half-eaten. Wessex placed his fingers lightly on the side of the tureen that stood on the sideboard.

"The soup is still warm," he announced.

"Could they have been taken by the soldiers?" Koscuisko asked.

"But why?" Wessex asked. "I suppose it's too late to wish I'd read Magie rather than Classics at University." The life of a spy was always uncertain, but on this occasion the stakes were as high and the odds as long as any in his career, and this time Wessex knew he could not console himself with the knowledge that another agent would take his place on the Chessboard of Night if he failed. If he failed here, there would be no recouping the terrible loss. This time, all that stood between Civilization and a Long Night of unimaginable barbarism was the Duke of Wessex.

Koscuisko shrugged. "If d'Charenton's mad anyway, he's probably not following a recognized magical system. But if the army has taken these people on d'Charenton's orders, it means that they are still backing him, and that's not good."

"We'll leave the horses here anyway," Wessex decided. "Horses would draw too much attention. We need to get to the house on St. Philip—without being arrested, for preference."

It was the end of October, and even at this hour the sun was already westering. In a few hours it would be dark.

The first word they had of trouble ahead came when the flatboat upon which Sarah and Meriel rode was hailed by a man on the side of the river.

"If you're bound for Dixie,[57] you're out of luck! The docks are closed!"

"Closed!" the captain shouted back. "What do you mean?"

"Put in!" the other roared. "You're a fool to go on!"

Swearing furiously, the captain gave the order to put in. It took

---

57. New Orleans.

an hour with the sweeps and bushwhacking[58] to bring the hundred-foot-long plankboat to shore, but when it had moored, the man who had hailed them from shore hopped aboard. Fortified by a dipper of Nongela,[59] he told his story.

"Day before last, the soldiers come down to Tchoupitoulas Street and start cutting the barges loose to drift downriver. You never seed such consternation, with the hoors skreelin and men cursin' and the like. The crews tried to stop 'em, and the bluebacks opened fire. Kilt a couple dozen or so, but we was holdin' our own until they brought up the cannon. I wasn't minded to face chain,[60] so I up and lit out, but I heered Dixie's been closed up tighter'n a sporting-house[61] on Sunday."

"Is it plague?" the captain asked, puzzled. "This isn't fever season."

The man shrugged. "All I know is, if you're bound for Dixie, you might as well go home now. Won't get shot at so much, anyway."

"Excuse me, sir? Is there a problem?" Sarah asked. She'd been listening all along with growing concern, for Meriel's mysterious business was what drew them to Nouvelle-Orléans. She was careful to speak submissively, for the rivermen were always eager to pick fights with the Indians, and the disguise that concealed her sex was a fragile one.

But the captain was too occupied with his own problems to pay much heed to her. "Are you deaf, boy? There's trouble in Dixie. I dasn't go down river until I find out what it is."

"I could go for you," Sarah offered carefully. "My people are waiting for me. Perhaps they have heard something."

---

58. To pull a keelboat against the current by means of putting a line around a tree on shore and hauling the boat upriver by muscle power.

59. The keg of whiskey kept aboard for the refreshment of the keelboat crews was known universally as "Nongela," from its brand name, Old Monongahela rye whiskey.

60. Chain-shot. Cannon were sometimes loaded with small pieces of scrap-iron, including short lengths of chain, and the load discharged against advancing troops. The result was a lethal spray of shrapnel which was daunting to face.

61. brothel

Now the captain did look at her, studying her face hard and long as if to read her soul.

"There's a dollar[62] in it for you if you do," he finally said, showing her the coin and then returning it to his pocket.

"Thank you, sir," Sarah said, doing her best to sound like one of her own coachmen. She turned and hurried back to Meriel.

"We have to get off here. There's trouble in the city."

"Yes," Meriel said, her voice remote. Sarah felt like shaking her friend, but dared not while they were among these rough strangers.

"Come on, then," she said.

The two women went over the side, and floundered through the knee-deep shallows to the shore. There was a broad and well-traveled tow-path there, and only twenty miles or so separated them from the northern border of the city. The morning air was chilly, but the walk would soon warm them. Sarah set off at a brisk trot, Meriel behind her.

She slowed once she was out of sight of the keelboat, but kept on walking. This was a well-traveled area, and the keelboatmen—the mauvais Kaintocks with which local mamas threatened their children if they misbehaved—were not people she truly wished to meet. Soon she found what she was seeking—a narrow track, almost invisible, that led them off the tow-path.

"Where are we going?" Meriel asked, when they were well off the main track.

"Nouvelle-Orléans—I hope," Sarah answered, pausing to take a sighting from the sun. "There seems to be trouble there."

"Yes. . . ." Meriel answered slowly. "A great evil seeks to be re-born in that place."

"Meriel, if you would plainly tell me what you know and why we are going to Nouvelle-Orléans—and what you are going to do when you get there—it would be a great help to both of us," Sarah said with barely-concealed exasperation.

There was a pause before Meriel answered, and Sarah could see

---

62. The dollar, a Spanish coin, was in common circulation in the New World side-by-side with other coinage until the middle 1800s.

her, once again, considering how much of the truth she could tell her friend. In that moment Sarah could happily have shaken Meriel until her teeth rattled. There was no need for all this mystery!

"We must go to the Cathedral de Saint Louis," Meriel said. "I can find the way, once we are there. That is all I can tell you, Sarah. Please don't ask me anything more."

"To the Cathedral," Sarah said with a sigh. "Well, perhaps the holy fathers will give us sanctuary once we get there—I have a feeling we're going to need it. Come on, then. It will take us most of the day on foot to get there." Trying not to be as irritated as she really felt she had a right to be, Sarah turned and began walking in the direction of the city once again.

His body hurt. But he was still alive, and he did not think he had talked. It was a small but real consolation to the man who hung in chains in a niche in one of the dark catacombs beneath the city.

Charles Corday still did not know what had happened to bring him to this fate. Perhaps there was no reason for his arrest. Perhaps it was only another symptom of d'Charenton's growing madness. He remembered coming to the Governor's office—the soldiers—and then awakening, chained half-naked to one of the drawing engines deep below the Cabildo.

D'Charenton had been there, with the terrible child he had made his pet. He had accused Corday of treason, of esoteric crimes that Corday barely understood. He had accused him of being Talleyrand's creature—half-true—but then, mysteriously, began to rage against him for stealing from him the treasure d'Charenton had come to the New World to find.

Corday had protested his innocence, but then d'Charenton began to turn the wheel, and all he could do was scream. As he lay there in agony d'Charenton had played with him as if he were a living puppet, cutting him with a razor, over and over again, to see the bright blood flow.

He would have begged for mercy, Corday thought, if Mam'selle McCarty had not been there. The avidity in her bright eyes sickened him; the way she dabbled her hands in his blood as if it were a child's paints and licked her fingers afterward.

He *did* beg, later, when the hot irons were brought and applied to his feet. It seemed that the room was filled with shadows, nebulous hooded shapes that stood behind d'Charenton, waiting. He had begged them to make d'Charenton believe him, he had sworn that he had stolen nothing from his sadistic master. He even confessed to being Talleyrand's creature, but vowed—and it was true—that since he had come to Nouvelle-Orléans he had told the Black Pope nothing—*nothing!*

But his words did not help him. D'Charenton continued to toy with him, until at last the hooded shapes had drawn nearer, muffling Corday in their dark cloaks. After that he remembered nothing, until he had come to himself here, goaded back into consciousness by pain.

I am afraid, he thought in shame. *I cannot bear for him to do that to me again.* But d'Charenton's victims lived days, even weeks, in his care, and d'Charenton would surely come to him again. Corday would have wept, but no tears would come, only an empty burning behind his eyes. *Blessed Virgin, you have a soft spot in your heart for sinners like me. Holy Mother, take away my fear. . . .*

There was the sound of footsteps along the passage that led to his place. Corday whimpered, heart hammering in his chest, desperately trying to console himself with the knowledge that it was many footsteps, heavy footsteps, and d'Charenton did not bring soldiers with him when he came to amuse himself with his victims. Blurrily, he saw the light of a torch—one eye did not work, for some reason, and the other was blinded and watering at the sudden harsh light. But Corday could see that d'Charenton was not with them, and the knowledge made him weak with relief, though the muttered oaths of the soldiers when they saw him was worse than any mirror. Several crossed themselves, and one turned aside to avoid looking at him.

"Are you men or old women?" the sergeant demanded roughly. Jingling the keys, he advanced on Corday and loosened his shackles.

To have the weight taken off the torn and abused muscles of his arms and shoulders was a blessed relief, but then his feet touched the floor and the pain of the harsh stone on the livid burns made

Corday scream. The sound was harsh and faint, forced through a dry throat and over cracked and bleeding lips.

"Get up." The sergeant kicked his ribs with relish. "God's Death, but it's cold down here," he observed to no one in particular. "Never mind. You'll be warm where you're going, eh?"

Corday forced his good eye open. "Where . . . ?" he managed.

"Where all good heretics and traitors go. Into the fires of Hell. Bring him. If he can't walk, drag him."

They dragged him out into Cabildo Square, the place of execution. For a brief instant, he felt almost grateful that he was to be spared d'Charenton's further attentions, but then the knowledge of his fate made him recoil with horror.

He was to be burned alive.

Wessex and Koscuisko entered the city proper an hour before nightfall. Most of the houses they passed on the way into the city had boarded-up windows—another gubernatorial edict, Wessex had learned when the two of them at last reached the Maison Lafitte on St. Philip. The door of that house was opened to him by a young man who introduced himself as Pierre Lafitte[63] and quickly swept them inside.

"I am Jean's brother—we do not look so much alike, eh?—and you must be the men he told me to expect. He said nothing of a priest," Pierre finished doubtfully, looking at Koscuisko.

"Never mind that now," Wessex said. "What do you know of the state of things here?"

Pierre was able to tell him little that had happened since the soldiers had begun confining the citizenry to its houses at dawn this morning. Even the slaves were forced to remain indoors. The city was under martial law enforced by d'Charenton's soldiers and the special militia he had recruited. The Swamp had been burned, and

---

63. Jean Lafitte's brother—some say half-brother—was his principle business agent, living in a lavish house at the corner of Bourbon and St. Philip. The blacksmith shop, which served as a conduit for the dissemination of smuggled goods, was just down the street from the house.

the flatboat city on Tchoupitoulas Street had been cut loose to drift downriver. Those who opposed the Governor's edicts, or who did not have homes to go to, had been confined in the Arsenal next to the Cabildo. He had heard rumors that the convent had been burned, that those who opposed the Governor's orders were being shot without trial, that the militia and a squad of quickly-deputized bullies recruited from among the Kaintocks were looting the city and keeping the people in their houses, killing any they found on the streets. . . .

"Rumors are all we have, my friend," Pierre said, pouring glasses of wine for his guests. "We heard the militia go by a few hours ago, and many people were taken away, but surely they were too many to burn? It must be only that the governor wants witnesses to his latest folly. He is a man of much punctilio, is the Duc d'Charenton."

Pierre had brought the visitors into the dining room, where the windows were hung with heavy black cloth to keep the light from showing to any watchers in the garden outside. Without question, the brother of Jean Lafitte was used to the niceties of receiving clandestine visitors. He poured a decent vintage, too, and Wessex found his nerves glad of the anodyne. This silent, deserted, *victimized* city was like nothing he had ever encountered in all his years of playing the Shadow Game.

"He cannot expect to keep the people imprisoned like this for long," Koscuisko said, shaking his head. "They won't stand for it. They'll be out of food soon—if they aren't already—and willing to risk the soldiers."

"Perhaps d'Charenton doesn't care," Wessex said. The actions of a madman did not follow the dicta of common sense, and despite Corday's opinions, Wessex was certain d'Charenton was mad beyond the constraint of greed or self-preservation.

"Perhaps once the executions are over, we will be let to come out again," Pierre offered. The light from the candles flickered over his face, making it difficult to judge his expression, but his voice was hopeful.

"Have you heard who is to be killed tomorrow night?" Wessex asked, probing for fresh intelligence.

Pierre shrugged fatalisticly. "I do not know who is to be burned with poor Corday, but the Governor never executes fewer than a dozen. At first—the city was a wilderness, and any measure that would end the lawlessness seemed good. But now . . . ? It has gone on too long."

Wessex glanced at his partner. Koscuisko looked unwontedly grave.

"Pierre, I need to get to the Cabildo to see the Governor," Wessex said. "What is the shortest way?"

"You cannot possibly," Pierre protested. But Wessex insisted, and Pierre finally produced a map of the city—complete down to the location of each outbuilding and garden—and showed Wessex how he must go to reach his destination.

"Stay off the streets, my friends," Pierre said. He moved the candelabrum to the edge of the map, away from the detailed drawing of the Vieux Carré. Single candlesticks, their candles unlit, held down the corners of the curling roll of parchment. "If you go through the back gardens—and take care not to be seen—you should arrive safely at your destination, God willing."

Wessex drained the last of his wine and set down his glass on the polished red mahogany surface of the table. He got to his feet, reclaimed his cloak and hat, and checked his pistols. There were no more preparations to be made. It was time to go, and to take what the Fates sent him.

Koscuisko stood as well. "I'll go with you as far as the Cathedral and see if I can free the good fathers. If I can create a distraction there, you may find it easier to get to d'Charenton."

A successful distraction might well cost Koscuisko his life, something neither man mentioned. This was their job. The sacrifices were familiar ones, if not easy. And Wessex had come to realize that there came a day when they were at last impossible.

But not today. Today I will do what I came to do. Whatever the cost, I will prevail.

Pierre put out all but one of the candles and led the two politicals into the kitchen before dousing that last feeble flame. In the darkness, the agents slipped from the house and across the back garden of the house on St. Philip. The moon was dark, so they did not need to fear being seen by its light . . . or by any other, because no lights showed, anywhere in the city.

13

Queen of Heaven, Queen of Hell
(Nouvelle-Orléans, October 29, 1807)

The Duc d'Charenton ran his fingers—their long nails black and encrusted with dried blood and worse—over the surface of the elaborate horoscope that was spread out upon his desk. It had taken him months to complete, working on it only on those nights when the moon was void-of-course,[64] drawing the sigils in the blood of an unbaptized virgin, and he believed what it told him absolutely.

The time for the sacrifice was now, tonight. The blood would spill, the screams of the damned would ascend to Heaven, and among them would be the sacrifice that would call the Grail out of hiding and into d'Charenton's grasp. This was what he had promised to his Master, and the time left in which d'Charenton could fulfill his bargain grew short.

The Grail for his life. The Grail for his freedom from the pains of Hell, and for power and dominion Eternal. He would call the Cup

---

64. "Void-of-course" meaning that the moon is in transition between two of the houses of the Zodiac, and thus not in either of them.

to him with the sacrifice of royal blood, and profane it with the blood of innocents. Through their deaths he would secure all that his Master had promised him so many years ago.

He had meant the sacrifice to be Louis de Bourbon, for the blood of the Young King was the most powerful that d'Charenton could secure. Lafitte had balked him there, but d'Charenton had made other arrangements. Jerome Bonaparte, brother of the Emperor, stood chained to a stake in the square, and beside him the Bishop of Nouvelle-Orléans—a prince of the Church—and Charles Corday, a lord in his own land, and a representative of the power of France. The power of the Old World and the New, and of the Holy Church—surely the three of them would constitute a fitting sacrifice in Louis' place?

If there were blood enough spilled, it must be so. And d'Charenton planned to deliver up the entire city in sacrifice. At the moment the pyres beneath the three stakes were lit, so would the fuses be lit throughout the city. There would be explosions, and, through the wreckage, fires would spread taking everything with them, until the entire city had become a holocaust to the greater glory of d'Charenton's Master.

He went to the window and looked out. Barricades had been built around the square to hold back the crowds that the soldiers were herding here to bear witness—all the aristocracy, all those who had mocked d'Charenton and opposed his will. The power of the blood was stronger than their empty piety, and their corruption would add power to what he planned here.

The blood . . .

From his vantage point, d'Charenton could see over the wall of the holding pen that was filled with young female slaves commandeered from homes throughout the city. He had wanted to use the virgin daughters of the aristocracy, for bloodline and breeding were important to him, but prudence had counseled that he begin more simply. The people would contest the destruction of their property, but would bear it as another tax imposed by France.

But the deaths of the Negresses would only be the beginning. The square would run red with blood, and hot with the power released with its spillage, and then would come the burning, and in the smoke of that sweet incense his reward would come. D'Charenton felt a warm coil of pleasure at the thought. So much blood. So much terror—the *jeunes filles* watching as their sisters died, knowing their turn was next. Surely it would be a pleasing sacrifice to the Lord of Despair.

He turned from the window to his mirror. As befit an aristocrat upon such an important and formal State occasion, d'Charenton wore an elaborate dress of black velvet worked with rubies and gold upon the cuffs and facings. Over that, he wore a hooded sleeveless robe of red silk, open at the front, embroidered with cabalistic symbols worked in the hair of virgins. He had robed himself in magic, and the multitude would adore him, just as it would adore his Master.

Turning from the mirror, d'Charenton checked the clock that stood in the corner, and consulted his horoscopes one last time.

It was the appointed hour.

It was time to begin.

The sergeant had given him water infused with *coca* leaves after they had chained him to the stake. Not out of pity, Corday realized, but so that he would be alert for what was to come. His face ached with a deep burning pain, and he suspected his right eye was damaged beyond healing, little though that would soon matter. The wood beneath his bleeding feet was dry and well-seasoned, promising a slow and agonizing death.

The square between the Cabildo and the Cathedral had been dressed as if this were a saint's day. The barricades were draped with colorful bunting, and the square was surrounded by torches. There was a reviewing stand filled with the notable personages of Nouvelle-Orléans, and barricades behind which were the folk of the city—proud Creoles and wealthy Frenchmen, burly Kaintocks, and haughty free men of color, herded here in the dying of the day, all jammed together like sheep in a pen and hemmed about by armed soldiers to keep them docile. They were not all the population of the city, but enough to fill Cabildo Square as far as the eye could see, save for the small space between the Cathedral and the stakes.

Men were tied to the stakes on either side of him. Their heads were covered with black hoods, though Corday's head had been left bare. One was in a uniform that Corday did not recognize—he struggled constantly and shouted, his voice muffled to unintelligibility by the hood.

The other wore the robes of a Prince of the Church, and stood quietly, though Corday could hear the rhythm of his prayers. Even in his injured condition, facing horrible death, Corday felt a pang of deeper grief. What was being done to him, some might say, was no more than justice for all the lives he had taken in his career as an assassin. But for d'Charenton to burn a Bishop of God's Holy Church implied a confidence on the Duc's part that must have a basis in far more terrible pacts and abominations than those Corday had witnessed.

There was a military band on the Cathedral steps behind him. Corday could hear them as they tuned. From within a makeshift pen off to his right came outcries and prayers. Women's voices, more sacrifices to d'Charenton's endless bloodlust. Even knowing how he was to die, Corday suddenly wished it would be over with now. He did not wish to see what he knew he would see here tonight before he died.

He could not even pray. Somehow he felt he had lost the right. All he could think of was that this thing was not right, that it should not be. He faced death and probable damnation, and all Corday could find in himself to wish for was that in his life he had been kinder and not so clever. . . .

The flickering of moving torches caught his attention, and he turned to look. D'Charenton was coming out from the Cabildo, flanked by six soldiers of his personal guard, wearing black and scarlet livery and carrying muskets. Behind him, Mam'selle McCarty walked proudly, all dressed in white lace and crowned in flowers. She carried a Bible in her hands, like a child going to her Confirmation.

D'Charenton himself was wearing a mockery of priest's robes, and for a moment Corday was filled with hope. Surely *this* would be enough to make the spectators rise up in protest. The soldiers could not kill them all if they chose to riot. They could save the innocents that were to die tonight. They could save themselves.

But no one moved.

What is wrong with everyone? Corday thought in despair. Couldn't they see what was going to happen? Didn't they care?

He tried to shout at them, to rally them to fight, but his voice came out in a cracked whisper, and the band began to play, drowning him out. It was playing the "Marseillaise," the anthem of Revolutionary France. Some of the onlookers began to cheer, and in his frantic despair, Corday felt the ghostly breath of King Mob wash over his skin. A mob was nothing more than a murderous animal, and d'Charenton would do his best to call that spirit into these good, frightened, confused men.

The music came to an end, and d'Charenton stepped forward to address the spectators, his silver hair making him look like a benign old priest. Behind him, one of the soldiers escorted Mam'selle McCarty to a chair of honor among the dignitaries in the stands, where the child would have a good view of the horrors that were to come.

"People of Nouvelle-Orléans!" d'Charenton cried in a huge voice. "Tonight you are privileged to witness a blessed birth. Tonight, Nouvelle-Orléans shall be reborn from the ashes of suspicion and doubt into a new and shining paradise, purged of all infirmity!"

He raised his hand in a signal, and now Corday heard the booming of drums—voudou drums, their rhythm calling the Gods, the Voudou Magnian, who lived both in the world and in the human heart. Corday felt a flash of painful pity for the musicians who had been broken so far as to profane their art for d'Charenton, but he did not blame them. He blamed none of d'Charenton's victims save himself. How could he have gambled with so many lives, knowing what he knew?

The stockade door opened, and the first of the victims was led out—a girl of perhaps fifteen, her eyes white with terror. D'Charenton held out his hand, and the captain of his guard placed a long knife into it.

The blade flashed silver in the torchlight. Corday screamed, and could not even hear himself. He closed his good eye. In his self-imposed darkness, he heard the spectators cry out at last, but mingled with the sounds of disbelief and anger was a curious anticipation.

✻   ✻   ✻

"Something's wrong," Koscuisko announced in a whisper, coming to a stop. A moment later, sound filled the air: drumming.

Wessex recognized it as the same cadence he had heard in the bayou when he had stumbled upon the voudou ceremony, just before Annie Christmas had knocked him unconscious.

"Ceremonial drums. Corday said that d'Charenton was experimenting with the local witchcraft," Wessex said.

In answer, Koscuisko pointed.

Between the buildings just ahead, a faint wash of light could be seen.

Torches in Cabildo Square.

And beneath the drumming, the sound of screams.

The roaring of a crowd followed the sound of the drums, blending with it and deepening its thunder. The rhythm of the distant cheers set Wessex's teeth on edge, and after a moment he recognized why. So had the mob which gathered to watch Madame Guillotine do her bloody work cheered each execution.

To the devil with circumspection. Such an audience would have eyes for nothing but the bloodshed before it. Wessex began to run toward Cabildo Square. Koscuisko, running after, grabbed him just as he reached the front of the Theâtre d'Orléans which stood behind the Arsenal.

"No!" Koscuisko said urgently, yanking him back into the shadows.

Wessex blinked, shaking off the furious spell of memories called up by the drums and the cheering. It was foolish of him to think he could stop the executions. As always, he must let innocents die to save himself.

"It seems," he said, his voice tight with anger, "that d'Charenton has moved his timetable forward. I expect I had best to kill him now."

"You can't get to him," Koscuisko said. He was stripping off his soutane—there was no point now in the disguise. Beneath it he wore a dark knit shirt and breeches.

"Perhaps not," Wessex answered, looking about himself. He smiled with savage triumph, seeing a path to his enemy. "But the show must go on, don't you think?"

Sarah and Meriel reached the edge of the city just after full dark. There would be no moon tonight, and Sarah had hoped for a lantern to guide her way, but the city was dark save for a glow upon the horizon as if some great bonfire burned somewhere within. The land about the city was still, unnaturally so—no dogs barked, no owls called.

"You see before you the end of all we are, Daughter of Kings."

Sarah turned toward the voice, swinging up her rifle in alarm. Meriel was nowhere to be seen. The sky shone moon-silver, bright with an impossible light, and the world was even more still and silent than a moment ago. Before her stood the Elderkin who had come to her upon the banks of Moonmere. Always before she had seen him clearly, yet this time, though the light was bright, somehow she could not look at him directly. Each time she tried, his form seemed to slide away, until he was only a flicker at the edge of her vision.

"I'm sorry," Sarah said, still not understanding. "I did all I could. And I will continue to do all I can."

"After tonight, the path of What Will Be is set. This land will no longer be a refuge for our kind. We must flee from Man's cities until at last we have no more foothold here.

"But do not despair, Daughter of Kings. We have departed from worlds before, and when it is time to go beyond the mountains to a new land we will go. Yet we will never leave you entirely, just as Land will never part from Land. And this last gift I give you."

He reached up to touch her between the eyes. Sarah recoiled, startled, and once more felt the rush of breeze and the gentle sounds of the river. All around her, objects appeared as sharp and clear as if they were well-lit, though the darkness was still as thick as before. Meriel was still gazing toward the city, as if she had noticed nothing.

Perhaps she has not, Sarah thought. *Perhaps the magic of that cup shields her from the Elderkin's magic. Was that what he meant? Is that what will drive his folk from the world?*

She did not know, any more than she knew what quixotic gal-
lantry had moved him to bestow upon her the faery-sight that turned
darkness into day and would make her journey into the city so much
easier. She did not trust what she didn't understand.

"We'll wait till morning," Sarah decided aloud. "I don't like this
at all."

"No," Meriel said. She dropped her cloak and was shrugging the
straps of the basket off her shoulders. "We must go now. It is already
nearly too late."

"Too late for what?" Sarah demanded in exasperation, but the
words died in her throat.

The cup was glowing.

Meriel cradled it reverently, one hand cupping its base, one
steadying its stem. The cup gleamed all over with a soft golden light,
as though it were lit from within, its gold as transparent as glass, or
as if sunlight from somewhere fell upon it alone.

It is bright enough to cast shadows, Sarah thought numbly, looking down at the ground.

"We must go now," Meriel repeated. "Please, Sarah. Help me.
Trust me."

Everybody wishes for me to trust them, and no one will explain!
Sarah thought indignantly, but Meriel had begun walking toward the
city without waiting for an answer, holding the cup before her like a
lamp.

Sarah shook her head. This was madness, and foolhardy besides.
But she slung her rifle off her shoulder, checked that her ammunition
was ready to hand, and followed Meriel past the first of the outlying
houses.

It was as if they walked through a city of ghosts—as if a city were a
living thing, and this one a corpse of a city. All the buildings they
passed were deserted. Some were boarded up, others had open doors
and broken windows, but a terrible sense of *absence* seemed to ra-
diate from every structure, as though inanimate wood and stone
could suffer bereavement.

Sarah would gladly have fled if she could have managed to take

Meriel with her. This was a city like the ones in her vision, and she wanted nothing to do with it. But Meriel walked on, neither looking to the left or right, and so Sarah followed, dreading each step she took. There were houses all around them—outlined in the light of whatever fire lay beyond—and Sarah had begun to assume that all the thousands of people who lived here were somehow gone, when they rounded a corner and saw two French soldiers patrolling, one carrying a lantern, the other with his rifle at the ready.

The soldiers stared at them in disbelief for a long moment, and Sarah thought at last perhaps she would receive an explanation of what was going on here. But then the one with the lantern struck his companion minatorily, and the other raised his rifle.

They aren't even going to arrest us! Sarah thought indignantly. Without thought, she raised her own rifle and fired. The rifleman fell backward, bowling his companion over and breaking the lantern. The spilled oil ignited in a brief puff of flame, then guttered out.

Quickly Sarah dropped to one knee to reload, remembering just in time that this rifle loaded at the breech and not the barrel. She worked the slide and charged the gun quickly, wishing with some uninvolved part of her mind that Meriel would not stand so close with the light she held. The other soldier could see her too clearly.

But he did not fire. He dragged himself out from beneath the body of his dead companion and fled.

Sarah watched after him until the sound of his running footsteps died away, then looked at Meriel, puzzled. But no explanation was forthcoming.

"At least we can stay away from the fire," Sarah said, to break the silence. "I wouldn't like to know what they're burning there, after a welcome like this."

"I'm sorry, Sarah," Meriel said apologetically, "but that is where the Cathedral is. And I must go there."

The cup in Meriel's hands burned ever brighter the closer they came to their destination, until both women walked within a bell of golden light. It was as if the waves of a monstrous ocean of night beat against the fragile protection of the light, and Sarah had a sudden intuition that without that protection their journey would be even more terrible than it was.

The light toward which they walked was a different thing altogether. It was as red as burning blood, silhouetting the spires of the Cathedral against the sky. They could hear the roaring of a crowd as they came closer to the Cathedral de Saint Louis—an unpleasant sound that was more like the baying of dogs than the cheering of crowds, and Sarah flinched away from it instinctively. For some reason, she was very, very sure she did not want to see the inhabitants of the Square.

"Meriel!" she whispered urgently. "We can't go there. It's right by the fires—there are people there, and if they are anything like the soldiers, I don't know what they may try to do." She thought of asking Meriel to conceal the glowing cup, and hesitated to do so for the same reason. She did not think she wished to be here without the protection of that Light.

Meriel stopped, and for the first time in many minutes looked at Sarah as if she saw her.

"We have to. *I* have to," she said simply.

"But does it have to be through the front door?" Sarah asked plaintively. Though she had never seen even a drawing of the great Cathedral that dominated the center of Nouvelle-Orléans, it surely must be of a similar construction to the English churches Sarah was familiar with. There was usually a side door by the altar through which the congregation could enter, as well as a back door that led through the vestry. If they could gain either of the alternate entrances, they could get into the church without seeing—or being seen by—what lay in the square beyond.

"I have to put the Cup on the altar," Meriel answered, as if she were only now wondering why this might be so. She smiled, and it was as if Meriel's old self peeked out for a moment from behind a mask of worry and determination and too much knowledge for the human spirit to bear. "But I do not think that God cares *how* I get into the church."

Sarah smiled, but she did not have long to luxuriate in her relief. Over the oceanic sound of the roaring mob, she heard the sound of many booted feet approaching at a run.

"Come on!" Sarah grabbed Meriel and ran.

Away from the Cathedral.

The *Théâtre d'Orléans* was deserted, though it showed signs of opportunistic vandalism. Inside its walls the shouting and the drums were muted, and that made it easier for Wessex to think.

Too late now to consider questioning d'Charenton for information about Sarah. Too late for so many things, perhaps even to rescue Corday. Even if Wessex killed d'Charenton now, who knew what orders the army had been given, or when the bombs that Robie had seen laid in the houses would be detonated? Louis might once more find himself crowned King of Nothing, even if d'Charenton died tonight.

The two men reached the back of the theater. The door to the outside was chained shut, but a few blows from a discarded maul broke the lock. Koscuisko eased the door open a bare inch, then closed it again, shaking his head.

"We can't get out that way," he said. He looked around. There were windows high along the walls that could be opened for ventilation, reachable from the iron stairs that led to the catwalks above the stage. The theater, so hastily abandoned, was filled with paraphernalia suitable to Koscuisko's purpose.

"Look around. Poles—ropes—sandbags—if we can get to this roof, we can get to the next. And nobody ever looks up," Koscuisko added.

Armed with their plunder, the two men climbed the long spiral stairs to the window that opened sixty feet above the ground. It was a tight squeeze. Koscuisko went first, and Wessex stopped to remove his coat before going on, cursing the fact that the shirt beneath it was white, but there was no help for it. Without the coat's fashionable constriction, Wessex had the freedom of movement to follow his partner out the window and up the side of the building. Just as he had prophesied, the plans he had made—and for which he had dressed so elegantly—had not survived their first encounter with events, and he must make do with what Fortune had sent him.

They gained the roof, but their view of the Square was still blocked by the looming bulk of the Arsenal that stretched before them. The building stood beside the Cabildo—the city had grown outward from the government buildings at its heart—and across the square from the Cathedral, whose spires gleamed brightly in the wash of light from the torches below. The space between the theater and the Arsenal was narrow—perhaps twenty feet—but too wide to jump, even though the roof of the Arsenal was slightly below them.

Wessex walked to the edge of the roof and looked down. There were at least two thousand people gathered in the square below, if what he could see were any indication. While the two of them could blend into such a mob virtually unnoticed, the crowd made it impossible for either of them to reach d'Charenton.

"And now? We fly?" Wessex asked. He began knotting a weight into the end of a light coil of rope, knowing it was useless. He could toss the weighted line to the other roof, and even, if he were lucky, snag one of the gargoyles that ornamented the roof of the Arsenal, but it was unlikely the line would hold or the friable stone bear his weight.

"After a fashion," Koscuisko replied enigmatically. "I saw this done once in a circus in Venice. I've always wanted to try it."

He was testing the pole he'd carried up from below—a length of ash twelve feet long, with a hook at one end. It was used by the stagehands of the *Théâtre d'Orléans* to pull down the counterweights that raised and lowered scenery.

"Don't tell me," Wessex suggested. Koscuisko grinned and retreated to the far corner of the building, carrying the carefully balanced staff upon his shoulder. Wessex stood back, ready to take what came.

Koscuisko began to run forward, with an odd loping sideways gait, the rod balanced at his shoulder. He reached the edge of the building and Wessex tensed to pull him back from certain death. At the last possible moment, Koscuisko dropped the end of the pole. It hit the low brick edge of the roof and stuck.

The far end whipped into the air, carrying Koscuisko with it. For a moment the pole stood nearly upright, and Wessex watched as Koscuisko swung his body around it and soared outward into space, then let go. Released, the rod sprang back. Wessex dived and caught it before it fell to the ground below.

When he looked up, for a moment he did not see his partner anywhere. Where was Koscuisko? He scanned the opposite roof, and at last a flash of movement caught his eye. Koscuisko was getting to his feet, waving to show he was safe. The pole had enabled him to vault the gap between the two buildings.

"The things you learn at circuses," Wessex muttered. He took up the coil of rope and made sure it would run free, then stepped up and flung the weight tied at its end as hard as he could.

It took two casts, but then Koscuisko had it secure in his hands and was tying it off to one of the stone gargoyles that ornamented the Arsenal's roof, coiling the slack in his hands to take the strain.

Now it was Wessex's turn. He gathered the end of the rope in his hands—glad he was wearing gloves—and stepped off the edge of the roof into space.

For a moment he fell straight down, then the rope began to pull him forward. Like a pendulum, Wessex swung toward the other building feet first, as above, Koscuisko shortened the line to keep him as high above the crowd below as possible. The moment his feet hit the wall Wessex began scrambling up the rope as fast as he could, the soles of his feet smarting from their impact against the brick.

Koscuisko dragged him the last few feet and coiled the rope in after him.

"You'll be delighted to know that there's a trap door that leads down," he said, as Wessex struggled to catch his breath. "But I think you'd better look at the Square first."

Koscuisko's voice was tight with shock, for all the airy banter of his words, and Wessex steeled himself against the sight of something terrible. But even his worst imaginings fell fearfully short of the sight that greeted him.

In the uncertain light of the torches, he could see across the square to the porch of the Cathedral beyond. Bodies hung from a gibbet erected over the steps of the church, and beneath the corpses sat three men with their drums, their sable skin glistening with the sweat of their exertions. In the center of the square stood three iron stakes. Chained to the center one was Charles Corday. His body was a map of welts and bruises, and half his face was a bloody ruin, but he still lived.

In front of Corday stood d'Charenton in his scarlet Devil's robes, and around d'Charenton lay the bodies of half a dozen young women, their throats slit as if they were pigs. Save for a small area around the bodies and the stakes, Cabildo Square was filled with armed soldiers restraining a mixed mob of *Orléannais.* As Wessex watched, the soldiers brought d'Charenton another victim. The sound of her screams was swallowed up in the hungry roaring of the crowd as the soldiers forced her to her knees, as though her death fed their appetite as well as d'Charenton's.

For a moment Wessex's mind reeled, and he wanted nothing more than to turn his back on this monstrous horror. Then his will asserted itself. He reached for his pistol, then hesitated. It was long range for a shot, especially by torchlight. With unfamiliar weapons, he did not think he could make it.

"I have to get closer," Wessex said reluctantly. He looked at his partner. Another roar rose up from the crowd lining the square. Koscuisko turned away, his face pale but expressionless.

"Let's go down."

The trap door was chained from below, but there was enough play in the chain for Wessex to wedge the muzzle of one of his pistols through the gap and fire. The chain parted with a ringing sound and he raised the iron door. He did not worry about being heard—not with the inferno going on in the Square below.

The stairway below was empty, and when they reached the foot of the steps they could see—in the flickering torchlight that shone through the barred windows—that the store of powder and weapons that should have been here was gone. The two men looked down the stairs that led to the front door and the square beyond.

"Give me five minutes," Koscuisko said. "I'll find a window to shoot from. It will draw their attention."

"Hurry," Wessex said. Each moment they waited meant another life.

Koscuisko turned away. Wessex stood a moment longer in the firelit darkness, then drew his remaining pistol. He would have liked to have both, but it was too dark to reload. With his pistol in his left hand and his sabre in his right, he continued down the stair.

The Arsenal was an impressive building, built at the height of the power of the Dons. From the foot of the staircase the foyer stretched thirty feet to the enormous ironbound doors. Wessex crossed the expanse warily, straining to hear any sound above the drums and the crowd, but there was none. D'Charenton had concentrated all his forces outside in the Square.

Carefully, Wessex pulled open one of the double doors. This close to the carnage, the smell of blood was a thick fog in the air, and Wessex steeled himself against it.

D'Charenton was to his right, directly between the Cabildo and the Cathedral. The sorcerer was surrounded by soldiers. Blood gloved him, staining the once-white linen at his wrists, and even spotted his incarnadine robes, drying to an ugly russet color upon the red silk. Wessex raised his pistol, but was unable to get a clear shot through d'Charenton's guards. He had only one shot, and they would give him no time to reload—but as soon as Koscuisko fired, the soldiers would scatter, and then Wessex could fire with reasonable certainty of striking his prey. But the seconds stretched, and there was no sound of gunfire from the window above.

Why didn't Koscuisko shoot?

A moment later Wessex understood.

The drums fell silent in a ragged skirl, and Annie Christmas came walking through the crowd. The townspeople scrambled to get out of the black giantess's way, and even the soldiers drew back from her. She wore a white calico dress and a white tignon upon her hair. Her arms and neck were wreathed with live snakes, and she wore a necklace of skulls and alligator teeth. Upon her ample hips was tied a red fabric belt covered with scalps and barely identifiable scraps of dried flesh. Between her teeth she clenched an enormous black cigar, and blue smoke wreathed her features as she puffed on it.

"Wheah de scrawny w'ite mans whut gots mah Charlie?" she roared in her deep bass voice. "I be Annie Chris'mas, de na'chural dautah o' de typhoon an de lightnin'-quake. I gots blessin' in my righ' han' an cursin' in my lef'. I can raise up de daid an' cas' down de livin', an' I doan feah no mans o' woman born. Ah comes ter sets de hoodoo on de mans whut took mah boy!"

Amazingly, the crowd let her through—but if Wessex had learned one thing in his sojourn here, it was that the *Orléannais* feared the *Voudous* more than the powers of either Church or State. He understood why Koscuisko had held his fire. Annie Christmas just might have a chance to destroy d'Charenton, and to gain the sympathy of the mob at the same time.

"Gib' me whut yo' done stole from me!" Annie bellowed.

The serpents slid over her neck and shoulders, but she paid no attention to them.

"Kneel and I will let you live," d'Charenton answered. Beside Annie's vitality the diabolist looked even more like an old man rotted through with drugs and age, held to life by malice alone. He raised one bloated white paw and gestured toward her.

At first, whatever d'Charenton had done did not seem to have any effect.

Annie uncoiled an enormous black snake from around her neck, held it out in her two hands, and flung it toward d'Charenton. It should have struck him, but somehow it fell short, writhing against the blood-covered stones for a moment before squirming away, and it was as if that failure had hurt her somehow. Close as he was, Wessex could see the beads of sweat that sprang up against Annie's skin, and her face twisted as if she were suddenly in pain. She grabbed for another of her serpents, but this time the one she touched turned on her, sinking its fangs deep into her hand.

She cried out in shock and pain, and all the snakes she carried dropped away from her body as though she had suddenly shed a fabulous cloak. Wessex heard scattered outcries from the crowd as people jumped to avoid them, but still he could not get a clear shot at d'Charenton.

Now Annie coughed, and suddenly her mouth was painted red with fresh blood. She shook her head like a bull maddened by flies, and took a step forward, her hands outstretched, obviously intending to choke the life from d'Charenton.

She never reached him. At the next step her knees buckled beneath her and she fell, vomiting bright blood. She gazed up at d'Charenton, and Wessex saw her furious eyes glaze over in death. She died trying to reach her enemy.

"Does anyone else challenge my power?" d'Charenton cried in glee. The crowd murmured in confused agitation. D'Charenton bent over to kiss Annie's bloodstained mouth.

"Dead or alive, I believe the lady would find your attentions unwelcome," Wessex called into the silence as he thrust open the door of the armory. The soldiers guarding d'Charenton had been stunned by the uncanny nature of Annie Christmas' death. Still Koscuisko did not fire. This was the best chance Wessex would have.

D'Charenton recoiled at the sound of the familiar voice. His eyes widened as he recognized Wessex, but he made a quick recovery, rising to his feet and bowing slightly.

"M'sieur le Duc d'Anglais! How odd to find you here—but how fitting. You, of all men, should understand what I have come here to do, for death has always been your tool."

D'Charenton's guards looked behind themselves at Wessex, unsure whether he was friend or foe. They shuffled uncertainly—but the sight of a pistol raised against their master would decide them. Wessex lowered it and stepped forward.

"I do not care to listen to your ravings," he answered coolly. "I have come to destroy you, d'Charenton. If your power is as great as you say, you will not need your soldiers to stop me. If it is not, perhaps it is not enough to protect them, either."

It was a gamble—a calculated insult both to d'Charenton's vanity and his followers' self-interest. Wessex took another step forward, hoping his bluff would get him close enough to fire.

But d'Charenton threw up his hand, and the guards turned toward Wessex, closing ranks again.

"Throw down your gun, M'sieur le Duc d'Wessex," d'Charenton called from behind them. "I think guns are so uncivilized, don't you? The sword is the true weapon of the aristocrat. Throw down your gun, English spy, and perhaps I will let you try your steel before you die. *Do it!* If you do not, I will order them to shoot."

Still no shot came from above, and now Wessex feared that Koscuisko had met some foe of his own there in the darkness. Reluctantly, Wessex did as he was bid, turning the pistol to shake the powder out of the pan and then tossing it to the stones. D'Charenton beckoned him forward, mad eyes alight, and now the soldiers fell back.

Wessex stepped from the doorway into the square. His boots slipped on the blood-wet stone as he came ever closer to d'Charenton. The point of his sword angled upward *en garde*, moments away from finding its home in the diabolist's heart, and he wondered what d'Charenton could hope to gain by this mummery. Even if he used against Wessex whatever force had slain Annie, Wessex would have enough time to plunge the point of his sabre into d'Charenton's heart before he died.

Slowly the air seemed to grow darker, as if black flames licked at the edges of Wessex's vision. He knew better than to take his eyes from d'Charenton's face, but even the torches behind the diabolist seemed to be growing dim. Somehow, though, that seemed only to be expected, a natural and unremarkable event. Wessex's sword-point remained steady as he paced forward to within striking range.

But the metal burned his fingers in a puzzling way, and his fingers seemed suddenly clumsy. Wessex stopped and shook his head violently to clear it, but d'Charenton did not take advantage of his inattention to riposte. Heartened by his luck, Wessex paced forward once again, beginning to wonder why he had not yet reached striking distance.

He was cold.

It was that sudden lash of unnatural sensation that galvanized Wessex out of the daze into which he had fallen. He swung his sword in a wide arc, staring around himself, but there was nothing. Only the blackness of shadows, and d'Charenton's white face shining before like a captive moon. The man was smiling, daring Wessex to come against him, and Wessex knew that somehow he had fallen into a trap of *magie* worse than the one that had killed Annie Christmas. He lunged, committing everything he had in one great attack.

Now Wessex ran forward, slashing with his blade as though he engaged a multitude. He knew he must be in position, but somehow the sword-thrust did not reach d'Charenton, though d'Charenton had not moved. He *must* reach his foe—he *had* to have reached him by now, but still d'Charenton stood, inviolate as the moon, and Wessex felt his limbs tremble with mortal fatigue. He would never move, and Wessex would never reach him.

"You see, M'sieur le Duc?" d'Charenton said pedantically, as though the two of them were scholars engaged in the bloodless pursuit of knowledge. "My power is greater than yours, as Magic is greater than Science. The pallid day of Reason is past, and I will usher in an era of eternal night."

Why doesn't Koscuisko fire? Wessex wondered desperately. Koscisko could see the square—he must see that Wessex was in trouble.

Unless Illya Koscuisko was already dead.

"It is, in its way, a pity. You could have been so much more fitting an opponent for me than you chose to be. But you restricted yourself to mechanical tricks, renouncing the hermetic birthright of your noble blood. You stood upon the shore of a vast sea of knowledge, and you never even played among the waves."

D'Charenton's voice grew somehow larger. Wessex's sight was fading, and his fingers were already so numb that he could not tell whether they still grasped the hilt of his sword or not, but as his senses had dimmed d'Charenton's voice had taken on shape, and color, and texture, until each word he spoke was somehow a separate entity, and Wessex stood amidst them, surrounded by his enemies.

I have lost, he thought in a last brief moment of clarity, and cursed his own arrogance, for even when he had seen what d'Charenton had made of Nouvelle-Orléans, he had thought the man's Satanic games of torture and humiliation only a nasty recreation for a madman, and not that they had true power. . . .

In the darkness, Illya Koscuisko waited at the window overlooking the Square, waiting for Wessex to appear. He did not see Annie Christmas approach and die, nor the moment when his partner stepped out of hiding. He gazed down at the Square, and did not see that the images before him were tangled in a terrible web of

potential, forever on the verge of action, never yet reaching that
moment.

And so he waited. . . .

Their progress toward the Cathedral became a terrible game of cat
and mouse. Sarah and Meriel fled across back gardens and through
alleyways, always away from the sound of marching feet. Each time
they thought they had lost the soldiers and began heading for their
destination, the sound of booted feet followed, forever between them
and their destination, harrying them away. If not for her faery sight,
which showed them every escape route, the two of them would have
been caught and killed already.

Meriel's face was streaked with frantic tears, and as the minutes
stretched to hours, a slow terrible anger grew in Sarah, until it shook
her with every beat of her heart. They had reached the street once
again, six hundred yards from their destination, and ahead of them
Sarah heard the tramping feet once more.

Meriel cowered back against the steps of some absent Creole's
fine house, her face drawn with weariness and the anguish of failing
once again.

I will not permit this to go on, a voice from Sarah's deepest self
said slowly. *It is not right.*

It was as if her will alone became her weapon, her sword and
shield against the darkness.

"Meriel," she said gently. "Will you do something for me?"

"Of course—if I can," her friend answered in a low whisper.

"When the soldiers come, run. Run around them, run toward
the Cathedral as fast as you can," Sarah said. "Do not wait for me."

"But—but where will you be?" Meriel asked. The cup trembled
in her hands with the exhaustion of the hours of running.

"I will be here," Sarah said, baring her teeth in a terrible smile
of anger. "Now stand back in the alley where they will not see you."

Meriel nodded, and Sarah knelt behind the brick steps of the
nearest house. The moment the light cast by the cup left her, Sarah
was drowned in a suffocating sense of terror and despair. The soldiers

would fire when they saw her. She was asking Meriel to run into a hail of bullets. This plan would not work. It would fail. She would fail. They would both die here, for nothing.

No. The denial came from a place deeper than reason, deeper than sense, from the place where the instinct for survival lives. But Sarah's instinct was not for her own survival. It was for the victory of the Light over the Dark, an instinct as uncompromising as a mother's need to protect her child. In its service men had died upon sword-blades and upon the gallows, and now Sarah was one of their number. She swung her ammunition bag down off her shoulder, pulled back the rifle-bolt, and waited, her entire being concentrated down to one tiny ferocious flame of indomitable will. She would triumph here, even in death.

No matter what, she would not run.

The soldiers appeared—twelve men and their leader—their faces clear to her magical sight. And it seemed to Sarah now that she saw them that there was something oddly beast-like about their faces—not in the way that Grandfather Bear was a beast, but as if whatever was human in the spirit of these men had suffered some terrible injury, and their faces bore the scars. The leader of the soldiers pointed toward Sarah, and red firelight shimmered down the blade of his sword.

Sarah fired, kneeling. And then lay down behind her cover, re-loaded her breech-loading rifle, and fired again.

A soldier of His Majesty King Henry could fire three shots a minute with the Baker rifle, but the Baker had to be charged with ball, powder, and patch, and the whole rammed home down the length of the barrel with the ramrod. The Farland she bore loaded at the breech, and did not take a ramrod. Every fifteen seconds—four times each minute—working in the darkness with the certitude of one who might have been blind for life, Sarah fired again. She did not have to rise to her knees to load. She did not have to expose herself to the enemy. She fired again and again, as steady and re-morseless as a ticking clock, as the soldiers' shots exploded around her, spraying her face with brick dust and filling the night with rolling clouds of black powder gunsmoke.

She did not hear the moment when Meriel fled toward the church, and blinded by the repeating flash of gunfire, Sarah did not see the Grail's glow depart. Walls of gunsmoke rolled through the street, and Sarah knew that soon the enemy soldiers would flank her, would catch her in an unanswerable cross-fire, and her life would be over.

But Meriel would get through to do the thing that the enemy would kill to prevent. Sarah would have the victory she fought for.

Another bullet struck the bricks, but this one came from behind. Sarah swung her rifle around and fired at the flash. She heard a scream, and dropped to load again.

It was only a matter of time.

Hurry, Meriel!

She had thought she would never be able to run out into the shots as Sarah had asked, but the guns began to fire and Meriel found herself bolting, without remembering how she began. Ahead lay the black bulk of the Cathedral, and for the first time there were no soldiers between her and her goal.

And then all at once the stones of the church were under her free hand. She groped blindly along the wall, panting from her run and trembling from the hammering of her heart, until the door's handle was beneath her hand.

She tugged, but the vestry door did not move. From within, Meriel heard the clink of chain. Locked. She began to panic and hurried on, looking for a second door by the light of the Cup she bore.

But the side door of the church was locked as well, and would not open. For a few moments Meriel tugged at it, unable to believe that she had come so close only to fail. She was now on a direct line with the square, and the door beneath her hands was lit both by the Grail and the light that came from the torches the soldiers held, but Meriel would not look toward the Square. She did not want to see what was there.

"I have come all this way," she whispered to the Cup. "I have done all You asked. Sarah has done all *I* asked. And now this? Why? You made the waters smooth—you could open this door as well."

There was no answer.

She knew what she had to do, little though she wished to. There was one more door for her to try, but to dare it she must walk into the strength of the dark power that had taken this city for its own. Fresh tears spilled down her cheeks and she wept at the unfairness of it, begging for any other choice than this. But there was no answer, and timidly Meriel turned toward the fire. She walked forward as slowly as if she waded through deep water, filling her eyes with the shining Cup she carried, willing herself to see nothing beyond it, no, not even if she died for refusing to look. Slowly, with small dogged steps, she made her way around the side of the Cathedral into the full view of the square beyond.

The steps had been fouled with animal bones and other trash, and on a rude gibbet erected across the doorway hung the bodies of six priests in their black and white vestments, swaying slowly at rope's end like a strange harvest. To enter the Cathedral Meriel must pass directly between the murdered bodies.

She wanted to cross herself, but her free hand was shaking too hard to complete the gesture. She wanted to pray, but the only words that ran through her mind sounded more like a child's angry accusation: "You *promised* me—You *promised* me—You *promised*—"

The robes brushed her face as she passed between the dead men. They smelled of incense and linen, the good holy smells of her childhood Sundays that was now the scent of love and eternal security betrayed.

Before her the wide oaken doors of the Cathedral stood closed. The sight of that last barrier was almost enough to make her weep. Closed, and locked like all the others, and everything she had done to get here for nothing, all for nothing.

But Sarah had come nearly as far without even faith to guide her, and so Meriel owed it to Sarah to try until there was nothing left to do. She reached for the door, screened from the watchers across the square by the bodies on the gibbet, and tried the hammered iron handle.

The door opened.

Intoxicated with mingled terror and hope, Meriel staggered forward, across the threshold of the church. The door swung closed behind her, and by the light of the Cup she carried, Meriel could see the inside of the Cathedral.

The painted saint's statues had been cast down from their niches and broken, and the whitewashed walls had been splashed with blood. Buckets of offal had been flung over the altar, and the meat seethed there, black with buzzing flies. A sob caught in her throat, but she did not falter.

I will not stop now, Meriel told herself. These sights were almost commonplace next to the horrors her mind had conjured and the deaths she had already seen. She walked down the blood-slick carpet of the center aisle until she reached the altar, slipping in the blood and filth beneath her feet. But when she passed the Sanctuary rail before the altar, she found she could not force herself to go closer. The smell of corruption, the buzzing of the flies, the glistening of the entrails made her cringe. She could not bear the thought of touching the offal, and if she recoiled from touching it, how much more should she balk from placing the Grail, the symbol of purity, upon this debased surface?

Was it wrong to go on? When the blessed angels had told her to bring the Grail here, surely they had not known what this place would look—and *smell*—like, how terrible it would have become. They would not have asked her to do this if they had known.

She listened for guidance, but no word came. The light of the Cup in her hands, that had been so bright when she entered the church, was fading now, and in only moments more she would be alone in the dark.

I will do what I said I would do.

Before she could stop herself, Meriel grasped the Grail firmly in two hands and thrust it down into a pile of entrails. They squished as the Cup touched them, and she pressed hard, and went on pressing, until its base touched the altar beneath.

There was a sizzling sound, as though she had dropped an icicle into hot fat, and the light flashed suddenly, terrifyingly bright. Meriel cried out, startled, and recoiled, slipping on the blood beneath her moccasins and falling backward down the three steps that led up to the altar.

And then there was nothing but the light.

You never had much faith in magic, Wessex thought to himself. *That's why you're in so much trouble now.* It was an interesting idea.

There was something he should be doing besides musing idly over his shortcomings, but somehow Wessex's mind refused to give up that knowledge, interested instead in an internal debate Wessex had engaged in so many times before. If Magic had held true power, would the Old King have died? Would the atheist Napoleon reign now in his place?

Magic. It was an acknowledged part of everyday life, especially among the aristocracy, but to Wessex the *Art Magie* had always seemed more a game of lies designed to trap and befool the wielder than any sort of clean-cut science. He had been embarrassed more than uplifted by the ancient ceremony of his Pledging on the day— too long ago!—when he assumed the titles and dignities of the Duke of Wessex. It had seemed to him then to be nothing more than foolishness, antique mummery beneath the notice of a rational man. He had poured the libations, kissed the Stone, left his gift, and gone back to the world of sunlight and law in which he belonged, thinking nothing more of the matter. But as the years passed, it began to seem that all the troubles, all the conflicts of Wessex's life had originated in that place, when he had confronted that which he could not accept. He had put it behind him as best it could, but now it seemed he had returned to his beginnings at last.

The night, the square, d'Charenton, the eternal Darkness, all were gone. Wessex stood once more upon the Sussex downs, barefoot in a white linen shirt and breeches, standing before the Pledging Stone. He was fourteen years old.

The Stone was an impressive rough-hewn pillar that stood unmolested between the field of one of his tenants and a small woods. The country people decorated it and danced before it, even though they were good Christians, and the country curate turned a blind eye to their ancient veneration of those powers that were old when his own faith was yet unborn.

All was just as it had been upon that day, but this time, instead of his father's game keeper, an old man who had been as ill at ease in the Pledging as the young Duke had, a woman stood beside the Pledging Stone.

She was tall, taller than any human could be, as tall as the stone itself and as fair as the day. She wore a cloak of wolfskin about her shoulders and carried a shield and spear. Her eyes were a bright and terrible blue and her lips were as red as fresh blood.

"I am Brigantia. I am England. How will you serve me, Rupert, Duke of Wessex?"

The question was nearly the one he had been asked on that other day that was somehow this one come again. *"How will you serve the land?"* He knew the proper response, but this time the answer took on a terrible burden of significance. The words he spoke would be more holy than any oath, binding him more terribly than any worldly obligations he could assume. But he could not stand mute and refuse to answer. He was Wessex, and his family had been old in England long before foreign kings[65] had come to rule them.

"Here in this time that is not a time, in this place that is not a place, I answer: with all my heart, with all my strength, with all my soul, I will serve You. Body and will shall serve You, and when I die, let me be laid in the earth to serve You still."

The terrible Goddess smiled, and Wessex knew in that moment that he would forever seek Her in all women, hoping to find Her again in all of them.

"And so you will, Rupert, and your children after you. My word to you. Your line will serve the Land until the Land itself shall pass away." Brigantia reached out her hand and touched him, lightly, above the heart.

It felt like a hammerblow exploding in his chest. In a flash like

---

65. The foreign kings Wessex is thinking of here are the Normans, who invaded England in 1066.

dark lightning the summer countryside was gone, and Wessex was on his knees, gasping for breath above d'Charenton's slain body.

And then there was nothing but the light.

❖   ❖   ❖

For one confused moment Sarah thought the sun had risen, but what illuminated the street was not the golden light of the sun. It was white, whiter than anything she had ever seen, filling the Cathedral like the force of a raging torrent and spilling through the doors, the windows, the very chinks in the stone, filling the sky above and the street below with brightness, blowing away the clouds of smoke as though it were a current of pure force.

As the light touched the soldiers, they screamed, though Sarah felt nothing. They threw down their weapons and clawed at their faces, howling as though they burned. Sarah would have leapt to her feet then and run for the Cathedral, but when she tried she felt a burning pain and weakness all along her right leg, and when she put her hand to her thigh, it came away wet. And so she stayed where she was as that impossible light turned the night to day and her enemies fled before it, crawling and staggering as though somehow they were horribly burned.

And then there was nothing but the light.

There was nothing but the light. It tore through the fabric of the Place he had created, weakening the armor of the magic he had forged. And through the holes in the darkness, the Duc d'Charenton could sense the approach of a greater Darkness still, a Darkness that had existed from the beginning of time, coming now to claim him.

"No! You told me the Grail was here! I have searched for it everywhere, and I have not found it. You told me it would be mine!" He stood before the Darkness, knowing that all it had promised him was gone, and only darkness remained. "You lied," d'Charenton whimpered.

I TOLD YOU IT WOULD BE HERE. AND SO IT IS, the remote inhuman voice corrected him. FOR I DO NOT LIE, THOUGH YOUR KIND WOULD LIKE

TO THINK I DO. BUT YOU HAVE NOT BROUGHT IT TO ME TO PROFANE UPON MY ALTAR. AND SO YOUR LIFE AND ALL YOUR WORKS ARE FORFEIT.

And then there was nothing but the darkness.

Koscuisko blinked and recoiled, startled by the flash of light. He looked down—where was Wessex?—but could see nothing but the light, a lightning-flare unnaturally prolonged. He cursed, flinging himself to his feet and staggering to the stairs.

He flung open the door and started out into Cabildo Square. Across the way, the Cathedral's stained-glass windows sparkled brilliantly, as if lit from within by a thousand thousand candles.

Wessex was kneeling among the corpses, his body across d'Charenton's, his bloody sword still clutched in his hand. Koscuisko dropped to his knees beside his friend, but Wessex was already trying to rise.

"Is he dead?" Koscuisko asked urgently.

"Yes. I think—" Wessex began. But whatever he had meant to say was muffled beneath the roar of the captive mob as it turned upon the soldiers who held it. The human tide broke over the reviewing-stand like a savage torrent, seeking to destroy the minions of their oppressor.

Few of d'Charenton's associates survived that night. And no one in Nouvelle-Orléans ever saw Mademoiselle Delphine McCarty again.

The Duke of Wessex could not afterward precisely remember the details of the riot, nor how he and his partner had escaped annihilation. Once he and Koscuisko won through to the stakes and freed the prisoners, the Bishop and the Admiral were able to unite their followers to restore a semblance of order to the immediate area. Even Corday, who Wessex had taken for dead, had been able to rally the militia before collapsing.

In the lull that followed, Wessex quickly took charge of the bewildered mass of *Orléannais*. There was one last task to perform, or else all that went before it would be in vain.

❀   ❀   ❀

The sun had been up for several hours before the last citizen-patrol reported that its district had been cleared. Wessex had set up a command post in the Arsenal, not daring to risk using the Cabildo, and from it he had overseen the removal of the bombs that ringed Nouvelle-Orléans.

No one had questioned his right to give orders, but they soon would. The crisis was past. General Victor was dead—reports said he had been killed sometime early yesterday—and the *Orléannais* had killed any of d'Charenton's soldiers they could find. The majority of the troops had stripped off their uniforms and were probably somewhere in hiding.

A few hours ago Jerome Bonaparte's flagship had anchored at the bottom of Toulouse Street, and a squad of Marines led by the ship's officers had come seeking their Admiral. They, too, had helped to restore order to the fractured city. If the Imperial Fleet had engaged the Baratarian navy, no one had thought it worthy of mention.

There were still bands of drunken looters roaming the streets, but their depredations were no worse (so Corday said from his bed in the makeshift hospital in the Arsenal) than what one might see at Mardi Gras. Word had been passed, and the surviving leaders of the intended revolution had gathered; Corday was being proclaimed as Governor, but that, too, would change quickly.

"I suppose we can vanish into the mist, now?" Koscuisko asked hopefully.

"I think so," Wessex answered. "Let us see if Pierre Lafitte's house still stands. D'Charenton is dead, and I am too tired to think of anything else but sleep."

But as they came down the steps of the Arsenal, both men gazed as if summoned toward the Cathedral across the square. Wessex thought of asking Koscuisko what had really happened last night— or at least what his partner had seen—but hesitated, realizing he truly did not want to know the answer. But it seemed somehow fitting, with the miracle of their survival growing more ordinary with every moment, to give thanks for their salvation in the Christian place nearest to it.

The doors of the Cathedral stood open. The bodies of the murdered priests had been taken down from d'Charenton's gibbet, to wait with the others for inhumation in mortuary tombs in St. Louis Cemetery, and volunteers were aiding the Bishop in cleansing the building of its defilement.

A strong scent of lye and incense greeted Wessex as he stepped inside. The church looked as if it had been stripped bare of all decoration, and faded bloodstains still covered the walls. Part of it had been converted into a makeshift field hospital, but the pews were also full of *Orléannais* giving thanks for their deliverance.

Koscuisko moved forward confidently—the man was a Catholic, after all—but Wessex hesitated in the doorway, not certain, now, what he had been seeking here in the sanctuary of an alien faith. Last night he had done the King's work, and the White Tower's, and perhaps God's as well. He was thankful, but not certain whether he should render thanks—or to whom, in the final analysis. It was an uncomfortable thought.

"Rupert!" a beloved voice cried, cutting through the murmur of prayers. Wessex looked around, and saw an Indian youth hobbling toward him on a makeshift crutch. Then he knew it was Sarah, and a moment later she was in his arms.

"Wessex! What are you doing here?" his bride demanded indignantly. She smelled of smoke and blood, and there was a thick bandage upon her leg, but she was here, alive, and whole. "Meriel is here, and I—"

"I don't care," Wessex answered, burying his face in her throat.

14

The Leopard Triumphant
(December 25th, 1807)

The King of Louisianne was officially crowned on Christmas Day.

The two months since d'Charenton's death had been busy. Admiral Jerome Bonaparte had sailed his ships out of the port on November 14th, bearing a copy of Louisianne's Declaration of Independence to the Emperor, his brother. Unlike most messengers with such unwelcome news, Jerome Bonaparte was almost certain to survive the delivering of it.

Envoys had gone to the Lord-Lieutenant of New Albion and the King of England as well, for Louisianne intended cordial relations with her sister powers. Within a fortnight of Louis' assumption of this newly-created throne—he would be the head of a constitutional state, though the Constitution was yet to be written—the Port was once more filled with shipping, as the word spread that the ruinous tariffs of the previous several months had been overturned.

Other matters would take longer to unravel. Though the buying and selling of slaves had been abolished immediately, as had the provisions of the draconian Black Code, the slaves' full manumission would be the slow work of months, for more than half the present inhabitants of Louisianne were property, and without their labor, all of Louisianne would starve. They must be educated to freedom, the large landholders persuaded to take responsibility for cultivating their independence and preparing them to sell the labor that had once been extorted from them.

But that was the work of politicians and statesmen, and undoubtedly Louisianne's new rulers would contrive something, Wessex thought. The daily minutiae of government had never been of interest to him, and just now, it was even less so. For the last two months, the Duke and Duchess of Wessex had lived in a rented house on Rampart Street, attended by Atheling (who had arrived on the Duke's newly purchased yacht only a few days after the news had reached Baltimore of the revolution in Nouvelle-Orléans) and entertained by Illya Koscuisko—and, occasionally, by Lafitte's young companion Robie, now recovered from his wound and complaining bitterly that the days of adventure seemed to be over.

It had been a curious and oddly pleasant interlude. The Wessexes planned to return to England when the spring sailing season began, but Wessex's resignation from the Order of the White Tower would precede him there by some months. He did not know just what the future would hold, but he knew that no longer could he travel a road of divided loyalties. He was the Duke of Wessex, the King's man, and he could no longer play the Shadow Game.

Her husband had told her very little of his adventures; Sarah had pieced together the truth of that terrible night from things M'sieur Corday let fall and from marketplace gossip. Louis had told her more, when she had finally been able to pry him from Meriel's arms, but Meriel had told her nothing at all. The Cup she had carried here from the banks of the Ohio through such trouble and privation was gone once more, and for Meriel that was the end of the matter.

The young friends spoke instead of the future: Meriel's, to reign as Queen-Consort of this strange new country that seemed to Sarah like an odd mirror-echo of her own lost United States; Sarah's, to return to England and her place as Wessex's Duchess. At least Wessex seemed now to be at peace, far more so than she had ever yet seen him. It was as if, in the months he had been parted from her, he had faced some strange trial of bravery and won home to her arms, content at last.

Sarah was content as well. Ever since her arrival in this world she had fought against its strangeness and longed for the one she had lost, but no longer. If her adventure had taught her anything, it was that she did not want merely to take up her old life once more, even if she had been able to. She was no longer that young Colonial who had looked upon the Bristol Docks with such wide-eyed awe. She belonged to England now . . . and to Wessex. Together they would work for England, so that the terrible vision of Sarah's spirit-quest would never come to pass.

The coronation was the vindication of all that the *Orléannais* had done to sweep the memory of d'Charenton from their city. St. Louis Cathedral was filled with dignitaries from throughout the Grande Alliance. Thomas Jefferson, the Lord-Lieutenant of New Albion, had come with his new bride, the former Sally Hemings, and the governors of Maryland and Virginia had come as well. The chiefs of those tribes which shared Louisianne with the Europeans sent envoys and gifts, and in the end the occasion, if not as splendid as its European counterpart, was as sparkling and lavish a day as Nouvelle-Orléans had lately seen.

At nine o'clock that December morning, an open carriage pulled up before the house on Royal Street that was home to the young King-Elect and his wife. They had risen early that morning to hear Mass in a private chapel, and then separated to don the clothes they would wear at the ceremony.

Louis wore a fabulous formal dress of white velvet, with satin shoes and a satin waistcoat. His person glittered with diamonds— many of them borrowed—for the proud *Orléannais* were determined that their King would outshine even his Old World counterparts. Jean Lafitte, the new First Minister, had provided much of the fabric, as well as the gold and some of the jewels for the coronation. His pirate empire of Barataria had been legitimated—to the disappointment of many of its inhabitants—and came, now, under the umbrella of Louisianne law and the Constitution that was still being toiled over.

Meriel wore a gown with a short train all of white satin. The underdress was sewn with pailettes of white gold in a pattern of vines and flowers, and the split skirt of the overdress was trimmed in silver lace. Around her neck she wore an ornate antique necklace of diamonds and pearls, and upon her head, a veil of antique lace. She more resembled a bride than a matron, but today she would become a Queen.

Life is so very peculiar, Meriel thought, pausing one last time to inspect herself in the drawing-room mirror. *Geoffrey*[66] *schemed and plotted to make me a Queen. And now I shall be, though of a different realm than ever he imagined.*

"Are you nervous?" Louis asked, coming in. He looked pale but composed, his blond hair swept back and pomaded into a shining sweep.

"A little," Meriel said. "But I know my part. And it will not be so very different from everything else we have done, my love. It is another masquerade, that is all."

Louis seemed more resigned than enthusiastic about what was to come, but Meriel knew he would accept it in time. Louis was of Royal blood, and some truths simply could not be ignored.

"When I thought I had lost you, I realized how foolish I had been to expose you to such danger. If you are beside me, even this masquerade will be endurable." He took her hand.

"The carriage is here!"

Robie burst into the room with little regard for decorum. Louis had been his prisoner once, and even though he was now the King's Page—Jean had thought the post would have a refining influence upon him—he apparently saw no reason to treat his new master any differently. All that had changed was his costume, for he now wore the red and powder-blue livery of the new Louisianne Royal House.

"Come on, Louis! You'll be late," Robie amplified.

---

66. Geoffrey, Earl of Highclere, wished his niece to marry Prince Jamie so that he could influence, and eventually undermine, the Protestant crown of England.

"Anyone would think you wished me to be King," Louis said. "You will have to treat me properly then, Robie. You will no longer be able to threaten to shoot me with impunity."

The young pirate-turned-page shrugged philosophically. "Ah, well. I dare say there will be someone I can shoot." He led the way down the steps to the carriage.

The street was filled with crowds who had been waiting since dawn to get a glimpse of them, and the gathered spectators broke into noisy cheers when Louis and Meriel appeared. The Civil Militia lined the street, as much as an honor guard as to control the crowd.

Meriel descended the steps as if she were floating, her head held regally high. Her husband, watching her, realized that Meriel knew far more of being a Queen than he did of being a King. *But never mind,* he thought to himself, *that will come with time. What do any of us—Lafitte, Corday, Baronner, any of us—know about being kings and dukes and ministers and rulers? This is a new land, and we all shall have to learn new things.*

The carriage moved slowly through crowded streets toward Cabildo Square. The winter air was cool and sharp, but snow was a stranger here, and Louis and Meriel were comfortable in the open carriage with no more protection than their cloaks.

By now, all trace of d'Charenton's jurisdiction had been erased both from the Cabildo and the square, and each had been returned to its proper use. Engineers were studying how to close up the network of tunnels which had been discovered beneath the city.

A red carpet stretched from the steps of the Cabildo to the doors of the Cathedral, for Louis would first take a civil oath before the Court and then be crowned by the Bishop. Those observers without places within the Cathedral were gathered in Cabildo Square and the streets beyond, waiting for the first sight of their new King. They cheered as the carriage stopped before the Cabildo and Louis dismounted.

"I will see you in the church," Louis told his bride. "You know what to do, don't you?"

"I'll take care of her," Robie said impatiently. "Now go on—I want to get this over with so I can go to the banquet."

Meekly, Louis allowed himself to be ordered off, and the carriage pulled slowly away. Alone, he walked up the steps of the Cabildo.

Corday was waiting for him inside. The eye-patch he wore to cover his mutilation at d'Charenton's hands gave him a rakish appearance, and the passage of time had healed him in body, but he still bore the intangible scars of that terrible night. Louis clasped his hand warmly.

"De ot'ers are waitin' inside, Your Majesty," Corday said in his broad Acadian *patois.*

"Oh, don't call me that!" Louis begged. "The others, perhaps— I know Lafitte enjoys it—but not you."

"Ver' well," Corday relented, smiling crookedly. "But perhaps I will, a liddle, when ot'ers can hear. Jus' so dey will respec' you, hahn?"

The two men walked side by side into the courtroom.

The flag of France and the Imperial arms were gone, and the new flag of Louisianne was proudly displayed: the Lilies of France in silver and blue quartered with the Tower of Castille in gold and red, and superimposed upon them the heraldic pelican feeding her young with the blood from her own breast, and the motto: *Piété, Justice, Liberté.*[67]

Louis' chief ministers and generals were gathered here—the head of his fledgling army, the captain of the Civil Militia, the admiral of his navy (who was also his First Minister), his ministers for Acadian Affairs, for the Affairs of Persons of Color, his Ambassador to the Parliament of Tribes—all in their best clothes, and wearing newly-created honors gleaming in gold and bright enamels. Before the dais, the Chief Justice stood in his scarlet robes and powdered wig, preparing to administer the civil oath that would have the force of law.

Louis stood before him as the judge raised the Book for Louis to kiss, and then the young King raised his hand and swore his sacred oath.

"I, Louis-Charles Philippe Capet d'Bourbon, who will reign as Louis I of the House of Orléans, do vow and undertake before Almighty God and Christ our Lord to uphold the Constitution of the

---

67. Piety, Justice, Liberty

Kingdom of Louisianne, to uphold the rule of Law, to subordinate myself to both of these things as much as any of my subjects, and to rule justly as a Christian King of a free, tolerant, and Christian nation, renouncing my crown when I feel I can no longer do so."

When he had spoken the words, the knot of tension in Louis' stomach eased. What would follow in the Cathedral would only be pageantry and gilding upon the oath he had taken here.

When he stepped back Lafitte embraced him roughly and kissed him on both cheeks. "When I saw you, I knew you were the King— and it is I who have brought you into your kingdom!" the pirate exulted.

"And I will remember that, Jean," Louis answered, smiling. He shook the hands of his witnesses—some friends, some only allies, all as uncomfortable with kingship as Louis himself was.

"Only one last journey," Corday said, beckoning.

Now came the passage across the square, his footsteps muffled by the red carpet laid down from the door of the Cabildo to the door of the Cathedral. Louis walked alone—the last time, perhaps, he would ever do so—with his ministers following behind.

The doors of Saint Louis swung open at his approach, and he saw the interior of the Cathedral, scrubbed and blessed and gilded, filled with those who had come to see him crowned. Steadily, looking neither to the right or left, Louis walked down the aisle.

"I always seem to be standing about in churches waiting to see someone crowned," the Duchess of Wessex whispered to her husband. "I wonder where Meriel is?"

"The last time was six months ago, when Stephanie was married and created Princess of Wales," her husband answered in an equally low voice, "so you may not tease me with this Banbury tale of coronations filling your days, my wife. And you shall see Meriel soon enough, for she will be led out to be crowned as soon as Louis has been."

Six months! Such a short time to have encompassed all the events that had befallen her. She had come from London to Wiltshire, and thence to Baltimore, and from there on a journey that had led in and out of the world, through perils unimaginable, until at last it had ended here.

Louis reached the altar and stopped before the Bishop. There he turned and faced the congregation, the Bishop standing behind him.

"Is it by your will and with your consent that I crown this man, Louis-Charles de Bourbon—king of the sovereign nation of Louis-ianne?" the Bishop asked.

"Yes!" the people shouted—and, a moment later, as the question was relayed to the people outside—their cheers of assent came as well.

Now Louis knelt before the Bishop upon a plump violet cushion with gilded tassels and swore to the Bishop as he had to the judge:

"I, Louis the First, do vow and undertake before Almighty God and Christ our Lord to be a true King and husband to Louisianne, to love and respect my subjects and to cherish them as my own children, to rule over them in accordance with the Constitution and the Law, and to uphold the power of the Church. I further pledge that Louisianne shall be a state under God, united in purpose and ideals, confident that justice shall prevail for all of those abiding here."

Then Louis rose to his feet, and as the choir sang the "Miseri-cordia," Louis seated himself upon the Coronation Chair that had been carried out from the vestry. The anointing oil was brought, and poured out by the Bishop onto his head.

Now peers of the new realm brought the robe of gold tissue and the cloak of red velvet trimmed with ermine, concealing every inch of the white velvet suit and turning Louis from a living man into a gilded statue. As the choir sang, the Bishop presented him with a sword that symbolized his might and justice, and a Bible, jeweled and bound in gold, to symbolize his wisdom and mercy. Each was carried forward on an opulent cushion by men who had been private citizens four months before, and who now must make the stuff of government from nothing more than their goodwill and honor.

Then the Te Deum rang out through the Cathedral, and the Bishop lifted the crown. It was a simple gold coronet, for the gold-smiths had not had time to create anything more elaborate, but it had been blessed and sanctified, and was the tangible symbol of all that was done here today. He raised it high above his head, displaying it to the congregation, before placing the crown upon Louis' head.

Now Meriel was led out, with Robie carrying her train, to kneel before her husband and sovereign as the first of his subjects to do him homage. She swore her oath of fealty to him in a clear, steady voice, her green eyes shining as she gazed up at him. The Bishop placed a coronet of pearls upon her dark hair, and a cloak of velvet and ermine about her shoulders, and she was raised up to stand beside her husband.

The thing was done.

The church bells of the Cathedral de Saint Louis began to ring—joined, one by one, by the carillons of churches all over the city. Beneath that joyous sound came the dull booming of the guns along the riverfront, and the choir broke into the joyous strains of the Recessional.

There was more to follow, of course—feasts and celebrations public and private, dancing and fireworks and horse racing—but the new nation now had its king and queen. Louis led Meriel back down the aisle to the church door, and the two of them stood upon the church steps in the pale winter sunlight as the assembled crowds roared their approval.

"It's like watching a fairy tale come to life!" Sarah said, craning to get a better view of Louisianne's fledgling Royal couple. "I hope that everything to come will be as wonderful as today."

"I think," said the Duke of Wessex, gazing at his beloved wife fondly, "that this is the best of all possible beginnings."

ABOUT THE AUTHORS

ANDRE NORTON is one of the best-loved and most famous science fiction and fantasy authors of all time. She was named Grand Master by the Science Fiction and Fantasy Writers of America and was awarded a Life Achievement Award by the World Fantasy Convention. She lives in Murfreesboro, Tennessee.

ROSEMARY EDGHILL has written nearly three dozen novels in the last fifteen years. Her books for Tor include the critically acclaimed *Bast* mysteries. She lives in the mid-Hudson Valley, where she is hard at work on her half of the next *Carolus Rex* novel. Find her on the web at: HTTP://WWW.SFF.NET/PEOPLE/ELUKI.